DEADLY ARTIFACT

DEADLY ARTIFACT

CLASSIFIED SKIES

BOOK 1

DANIEL J. KOCH

For my wife—my first reader and my last love.

CONTENTS

This book is a work of fiction about unidentified flying objects, or UFOs. Nowadays, many refer to them as UAPs instead—unidentified aerial phenomena. I'm rather old-school, so I'll stick with UFO throughout.

By the way, in case you didn't know—UFOs are real.

Don't take my word for it. The U.S. Government has formally acknowledged their existence through congressional hearings, Pentagon investigations, and the establishment of official reporting programs dedicated to tracking them. They have stopped well short, however, of saying exactly what they are.

One of the more famous mass sightings of the past century occurred in Phoenix, Arizona, in March 1997—now known as the Phoenix Lights incident. What most people don't realize is that there were actually two separate phenomena that same night.

The first was a massive V-shaped formation of lights that tracked southward from the Las Vegas area, through Phoenix, and possibly as far as Tucson. The second was a curved arc of lights that hung over the Sierra Estrella Mountains west of the city. Most people have seen a video of the second incident—it is striking footage that has been replayed countless times. Clips purporting to show the first incident exist online, but none of them match what I personally observed.

Yes, I was there. I spent 32 years as a meteorologist with the National Weather Service, and in March 1997 I was stationed at the Phoenix office. I was on duty the night it happened. A colleague and I watched the first incident from the roof of our building, and what we saw was unlike anything either of us could explain.

This novel begins with a fictionalized version of that night. I want to be clear: what follows is not an eyewitness account. The events have been significantly dramatized for fiction, and the characters—while inspired by that world—are not real people. But the phenomenon itself? That was real. I watched it cross the sky.

Many believe it is only a matter of time before the full truth of what governments know about these phenomena becomes public. Until that day arrives, the rest of us are left to wonder—and to imagine.

MARCH 13TH, 1997

Southwest Airlines Flight 270 climbed into the night sky over the Nevada desert, banking southeast after departing Las Vegas's Runway 7L. A flash of amber light to his right caught First Officer Dave Mendoza's eye.

His fingers locked around the throttle, and he swallowed hard. Mendoza pointed at the starboard window, where five amber lights hung in defiance of physics against the black sky. "Hey, Cap, what in the hell is *that?*"

Captain Frank Reeves squinted through the windscreen, his twenty years of flight experience rendered useless. "Jesus Christ," he said, his grip on the yoke tightening until his fingers ached. "Five amber lights in perfect formation. I'm not seeing much movement with them."

Mendoza's eyes darted to the radio then back to the lights. "We calling this in?"

Reeves nodded, jaw clenched, and reached for the transmitter with an unsteady hand. His finger hovered over the button. "Departure's gonna think we're nuts."

Mendoza felt his mouth go dry. "Maybe we are."

Static hissed through the cockpit as Reeves's thumb found the transmit button. "Las Vegas Departure, southwest two-seven-zero, we have a PIREP. At fifteen thousand feet, approximately thirty-five nautical miles southeast of Las Vegas, we're observing an unusual formation of lights, five amber orbs in a V configuration, tracking southbound, no navigation lights visible, no apparent collision strobe. Slow-moving. Request you note for traffic."

Inside the Los Angeles Air Route Traffic Control Center, another call came over Supervisor Donna Keller's headset, relayed by Las Vegas Departure. She covered her free ear, hunching forward in her chair.

"That's the seventh report in twenty minutes," she said to her colleague.

The digital map behind her showed a constellation of blinking aircraft identifiers across the southwestern United States. Her screen flashed with another incoming transmission, this one from a FedEx cargo pilot over Kingman.

Keller called out, "Get me the National Weather Service now. Ask if they've got any balloons up in that airspace." She glanced at the radar screen again. "Try Las Vegas first, then Flagstaff. I want answers five minutes ago."

From the room's far end, a sharp whistle sounded. Johnson leaned over his screen, waving one arm without looking up. She hurried over, coffee sloshing onto her wrist.

He eyed a faint, ghostly smudge that appeared, vanished, then reappeared on the black radar display. "There, see it? Primary's picking up something massive, but the moving-target indicator keeps filtering it out as ground return." The smudge pulsed again and disappeared as the sweep continued.

Keller leaned in close. "What is that? Give me vectors and velocity," she said.

Johnson's eyes narrowed as the green line swept across the screen again, revealing the anomaly. "Heading one-six-zero at five thousand, speed one-niner," he said.

Keller's coffee mug froze halfway to her lips. "Nineteen knots? That's commercial blimp speed with jet aircraft positioning. Nothing moves like that."

Johnson's face drained of color as he stared at the screen. "That's impossible," he said, voice dropping to a whisper. "The signature just jumped thirty-five nautical miles south-southeast. No transition. Gone one second, there the next."

"What in God's name is that thing?"

It had started out as a quiet night at the National Weather Service in Phoenix. Jack Davis was in his cubicle, working on a project after hours...or at least that's what he told himself. The truth was simpler and less flattering: there was nothing to go home to.

His wife Maggie had been in Houston for six weeks, staying with her sister. They agreed on a trial separation, so they could figure out what comes next. They were college sweethearts and made love look easy; until it wasn't. She was coming back in a few days, and they were planning to talk things out. Hopefully.

So he stayed late. He always stayed late these days.

The first sign of trouble was when a hotline between Flagstaff and Phoenix rang. The Flagstaff office was calling with urgent reports of an unidentified flying object traversing the skies over northwest Arizona. Calls had been coming in at a frantic pace from the Federal Aviation Administration (FAA) and the public.

They warned Phoenix that the mysterious object was now headed into their area. It wasn't long before the Phoenix control tower spotted the mystery lights to the north and closed down the airspace.

Jack came out of his cubicle into the main operations area. At twenty-seven, he was the youngest meteorologist on staff, though you wouldn't know it from the confidence he carried. Nearly six feet of neat khakis and a polo shirt, brown hair styled just so—he looked more like he belonged at a country club. "If you guys don't mind, I'm going up to the roof. Maybe I can spot these lights myself."

"Don't fall off," said Gene. At fifty-five, the senior meteorologist was still built like a man who took care of himself, his silver-gray hair neatly trimmed, wire-rimmed glasses perched on a round, unworried face. He radiated the kind of steady competence that kept a night shift from unraveling.

"I want to go too!" said Garrett, spinning in his chair. He was a head shorter than Jack and a few years older, with a brown mullet that hadn't been fashionable for a decade and a perpetual shadow of stubble on his jaw. His shirt was untucked and slightly rumpled, which was pretty much his default state.

Gene shrugged. "Knock yourself out."

"Hey Nate," Jack called across the operations floor, "hold down the fort."

Nate looked up from his console, jaw tight, brown hair falling across his forehead. He was Jack's age, give or take, but wore it differently—eyes skeptical, posture coiled like he was already anticipating something to argue about. He gave a short nod and said nothing.

Jack said, "Hey, let's grab the video camera and maybe that new digital camera too. Get the binoculars and the clinometer if you can find them."

"I spotted them in the storage room yesterday," said Garrett.

He carried both cameras and handed Jack the clinometer and the binoculars. The clinometer was a unique instrument used to track a balloon's angle after launch, but Jack had another idea for it.

It resembled a longneck beer bottle painted black with a protractor-like device attached to the bottom. The familiar weight of the tool reminded him of the countless times he used trigonometry to track rising balloons.

As the pair pushed into the hallway, they realized they didn't have time for the five-minute walk to the roof access door, so they sprinted as fast as they could.

When they finally reached it, Garrett was bent over, his hands on his knees, wheezing. Jack leaned against the wall, chest heaving as he reached for the door handle.

Garrett fumbled with the key in his trembling hands, shouldering past Jack in his eagerness. The metal scraped against the lock as he twisted it until the door finally yielded.

The hinges squeaked, and the metal door clanged against the concrete block wall. Within was a small room with a second exit leading outward. Garrett crashed through the outer door first.

Darkness bathed the roof, and many pipes, conduits, and air-conditioning units formed an obstacle course for them to navigate. They finally made it to a prime viewing spot as the night air whispered across their skin.

From their vantage point, they had a commanding view in every direction except to the north, where the Papago Mountains rose to obstruct the lower horizon. Beyond that was Camelback Mountain, a well-known landmark.

According to the reports they'd received, the mystery lights should be approaching from that direction.

Full of anticipation, they scanned for the lights, but the darkness revealed nothing but the usual night sky.

"I'm not seeing shit," said Garrett.

As soon as he said that, a bright light punctured the darkness, left of Camelback Mountain.

"Wait! There it is!" Garrett said, pointing to the north as several more lights appeared in succession.

"Roll tape on the video recorder!"

The five amber lights approached at a steady pace from left to right. Jack said, "The callers were reporting a V-shaped object. That sure looks like it to me!"

The formation dominated the horizon, its scale difficult to gauge in the darkness, somewhere between five and ten miles distant, Jack estimated, though nighttime made precision impossible.

"Garrett, you know I'm a skeptic, but I'm struggling here. What else could we be looking at?"

"Military aircraft maybe, but they should have their transponders on, and should be talking to air traffic control. Obviously, they're not."

"They would also have to be flying in perfect formation, because I'm not seeing any of the lights sliding out of alignment. Unless we're looking at the Thunderbirds or Blue Angels here," said Jack.

Garrett struggled in the dark with the video recorder. "I'm having trouble focusing in the dark, so I'm adjusting it manually."

Peering into the darkness between the lights, Jack struggled to discern their true nature. Was it one massive craft with five illuminated points or five separate objects moving in perfect formation?

"I think it's about even with Camelback now, about five miles away. It's getting bigger by the minute."

Jack reached down to grab the digital camera. "Time to take some photos!" He snapped a few shots. "What do you think, Garrett? I think it's right next to Camelback. It can't be over three hundred feet higher than the peak."

Garrett nodded, still focused on the recording. "Yeah, I'd say that's pretty close. I'm getting a little worried about being exposed up here."

The formation grew brighter with each passing second, the lights glowing amber against the night sky.

"Christ," Jack said, "I think it's heading straight for us. It's blocking out the stars!" His finger trembled as he pointed north. "See that bright one? That's Polaris. Watch." The pinpoint of light vanished behind the approaching object. "No doubt about it now, it's a solid object."

Soon, the forward part of it loomed less than a mile away. One glowing orb hovered ahead, accompanied by pairs extending left and then right. The angle revealed a massive and V-shaped object against the night sky.

Garrett said, "It's going to go right over us! Do we stay out here or run back inside?"

"We may never have an opportunity like this again. You can ditch if you want, but I'm staying right here!"

"Okay," Garrett said.

Jack grabbed the clinometer. "Hey! I'm going to take some angular measurements. Any chance you can write some numbers down?"

"I have a pen in my back pocket, but I didn't bring any paper!"

Jack glanced at the video camera case and spotted a glossy quick-start manual protruding from an internal pocket. "Grab that thing," he said, pointing to the manual.

Jack's heart beat faster as the front of the craft was almost overhead. "Look at the size of this thing! It's bigger than an aircraft carrier!" He lined up the clinometer with the craft and started calling out numbers to Garrett, who scribbled them down.

The air buzzed with an invisible energy as the craft passed directly above them. Jack felt his arm hairs stand at attention, and for a brief moment the world seemed to tilt slightly beneath his feet.

Despite straining his ears, Jack couldn't identify anything beyond the normal din of city traffic and the mechanical drone of the rooftop air-conditioning units.

The craft was featureless, at least in the dark, save for the glowing orbs of light.

Jack's attention snapped northward as twin pinpoints of light sliced through the night sky, banking hard and racing toward their position. "Hey, what's that?"

"Jet fighters!" Garrett said. "F-16s out of Luke, I'd bet." Garrett was an Air Force veteran, and Luke Air Force Base was on the west side of Phoenix.

The fighter jets tore through the night toward the colossal V-shaped object. As they came closer, the craft ceased to exist—there one heartbeat, gone the next, leaving nothing but stars where its massive shadow blocked them seconds earlier.

They both shouted at once, shocked.

"It just disappeared!" Garrett said.

"What the hell?" Jack shouted.

The fighter jets streaked closer through the night sky while Garrett swung the video camera across the horizon, frantically searching for the UFO.

The jets flashed silently overhead, then a heartbeat later twin thunderclaps slammed into them with physical force. *BOOM! BOOM!* The roof beneath their feet shook and undulated as the sonic booms rolled across the city. In the parking lot below, dozens of car alarms erupted in a frenzy.

"Those guys are supersonic! They aren't messing around!" Garrett said. They continued watching the receding jets as they raced through the empty sky.

After another minute ticked by, Jack said, "I guess the show is over. Let's hurry back downstairs. They're not going to believe this!"

P hone calls were overwhelming the weather office. Gene had just hung up the receiver when the building shook from the sound of twin thunderclaps.

Nate shot up in his seat. "What the hell was that?"

"Well, we know it's not thunder. I wonder if something exploded somewhere."

The ringing of the phone interrupted their thoughts. Nate grimaced as he took another UFO report. He slammed down the phone. "Why in the hell are the 911 centers sending these calls to us? It's 1997 for Christ's sake!"

"Nate, it's been like that for decades. It all goes back to when the Air Force started dismissing UFOs as weather phenomena. They'd tell people to call us, like we'd have the answers," Gene said. "Some things never change."

"Can we shut the damn line off? I'm not getting any work done," said Nate.

They weren't able to do their jobs with the phone ringing constantly, and there wasn't anything they could do about the situation, genuine UFO or not. "You know what? Go ahead," said Gene.

The technicians had installed a toggle switch in the back room that would cut off the public line, and he dashed over to cut it off. They didn't use the switch very often, usually during the most intense weather events where the call volume could overwhelm the forecasters.

The sound of a door opening and footsteps approaching drew their attention. Jack and Garrett hurried in.

Gene swiveled around in his chair and eyed them both for a moment. "What happened out there? We heard a thunderous noise that shook the office."

Garrett said, "Fighter jets! Two of them were chasing this massive UFO, breaking the sound barrier!" Slapping the camera case, he grinned. "Got it all right here on this tape."

Watching the exchange from across the room, Nate furrowed his brow. "You're telling me you caught it on tape? A UFO? Really?"

Garrett nodded with enthusiasm as he caught his breath. His hands were shaking as he handed it to Gene. "It's the craziest thing I've ever seen," he said. Nate folded his arms across his chest, looking unconvinced.

Gene opened the small screen on the video recorder, rewound the tape, and hit play. The three huddled around it, with Nate keeping his distance.

Jack frowned as the grainy video unfolded on the small display. The equipment performed much worse in the dim light than he expected.

Garrett pointed at the screen, the excitement rising in his voice. "There, right there! That's when it first came around Camelback Mountain." The video played throughout the encounter, Garrett narrating every step.

Gene was unmoved as the tape wrapped up. He glanced up at their expectant faces. "Guys, I hate to be the one to say it, but all you've got are lights in a dark sky. Nothing here would convince anyone who wasn't standing right beside you."

Garrett plopped down in an office chair and slouched.

Jack stepped forward and said, "Gene, I know what we saw. The camera might have failed us, but when that thing passed overhead, it was unmistakable. I'm staking my professional reputation on this. It wasn't natural."

"Are you sure it wasn't a classified military prototype? The Air Force tests experimental aircraft in the desert all the time."

Jack shook his head. "Gene, you know they wouldn't do that over a major city. The FAA had to shut down an airport and a flight corridor."

Gene raised his hands in a conciliatory gesture. "All right, fair point. Let's regroup. Garrett, go set up that tape on the big screen in the office library. The resolution might show us something we're missing on this tiny viewfinder. Jack, give me all the details of what happened."

Jack recounted the encounter from start to finish.

When he was done, he remembered the camera, ejected the card, and handed it to Gene. "Let's check this to see if we captured any decent photos."

Jack was disappointed. The still camera images were no better than the video. The glowing lights were visible, but the image quality reduced them to fuzzy, pixelated smears against the night sky. Mountain silhouettes provided the only sense of scale, and the images were too dark to reveal evidence of the craft's body.

In the library, Garrett had no more luck with the video replay on the larger screen. The phenomenon was visible, but even on the larger screen, significant detail was missing. The camera didn't capture the most incredible part, when the craft vanished. It all came down to bad timing. Garrett had turned the camera toward the incoming fighter jets one second before it happened.

Gene rubbed his jaw, his gaze fixed on the wall map but seeing something else. "There is little doubt you guys saw a genuine UFO." He gestured at the grainy footage. "But to anyone else, these are just strange lights in the sky."

Jack sighed. Garrett stared at the floor, their excitement now deflated.

A thought popped into Jack's mind. "Hey! I almost forgot. Garrett, where's that camera manual?"

Garrett dug through the case and handed over the booklet, its back cover scrawled with Jack's measurements.

Jack turned to Gene, tapping the written figures. "I took angular measurements with the clinometer while it passed overhead. We estimated it flew 1,800 feet above our heads based on its appearance beside Camelback. I can work out the actual dimensions."

Gene tilted his head to the side, intrigued.

Jack hunched over the desk, pencil scratching across paper. He punched numbers into the calculator, converting angular measurements into dimensions.

Jack sat back in his chair and slapped down his pencil. "About 2,500 feet wide by 2,800 feet long."

Nate let out a sharp laugh. "That's over half a mile long. You've made a mistake somewhere."

Jack rolled his chair across the floor to Nate's desk and handed him his calculations. "Oh yeah? Check them yourself." Nate stared at the paper, then reached for his calculator and a clean page in his logbook.

After several minutes of working through the equations, Nate swore, tore up the sheet of paper, and started over. After repeating the process twice, he agreed the numbers were correct; however, he still couldn't let it go. "Your altitude estimate of 1,800 feet is flawed. That has to be the critical error."

Jack raised an eyebrow. "You're suggesting the craft flew higher?" He tapped his pencil against the paper, circling a figure. "Run the numbers again. If anything, we've been conservative. The higher its altitude, the larger this thing would have to be, based on my measurements." He rubbed his chin. "I watched it glide past Camelback, and it wasn't lower than the mountain. My estimate is solid, Nate."

Nate's lips tightened into a thin line as he stared at the calculations. "You must have made a mistake in your measurements then."

"Like hell I did! Even if you figure I made small random mistakes in my readings, that doesn't change the overall scale of the object. It was massive."

"Maybe Garrett wrote some numbers down wrong."

"The numbers on the paper look right to me," said Jack.

Nate's face was getting redder by the minute. The debate continued, arguments circling back and forth, until the energy drained from the room. Each man retreated into his own certainty, the silence between them as vast as the night sky that started it all.

After several minutes, Nate went to the break room to grab a soda. Jack pushed back his chair and rose to his feet, rolling his neck until it cracked. "All of this excitement has worn me out. My mind's racing too much for sleep, but I need to process what we experienced."

Garrett caught his arm as he turned to leave. "Hold up. Any chance you have a home setup that can make copies? There is a video lab on Central Avenue that specializes in cleaning up low-light footage. I'd rather not hand over our only copy."

Jack said, "I have two VCRs in my office for that purpose. I'll work on it as soon as I get home." He touched his shirt pocket where he slipped the card. "I'll copy these to my computer too. Maybe I could enhance the images."

With several hours of his shift still ahead, Garrett couldn't contain himself. He paced the room, rehashing details of the incident for the twentieth time. Gene nodded along, muttering affirmations, while Nate strangled his pen.

Jack had gone home, so it was just the three of them now, the office quieter than it had any right to be after a night like this.

Garrett's fingers kept finding their way to his right shoulder blade, the skin transitioning from a mild irritation to something more insistent—a hot, needling sensation that demanded his attention.

He reached back and pressed two fingers against the spot. The contact sent a sharp sting rippling across his skin, and he hissed through his teeth.

"You all right?" Gene asked.

"Something's gotten to me up there. Feels like a burn. A bad one." He winced and with an awkward motion tried to reach behind himself. "Gene, I need you to look at my back. Did I get stung by something?"

"Sit down."

He motioned for Garrett to roll his chair toward him. Garrett's shirt bunched up in his hands as he lifted the fabric. He went still.

Five red welts marked Garrett's shoulder blade. Five perfect circles, each the size of a small pea, arranged in a distinct V-pattern across his skin. The same V-formation he'd been describing for the past two hours.

Gene said nothing for a long moment.

"What do you see?" Garrett asked.

"If this is some kind of prank, it isn't funny."

Garrett's eyes narrowed. "What prank? I don't understand."

Gene straightened up and looked across the room. "Nate. Come over here."

Nate pushed back from his desk with a sigh, clearly expecting some new piece of UFO nonsense to roll his eyes at. He walked over and looked down at Garrett's back. His expression changed instantly.

"What the hell is that?"

"That's what I'm trying to figure out," said Gene.

Garrett twisted in his chair, his arm contorting as he groped behind his back, trying to feel what they were looking at. "Jesus Christ, would one of you just tell me what you're seeing?"

He rested a hand on Garrett's shoulder to keep him still. "I'm looking at five circular marks. Burns, or something like burns. They form a perfect V-shape, identical to the formation you described."

The room went quiet. Even Nate, who had spent most of the last hour poking holes in Garrett's story, had nothing to say.

Garrett jumped out of his chair and sprinted toward the front door, disappearing down the hall. Gene and Nate exchanged a look.

The door banged open a minute later. Garrett stumbled back in, his face the color of old chalk, one hand still pressed against the back of his shoulder.

"You guys weren't kidding," he said. "Those marks are in a perfect V. Almost like something branded me."

He dropped into his chair and leaned forward with his elbows on his knees, staring at the floor. The room felt smaller than it had a moment ago.

Gene pulled up a chair and sat across from him. "Garrett, I need to ask you something, and I need you to think carefully before you answer. At any point on that roof, when the craft was directly overhead, did you feel anything? Heat? A tingling? Anything at all?"

Garrett looked up. He rubbed the back of his neck. "Yeah. I mean, I thought it was the adrenaline. My skin felt prickly."

Gene laced his fingers together and rested them on his knee. "I saw training films when I was in the Air Force. Radiation exposure. Skin effects." He paused. "Those marks look consistent with what I saw in those films."

"Radiation," Garrett said. "Are you kidding me?"

"I'm not kidding you."

Garrett stood up and paced to the window, staring out at the parking lot. His reflection looked back at him from the dark glass. "So, what does that mean? What are we talking about here—like, cancer? I'm going to get cancer from a UFO?"

"I'm not saying that. I'm saying you need to see a doctor. Tonight, if possible. First thing tomorrow at the absolute latest. Don't let this sit."

Nate had drifted back toward his desk but hadn't sat down. He was watching Garrett with an expression that, for once, didn't look like skepticism. It looked like unease.

Garrett turned from the window. "I was only up there for a few minutes."

"I know," said Gene.

"Jack was up there too. Same amount of time."

Gene's expression didn't change, but something shifted behind his eyes. "Yeah," he said, "he was."

Calls to the 911 center were lighting up again. Observers in the western suburbs described a similar phenomenon. People were reporting glowing amber orbs in formation, suspended above the Sierra Estrella Mountains.

The lights hung in the sky, motionless against the desert night, tracing what appeared to be a perfect arc. Some imagined it looked like the leading edge of a giant flying saucer.

Several 911 callers found themselves redirected to the National Weather Service only to hear endless ringing on a silenced line. Nate had forgotten to turn it back on after all the excitement.

Meteorologists staffed the weather office around the clock in rotating weekly shifts. When the midnight shift arrived, the talk was all about the earlier incident. Garrett waved his arms as he recounted his experience and showed off what appeared to be a burn on his shoulder. The incoming shift exchanged sidelong glances, their arms folded across their chests, unsure of what to make of it all. As they glanced over at Nate, he rolled his eyes and shook his head.

This was Glen Harmon's first midnight shift, and he was quite tired. Staying awake became more difficult after he turned forty, and he dreamed of a daytime desk job. He eased into the faded blue office chair and let out something between a yawn and a groan.

His eyes burned from the poor attempt at a nap he'd grabbed in the evening, and the muscles at the back of his neck throbbed with a familiar, pulsing ache. No caffeine in the world could shake it, especially not the sludge from the crusted-over office coffee pot.

His eyes wandered around the main operations area. One of the overhead fluorescent lights buzzed in its harsh white glow. His colleague, Terry, was busy over at his station, pecking at the keyboard with jittery, birdlike taps.

The night seemed to drag on forever.

Glen was half asleep when the phone rang at six a.m., jolting him awake. On the line was Jeff Hart, a popular morning radio host whose catchphrase "Rise and shine, it's party time!" had become synonymous with the Phoenix morning drive.

Jeff wanted the St. Patrick's Day forecast for his show. He wanted to interview Glen and needed something solid to tell his listeners about the weather. Rumors of rain had been circulating.

Before they went on air, Glen cleared his throat. "I thought you might be calling about what happened earlier," he said, "the UFO thing."

Jeff's voice perked up. "Those lights hovering over the Estrellas? Man, the night crew told me the public jammed our phone lines, going nuts. Some lady in Goodyear swore it was the mothership coming to take her home!"

Glen blinked. "Huh, I didn't know about that one. Right here at our office, we had our own visitor, some V-shaped craft with glowing orbs that passed overhead. Two of our guys rushed up to the roof with a camera. They got it on tape and took measurements too," he said.

For the first time in his broadcasting career, the infamous motor-mouth Jeff Hart couldn't find his voice. When he managed to speak, it came out in a rush. "Hold on! Are you telling me the National Weather Service has actual footage of a UFO with measurements to back it up?"

At that moment, Glen realized just how badly he'd messed up. He tried to redirect the conversation. "Uh, well, perhaps we should focus on the St. Patrick's Day forecast."

But it was too late for that. Jeff's tone changed over the line, a subtle shift that signaled the radio host recognized the sound of a career-making scoop.

Jeff Hart never got his weather forecast. Glen mumbled something about having to go, his stomach sinking as the line went dead.

Less than fifteen minutes later, Glen's phone rang again. On the other end of the line was Walt Greer, a fellow meteorologist, calling from home.

"Turn on Rise and Shine, Party Time," Walt said. "Jeff Hart's telling all of Phoenix that the weather service has scientific proof of a UFO, says we measured it and everything. Other people are calling, saying they saw it too. What the hell is going on?"

Glen's shoulders fell. His eyelids crashed shut as his hand found his face, fingers digging into the bridge of his nose to block the migraine he knew was coming.

"Oh no," he said.

4 / SHIFT CHANGE

Coffee sloshed in the ceramic mug as Ray Kallas cruised through the office door. This workplace had been his domain for five years, a position that still brought him satisfaction.

At fifty-eight, retirement loomed on the horizon, close enough to contemplate but far enough to keep him engaged. Ray carried himself with the confidence of someone who had found his place in life. His tall, lean figure, olive skin, and the shock of jet-black hair that hadn't yet turned gray spoke to his Mediterranean heritage.

Ray walked into the shift change briefing. He side-stepped a cluster of meteorologists in muted conversation.

Overnight staffing consisted of three people but ramped up during the day to fifteen, including the administrative staff. He claimed an empty chair and said, "Good morning! What's up, fellas?"

The forecasters exchanged glances, their faces tense. Glen broke the awkward pause with a throat-clearing cough. "Uh, we've had a few things happen in the last twelve hours that you might need to know about, boss."

Glen recounted the UFO incident that unfolded at the office, at least to the best of his knowledge. Ray's expression shifted from confusion to disbelief, his thick eyebrows inching higher with each detail. When Glen finished, Ray opened his mouth, but he held up a hand. "There's more," Glen said, wincing. "I wasn't thinking straight and said something about the event to Jeff Hart this morning when he called for a weather update. His station has already run a segment about it, and now other radio and television stations are calling. We've been deflecting their inquiries so far, telling them we have no comment."

"Jack and Garrett were involved? Please tell me this is one of their jokes."

Glen shook his head. "No, Ray. They swore up and down that it was authentic. They got a video, a tape of lights in formation flying overhead. Garrett was giddy all night."

Ray was silent for a long moment. "Okay," he said, "let's downplay this and keep declining to comment on the story. I'm going to call regional headquarters for guidance. Where is Eddie this morning? Has anyone seen him? Let me know the second he gets in. And where is this alleged tape of lights?"

Glen said, "To the best of my knowledge, Jack took it home to make a copy."

"Wonderful," Ray said as he got up from his chair and turned back toward his office. "And Glen? I need to see you when you're done out here."

As Ray retreated, Glen sighed. All he wanted was to clock out, drive home in silence, and disappear under his comforter for a minimum of six uninterrupted hours.

Glen found Ray behind his desk.

"Close the door," Ray said.

Glen eased it shut and settled into a chair.

"Tell me what you said to Jeff Hart. As best you can remember."

Glen walked him through it. When he finished, there was an extended period of silence.

"You told a radio host with a hundred thousand listeners," Ray said, "that our office filmed a UFO. And took measurements. Did I get that right?"

"I didn't intend to…"

"But that's what he heard. And that's what he broadcast." Ray leaned back, deep in thought. "Glen, do you understand what we do here? What people rely on us for?"

"Yes."

"We issue forecasts. Severe weather warnings. Flood warnings. When people hear a warning from the National Weather Service, they trust us. That trust took decades to build. What do you think happens when every newsroom in the state is running a story about how we measured a flying saucer?"

Glen had no answer.

"There is a protocol for media inquiries, and it exists for this reason. You don't improvise with a reporter. Never. Especially on a midnight shift."

"You're right," Glen said. "I know."

"I need you to mean that." Ray held his gaze. "Because if something like this happens again, it won't be a polite conversation. Do you understand what I'm telling you?"

"Yes," Glen said. "I do."

Ray nodded once, the matter apparently closed in his mind. "Go home and get some sleep. You look terrible."

Glen stood, relieved to be moving. He had his hand on the door when Ray spoke again.

"And Glen." He didn't look up from his desk. "Next time Jeff Hart calls for a forecast, you tell him it's going to be sunny, and to have a nice day. That's it."

Eddie Callahan strolled into the office past his usual arrival time. Three separate accidents turned the freeway into a parking lot this morning.

Though second-in-command to Ray, who oversaw all the weather offices throughout Arizona, Eddie ran the day-to-day operations in

Phoenix with the same efficiency and professionalism he honed in Brooklyn. At fifty-two, he was a broad man whose scraggly gray beard and close-cropped hair the color of dirty snow gave him the look of someone who had stopped caring about appearances around the same time he stopped caring about other people's opinions.

Marco Rodriguez was the senior meteorologist on duty today. At forty-five, he had the kind of round, good-natured face that made people underestimate him, though anyone who'd worked with him long enough knew better. His black hair was pulled back in a ponytail, and he had a way of seeming relaxed at his station while actually tracking everything happening in the room—which, given his reputation as the office conspiracy theorist, made him well-suited for a morning like this one.

Marco glanced up and saw Eddie walking by. "Hey, Eddie, Ray wants to see you in his office right away. Looks like we have a big crisis brewing."

Eddie frowned. "For the love of God, Marco!" He rubbed his eyes and exhaled through flared nostrils. "I spent forty minutes watching some jackass in a BMW try to merge across three lanes. Can't a man drag his ass to the coffee pot before the world falls apart?"

Marco raised his palms in mock surrender, his toothy smile never faltering. "Hey, I'm just the one delivering the news!"

Eddie turned and ambled toward his office. "Yeah, yeah, alright."

Five minutes later, coffee mug in hand, Eddie walked across the operations area to Ray's office.

Ray paced behind his desk when Eddie entered, waiting for his colleague to take a seat before lowering himself into his own chair. Even seated, he maintained the posture of a man ready to spring back up, leaning forward with his elbows planted on the desk blotter and fingers interlaced tightly.

"You've heard," Ray said.

"Heard what?"

Ray sat back in his chair with a heavy sigh. "Jack and Garrett were on shift last night when they spotted something in the sky. Not just lights, a massive object. They got it all on tape, and Jack even pulled out the clinometer to make measurements. The thing measured several thousand feet from end to end."

Eddie snorted. "UFOs? Really?" He gestured toward Ray's coffee mug. "You sure that's regular brew in there this morning? Maybe a little Irish coffee instead?"

Ray's face hardened. "I'm dead serious, Eddie. And here's the kicker. Glen answered a call from a morning disc jockey and spilled everything. By noon, every news outlet in the valley will be running with it. That man couldn't keep his mouth shut for ten minutes if his life depended on it. The media have been all over this since then. Six different outlets called before I could finish my first cup of coffee. At this point, 'no comment' is starting to feel like my new middle name."

Eddie scoffed, "You're not buying this UFO business, are you?"

"Whatever they witnessed last night isn't even the issue here. Our regional headquarters is now involved. Their position is clear: absolute silence. 'No comment' to every question, kick everything upstairs, and whatever we do, don't acknowledge the existence of any recording." Ray released the tension in his shoulders and slumped back in his chair. "That handles the press, but we've still got a three-ring circus going on in here."

"Garrett and Jack."

Ray's eyes narrowed. "The problem is they documented it; video footage, photographs, all of it, using government equipment. And rather than following proper channels, the whole thing leaked through Glen to some radio idiot." He massaged his temples and gestured toward the window. "Channel 4's news van is already camped in the parking lot. My staff are huddled in corners, trading rumors. This is getting out of hand."

The meeting continued for another ten minutes as they strategized on how best to handle the situation.

When Eddie emerged, his face had hardened into a mask of irritation. He walked past Marco's workstation and muttered, "Check the schedule to see what shift Jack and Garrett are working next. I need to sort this out."

Eddie turned to walk toward his office when Linda Summers, the secretary, came up behind him. "Eddie, there are two men here from the Air Force who want to speak with a manager. Ray got back on the phone with regional headquarters. Is it okay if I send them to you?"

"Yeah, that's fine," Eddie said, thinking to himself, *This had better not be about that damned UFO.*

Linda ushered a pair of visitors toward Eddie's office. Their polished shoes clicked against the floor as they passed the operations area. Marco's eyebrows shot up at the sight. Each man wore an identical black suit, a crisp white shirt, and a black tie knotted in perfect symmetry.

When the journeyman meteorologist glanced over, Marco gave him a wide-eyed look. "Men in black!"

Linda pulled Eddie's door shut and retreated to her desk up front. Marco tilted his head toward the closed space, catching only the rise and fall of voices, nothing distinct enough to piece together.

The clock hadn't even ticked through ten minutes when the door swung open and the men emerged and strode toward the exit.

Eddie came out of his office, face wrinkled. He stopped at Marco's desk and leaned in close. "Find Jack and Garrett," he growled through his teeth. "I need them here right now!" He straightened up and made his way across the operations floor, heading straight for Ray's office.

Jack's eyes burned after two hours of hunching over his monitor. Coaxing details from last night's digital images was tedious. Without access to professional software, he used basic adjustments: contrast, brightness, and sharpening.

After tinkering with various adjustments repeatedly, Jack bolted upright in his chair. There it was! The V-shaped craft finally emerged from the pixelated darkness. He wasn't a magician, but this was as close to magic as he would ever come. The photos were still grainy and somewhat indistinct, but these were fantastic compared to the murky originals.

He leaned back and took it all in, allowing himself a moment of satisfaction. At last, proof that would force the skeptics to face what he'd known all along.

The sudden ring of his phone cut through the silence. The caller ID flashed "NWS Phoenix." A mischievous smile crossed his tired face as he picked up the receiver and affected his best deep voice. "Mesa Police Department, what is your emergency?"

The line went dead silent as Marco, thrown off balance, tried to make sense of the voice on the other end.

"Uh, is Jack Davis there?" Marco asked.

Jack started laughing.

"You idiot! You had me for a second! Hey, I'm calling because Eddie wants you to come into the office right away."

Jack's gaze lingered on the V-shaped formation glowing on his screen. "I'm in the middle of something pretty important right now," he said, fingers hovering over the keyboard. "Let's say it's otherworldly."

"Yeah, I heard!" Marco said with excitement. "Everyone is talking about it. I sure wish I'd been on shift last night! Anyway, you need to get in here. This whole thing has both Eddie and Ray upset. I talked to Garrett, and he's already on his way as we speak."

Jack sighed, "Shit. This is my only day off. I'm claiming comp time if I have to come in."

"Whatever. Get here as fast as you can!"

Forty-five minutes later, Jack sauntered through the office doorway and nearly collided with Eddie. "Oh, hey there!"

Eddie's gaze swept over Jack, taking in his appearance. "Garrett's been here for twenty minutes already. What's your excuse? Stop for the breakfast special at Denny's?"

Jack, patting Eddie's rounded belly, said, "It doesn't look like you missed breakfast this morning!"

"All right, smart-ass! Get into the library. Garrett is in there, and Ray and I are joining you too. We're gonna have a nice chat. I've already visited with a couple of black-suited kooks from the Air Force."

"Wait, what?"

"Yeah, didn't you hear? Motormouth Glen spilled his guts to a radio station this morning, and now the news is all over the state. The Air Force, or whoever the hell these guys are, took a special interest in your little sighting and the mention of your videotape."

As they walked down the hall to the library, Jack tried to absorb the recent development.

The station library doubled as a conference room. Two walls featured book-lined shelves with a lengthy table occupying the center of the room. Garrett and Ray sat on opposite sides of it, and Jack took a seat by Garrett. Eddie closed the door and sat next to Ray. Jack inhaled the familiar scent of aging paper and dust that always lingered in the library, faint but unmistakable.

Ray leaned back in his chair, arms folded across his chest. "Congratulations, gentlemen. You've torpedoed what was supposed to be eighteen holes at Papago this afternoon. As the station manager, I've witnessed my share of headaches, equipment failures, budget cuts, and that time John brought a rattlesnake to work, but this is the most absurd breach of protocol I've seen in years. Flying saucers? Really? When Glen briefed me this morning about lights in the sky, I figured you jokers were pulling another one of your stunts."

"It wasn't a flying saucer, Ray. It was a V-shaped craft," Jack said.

Ray slammed his palm on the table, his voice rising to a pitch none of them had heard before. "I couldn't care less if you witnessed the Queen Mary sailing through the clouds." He jabbed a finger in Jack's direction. "You weren't even supposed to be here last night. And Garrett, why were you out on the roof in the middle of your shift?"

Jack felt his cheeks redden with anger. "Come on, Ray, you're a scientist! Aren't you the least bit interested in what's flying over our heads? Because it wasn't a human-made craft. This might be a huge scientific discovery!"

"For your information, it *was* a human-made craft! It was a top-secret government prototype that you filmed. It was off course and wasn't supposed to be over Phoenix. We have already complied with the military's request to destroy all our logs and phone records from last night, and we need you two to hand over any photos or videos you have. Neither you nor anyone else in this office will ever speak of this incident again if you know what's good for your career. Do we understand each other?"

Jack could feel his blood pressure surging. "The hell it was a government craft! It was a half-mile long, silent, and glided like a feather across the sky. When fighter jets approached, it instantly disappeared! Does that sound like our technology to you?"

Ray deepened his voice and lowered the volume, but it was obvious the point was not up for discussion. "It doesn't matter what you or I think. It's no concern of ours. Go home and bring those photos and videos back. This topic is closed."

Before Jack could muster a response, Ray swiveled away, pushed himself to his feet, and stormed out of the library, the door swinging shut behind him with a decisive click. Jack looked toward Eddie. "What the actual fuck was that?"

Eddie held up a hand and cut him off before he could continue. His tone softened, which was a rarity. "Listen, I appreciate your position, but you don't know the entire story and everything we've had to deal with this morning. Drop it, Jack. You have a promising career ahead of you. You're going places, but if you keep this up, we're all going to end up jobless.

Jack fired back, "No way those guys were from the Air Force, and I can guarantee you one hundred percent that was not a top-secret government aircraft."

"No shit, Sherlock. You think Ray and I don't know that?" The sarcasm returned to Eddie's voice. "Bring those tapes and photos in here ASAP."

Throughout the heated exchange, Garrett remained silent. Finally, he stood up and started unbuttoning his shirt.

"Hey, hold up there, Romeo! What do you think you're doing?" said Eddie.

Garrett's shirt was now all the way off, and he turned to show his shoulder blade to Jack and Eddie.

"What the hell are those marks?" asked Jack.

"I'm going to the doctor after this to have it checked. It's itching and burning like a bitch. Gene told me it looks like a radiation burn."

"Radiation burn? Yeah, right," said Eddie. "I'll bet it's a couple of spider bites."

Garrett put his shirt back on. "It's in the exact pattern as the lights we saw last night." Garrett thought for a second. "You want us to keep quiet about this? Fine. I've got bills to pay, and I like my job, but we know the truth."

Jack weighed his options. "Okay, Eddie, you win. I'll bring all my stuff in," he said with some difficulty, "but don't expect me to pretend this never happened."

Eddie pushed back his chair and stood, his throat catching on a dry cough that punctuated the tense silence. He shook his head and walked out the door.

Jack whispered under his breath to Garrett, "I have a copy of the videotape, and I backed up the memory card on my home computer. Nobody else has to know about it."

Garrett gripped the doorframe until his hand trembled. "This thing hit me with radiation last night. I'm a little freaked out. If you want to keep pursuing this, more power to you, but I can't be part of it."

Jack remained in his chair, the empty library closing in around him. Finally, he pushed himself to his feet, his movements stiff as he navigated the hallways, shouldered through the exit doors, and slid behind the wheel of his truck. The engine roared to life, and he started toward home.

Jack's pickup slowed as he approached the driveway. His foot froze above the brake pedal. The front door gaped open several inches.

He killed the engine and sat motionless for a moment, listening. The neighborhood was quiet. A sprinkler ticked somewhere down the block.

He reached behind the driver's seat and closed his fingers around the grip of his 9mm pistol. He checked the magazine by feel, snapped it back in, and chambered a round as quietly as he could manage.

Jack moved toward the front door in a low crouch, his back against the exterior wall, and peered through the gap. Nearest the door he saw books on the floor and a drawer dumped across the carpet. Further into the living room he saw overturned furniture, and the television lying on its side.

Two men in black suits stood on the far side of the living room. One had a computer tower tucked under his arm. The other held two videotapes in one hand and the memory card in the other. They were moving toward the hallway, like professional thieves in no particular hurry.

Jack kicked the door open and came in with both arms extended.

"Don't move! Set it down! Now!"

The pair froze. The one with the computer tower turned first, showing no emotion. The other man's eyes moved to his partner, a micro-transaction of communication that Jack recognized.

"I said put it down!"

They ran.

Both men sprinted through the house, cutting hard left through the living room toward the back of the house. Jack went after them at full speed, vaulting the overturned coffee table, his shoulder clipping the doorframe to the kitchen as he made the corner. The back patio door was already open.

He came through into the backyard ten feet behind them.

His home had a concrete block wall at the rear of the property that was six feet tall. The first man hit it running and went over clean, the technique of someone who had scaled walls before. The second struggled, his wingtips scrabbling against the block, but he muscled over as Jack's fingers grazed the back of his jacket.

Jack holstered the gun, backed up three steps, and ran at the wall. His fingers caught the top edge and he hauled himself over, dropping hard into the alley on the other side. His knees absorbed the impact, and soon he was up and moving.

They were twenty yards ahead, still in their suits, running faster than men in dress shoes had any right to. The one who had the computer tower had ditched it somewhere. Both men were moving freely now, arms pumping, headed north up the alley toward the cross street.

Jack pushed harder. His lungs burned. He gained a few yards on the slower of the two, close enough now to see the coiled earpiece behind the man's right ear, close enough to hear the slap of leather soles on asphalt.

They cut right at the end of the alley without breaking stride.

Jack made the turn and closed the distance. Suddenly, both men threw themselves into the open rear door of a black sedan idling at the curb. Government plates. Engine running. The door wasn't even shut before the car accelerated away.

Jack ran after it. He followed it until the sedan made a left two blocks ahead and disappeared. He slowed to a stop.

"That's right!" His voice tore out of him, raw and ragged. "Run, you sons of bitches!"

The words bounced off parked cars and quiet houses and went nowhere.

He stood there breathing for a long moment, watching the empty intersection before he turned and walked back.

This time he went down the alley to the street, turned the corner, and went inside through his front door.

In the living room, the computer tower sat on the carpet where the first man must have tossed it down when he ran. He checked the side panel. Wrenched open. The hard drive bay was empty. They'd pulled the drive before he got home.

He moved into the office. Both videotapes were gone, along with the memory card. He knew it already, but he had to check.

He sank down against the wall until he was sitting on the floor, back against the baseboard, looking at what was left of his living room.

The television lay on its side. Maggie's jewelry box was upended in the bedroom. He could see the scattered earrings from where he sat.

They hadn't taken any of it. Not the jewelry, not the television, not the camera equipment on the shelf. They had known what they wanted and where to find it.

This wasn't a burglary. This was a message, delivered in the language of ransacked drawers and empty hard drive bays, signed by no one and impossible to report.

He picked up the cordless phone from the floor, checked for a dial tone, and called the office. He kept it brief. The tapes were gone. The memory card was gone. He wouldn't be bringing anything in.

He hung up and sat back down.

Maggie's flight landed at Sky Harbor in less than twenty-four hours. What would he tell her? That a burglar had broken into the house?

She'd go straight to the police, demanding a case number, a detective, and a follow-up call. She'd want answers, and Maggie's version of wanting answers involved crossed arms and a look that made people confess to things they hadn't done.

And there would be no case. No detective. No answers he could give her.

The truth was worse than useless. Government agents tore the house apart looking for UFO evidence. He could already hear her response to that: the particular silence that preceded the worst things she'd ever said to him.

Six weeks in Houston. Six weeks of phone calls and careful conversations and the fragile possibility that they might actually put it back together. And now this.

He noticed the quiet differently—not the quiet of an empty room but the quiet of a house that was missing something specific.

Annie. His wife's beloved Persian cat.

The front door had been open when he arrived. He was on his feet before he'd finished the thought, moving through the wrecked house calling her name.

She wasn't under the bed. Not in the closet. Not behind the washer or in any of the places she retreated to when something frightened her. He went outside and walked the yard, then the cul-de-sac, then the surrounding streets, stopping to ask neighbors who had seen nothing and probably thought he'd lost his mind.

The sun went down while he was searching. He was standing in his own driveway, about to give up, when he heard it.

A small sound. From above.

He looked up.

Annie sat on the flat roof over the garage, peering down at him with wide luminous eyes, white coat catching the last of the evening light, looking completely unbothered by the fact that she'd apparently spent the afternoon watching government agents ransack the house from the best possible vantage point.

"Of course," he said.

He wrangled the ladder off the wall in the garage and winced when the end slipped and banged against the concrete. He positioned it against the front of the house and climbed.

Annie watched his approach with disinterest until he finally made it onto the roof. Then she started to back up toward the peak of the gabled roof, considered the drop, and finally allowed herself to be picked up.

That was only half the battle. Jack now had to get ten pounds of Persian cat off the roof. He tucked her under his arm and began the descent. She yowled and twisted against his ribcage on every rung. When he finally reached the ground, she became still instantly, as if the protest had been entirely for show.

He carried her inside, set her down, and watched her shoot down the hallway and disappear under the guest bed. He stood alone in his wrecked living room for a moment.

Then he picked up a couch cushion and put it back where it belonged, and got to work.

Maggie was coming home tomorrow. He needed this to look like a house she might actually want to come home to.

Garrett had been told to arrive fifteen minutes early for his doctor's appointment. That was an hour ago, and he was getting irritated. "Why tell someone to show up beforehand if they're just going to make them sit and wait?" he grumbled under his breath.

Finally, the nurse emerged from a door and called his name. After checking his weight, they escorted him back to a treatment room and recorded his vital signs. "The doctor will be with you soon," the nurse said as she exited.

I'll believe it when I see it, Garrett thought. Thirty minutes later, the doctor came in.

He examined the angry red dots on Garrett's shoulder blade, his brow furrowing. "How did this happen?"

Garrett shifted in his seat, eyes darting to the floor. The doctor waited, clipboard in hand. After several uncomfortable seconds of silence, Garrett sighed and explained the UFO incident.

He looked at him suspiciously. "A UFO? Oh, really?" The doctor wasn't buying it. He tapped his pen against the clipboard. "I don't know what to make of your claim, but these marks are consistent with radiation exposure. Gamma rays in particular. We should run some blood work to check your marrow function, though I suspect the dose wasn't significant enough to cause that level of damage."

The doctor prescribed a three-part approach: a cream to reduce inflammation, medicine to fight infection, and special bandages that needed to be kept damp to help the skin repair itself.

Garrett gripped the side of the examination table, barely able to ask the next question. "Doctor," he murmured, "am I going to get cancer from this?"

The doctor removed his glasses, polishing them with the edge of his lab coat. "The blood work will tell us more about your exposure levels," he said gently, "but based on what I'm seeing, I don't think you need to lose sleep over this. From what I can tell, the radiation signature appears minimal."

Garrett felt the tension drain from his shoulders for the first time since he'd noticed those strange marks.

Jack limped through Sky Harbor's Terminal 4, sweat on his brow despite the frigid air being blown through the air conditioners. In a futile ritual, he kept checking the arrivals board. The plane was still on time; the baggage claim status unchanged. He hobbled back and forth between a coffee shop and floor-to-ceiling windows scorched by the Arizona sun.

It was Saturday. He was supposed to work the day shift today, but after everything that had happened, Eddie was quick to grant him time off. He hadn't slept well last night, as every little noise made him think the government spooks had returned.

Pacing would not make the flight arrive any faster, so he plopped down in a short row of chairs nearest the window. His mind drifted to the mess back home. Before leaving, he'd spent half an hour fixing the front door's battered deadbolt and another hour sweeping up the splinters and doing his best to fix the door jamb. Sadly, his amateur repair attempts were insufficient; he needed professional help. Jack wondered how much that was going to cost him on top of everything else.

Last night, he'd worked on the living room bookcase, which also held the TV. It broke and split clean at the joints. Jack resurrected it this morning with his electric drill, boring fresh holes and driving screws through the splintered wood. The repair job wouldn't win any design awards, but at least the shelving should hold up under the weight of their twenty-seven-inch television.

Jack had left the drill atop a nearby stepladder's third rung. While he was padding barefoot through the house in search of a misplaced screwdriver, his hip bumped the ladder's edge. The drill tumbled off its perch, the sharpened steel bit driving straight through the soft skin between his first and second toes. The injury wasn't as severe as he feared, but it required him to sterilize the wound with rubbing alcohol, which was more painful than the injury itself.

While he was trying to patch up his wound, the phone rang. He hopped one-legged over to it. The caller ID indicated a Houston number. It was Maggie. He tried to mask any sign of distress as he confirmed the details of her flight back to Phoenix. She sounded happy on the phone, so he didn't want to tell her what happened.

His mind back in the present, he got up and wound through the maze of seating, his foot throbbing. Maggie should be here any time now. How should he start the conversation? "Hi, honey, did you have a pleasant trip? Government agents ransacked the house, and I think someone might be following me." No, that sounded insane.

He recognized Maggie's walk before he saw her face, a determined, shoulders-back stride that broadcast a hybrid of self-confidence and mild impatience.

She came off the escalator, and the sight of her hit him the way it always did—like something he'd almost talked himself out of missing. She was tall for a woman, nearly his height, with shoulder-length hair that curled and waved in every direction it pleased, honey-brown with lighter streaks running through it. Her black-framed glasses sat slightly crooked on her nose, the way they always did by the end of a long travel day, and her blue eyes found him across the terminal before he had a chance to school his expression into something casual.

She was towing her wheeled suitcase, wearing her travel uniform: black yoga pants, and a faded University of Texas hoodie.

Jack plastered on a smile as she spotted him. He stepped forward for a hug, but the luggage handle and a pink canvas tote bag encumbered her. They made do with a one-armed, lopsided embrace.

"Hi," he said, detecting the faint odor of alcohol. "Hey, have you been drinking?"

She made a face. "There were some thunderstorms moving in from the Gulf, and the captain said we might have a rough ride, so I self-medicated. Good thing I did. The turbulence was bad. I think we flew straight through a storm." She looked him up and down. "By the way, nice shirt."

He looked down. The white t-shirt had a weather map with various symbols and phrases, ranging from "Shitty" to "Partly Shitty" to "Mostly Shitty."

"My sister sent it to me. She thought it would be funny."

"Jack! What if kids read that?"

Jack shrugged.

They turned and walked out of the automatic doors in tandem, heading toward the parking garage. The sidewalk outside was hot, but at least summer hadn't arrived yet.

"Are you limping?" she asked.

He tried to focus on the painted white crosswalk lines rather than her face. Jack lied and shrugged, "I twisted my ankle a little, but it's getting better."

"Anything else happen at home while I was gone?"

He tried to be as nonchalant as possible. "Nothing much, the same old routine. I had to decline salvation from a couple of Jehovah's Witnesses who came by."

"Did you tell them you were Catholic? They always love that."

"No, we didn't have much to talk about." They made it to Jack's pickup truck and loaded the suitcase in the back, and pulled up to the booth to pay the parking fee. As they exited the airport, he could feel Maggie's eyes on him, waiting for something.

"Did you remember to water my plants?" she asked.

"I did twice weekly, including the cacti," he said.

She frowned. "Jack, you don't water cactus plants that often. They'll die!"

He scoffed, "Well, they're still alive."

Several minutes of travel on the freeway passed in silence. He glanced again at Maggie. She was staring off at the mountains, her face intent, framed by sunlight and a few stray wisps of hair.

He tried to picture how she'd react to the truth. Fury? Fear? Maybe she'd laugh it off, or perhaps she'd want to run, change their names, move to Saskatchewan.

He drummed his fingers on the steering wheel. His pulse was a thunderstorm in his temples.

Maggie looked up. "You're awfully quiet. Are you sure you're okay?"

"Yeah, no, I'm good. Just a little tired."

They hit the Superstition Freeway and headed west, Jack with both hands on the wheel, fully aware of the silence between him and Maggie, not the companionable kind either. This was an uncomfortable silence.

Maggie kept her gaze on the windshield, sunglasses reflecting the endless concrete lanes of traffic.

Jack asked, "Do you want to stop and grab lunch somewhere?"

She shook her head. "No, I'm good. I want to get home and see Annie. I've missed that furball."

The mention of the cat hit him like a punch. He blinked hard, lost his focus, and drifted out of his lane, prompting an angry honk from a Honda in the adjacent lane.

Maggie turned, peering over her sunglasses. "What the hell was that? You've been acting odd since you picked me up."

"I thought I saw something on the road."

He exited the freeway and merged onto the main road leading to their neighborhood. The tension in his chest became palpable. He glanced at Maggie, took a breath, and blurted out, "Some people broke into the house while you were gone."

She blinked. "What?"

He kept his eyes on the road. "Yesterday afternoon. I had to run to the office, and some guys busted open the front door. When I got home, I caught them in the act. I even chased them down the street, but they got away."

Her face was turning red. "Why am I only hearing about this now? What did they take? What did the cops say?"

"Yeah, about that," Jack stammered, staring straight ahead. The last turn onto their block was coming up, and he could feel his heart stutter. "Thursday night, I was working late, and we had a minor incident at the office."

"A minor incident?"

Jack confessed, "I guess it was a pretty major incident."

"A major incident?"

"This is going to sound nuts, but I swear it's true. I was working late, and we started getting reports of a UFO heading toward Phoenix. Garrett and I ended up on the roof, and not only did we see it, but we also filmed it. It came straight over the office." Maggie furrowed her brow.

"Then Friday these government guys showed up, actual men in black. I was called into the office, and both Garrett and I got our asses chewed pretty good. The boss said these agents wanted the videotape and memory card with photos on it. By the time I got back home to get them, they had already broken into the house and were in the process of taking them. They left the house in disarray, a total mess."

"You and Garrett filmed a UFO? And men in black broke into our house? Tell me this is one of your jokes," she said in disbelief.

Jack shook his head and said no. She stared at him in silence.

They pulled onto their block, the red-tiled roofs all in neat, sterile rows. Jack slowed as they approached their driveway. The front door had a strip of mismatched wood patched onto it. The repair was ugly but effective.

Maggie gathered her things.

He killed the engine. The sudden quiet was almost painful. "I'm sorry," he said. "I should have told you sooner."

She didn't look at him. "Let's go inside," she said. "Is Annie okay?"

"Yeah. They left the front door open, and she got out, but I found her on the roof."

"The roof? How did she get up there?" Maggie asked.

"I think she climbed up the trellis."

"Is anything missing besides your UFO stuff? What about my jewelry? And the laptop?"

"They didn't take any of it," he said.

The front door was an eyesore. Even after Jack's repair job, it was obvious the door had been kicked open.

Maggie said nothing as she pushed it open. Inside, the house was quiet. Jack followed behind her, aware of every spot he'd missed.

The living room was back in order for the most part. He'd righted the couch, patched the gash in the side table and rehung the frames on the wall.

The carpet still revealed signs of a scuffle. There was a greasy boot print near the baseboard, a liquid stain he couldn't identify, and a few stray drops of blood leading to the bathroom from his foot injury. On the far wall, the repaired bookshelf and TV stand skewed to its side.

Maggie drifted through the room. Her eyes swept back and forth, taking it all in. She paused in front of the bookshelf, knelt, and straightened up a copy of *Pride and Prejudice*.

They walked the circuit of the house in silence. The guest bathroom was untouched, and the linen closet was undisturbed. However, in the bedroom, the intrusion was impossible to miss. The closet doors hung askew, hangers splayed at odd angles. Her jewelry box was on the floor, drawers half-open, necklaces spilled in a tangle.

She picked up a gold chain and let it dangle, the pendant spinning in the sunlight. Then she set it down and closed the lid with a click.

They moved on to the home office. The rolling chair was upright now, but two slashes marred its fake-leather covering. On the desk, the monitor was smashed, and cords dangled over the front. Both drawers of his metal filing cabinet had been forced open, their contents spilled on the floor.

Maggie took it all in, shook her head, and made a grunt.

While she continued her tour, Jack busied himself in the office, picking up debris from the floor.

This certainly hadn't been the return he'd hoped for.

Their relationship had been struggling for at least a year. His rotating shifts meant she spent most evenings and weekends alone. Time off during the holidays was rare. Jack had to work around a schedule that responded to weather patterns rather than anniversaries or dinner plans.

When they'd moved to Phoenix, she'd taken a teaching job full of enthusiasm. Eventually, she let it go when the exhaustion of managing a household solo made everything harder.

After a while, they'd stopped making plans together and stopped arguing about it, too. The silence that moved in where the arguments used to be was what finally sent her packing.

Maggie popped her head back into the office. "What happens now? Are they coming back?"

He'd been trying to avoid that question. "I don't think so. I hope not."

She sat down on the couch in the living room. "I feel like I'm being watched," she said, her voice small.

Jack sat beside her, not touching but sharing the same space. "I don't know how many times I can say I'm sorry," he said. "I truly am."

"Stop with all of that, enough! We should call the police."

He said, "What do we tell them? That government agents looking for UFO evidence made a mess of our house?"

Maggie set her jaw. "That someone broke in. That we're scared."

He nodded. "Yeah, maybe."

After a while, she stood and walked back toward the guest bedroom. Jack followed a short distance behind, unsure if he should. He watched her kneel at the edge of the bed and coax Annie out from underneath, murmuring until the cat slithered into her arms. She hugged Annie to her chest and buried her face in the soft white fur.

Maggie rocked the cat, returned to the living room sofa, and closed her eyes. At first glance, Jack thought she might be crying.

Then she opened her eyes and glanced down at the bottom rail of the mini-blinds in the front window. She crawled across the couch, bent lower, and shifted Annie to one arm. Maggie twisted up the rail to expose the bottom and detached a small, black rectangle, something electronic.

She turned it over in her hand, holding it between her thumb and forefinger. It was about two inches long and half an inch wide, thin and heavy, with no visible branding. She held it out toward Jack.

He stepped forward, took it, and examined it. It was warm to the touch. There was a tiny switch on the side, and a series of pinprick LED lights along one edge. Jack had seen nothing like it. Could this be a government surveillance device?

Maggie stared at him, eyes wide and unblinking.

Jack's spine went cold, like ice water dripping down his back. He flung the device to the floor and brought his heel down with a crack that echoed off the walls. The black casing split along invisible seams, spilling tiny copper and silicon guts across the hardwood. Three pinprick lights, red, green, blue, flickered twice then died.

Maggie's voice was a whisper, muffled against the cat. "What have you gotten us into, Jack?"

He stood there, empty hands hanging at his sides, staring at the little alien object, which made the house seem much smaller and less safe. For a second, he was sure he could feel the house itself listening, all its patched wounds and silent shadows waiting for his answer.

He had none.

In the months that followed the UFO incident, Jack's routine had returned to normal, not that rotating shift work was normal, of course. For meteorologists who lived with that kind of schedule, time moved differently. It was not uncommon for a shift worker to wake up and not know what day of the week it was.

The southwest monsoon had come and gone, which brought three months of above-average humidity and almost daily thunderstorms to parts of Arizona.

Aside from winter storms, the monsoon was the busiest time of year for meteorologists.

The topic of the UFO incident from March hadn't been mentioned at work again, not even in casual conversation. However, Jack couldn't shake the memory of what he'd seen that night.

At home, he leaned over his computer keyboard until his eyes burned, jumping from one UFO forum to another, dog-earing pages in worn paperbacks with titles like *Cosmic Visitors* and *The Truth Above.*

He filled his notebooks with cramped handwriting, dates, locations, witness descriptions, a growing catalog of unexplained phenomena from every corner of the globe.

Jack's interests expanded from simple UFO sightings to include alleged alien abductions, cattle mutilations, crop circles, and anything else that seemed related.

More recently, he had become involved with a local UFO group in the Phoenix area called CAPER, which stood for Central Arizona Paranormal and Extraterrestrial Researchers.

The group used to investigate ghosts and UFOs, but the ghost-hunting part had long since split off to form its own group, leaving the UFO researchers behind. However, they stuck with the acronym, even though it no longer made complete sense.

Between work and his newfound obsession, Jack's home life had deteriorated.

The dining table where they once shared meals now disappeared beneath towering stacks of dog-eared UFO magazines, printouts of grainy photographs with circles and arrows in red marker, and three-ring binders stuffed with newspaper clippings yellowing at the edges, the table's surface invisible except for a small corner where Jack's coffee mug left overlapping brown rings.

Maggie was becoming frustrated with Jack, unable to understand his obsession with the phenomenon.

When she spoke to him, his eyes remained fixed on his computer, his responses delayed and distracted. At night, she'd wake to find his side of the bed empty, the blue glow of the screen illuminating their home office until dawn.

With a long weekend approaching, Jack and Maggie had booked a quick getaway to San Diego. It was her idea; a last-ditch effort to remember why they'd fallen in love in the first place.

The timing couldn't have been worse when Jack's phone lit up with a call from his friend Pat at CAPER. A case had broken out in Sedona, where witnesses were reporting strange luminous spheres hovering above the western canyons. One person claimed to have spotted a classic flying saucer. He wanted Jack and his friend Steve on-site as soon as possible.

The Sedona case sent electricity through Jack's veins, but one obstacle stood between him and Sedona: Maggie. What if they redi-rected their getaway instead? A luxury spa in Sedona in lieu of San Diego. While Maggie indulged in massages and mineral baths, he could slip away with Steve to chase those luminous spheres. A gamble, but one he would take.

Jack weighed his options. The Cinnabar Canyon Resort would cost him almost triple what they'd budgeted for San Diego, but it was where he needed to be. The concierge promised views of red rock formations from the hot tub on their private balcony. He pulled out his credit card and booked it for four nights. He hoped the resort's extravagance would mask his deception.

Maggie's mood lightened at the mention of Sedona. "You're seri-ous? I thought you hated those new age tourist traps," she said, searching his expression. When he described the private balcony overlooking Cathedral Rock and the five-star spa treatments, her suspicion melted into the first genuine smile he'd witnessed in a long time. By the time he finished detailing the resort's amenities, she was full of anticipation.

He would need perfect luck to pull it all off.

The first night, while Maggie slept, Jack coordinated with Steve to confirm their plan. His colleague had already booked a room at the Desert Sage Motel. Steve had laid out a detailed itinerary for day one: at 10 a.m. they would interview the canyon hiker who had seen the glowing spheres, and at 2 p.m. they would meet with a couple who had shot video of a flying saucer. A late-night stakeout of the canyons was planned for after Maggie went to sleep.

Jack studied the resort's spa brochure, his finger tracing down the list of treatments. The ninety-minute hot stone massage would give him enough time to meet the hiker. For the afternoon interview, he'd need a better excuse, perhaps something about the resort's champi-onship golf course he'd mentioned on the drive up. He made a mental note to bring his golf clubs along, even though he did not intend to hit the links.

Jack couldn't believe his luck. The day was unfolding exactly as planned. While Maggie surrendered to the skilled hands of a masseuse, he and Steve extracted every detail from the hiker about the luminous phenomena.

Later, as she inhaled essential oils in her aromatherapy session, Jack shouldered his golf bag for show before slipping away to the couple's adobe home, where grainy footage of something disc-shaped hovered above red rocks.

Dinner had been perfect; their table had a view of the sunset as it painted the red rocks in shades of amber and rust. Now, steam rose from the hot tub on their private balcony as Jack topped off Maggie's champagne flute.

"This place," Maggie said, settling deeper into the jets, letting her head fall back. "How did you know I needed this?"

"Lucky guess."

She tilted her face skyward, her smile catching starlight. Something had unwound in her shoulders, in the lines around her eyes...a tightness he hadn't realized she'd been carrying until now, when it was gone. "God, I needed this," she said, voice soft with relief.

"I'm glad." He nestled the champagne bottle back into its bed of ice and sank into the bubbling water opposite her. Her gaze lingered, studying him. "Where are you right now? Because it's not here with me."

"Just unwinding." He smiled. "Takes me longer than you."

"Mm." She didn't sound convinced but let it go, nudging his leg with her foot under the water. "We should do this more. Get away. Just us."

"Absolutely," he said, and heard how automatic it sounded. He reached over and cupped his hand behind her neck, and she leaned in the way she used to.

He checked his watch under the pretense of adjusting his position.

Two hours and forty minutes.

She caught him. "Really?"

"Sorry," he said, "force of habit."

Maggie studied him for a moment. She slid her shoulder under his arm.

"I've missed you," she whispered.

He pressed his lips against the top of her head. The champagne tasted flat on his tongue. Somewhere below them, the canyon sat in darkness, and Steve was probably already running equipment checks, setting up the night-vision rig they'd hauled up in the back of his Jeep.

"I've missed you too," Jack said.

It wasn't a total lie. He had missed her. Or at least the version that wasn't high-maintenance. But even as he held her, his mind was drawing a map: the gravel road to the overlook, forty minutes round trip if he didn't linger.

She tilted her face up toward his. The candlelight twinkled in her eyes. There was a look of hope that made something twist uncomfortably in his chest.

They kissed. He realized that he might be late for his meeting with Steve.

The candles had burned low by the time they finally came inside.

Afterward, Maggie lay with her head on his chest, her breathing slowing, one hand resting open on his sternum the way it used to when they were first married. He'd held her until she drifted off to sleep.

He stared at the ceiling in the dark.

It hadn't been a performance, not exactly. She was warm and familiar, and he thoroughly enjoyed it. Despite that, a part of him remained at a distance, observing rather than feeling. In the way that you can watch a fire without being warmed by it. She deserved better than that. He knew it and couldn't do anything about it.

He waited another few minutes, listening to her breathe, before carefully lifting her hand and setting it on the sheet beside him. She murmured something and shifted, but didn't wake.

Jack sat on the edge of the bed in the darkness, buttoning his shirt by feel. On the nightstand, her champagne flute still had an inch left in it. A small smile crossed his face despite everything—she'd never been able to finish a drink.

He picked up his keys from the dresser, one careful finger at a time, wincing at the faint clink of metal, and slipped out the door.

As he made his way out of town, the headlights illuminated the dirt road in front of him, the color of dried blood. To his left and right, a tangle of scrub brush clung close to the road's edge, interspersed with a few boulders like discarded relics from some ancient event, their surfaces worn smooth by centuries of wind and indifferent heat.

The mountains were not far off, but were a silhouette at this hour. With imagination, one could perceive the great shelves of sandstone stacked each upon another, their faces striped in layers of burnt sienna and ochre.

Jack's vehicle rumbled over a little rise, and he could see Steve's Honda parked in a small clearing. He pulled up to the overlook and stepped out of the truck. It was a dark night, and the Milky Way was luminous. He hadn't seen stars this vivid in quite a while. There was no sound here that a person made, only the slight whisper of dry wind.

He walked up to Steve, who had set up a couple of folding tables and chairs in front of his car, the tables stacked with various devices.

"Did you get away okay?" asked Steve.

"So far, so good," said Jack. "She's sound asleep and never wakes until the alarm clock goes off. We can hang out until around 4 a.m., but I don't want to push it much further."

"Sounds good to me," Steve said. He gestured to the equipment on the table. "I've already got a still camera and a video recorder on tripods overlooking the canyon. These are extras you might use. I have two pairs of binoculars here as well."

They sat and watched the canyon for hours, with no activity happening. By 1 a.m., Jack was thinking about calling it a night when Steve spotted something.

"Jack, get your binoculars. See there," he said, pointing down the canyon. "A flickering orange light. It's faint but getting brighter."

Jack fumbled for the binoculars, scanning the darkness until the faint glow came into focus. "Got it," he said, steadying his elbows on the table. The orange pinprick hovered, barely shifting against the black canvas of the canyon. "Looks pretty stationary to me. Are you sure we're not watching some hiker's campsite? I see nothing that screams otherworldly."

Steve shrugged. "Maybe, but the movement pattern seems… unusual." They kept their binoculars trained on the spot until the light winked out as if someone had thrown a switch.

Jack said, "Maybe a camper had to take a piss and turned on a light."

"Maybe," said Steve.

Thirty more minutes passed in silent vigilance, their eyes straining against the darkness until they watered. As Jack's attention drifted, he decided to relieve his bladder. "I'll be right back," he said.

Jack stepped behind his vehicle, his flashlight beam cutting through the darkness. Maybe that's all they'd seen, some poor bastard taking a leak with a headlamp on. It made perfect sense. As he zipped up, the light caught something moving across the sand, a daddy longlegs picking its deliberate path between pebbles. Boredom and mischief stirred within him. He crouched, scooped the spindly creature into his palm, and made his way back to where Steve sat, hunched over his equipment.

He gently placed the hapless arachnid atop Steve's hair and sat down. The show was about to begin.

Jack counted under his breath until the tiny creature made its presence known.

The spindly legs tickled across Steve's temple, invisible in the darkness but unmistakable in sensation.

Steve's body went rigid before erupting into motion, arms flailing at phantom touches, voice cracking into high-pitched yelps that echoed across the canyon as he stumbled backward, almost upending their equipment in his desperate dance to escape the unseen invader.

Jack couldn't contain his laughter.

"You fucking bastard! You know I hate spiders!" he screamed as Jack continued belly-laughing.

Jack tried to reassure him it was only a harmless daddy longlegs.

"I don't give a damn what it was. You know I don't like that shit!" he said. "I'm going to get you back, you bastard!"

"There's only one thing I fear in the world: bears. So good luck with that!" said Jack.

"A Chicago Bears fan scared of bears. Imagine that," he said as he settled back into his chair. "You're going to get yours one of—"

Jack cut him off. "There it is again," he said as the amber light flickered back into existence.

Both men trained their binoculars on the phenomenon, tracking its rapid approach.

The light wound through the canyon's contours like a luminous serpent, covering the three-mile stretch with alarming speed, its intensity magnifying with each passing second.

"Well, it's obvious that isn't a hiker or a guy taking a piss," Jack said.

A bright white orb streaked into view from their left, well above the horizon. "What the hell is that?" Steve gasped.

As the white light continued darting to the right, the amber orb began ascending straight up, and after about twenty seconds it intersected with the white light and seemed to merge with it. The light remained the same white color but came to an immediate stop.

"The cameras are rolling, right?" Jack asked.

"Oh, we're getting all of this!" said Steve.

The white orb dropped back down into the canyon and hovered at the entrance, about fifty feet above the ground. It remained unmoving for about a minute before it changed back to an amber color. After about five seconds, it winked out of existence.

Nothing else appeared in the sky or in the canyon for the rest of their vigil. As the clock approached 4 a.m., Jack rubbed his burning eyes and reached for his keys. If he left now, he might salvage a couple of hours of sleep before Maggie awoke.

9 / SEDONA

Jack eased the vehicle into a parking spot and crept back to their room. At the entrance, he held his breath while sliding the keycard into the reader, wincing at the tiny electronic chirp. He pushed the door open with painful slowness, then closed it carefully, feeling the latch catch with an almost inaudible click. Only when he turned toward the bed did he see Maggie, motionless in the corner chair, her silhouette unmistakable against the pre-dawn darkness.

She flipped on a floor lamp next to her, and he knew he was in big trouble. She didn't pull any punches. "Where the hell have you been?"

"I couldn't sleep, so I went out for a bit," he said.

"Don't lie to me, Jack! I woke up at 11:30 to get a drink of water, and you were already gone. I've been sitting here for almost five hours. You had sex with me and then left after I fell asleep."

Jack sighed in defeat. The game was over, and he lost. "My friend Steve is up here, and we watched for UFOs all night."

Her fingernails dug into the armrests. "This whole resort idea, the couple's massage, the hot stone treatment, was all cover so you could hunt little green men?" she growled through clenched teeth.

"Why couldn't it be both?" he asked.

"Take me home right now. Not in the morning, but right now. We're done here, Jack. This whole marriage is one big fucking charade!"

The ride home was painful. Maggie kept her arms folded over her chest and uttered not a single word. Jack had tried to start up an apology of sorts a few times, but she ignored him.

When they turned into the driveway, she finally spoke. "Leave me here. Go back to your UFO chase. I need some time to think."

Jack didn't argue. He was bleary-eyed from a lack of sleep but turned the vehicle back toward Sedona.

Somehow he made it back without wrecking his vehicle. He put up the do-not-disturb sign and slept most of the day. Jack and Steve were refreshed and ready for another night of adventure.

Jack told him what happened between him and Maggie, shaking his head.

"Your marriage has been on the rocks for a while, my friend. This sped up the process."

They planned something adventurous for the evening. Carrying nothing more than hiking gear and their video cameras, they set out down the canyon where they'd seen the amber light emerge the night before.

According to their topographic maps, the canyon went back about three miles until it narrowed to a point where they could go no farther. A thousand-foot rock wall was present at the end.

The canyon's entrance yawned six hundred yards across, pinching inward until it measured a few hundred feet at its midpoint. Scrubby vegetation blanketed the canyon floor, but a dry streambed offered them a natural pathway through the wilderness. Jack cataloged the local predators as they prepared to enter: rattlesnakes coiled under rocks, mountain lions watching from ledges, packs of coyotes, and those tusked wild pigs, javelinas, that could slice a man open if provoked. And who knew what danger the mysterious orbs presented?

Sunset painted the horizon in fiery streaks as Jack and Steve descended into the canyon. Shadows lengthened between the narrowing walls, forcing them to click on their headlamps.

Their strategy was methodical: advance several hundred yards, extinguish all light, then crouch in darkness for ten or fifteen-minute intervals, straining eyes and ears for anything that didn't belong in the desert night.

Three and a half hours into their trek, Jack and Steve found themselves in a narrowing throat of stone. The canyon had constricted to 150 feet across, its floor tilting upward at a steep grade. As they rounded what proved to be the last bend, they confronted their terminus a few hundred yards ahead: a sheer rock face that soared a thousand feet skyward, blocking any further progress. Despite their vigilance, the night had yielded nothing extraordinary beyond the occasional rustle or animal cry that sent their hearts racing.

"Should we keep going all the way to the wall?" Steve asked.

"We've hiked this far, might as well," said Jack. "Let's sit for a minute and rest."

There was an outcropping of rocks next to the dry streambed, which was a perfect place to rest. As they sat back and scanned the night sky, Jack's mind wandered. What would he be facing when he returned home? Would all of his things be piled on the curb? Would she be gone?

The shrill cry of a bird coming from the rock wall ahead interrupted his thoughts. Something had disturbed it. Jack sat up to squint into the darkness, even though there was nothing there to see.

The rock face erupted with light as an amber sphere burst from solid stone halfway up the wall. It plummeted and halted abruptly, suspended about ten feet above the canyon floor before beginning a deliberate forward drift. Jack and Steve scrambled for cover, wedging themselves behind a massive boulder that jutted from the canyon wall.

The sphere drifted forward, maintaining perfect alignment

between the canyon's rugged walls until it decelerated above the very ledge where they had been sitting.

Jack's pulse hammered against his ribs like something desperate to escape, while cold perspiration slicked his brow. A wave of nausea rolled through him, turning his insides to liquid.

The orb hung in perfect silence. No heat radiated from its amber glow, yet Jack recognized what was happening to his body, the same reaction he'd had near the V-shaped craft. Though his ears detected nothing, the air seemed charged. Tiny pinpricks danced across his skin as the fine hairs on his forearms stood at attention.

For half a minute, the orb remained suspended in the air, then resumed its journey toward the canyon entrance, accelerating as it went. Jack and Steve exchanged glances only after it had passed from view.

Jack's voice caught in his throat, escaping as a ragged whisper. "Holy shit!" When Steve didn't answer, Jack clicked his headlamp on. The beam caught Steve's face, pupils contracting to pinpoints, skin drained of color like desert bone. His lips barely moved. "Got every second on video."

"Let's get the hell out of here!"

The orb had vanished into the night, leaving them to navigate the canyon's twisting path in tense silence. Jack's eyes darted between the trail and the darkening sky, where clouds had smothered the stars. The weather report had promised clear skies, but he knew better than to trust forecasts in this corner of the desert, where flash floods could transform dry beds into raging torrents without warning.

Within fifteen minutes, Jack's fears proved justified. Lightning flashed in the distance, momentarily illuminating the canyon walls with ghostly blue-white light.

The storm wasn't above them yet, but the increasing frequency of the flashes suggested it was advancing toward their position.

"We need to pick up the pace," said Jack. "This isn't a safe place to be in the daytime with a thunderstorm, let alone at night. This could go from bad to worse with little notice."

They moved forward at an almost reckless rate as drops of rain pelted them. Lightning flickered closer by the minute. They were only one hundred yards from the mouth of the canyon when Steve's foot got caught between two slippery rocks. He fell on his face and twisted his knee.

Torrential rain hammered down as lightning cracked above them, splitting the sky into jagged fragments. Steve's howl pierced through the storm's roar. Clutching his right knee, he rocked back and forth on the muddy ground, his face contorted in agony.

He hoisted Steve upright, his friend's body sagging against him, as he transferred his entire weight onto Jack's shoulder. A sharp cry escaped Steve's lips. His injured leg dangled uselessly, refusing to bear even the slightest pressure.

"We're almost there, buddy. Use your good leg and put your weight on me. We'll get out of this. We're almost to the mouth of the canyon."

With Steve's arm slung across his shoulders, Jack half-dragged, half-carried his friend just beyond the canyon's mouth. He eased him onto a flat-topped boulder, both men gasping for breath as rain pelted their faces. "The vehicles are a half-mile up that trail," Jack said, pointing into the darkness. "No way you're making that walk. I'll bring my truck down. Stay put and keep pressure off that knee."

Jack bolted uphill toward the overlook where they'd left their vehicles a half-mile away. Rain hammered his face as he navigated the treacherous slope, each lightning strike revealing the path for split-seconds before plunging him back into darkness. Twice, his boots lost purchase on rain-slicked stone, almost sending him sprawling. His pace was slow. Lungs burning, muscles screaming, he finally reached his truck, collapsing against the driver's door as thunder cracked overhead.

He cranked the engine and threw the truck into four-wheel-drive, tires spinning against mud before getting a grip. The headlights carved a path through the darkness as he navigated backward around the overlook, searching for a gentler slope. The truck lurched and slid down the incline toward the valley floor. When he reached the spot where he'd left Steve, everything inside him turned to ice.

Muddy water surged through the canyon exit where he had been waiting, the flat boulder now submerged beneath churning rapids. Jack's eyes swept the banks as his headlights cut through sheets of rain. Steve was nowhere. The realization hit that the flash flood must have taken him.

Jack flung himself from the truck into the storm, hollering Steve's name. His headlamp slashed through the darkness, revealing nothing but torrential rain. The canyon and its exit had transformed into a roaring monster. Water churned where there had been dry earth minutes before. Thunder cracked overhead, drowning out any human sound. The world had become nothing but noise and fury.

A jagged bolt split the sky, freezing the landscape in electric blue for several seconds. There, against the hillside to his left, Jack spotted a huddled form. Steve had somehow dragged himself fifty yards away and about ten feet higher from the surging waters below.

Jack scrambled up the slope, mud sucking at his boots with each desperate step. He hooked his arms under Steve's shoulders, feeling his friend's weight sag against him as they staggered toward the idling truck. Murky water now lapped at the front tires, the flood's advance quickening. He wrenched the gearshift into reverse, tires spinning like crazy before finding purchase, the vehicle lurching backward as the torrent clawed at their escape.

Jack's pickup clawed its way uphill, tires flinging arcs of mud until they reached level ground. The once-dusty access road had turned into a slurry that streamed alongside them.

His truck fishtailed as Jack navigated the serpentine path of crimson sludge toward Sedona. His mind raced through a mental map of the terrain. Were there places where the road dipped through low-water crossings? He didn't recall any, but in the darkness with rain hammering the windshield, he might not see rushing water fast enough. Many drivers in these parts had driven unwittingly into rushing water at night. He slowed down.

With good fortune, the road remained above the flood all the way to the highway. Jack's knuckles stayed white on the wheel until Sedona's lights appeared through the rain-streaked windshield.

Minutes later, fluorescent hospital signs guided him to the emergency entrance, where attendants rushed out with a wheelchair for Steve.

Jack slumped into a molded plastic chair in the waiting room, mud-caked and trembling, as the night's impossible events replayed behind his exhausted eyes.

Jack jolted awake to a gentle tap on his shoulder. His neck ached from the awkward angle against the waiting room wall. He didn't know how much time had passed. A nurse in blue scrubs stood over him.

"Are you the one who came in with Steve Diller?" she asked. When he nodded, she gestured toward the treatment area. "He's stabilized. You can see him now."

He followed her to a set of double doors. She pressed a wall-mounted button, and they swung open with a pneumatic hiss. Jack followed her through the sterile corridor to a row of curtained alcoves. She drew back the pale-blue fabric to reveal Steve, propped up in a hospital bed. Clear tubing snaked from an IV stand into his arm, while a thin oxygen line looped beneath his nostrils.

He was wide awake and grasped Jack's hand when he came up beside the bed. "You saved me, man! I guess I can forgive you for throwing that damn spider on me yesterday."

Jack squeezed his friend's hand and nodded at the bandaged leg. "So, what's the verdict? Should I shop for peg legs and parrot accessories?" His smile cracked through a thin layer of dried mud on his face.

"Thank goodness, no! The doc used some fancy term, a patellar contusion," Steve said, gesturing to his knee as Jack grimaced. "In plain English, I smashed my kneecap against those rocks and bruised the bone. But wait, that's not all. They think I might've torn something inside, the meniscus. Can't tell for sure until I get back home for an MRI. If it's torn..." He made a scissors motion with his fingers. "They'll have to go in and clean it up."

He shook his head. "It's my fault. I was pushing us too fast, trying to outrun the storm."

"Jack, if you hadn't pushed us, we'd both be dead, swept away in a flood. How the hell did you know what was coming?"

"Jesus, Steve, I'm a meteorologist. Do you know how many flash flood warnings get issued every year for things like that? Plenty!" he reflected for a moment. "And for what it's worth, I'm going to call up my colleagues in Flagstaff and bitch them out. It's their area, and they had no rain in the forecast."

After a quick shower at the resort, Jack stuffed his clothes into duffel bags, checked out early, then drove back to the hospital, where Steve waited with discharge papers and a knee brace.

With his knee immobilized, Jack took the wheel for the drive back to Phoenix. They'd arranged for Steve's abandoned car to be retrieved from the canyon overlook. As miles of red rock landscape scrolled past the windows, their conversation circled back to what they'd witnessed in the canyon: the glowing orb that had emerged from solid stone.

Steve shifted in his seat, wincing as he adjusted his leg. "What about the camera footage? That thing got drenched. I'd bet it fried the circuits."

Jack grimaced. "The camera's toast, but I extracted the tape. It looks to be water damaged, so I'm not very hopeful of recovering any footage from it."

Steve rubbed his temple, his eyes distant with the memory. "Jack, I keep seeing it in my head, that ball of light phasing through solid rock like it wasn't even there. What the hell could do something like that?"

He shook his head. "No idea, but think back to right before it showed up. Remember that bird that went nuts on the ledge at the end of the canyon? Birds have incredible sensitivity to electromagnetic fields. If these phenomena generate an energy signature, wildlife might detect it before our instruments do. Could be worth investigating as an early warning system."

Steve massaged his knee. "Birds as detectors? Interesting theory, but I wouldn't be happy about lugging a canary into every investigation." He winced as he shifted in his seat. "Something's bothered me since we left. That light, or whatever it was, how large would you estimate it was?"

Jack concentrated as he relived the scene in his mind. "Hard to judge with that brightness. Maybe it was a yard across. What do you think?"

"Could've been bigger. I kept thinking it was going to float around that boulder and...do something to us."

"Whatever that thing was, it wasn't some random phenomenon. The way it moved after we showed up, as if it was watching us. My hands are still shaking, man. Do you think it was some kind of craft under intelligent control?"

Jack stared ahead at the highway. "I keep coming back to plasma, you know, the fourth state of matter. Not solid like that rock face, not liquid like the floodwater, not gas like the air. Plasma is in an entirely different category. It's a superheated, electrified cloud that can pass through solid matter. That orb had many of the hallmarks."

"Isn't that what ball lightning is supposed to be like?" asked Steve.

Jack nodded approvingly. "Looks like someone's been reading up! Ball lightning is indeed a plasma phenomenon. But natural plasmas typically behave erratically and dissipate within seconds. The orb we saw exhibited some plasma-like characteristics, I'll grant you that."

"Some?" Steve asked.

Jack held up an index finger for emphasis. "Natural phenomena don't behave like that, maintaining form for that long, moving with such purpose, almost like something was directing it. You know what I mean?"

"Oh, I was scared shitless, Jack. I get what you mean."

Jack nodded slowly, his eyes distant with calculation. "Makes you wonder what equipment we would need to capture data on something like that next time. Maybe some kind of electromagnetic field detector or infrared. Something that wouldn't get fried in the process. I need to think about it for a while."

After he left Steve at his place, he steered toward home, as he imagined Maggie's reaction to his premature return.

Jack pressed the garage remote, and it was empty where her car should have been. He parked the truck and entered the house. The silence was overwhelming. In the kitchen, a single sheet of paper hung from the refrigerator, held by a cloud-shaped magnet he had received as a gift from her last Christmas.

The note confirmed what the empty closets already told him. Maggie had left for her sister's in Houston, taking Annie. Jack sank into a kitchen chair, a heaviness settling in his chest. He had stood on the sidelines as their marriage unraveled, and did little to stop it. Her dreams of stability pulled against his need for cosmic answers.

In the coming weeks, Jack wore out his phone dialing Houston, only to have her sister act as gatekeeper. "She's not ready." That became a mantra he could recite in his sleep. Every day, he checked his phone for missed calls, rehearsing what he might say when Maggie's name finally lit up the caller ID. Weeks blurred together, and his phone remained silent.

Jack made one last desperate call to Houston. This time, her sister didn't bother with the usual excuses. "She's with David now," she said. "He's someone she's known since high school. I think it would be best if you moved on." The line went dead before he could respond.

Not long thereafter, Jack answered an unexpected knock to find a man in a cheap suit holding a manila envelope. The divorce papers inside were as impersonal as the server's rehearsed speech. It wasn't a surprise.

By autumn, their marriage existed only in the past tense, a legal dissolution as complete as Maggie's disappearance from his life.

A heavy heart accompanied Jack as he acknowledged his share of the blame. In the end, they had agreed to a fair division of assets, with Annie remaining in Houston with Maggie. He had to sell the house and divide the proceeds. He rented a one-bedroom apartment in Tempe. At least he had a shorter commute to work, being only ten minutes away.

After a week in his apartment, Jack figured the worst was behind him.

Many people wouldn't think it, but a union governed federal meteorologists, the National Weather Service Employees Organization, or NWSEO. The office elected Frank "Duke" Deluca as the union steward three months ago.

Unlike typical unions, the NWSEO operated with significant constraints. Federal law prohibited them from striking, and a labyrinth of regulations dictated their every interaction with management. Whenever they raised objections, their complaints carried little weight.

Jack was getting ready for a day shift when the phone rang on the nightstand next to his bed. The caller ID flashed "Frank Deluca."

"Morning, Jack. Got some news for you, and I only found out about it myself five minutes ago. Eddie told me you are being brought up on disciplinary charges. They won't tell me what it's about. They're going to hit you with it when you walk in the door. The regional director from Salt Lake is here, and a couple of suits from DC, along with Ray and Eddie."

Jack was puzzled. "What? They have people here from Washington? What the hell did I do?" Had one of his pranks gone too far, or had he told an inappropriate joke in front of someone he shouldn't have?

"No idea, but you already know you have the right to union representation, assuming you want me there. Walt agreed to take over my fire-weather duties this morning, so I can help you."

Jack's heart raced. "Okay, thanks, Duke. I want you in there. I'm about to leave." He'd been reprimanded twice before and written up once. None of these disciplinary actions were because of his job performance. They were all because of his pranks. Jack had dialed the practical jokes back since then and couldn't imagine what he'd done this time.

Jack entered the office, and the stern gazes of Ray, Eddie, the regional director, and a man he didn't recognize swept over him. They were standing by the front desk, drinking coffee and chatting with the secretary.

Eddie said, "You're here. Let's get started in the conference room."

"I'll be right in. Let me put my lunch in the fridge."

The regional director held up a hand to stop him. "Bring it in here for now." That comment seemed unusual to Jack, and his heart started beating faster. They entered the conference room single file. Duke sat across the table, and a man in a suit sat next to him.

Silence prevailed for several seconds, apart from the sound of shuffling papers. Ray was the first to speak, turning to address Jack. "I know you must be wondering why you're in here this morning. Before we begin, I'll introduce our visitors. To my right is Harry Smith, our regional director. Anthony Samuelson, general counsel with our headquarters in DC, and Frank Lutz, U.S. Secret Service."

At the mention of the Secret Service, Jack's mind was reeling.

Several months ago, he and John had scanned a twenty-dollar bill into the computer and printed it on the new color laser printer. They cut the fake bill out, wrinkled it up a bit, and left it lying on the floor as bait for Nate. It looked quite real, unless you inspected it up close.

Nate was ecstatic when he found it, and then hilarity ensued when they revealed its phony nature. Nate mentioned they could get in trouble with the Secret Service for counterfeiting, so they destroyed their creation with haste. Was this what the fuss was about?

Ray said, "I've already briefed everyone on the alleged UFO incident that happened earlier this year."

Jack's pulse quickened. This was about the UFO? Again?

Eddie took over. "A brief media sensation occurred when one of our forecasters on an overnight shift mentioned the UFO to a morning radio DJ. We got that under control, but later two strange men visited us. They claimed to represent the Air Force and ordered us to destroy all evidence in our possession and to never speak of the incident again."

Ray picked up where Eddie left off and looked at Jack. "A little over a month ago, a reporter at the Arizona Republic received a letter detailing the entire event, including claims of a cover-up, claiming the office was forced into silence. Lucky for us, the reporter came to us before printing the story. You wouldn't know anything about that letter, would you, Jack?"

The question surprised him. "What? That's news to me. We all sat right here in a meeting where you told us to kill the evidence and forget it ever happened. I've held up my end of the bargain. It wasn't me!"

Regional Director Harry Smith said, "Mr. Davis, I'm having a hard time believing that." He nodded toward the Secret Service agent, who opened a manila folder and slid a paper over to Duke and Jack. Tiny, magnified yellow dots were visible on the document.

"What's this?" asked Jack.

Mr. Lutz leaned forward, his tie brushing the table. "Most people don't realize that color laser printers leave a fingerprint. Tiny yellow dots, invisible to the naked eye, appear on every page they print." He tapped the paper with his index finger. "Manufacturers built this into their machines at our request. Originally to catch counterfeiters, but these dots can identify any printer, including the one that produced this letter."

"And?" asked Jack.

Smith went on, "They traced the printer back to this office and identified the new HP model you've had for less than six months. We discovered the date and time it was printed, and which computer it came from: yours."

Jack's collar seemed to shrink around his neck as heat crept up from his chest to his hairline. The conference room lights pulsed in time with the blood hammering in his ears, and he swallowed hard against what felt like a mouthful of cotton. "Wait a damn minute! I did no such thing!"

The regional director said, "You were on shift when it happened, and we confirmed you logged into your computer five minutes before the document printed. That leaves no doubt who the guilty party is."

Jack gripped the edge of the table, forcing air into his chest. "Bullshit! Anyone could have used my login and hacked my password. I never sent that letter to any damn reporter!"

The room erupted into a shouting match, with Jack claiming innocence and accusations flying from every corner.

Finally, Samuelson, the lawyer from headquarters, made a loud whistling sound and banged on the table.

"All right, listen up! This is more complex than you think."

"Remember those Air Force men who came to visit the office?" he said. "They heard about the media leak and started following you around. It seems like you're spending a lot of your free time with some UFO research group, and they've documented you interviewing witnesses from the March incident." He opened his briefcase and tossed many black-and-white photos of Jack talking to witnesses onto the table.

"So? What I do outside the office is my business!"

The lawyer swallowed and then said, "Ordinarily, that's true. However, you were specifically told never to speak of this incident again, and here you are," he said, gesturing to the photos on the table, "violating the very principles of that agreement."

Jack sat quietly for a second. "Maybe so, but I didn't print that letter and send it."

Samuelson said, "It doesn't make a difference." He looked at the regional director, who gave a small nod. "As of this moment, you are no longer employed by the National Weather Service."

Jack couldn't believe it. "WHAT? Are you fucking kidding me? I'm being FIRED?"

The regional director interjected with a smooth demeanor that suggested this was not his first time giving this speech. "Not necessarily. We can fire you, as Mr. Samuelson has alluded, or you can resign of your own accord. Doing so will allow you to walk away without a blemish on your employment record. You haven't worked enough years to earn a pension, but you can keep your retirement savings account and roll it over with a new employer."

Duke, who had been silent throughout the entire exchange, said, "Listen, Jack, you don't have to resign. Let them fire you. The union will fight to get your job back."

"And how long will that take, Duke? Years? I need money. What should I do? Being fired from a federal job means I would struggle to be hired as a burger flipper at McDonald's."

Eddie cleared his throat. "I wish it hadn't come to this, but let me give you some advice. You'll never work as a meteorologist again if you get fired. But if you resign, there are plenty of jobs in the private sector, or you can find a job in television, or hell, you can go back and get your Ph.D. and teach. Tell them you couldn't handle the rotating shift-work, and nobody will think twice about why you resigned."

The regional director slid a small packet across the table to Jack. "I can't tell you what choice to make, Mr. Davis, but if you choose to resign, all you have to do is sign these papers. We've already filled them out."

"Gee, how convenient." He gathered his thoughts. "Will you excuse me? I need a minute to think."

"Don't take too long," said Ray. Everyone else filed out of the room, leaving Duke and Jack alone.

~

"Duke, I did not print and send that letter. Would you find out when this happened? I need to know who worked during that shift. While you check, I'll review these forms."

"I think they're trying to railroad you out of the organization, Jack. They'll invent fresh accusations no matter how you defend yourself. I don't think there is any way you're going to win at their game," said Duke.

Leaving Jack with the resignation papers, he strode into the hallway, searching for Ray. Five minutes later, he came back with a printed schedule. "It was on the twelfth of September, Jack," he said, examining the paper in his hand. "Looks like you, Glen, and Garrett were on shift that evening."

"That son of a bitch," Jack said. "It had to be Garrett! You may not believe me, but I know the truth, and I didn't print and send that letter. Garrett witnessed that UFO with me. That dirty bastard! I'm getting kicked out the door because of what he did!"

Duke grimaced. "Whoa, you don't know that Garrett did it. It could have been Glen, or perhaps someone else was in here."

"Glen, seriously? Mister goodie two-shoes? Not a chance. It was Garrett. I know it was."

The regional director poked his head through the conference room door. "Time's up, Mr. Davis. What's it going to be?"

Jack snatched the resignation papers, his pen scratching across the signature line with enough force to tear through to the next page. He shoved his chair back and thrust the documents at the regional director's chest, forcing the man to fumble to catch them.

"Screw you and the weather service! I don't want to work for a place that has its head up its ass!" Jack pushed the regional director aside and stormed out the door.

Duke called after him, "Hey, you forgot your lunch!"

Jack slammed the car door so hard that the window rattled in its frame. The engine roared to life, and he stomped the accelerator, leaving a short stretch of rubber on the pavement as he fishtailed out of the parking lot. The steering wheel vibrated under his grip as he cut off a delivery truck, the driver's horn blaring behind him. All he could see was the route to Garrett's neighborhood in Chandler.

Jack knew Garrett worked the swing shift yesterday. He might still be asleep. Jack clenched his jaw. "Garrett's in for a rude awakening." He stomped on the gas and roared onto the freeway.

The speedometer needle trembled at ninety as Jack weaved through multiple lanes of traffic. A flash of red and blue in his rearview mirror would mean the end of his perfect driving record, one more thing taken from him today. He eased his foot off the accelerator, watching the needle drop to seventy-five. Still too fast, but he couldn't bring himself to slow down any further.

Ten minutes later, Jack pulled into Garrett's neighborhood and nearly locked up the brakes, coming to an abrupt stop in front of the white stucco home. He glanced at the driveway to see if Garrett's wife, Karen, was home. All he saw was Garrett's pickup truck. Good. Jack preferred no witnesses to the ugliness about to unfold.

Jack pounded on the front door with fury, and after thirty seconds he alternated ringing the doorbell and pounding on the door. After a minute, Garrett finally opened the door, looking half-asleep.

"Jack, what the hell, man! Where's the fire?"

Jack lunged forward, thrusting his finger into Garrett's chest. "You leaked that letter to the newspaper, you backstabbing piece of shit!" Garrett stumbled backward, catching himself against the doorframe.

"What the hell are you talking about?" he shouted back, his face flushing crimson. "I didn't leak anything!" Their voices echoed down the street as neighbors' curtains twitched. Jack slammed his fist on the railing. Garrett jabbed a finger toward Jack's chest. Accusations flew. Voices escalated. Friendship crumbled. In the end, they resolved nothing. Garrett retreated inside and slammed the door, leaving Jack to drag himself home.

Back in his apartment, the reality of the situation weighed on him. Jack's career in meteorology, the only professional identity he'd known since college, had evaporated like morning dew in the Arizona sun. And by resigning, he lost any unemployment benefits he might have been eligible to receive.

What was he going to do now? Move back home to Chicago? He could call old friends and see if they could put in a good word for him somewhere. Perhaps one of those commodity trading firms was hiring. The bigger ones employed a small team of meteorologists to help determine when to buy and sell crop futures. Or he could try the airlines. Both United and American kept weather teams at O'Hare. Jack grimaced at the thought. Swapping one windowless office for another, abandoning the desert skies he'd grown to love.

It was October now, and soon snow and freezing winds would engulf Illinois. He shivered at the thought. But the rent wouldn't pay for itself, and his savings wouldn't last long.

He remembered that a bunch of folks from CAPER were getting together at the Depot Cantina, one of Jack's favorite Mexican food joints. He needed a sober driver tonight. Jack wasn't a heavy drinker, but tonight? He was planning to get drunk.

Garrett reeled from Jack's unexpected attack. He stood in his doorway long after the squeal of tires on pavement faded. His pulse was still hammering. He leaned against the doorframe and stared at the empty street, replaying the last two minutes, trying to find the moment where his morning had gone completely sideways.

He went inside, poured himself a cup of coffee he didn't want, and called the office.

Duke picked up on the second ring and broke the news without preamble: Jack had lost his job. The government was accusing him of leaking information about the UFO incident to the Arizona Republic. The letter had been traced back to a printer at the office, to Jack's login, on a shift they had both worked.

Garrett sat his mug down on the counter; his stomach dropped somewhere around the word *fired*.

So that explained the finger in his chest, the shouting, the look in Jack's eyes. Somebody betrayed him, and he lost his job because of it.

Jack had been more than a co-worker. They stood and witnessed that craft across the rooftop together, shouted at the same dark sky, shared the same stunned silence when it ceased to exist.

He hadn't sent the letter, nor had he breathed a word of the UFO encounter to anyone outside the office. After the radiation burns, the doctor's visit, and the quiet fear of not knowing what that exposure might eventually do to him, the last thing he wanted was more attention.

He made his peace with staying quiet. That peace had cost him something, but he'd paid it willingly.

If it wasn't him, and assuming Jack was telling the truth, then the math pointed to Glen.

Glen was the mature, responsible shift leader, always following the rules to the point of being irritating about it. It was hard to picture him composing a whistleblower letter in the middle of a shift.

But hard to picture wasn't the same as impossible.

Garrett decided to keep quiet for now. He'd watch, listen, and pay attention in a way he hadn't before. Something didn't add up, and the next time this happened, he wanted to make sure his name wasn't attached to it.

Everyone knew what happened that morning. Jack Davis was gone. That fact alone was enough to knock the whole office off-balance.

Jack was a practical joker, but he was also one of the most generous people in the office. He was the one who stayed late, on his own time, to walk interns through their forecasting work. Jack volunteered for extra shifts without being asked. He was the last person any of them would have expected to be escorted out.

If Jack was innocent, the unanswered question was: who really did it?

Garrett could feel the eyes of his coworkers upon him at every turn. Conversations suddenly paused when he rounded a corner, and people were whispering and keeping to themselves.

He knew what they were thinking. He and Jack had been on that roof together. Since Jack was gone and Garrett was still here, the math looked suspicious to anyone willing to consider it.

He sat down at his station and stared at his monitor without seeing it.

Should he say something or keep quiet? Left to its own devices, rumors tended to run out of control. He'd have to confront it. He just needed a little time to figure out the right words...how to say "it wasn't me" in a way that didn't sound like something a guilty person would say.

Sunset was a half hour away in Tempe, stretching the shadows of palm trees like dark fingers across the Depot Cantina's parking lot. Jack stepped out of the passenger side of Steve's Honda, his designated driver for the night. With good fortune, Steve had recovered from the knee injury and didn't require surgery.

"Hey, there are almost no cars here. What's up with that?" asked Jack.

Steve peered around the parking lot. "I don't know. Let's see if the rest of the guys are here."

Their group emerged from around the corner of the building, walking toward them with slumped shoulders.

Pat, a stocky man with a salt-and-pepper mustache who'd become the de facto ringleader of their UFO-hunting crew, trudged over with his hands stuffed in his pockets. "Restaurant is shut down," he called out, jerking his thumb back toward the restaurant. "Something about a plumbing problem. The place reeks. I can smell it outside the front door."

"Damn it, I was looking forward to some amazing fajitas," said Steve.

The group huddled together to make alternative plans. Jack

didn't really care where they went, as long as the beer was cold. Someone suggested Casey Moore's, an oyster bar about a half-mile away. They erupted in a chorus of objections. "Oysters? I can't stand those slimy things," grumbled Pat, while Steve threw his hands up. "Last time I went there at night, it was pretty crowded. Hard to hold a conversation."

Jack cut through the debate with a sharp wave of his hand. "Look, Casey Moore's has everything: steaks, burgers, the works. Plus, we can grab a table outside. It's not too noisy out there, and there's plenty of seating. Perfect night for it, too. I didn't lose my job today to spend the evening bickering about dinner plans. I had enough of that during my marriage!"

That was met with a few laughs, and the party reluctantly agreed. Jimbo chimed in, "I heard a rumor that the place is haunted."

"Where did you hear that?" said Jack.

"I saw something in the Phoenix New Times, I think," he said.

Steve interjected, "Well, ghost or not, nothing will bother you outside, so you're safe, Jimbo."

The CAPER group had settled into the yard at Casey Moore's, seated at a picnic table in the corner. A young, shapely waitress had taken their drink orders and left them with menus. Two guys were prodding Jack to hit on her. Steve, in particular, wouldn't let up. "She's cute, man! Look at her sweet face and that blonde hair! You're single again. You need to get back out on the playing field!"

He rolled his eyes. "I'm not hitting on a waitress who has to rush home after her shift to finish her college homework."

The debate continued on about Jack's love life, or lack thereof until Pat's cell phone rang. Most people relied on pagers or bulky car-installed phones if they needed to be reached on the go. Seeing a person pull out a Nokia or Motorola StarTAC was like spotting someone from the future. Pat always placed his phone on the table, as if casually forgetting a rare jewel where everyone could admire it. The monthly payments for that sleek little rectangle ate up more of his salary than he could afford, but that was typical Pat behavior.

Pat excused himself and stepped away to take the call. In the meantime, the waitress brought their drinks out. The guys shook their heads when she asked if they were ready to order. Jack caught her before she left. "Actually," he said, leaning in with a sly grin, "could you bring a dozen raw oysters for our friend who's on the phone?"

The waitress glanced at Pat's empty chair and nodded, pen poised over her notepad. Around the table, shoulders shook with suppressed laughter as she walked away.

Jimbo could hardly contain himself. "Pat's going to kill you! He hates oysters!" Jack's life had crumbled around him piece by piece, but as he watched his friends try to stifle their laughter, he realized an essential part of himself had survived the wreckage.

Pat slid back into his seat, his eyes wide with excitement. "Jack, remember that silver-haired guy who was at our presentation in Scottsdale last month? The Paradise Valley guy? Claimed he watched the whole V-formation cruise right over Camelback from his back patio?"

"Yeah, kinda. He was asking a lot of questions."

Pat's eyes lit up. "That guy, he's loaded. He is an Arkansas business mogul, and he's got a winter mansion nestled right against the base of Camelback Mountain. Back in March, he was lounging on his patio when the V-formation cruised right over the peak. Said it was so close he could've hit it with a rock." Pat took a swig of his beer. "Anyway, he's dying to talk to us. I told him to swing by for drinks."

Jack's beer bottle paused halfway to his lips. "Rich guy from Paradise Valley wants to talk UFOs on the night I'm drowning my sorrows?" He shook his head and took a long pull from the bottle. "Tonight's about forgetting my problems, not rehashing them for some snowbird millionaire."

"Hey, the dude said he'd buy all our drinks tonight. You want him to go away, you can tell him yourself," Pat said.

Jack shrugged. "Well, if he's buying, he can talk my ear off."

~

The CEO of Sinclair Consolidated Companies, Bob Sinclair, had built his empire through several profitable businesses across Arkansas, including Sinclair Farms Poultry, Delta Gold Rice, and Sinclair Trucking. Jack watched Pat's eyes light up with each additional detail about Sinclair, like a kid reciting baseball statistics.

Pat leaned over the table, lowering his voice. "This guy's worth a fortune, but you'd never know it. Drives an Audi when he's at his Arkansas headquarters. No gold Rolex, no name-dropping. Complete opposite of most rich guys."

Pat continued, "I've heard he's not your typical corner-office type, remembers every employee's birthday and knows all their kids' names. The kind of boss who listens when he asks how your weekend was."

Jack rolled his eyes and drained the last of his beer. "That's fascinating, Pat, but I didn't come here for a biography. Unless he's buying the next round, I couldn't care less."

Despite Pat's insistence about Sinclair's modest tastes, Jack couldn't help but raise an eyebrow when a gleaming Bentley Continental glided into Casey Moore's parking lot, wedging itself between a rust-speckled pickup and a dented Honda Civic.

Jack nodded toward Pat. "So this is your restrained billionaire you've been telling me about? That sure doesn't look like an Audi to me."

"Well, that's just what I've heard," said Pat.

Jack watched a man cross the parking lot—tall, lean, white-haired, moving with the unhurried confidence of someone who had never once needed to rush to make an impression. His hair was thick and swept back cleanly from a tanned, angular face, and he wore a light blue dress shirt with no tie, open at the collar. No jewelry that Jack could see. No flash of any kind. He walked up to the bouncer, who took one look at him and nodded without a word. He carried himself the way men with real money did, with a settled, unshakeable ease that parted crowds.

The man waded through the sea of college students—the laughter, the bare shoulders, the mingling perfumes and bar food—and when his eyes swept the courtyard, Pat sprang from his chair and wove through the crowd like an eager retriever.

"Mr. Sinclair, good to see you again! I'm glad you could make it," Pat said, steering him toward the table. "Guys, allow me to introduce Robert Sinclair, the man I've been telling you about."

Up close, the man had the kind of face that aged well—sharp cheekbones, clear blue eyes that moved over each of them with genuine attention rather than the glazed social scanning of someone working a room. He shook their hands around the table, and when he reached Jack, his grip tightened.

"Your Scottsdale presentation on the March thirteenth incident, remarkable work. I was a skeptic my whole life until I saw that formation over Camelback Mountain. That changed everything for me. In fact, I haven't been able to stop thinking about it. Some truths can't be denied once you've witnessed them firsthand," he said.

"I understand. I was a skeptic myself," Jack said. He gestured for Bob to sit next to him.

At that moment, the waitress materialized beside them, balancing a platter of glistening oysters nestled in their half shells, which she deposited with a flourish directly in front of Pat. His face contorted as if he'd just bitten into a lemon.

"What in the hell is this shit?" he demanded, triggering howls of laughter around the table.

Jack leaned back with a mischievous grin. "A special order for you, Pat. Nothing but the best for our resident oyster connoisseur."

Pat glared at Jack, his lips pressed into a tight line. "Hilarious." He tilted the plate toward the edge of the table, the oysters sliding precariously near the rim.

Jimbo lunged forward, his hand clamping onto Pat's forearm. "Whoa there! Don't waste those beauties. I'll take them off your hands."

Pat shoved the plate across the table with a theatrical grimace. "Be my guest. I'd rather starve!"

The plates were cleared, and beer bottles multiplied as the night wore on. Jack leaned closer to hear Bob over the escalating laughter of his friends. With a subtle nod toward an empty table nearby, Bob rose from his seat. Jack followed, leaving behind the boisterous group for the relative quiet of their new sanctuary.

Bob sipped his drink, leaned in, and said, "Have you noticed how the media's buried what we saw that night? They've branded everything as the 'Phoenix Lights' now, but they only ever discuss those lights over the Estrellas. The V-shaped craft, the real UFO, it's like it never happened." He tapped his finger on the table for emphasis. "Why do you suppose that is?"

Jack shook his head. "The lights over the Estrellas make for good TV, and they were easy to replay. What people don't know is that we..." His jaw tightened as Garrett's face flashed in his mind. "I had footage of the V-shaped craft. But the government spooks broke into my house and took everything. If that footage had made the evening news, nobody would remember the second sighting."

"The Air Force claims those lights over the Estrellas were military flares. You buying that explanation?"

Jack considered that for a second. "There's this analysis floating around that shows how those lights winked out at a consistent rate and disappeared where they'd hit the mountain ridgeline. That's some pretty compelling evidence backing up the flare theory." He leaned forward. "But there are still several unanswered questions. Why did those lights appear there in that formation on the exact night the other craft was sighted? Some people are asking if it was a large UFO descending toward the desert surface. Wouldn't the lights disappear at the same place flares would? I don't have enough evidence to make a call on that one."

Bob leaned back, the ice in his whiskey glass clinking as he took a thoughtful sip. His expression changed, the casual demeanor giving way to something heavier, more deliberate. "You know, Jack, I lost my wife, Elaine, three years back. Cancer. Forty-nine years old. Makes a man wonder what's waiting on the other side." He tilted his head toward the night sky visible through the patio's pergola. "Or who else might be out there looking back at us. After losing. her, I walk through most of my days like a man moving underwater, everything muted, slowed down. Funny how a person can own three houses, have more money than he could ever spend, but still feel lost in this world."

Jack nodded and said, "I'm sorry to hear about your wife. Cancer is a bitch."

"It is indeed. But I'll tell you, something changed in me that night last March. It awakened an intellectual curiosity, a desire to know more about what's out there. Like you, I've been reading up on many unexplained events around the world. It's given me something new to focus on in life. In fact, because of that, I'm stepping down from my role as CEO in December and turning the reins over to my eldest son. I have a new passion in life, and that is the quest for knowledge, specifically this UFO phenomenon. I have so many questions, and I want answers."

The beer in Jack's hand had gone tepid, forgotten during the time he'd been absorbed in Bob's story. So much for drowning his thoughts in alcohol tonight. His mind was too busy swimming in the potential scenarios this conversation had opened. "Every night when my place gets quiet, my thoughts drift away, thinking about all the possibilities. Are we looking at visitors from another star system? Or maybe it's more complex, beings slipping through the fabric of time or even breaking through from parallel realities we can't even comprehend."

Bob leaned forward, his whiskey glass cradled between his palms. "Few people know this, but I want to let you in on something. I've been assembling a team, my funding, with the goal of conducting serious research into the phenomenon." His eyes locked onto Jack's. "Your Scottsdale presentation is when I knew I needed your mind on this. I was planning to approach you after the new year when I hand over the company keys, but after what happened at your office today, the timing's changed. I can't risk someone else snatching you up."

He opened his mouth, but Bob raised a hand, his eyes gleaming with intensity. "So what do you say, Jack? Can I convince you to join my team? I'll triple whatever the weather service was paying you, plus health benefits, retirement contributions, and all that. There's one thing. We'll be operating out of Little Rock, so you'd have to move. I'll cover all of those expenses, of course."

Jack sat back and pondered the question. If he'd asked him yesterday, he would have turned him down. But after today, he had a lot less to lose. "That's a generous offer," he began. "And I have a newfound passion for UFOs. But do I want to abandon everything I've ever known? My skills, my training, it's all in meteorology. I'm not blowing my horn here, but I'm one hell of a meteorologist. I can find another job in the field. It might take some effort, but I'll land on my feet." Bob was about to say something, but Jack held up his hand, "And your UFO research group? What if things don't work out? Hell, what if I'm the one who doesn't work out? Then what? I'm back to square one."

Bob was staring at Jack but remained silent.

"Hell, I don't know, Bob. I want to say yes. My heart wants to say yes. But my head is telling me to think this through. How many people are we talking about in this group you're putting together? It's not just another person and me, is it?"

Bob nodded appreciatively. "That caution shows good judgment. This isn't some amateur UFO-hunting club. I'm investing serious capital, north of thirty million." He leaned forward. "The scientific team I've assembled would make NASA jealous. We've got hard sciences covered from every angle—chemistry, physics, geology, astronomy. Experts who can analyze materials, biological samples, and optical anomalies. Plus specialists to handle the human element —psychology, sociology, medical implications, and several engineers of various backgrounds. Not to mention, a bunch of techs that will handle a lot of the grunt work." He tapped the table with his index finger. "The only missing piece is you."

Jack raised his eyebrows and let out a low whistle as he leaned back in his chair. "That's a legitimate scientific undertaking. I had no idea you were assembling something on this scale. Wow! I mean, if things didn't work out with me, I guess I could always fall back on a job in meteorology," he said.

Bob watched Jack's expression shift from hesitation to curiosity, recognizing that familiar gleam in his eyes, the same look he'd seen across countless boardroom tables just before handshakes closed million-dollar contracts.

Jack extended his hand, pulled it back halfway and hesitated, then extended it again. "Okay, Bob, you've convinced me. Count me in!"

Bob's face lit up. "Now there's the spirit! Welcome to the team!" He produced a business card from his wallet and pressed it into Jack's palm. Bob rose from the table and turned back toward the main group. "I've got to head back to Paradise Valley tonight, but call me tomorrow. We'll iron out all the details then. I'm sure you'll have more questions." Bob gave a firm nod and returned to the guys to exchange farewells. After a few minutes of polite conversation, he threw a couple of hundred-dollar bills on the table and slipped away into the night, leaving Jack staring at the embossed card between his fingers.

"Hey, Jack, I thought you were getting drunk tonight! We're way ahead of you," Steve said as he got up and staggered into the restaurant, looking for the restroom.

He watched Steve's unsteady retreat and shook his head with a wry smile. "So much for my designated driver. Looks like our roles reversed," Jack said, prompting chuckles around the table.

"So what did you think of Bob?" Pat asked.

He twirled Bob's business card between his fingers, a grin forming. "It looks like I will be trading the desert heat for Arkansas humidity."

Six weeks passed since that fateful night at Casey Moore's, where Jack accepted Bob's offer to join his research team. Bob, a generous man, gave everyone a $50,000 signing bonus. He used the bulk of the money as a down payment on a home in Maumelle, a quiet suburb of Little Rock.

It was the early part of winter in Arkansas, and although it was mild by Chicago standards, the weather was much colder than Jack liked. Since his arrival, it had been unseasonably cold with many cloudy days. Overnight lows were in the teens over the past few days, with highs struggling to climb above freezing. He didn't like it one bit.

Fresh from signing the final papers at the title company in Little Rock, Jack tossed the new set of keys into the cupholder as he drove toward Maumelle. He couldn't believe his good fortune, being able to afford a house like this.

His money stretched further in Arkansas than it ever had in Arizona. The new salary, combined with the lower cost of living, meant Jack could afford a luxurious four-bedroom home on the fourth hole of a country club.

The thought nagged at him, knowing he had several unused bedrooms. What did one man need with that much square footage?

But then again, real estate in this area was guaranteed to appreciate. He'd tell anyone who asked that it was a smart financial move.

Living in a hotel room since arriving, Jack couldn't wait another night to claim his new home. The bare floors would have to do for sleeping, since his furniture wouldn't arrive for two days. A pillow and blanket would be his only companions tonight. The prospect of a hard floor didn't bother him much; he spent many nights over the past several years camping in the Arizona desert with nothing more than a tent canvas and a sleeping bag between him and the ground. This should be an improvement over that.

Jack's footsteps clattered against the bare floors, bouncing off empty walls. This wasn't a home yet, more of an expensive shell waiting to be filled.

He stared out the window. Winter had stripped the landscape bare—straw-colored grass lay flat against the earth, skeletal trees reached toward a colorless sky, and the usual chorus of birdsong had fled south with its creators.

He closed his eyes and tried to imagine what it would look like come spring. The azalea bushes up front would explode into a riot of fuchsia and magenta, their petals so delicate they'd tremble in the slightest breeze. Bradford pear trees would transform into clouds of pristine white blossoms, their fragrance drifting through open windows. The dormant Bermuda would awaken into a carpet of emerald, demanding the whir of his not-yet-purchased lawnmower. Mockingbirds would trill their varied melodies from dawn till dusk, cardinals would flash like rubies among new leaves, and perhaps even hummingbirds would visit, their wings a blur as they hovered near his future feeders. It would be worth the wait.

He imagined the white-hot Arizona sun beating down, felt the sweat evaporating from his skin before it could even bead. Behind his eyelids loomed those serrated mountains, purple-shadowed at dusk, and the silhouettes of saguaros standing like sentinels with upraised arms. His throat tightened. Then he opened his eyes to the Arkansas winter again—brown and withered now, yes, but only sleeping. In three months, this dead landscape would erupt with color and life, while back in Phoenix, the same ancient cacti would stand guard over the same sunbaked earth they always had.

Jack exhaled. He ached for Arizona's familiarity, but beneath it was something unexpected, a curiosity about the seasons to come. Perhaps these dormant months were just the prelude to something worth waiting for.

Several days later, Jack had finally settled into his home. The movers had delivered his furniture the previous day, and he was ready to report on his first day of work. The rest of the team members had been in place for weeks, in some cases months, and Jack was the last member to arrive.

In downtown Little Rock, Bob had purchased the former headquarters of a small corporation that had moved after expanding beyond the building's capacity.

As Jack pulled up, he could see that it featured a podium design with an open-air parking level on the ground floor and massive concrete columns supporting the building above.

From the outside, the structure presented itself as a perfect square of obsidian glass that would have formed a flawless cube if only it had risen a few stories higher.

In front of the building, black granite rose from a bed of crushed white marble, its polished surface catching the winter light. Etched into the stone were sleek sans-serif letters that matched the building's modern aesthetic: "SPIRE," followed by the address in smaller text beneath. He couldn't remember what SPIRE stood for, but he knew the first word was Bob's last name, Sinclair.

Jack pulled into an empty spot under the building and secured his vehicle.

The parking level housed two banks of elevators flanking a freight lift, with a stairwell tucked into the corner. Since he needed to ascend just one floor, Jack opted to bypass the wait and take the stairs, welcoming the chance to work out the stiffness in his legs after the drive.

The name SPIRE was on the door again, and underneath it read, "Sinclair Paranormal Investigations and Research Enterprise." Shit. Paranormal? He hoped Bob wasn't planning to chase ghosts.

The heavy fire door swung open under Jack's hand, revealing a first floor that stopped him in his tracks. After years in sterile government facilities with their fluorescent lights and beige walls, the contrast was jarring. Bob had transformed the former corporate space with understated luxury—Italian marble floors that caught the light, rich teak paneling that warmed the walls, and recessed lighting that cast a gentle glow from the paneled ceilings above. Expensive, but with a tasteful restraint that impressed Jack despite himself.

Behind a sleek desk sat a woman whose auburn hair cascaded in waves past her shoulders. When she lifted her gaze to meet Jack's, her pale-blue eyes seemed to evaluate him with immediate warmth. The bright smile that followed, confident and inviting, brought a subtle glow to her fair, freckled skin, as if she already knew something about him he had yet to discover.

She rose to her feet and strode toward Jack, extending her hand. "Mr. Davis, welcome! Mr. Sinclair mentioned you'd be arriving this morning. He's expecting you in his office."

The woman's familiarity caught Jack off guard. "Morning," he said, his expression betraying his search for a name tag or some hint of her identity.

"I'm Patty!" Her voice rang with enthusiasm. "Welcome to SPIRE!"

Jack returned her smile, though his didn't quite reach his eyes. "Glad to know I'm in the right place."

"Let me show you to Mr. Sinclair's office," she said, already moving. Jack followed her down a corridor that branched left from the lobby. At its end stood a pair of imposing double doors, their dark wood carved with intricate patterns that seemed to absorb the hallway's light.

She gave a firm knock at the door and heaved back on one of the heavy doors. Bob was on the phone inside and made a brief gesture for Jack to come in.

Jack paused at the threshold, taking in the office. The space surprised him, generous without being extravagant, refined without flamboyance.

Teak-paneled walls rose around him, interrupted only by built-in shelving illuminated from within.

The substantial desk dominated the center of the room—a broad expanse of polished wood supporting only the bare essentials: a sleek computer monitor, a leather desk pad, and a few meticulously placed items, nothing superfluous or out of alignment.

Facing the desk, comfortable seating formed a semicircle, designed for conversation rather than confrontation.

As Bob concluded his call, Jack lowered himself into one chair facing his new boss. Bob stood up and came out from around the desk to shake hands. "Jack, Jack, Jack! So good to see you this morning!" He motioned for him to stand and follow him. "Come with me. I want to take you on a tour of your new workplace. What do you think so far?"

"Very impressive. I've worked in government offices my entire career, so this is quite a change."

Bob gripped the brass handle of one of the massive doors and swung it wide, stepping aside with a slight bow. "After you," he said, gesturing Jack forward with an open palm.

He took Jack on a tour of the first floor, which included administrative support staff, an IT department, and small departments for accounting, personnel, and payroll. The scale of the operation stunned Jack. This enterprise had the infrastructure of a Fortune 500 company.

Next was the second floor, which was more utilitarian in design, with space for various technicians and personnel who supported the scientists. By the time they finished, Jack's hand was going numb from all the introductions. Bob clapped him on the shoulder with a grin. "I hope you've been taking notes. There might be a pop quiz on all these names tomorrow morning."

The elevator doors parted to reveal the third floor, and Jack's breath caught in his throat. Before him stretched a facility that would make an Ivy League research lab look like a high school science classroom. Sleek workstations exuded an aura of extreme processing power, their monitors displaying complex simulations that twisted and morphed in real-time. Through glass partitions, he glimpsed several specialized laboratories—pristine environments full of equipment Jack couldn't even name. The most striking feature was the southeast corner of the space, where floor-to-ceiling shelving housed what appeared to be thousands of cataloged UFO reports, their spines organized in a system he couldn't yet decipher. Between these zones of intense focus, a comfortable lounge offered respite, along with a common area with plush seating. The modern furnishings suggested places where breakthrough ideas might emerge over coffee.

Bob's chest puffed as he gestured toward the equipment. "What you're looking at here is cutting edge across every discipline. If we are fortunate enough to recover physical evidence, whether it's a mysterious alloy or tissue samples that defy classification, we'll have answers within days or weeks, not decades."

"Amazing," said Jack.

The elevator ascended to the fourth level, the domain of the scientists. When the doors slid open, Jack stepped onto a polished white marble floor with black marble accents. Silver sconces cast a warm glow against the walls at regular intervals. Bob led him to the right, their footsteps echoing in the hushed corridor, before stopping at the second door. "Your new home away from home," Bob announced with a slight theatrical flourish. "Care to try out the chair?"

Jack froze in the doorway, his mouth agape. "You can't be serious," he finally said, his voice a whisper. Bob's only response was to tap his finger against the brass plaque mounted on the wall that read in engraved script, "Jack Davis - Meteorology."

Jack crossed the threshold in silence, absorbing his surroundings. Though not as opulent as Bob's domain, the office carried its own understated sophistication. Floor-to-ceiling windows bathed the room in natural light, framing Little Rock's modest downtown skyline. Vertical wooden slats in warm chestnut tones wrapped the walls, complemented by dark hardwood flooring that disappeared beneath a cream-colored area rug.

A sweeping desk commanded the room's center, its curved form both modern and elegant. The gleaming surface held only the necessities: a slim laptop, a lamp with its silver neck bent over the workspace, and a few carefully arranged items. The executive chair behind it stood ready with a tall back that promised authority and comfort. Across the room, a dedicated workstation bristled with multiple wide-screen monitors, poised for the most demanding tasks. Soft leather chairs sat nearby and to the side along the windows, angled for conversation.

Never in his government career had Jack seen an office like this assigned to someone at his level. Jack ran a finger along the polished edge of the desk as he made his way around to the back. He sank into the leather chair, running his hands along the sturdy armrests.

"I can't believe this is mine," he said, shaking his head. "My last workspace was not much bigger than a closet, all fluorescent lights and those sad government-issue dividers. Does everyone here get this kind of treatment?"

"All except Dr. Janssen. He's our astronomer and is in charge of everyone on the fourth floor. His office is larger and a little nicer." Bob let Jack take it all in. He glanced at his watch. "The rest of the team is waiting for us in the conference room. I think you'll find them to be an impressive bunch, each one a leader in their field." He gestured toward the door with a slight bow. "Shall we? I'm eager for you to meet your new colleagues."

Jack followed Bob down the hall to a glass-walled room on the right. After the warmth of his new office, the stark contrast of this space hit him like a blast of arctic air. The sleek, intimidating design made Jack straighten his posture. If Darth Vader himself had commissioned a conference room, Jack thought, it would look like this: imperial, cold, and designed to make one feel small in the presence of power.

Dominating the room was an imposing conference table, obsidian black and reflective as still water, narrowing to a commanding point at its head.

Bob positioned himself at the head of the table. "Ladies and gentlemen, it's my pleasure to introduce you to Mr. Jack Davis. He worked as a government meteorologist and holds a master's degree in meteorology from the University of Illinois and a bachelor's degree from Northern Illinois University.

"Jack was the scientist who tracked, filmed, and documented the V-shaped craft over Phoenix last March. The government came after him hard. They broke into his house, stole the evidence, and torpedoed his career over it."

The scientists offered polite applause. Jack acknowledged them with a slight nod, his hand half-raised in an awkward gesture.

"Now, let's go around the room and have everyone introduce themselves and their specialty. And for fun, let us know where you're from. We'll start with Hendricus here on my left."

A man with wavy, faded blond hair spoke up with a very slight Dutch accent. "I'm Doctor Hendricus Janssen, astronomer and chief scientist. I'm from the Netherlands. Welcome, Jack, it's great to have you here."

The introductions continued without interruption, representing most major scientific fields. As each scientist announced their credentials, Jack counted those with doctorates, the majority, and started to feel small with just a master's degree.

Jack nodded at everyone, noting the genuine smiles versus the clinical assessments. A few gazes lingered too long, making him uncomfortable. By the time they reached the last seat, Jack had already constructed a mental map of who the power players were.

"Doctor Jessica Bowden, astrophysics, Wisconsin." The woman

at the end of the table had honey-blonde hair that fell in loose waves past her shoulders. When her green eyes met Jack's, something in them registered his presence in a way that was different from the others. Not assessing. Just aware. "Welcome, Mr. Davis."

Jack was talented at reading people. When she looked at him, he felt drawn to her. A kindred spirit, or something else? Suddenly, he heard his name mentioned and realized he wasn't paying attention.

"A few of our people are out on assignment. I'll have them come by and introduce themselves when they return," said Bob.

Bob straightened in his chair, shifting into a more formal register. "Before we break, I want to go over a few administrative items. HR has asked me to remind everyone that time-off requests need to be submitted a minimum of two weeks in advance through the personnel portal. No exceptions for anyone, including for you, Hendricus." A wave of laughter moved around the table.

"Expense reports are due the last Friday of each month. Field assignments are the exception; those get submitted within seventy-two hours of returning. And for those of you who have not completed your building security orientation, that needs to happen this week. Frank in facilities will schedule you." Bob glanced around the table. "Safety walk-through for the third-floor labs is Thursday at nine. Attendance is mandatory. We had one near-miss with the spectrometry equipment last month, and I don't want a repeat." He closed his portfolio.

"That's all. Thank you for your time," he said.

The group broke up, and the scientists started streaming out of the room in small groups. Jack found himself in an unusual position, not knowing what to do next. Escaping to his office seemed to be the wisest move for now. He pushed back his chair and stood, only to feel fingers brush against his sleeve. Startled, he turned to see Dr. Bowden standing at his side.

"Oh, hello, Doctor Bowden."

"Oh, please, call me Jess. We don't stand on formalities around here." She reconsidered that for a second. "Well, most of us don't. You'll figure that out soon enough."

"I've already got a few general ideas of who those folks might be," he said, making Jess snicker. On a whim, he added, "I'm going to go back to my office and familiarize myself with the place. I'd love to chat with you for a bit if you've got the time."

She responded by holding the door open to the hallway and gesturing, "Lead the way."

Jack settled into his chair, allowing himself a moment to get a good look at Jess for the first time. Light danced across her shoulder-length hair as she moved, the blend of caramel and honey tones framing an alluring face. High cheekbones and piercing green eyes.

Jess settled into one of the leather chairs angled toward his desk and crossed one leg over the other, the navy blazer she'd worn to the meeting draped over the arm of the chair.

"So," she said, "you're the man who measured a half-mile-long spacecraft with a balloon tracker and scribbled notes on a camera manual. I have to ask what was going through your head when you first saw it?"

"Hmm, my first thought? I'm going to need more paper!"

She laughed and leaned forward slightly. "That is the most genuine answer I've ever heard."

They fell into easy conversation, the topic moving from the Phoenix incident to the broader topic of UFOs.

Several colleagues drifted past the open door over the course of the morning, glancing in, then moving on without knocking.

When she leaned forward to make a point about quantum entanglement as a possible mechanism for apparent faster-than-light travel, Jack noticed how her green eyes caught the light. He also noticed that he had stopped thinking about UFOs entirely for the last forty-five seconds, which hadn't happened since March 1997.

He guessed she was a few years older than him, late twenties or early thirties. She wore almost no makeup; she didn't need to, and there was a quiet self-possession about her that spoke to her knowing exactly who she was.

First day on the job, he reminded himself. Pay attention.

Jess snapped her wrist and checked her watch. "Oh, Jesus, look at that. It's 11:30. Where did the time go? Do you have any lunch plans?"

"I hadn't given it much thought. The morning went by quicker than I thought."

She tilted her head, eyes sparkling with mischief. "I know a place that does something magical with chicken. Interested?"

Jack laughed, "Sure, as long as it's nothing weird."

Jess smirked. "I promise, it's chicken that'll make you forget about anything else for at least an hour. Two blocks from here, there's this little barbecue joint where the owner makes what he calls 'Dixie chicken.' He prepares only twenty servings daily, first-come, first-served. Twelve hours of slow smoking over this crazy blend of wood. Last time I was there, he was showing off his woodpile: pecan, cherry, apple, even sassafras, I think. The smell alone is worth the walk."

"Sounds good to me!"

Jess was right. The chicken was amazing and might have been the best he'd ever had. Over lunch, she had floated from topic to topic and asked him about his move, his new home, and whether he was settled in yet.

Somewhere in all that, she set down her fork and tilted her head. "So, is it just you rattling around in that new place of yours?"

"Four bedrooms," he said. "Just little old me."

"That's a lot of square footage for existential contemplation." The corner of her mouth lifted. "I'm in West Little Rock. Quiet neighborhood, decent wine selection, and I make a very respectable bruschetta. You should come over tonight and continue the debate about Levelland. I'm not done with you yet."

He looked at her. She looked back, not quite smiling.

"That sounds like a trap," he said.

"It's bruschetta and astrophysics. The worst that happens is you learn something."

"In that case," he said, "absolutely."

She smiled then—the full version this time, unhurried—and reached for her glass. "Good. Don't bring anything. I have everything we need."

When they got back to the office, Bob pulled Jack into a small group discussion to get a meteorologist's perspective on a longer-term project that was underway. The meeting lasted all afternoon, and when Jack finally returned to his office, Jess was already gone. She'd left a handwritten note on his desk—her address, number, and underneath it a small drawing of what was unmistakably a flying saucer with an arrow pointing to it and the words conversation starter written beside it.

He caught himself raising the note to his nose, where a whisper of her scent still clung to the paper.

Oh, for the love of God, he thought.

He knew workplace romances were a bad idea and almost never worked out. In his freshman year, he'd crashed and burned with a classmate in the meteorology program—three months of bliss followed by three and a half years of strategic seating and averted gazes in a department of twenty people. He had sworn, emphatically and repeatedly, never again.

And yet, here he was, already planning his route to West Little Rock. He'd known her for less than eight hours, and he already had it bad.

13 / PINOT NOIR

Jess rushed home after work and began a frantic clean-up. Her apartment was presentable enough, though evidence of her harried morning routine was scattered about: a blouse draped over a chair, a half-empty mug with a lipstick stain on the rim, yesterday's mail spread across the coffee table. She darted from room to room, snatching up the detritus of single life, stuffing it into drawers and closets where it couldn't betray her. She dragged the vacuum over the carpet, its roar drowning out her anxious thoughts, then attacked the kitchen tile with a mop, leaving gleaming trails in its wake.

Jess was rather reserved with men, and she had dated no one for over three years. She hadn't been intimate with anyone since then either. She replayed her encounter with Jack, puzzling over her own behavior. Her heart had fluttered in her chest the first moment their eyes met. Then somehow they were talking, words flowing between them without effort or awkwardness, as if resuming a conversation paused years ago. Even now, hours later, she could still feel the strange current that had passed between them, something unfamiliar yet unmistakable.

With the house cleaning done, she hopped into the shower to get ready for tonight. Her mind wandered as she bathed. She knew what was going to happen; she knew it, and Jack knew it. She had to stop and ask herself what the long-term implications might be. They were coworkers, and she had just met Jack this morning.

The thought crept in: would she seem too eager, too available to him? And what about Bob, her boss, if office whispers reached him? She pictured his face, that easy smile that had convinced her to leave Baton Rouge twelve weeks ago. Would that smile harden if he discovered something between her and Jack? She couldn't read him yet, not really. Her fingers paused on the soap, slick against her skin. These weren't the thoughts that made her pulse race under the shower's spray.

At precisely 6:32, the doorbell's chime sent Jess's heart into her throat. She held back from sprinting toward the door, forced her breathing to steady, and smoothed her blouse with damp palms. When she turned the knob, Jack stood in the doorway, his eyes bright with anticipation, cradling a bottle of pinot noir that gleamed in the porch light.

"Pinot noir?" she asked.

"Patty said this was your favorite."

"So you thought you would ply me with alcohol tonight and take advantage of me?" Jess asked.

Jack stammered, at a loss for words. "Well, no, I..."

She laughed and assured Jack that she was kidding. "Get in here, and let's get this cork out of the bottle!"

They talked about every subject imaginable for the next hour. Finally, the bottle of wine was empty. Jess had reclined on her back and was using Jack's lap as a pillow.

Jack began gently stroking her hair, and their eyes met. They held that gaze for several seconds. Finally, she raised up at the same time Jack moved in. His mouth found hers. When they parted, Jess found herself breathless.

Jack broke the silence. "So..."

Jess never broke eye contact with Jack. "So..."

"Ever since I met you this morning, I've felt this attraction toward you."

She didn't let him finish. "I felt it too..."

His fingertips brushed her wrist, and a current shot through them both. "I can barely breathe when I touch you," he said, entranced. "We just met today, but it feels like I found something I didn't know was missing."

She swallowed, her throat dry. "I know what you mean." She gestured between them. "This isn't the kind of thing I do all the time. It's been three years," she whispered, the confession warming her cheeks even as it left her lips.

"I understand. And you know, we should put the brakes on and step back. We're coworkers, after all," Jack said.

Jess's fingers traced the collar of his shirt. "Is that what you want? For us to stop?"

Jack's eyes darkened. "No, that's the last thing I want." His fingers traced the curve of her jaw and lingered at the pulse point beneath her ear. "I don't think I've ever felt this way before, Jess."

Their mouths met again, hungry and searching, as Jess's fingers found the hem of her blouse. She pulled it upward and off in one smooth motion. Without breaking apart, they stumbled down the hallway, nothing but a tangle of limbs and half-whispered breaths. Once they reached the bedroom, the edge of her mattress caught the backs of her knees, and they tumbled together onto the sheets.

Night had passed to morning, and Jess awoke slowly. Awareness arrived before she was ready for it. The sheets were warm, and there was a weight beside her. Jack. Then she remembered everything; this wasn't typical behavior for her.

She lay still, listening to the cadence of Jack's breathing. Three years was a long time, and she had grown comfortable in her solitude, had even convinced herself it suited her. She was good at her work, good at being alone, good at not needing things she couldn't have. Last night had dismantled that argument entirely.

She had expected awkwardness, the inevitable stumbling of two strangers finding each other in the dark. There had been none. That was the thing she kept returning to. It had felt like a continuation of something she didn't realize was already in progress. She wasn't someone who believed in that sort of thing. She dealt in evidence, in data, in what could be measured and verified. And yet here she was, unable to explain what had happened between them in any terms that satisfied her scientifically.

The alarm cut through her thoughts with its usual lack of mercy. She silenced it on the third try, then turned over to find Jack already awake.

"Hi," she managed.

"Good morning," he said. "How are you feeling?"

She considered the honest answer. It was the only kind she knew how to give. "Like I've been walking around half asleep my whole life until now." She pressed her fingertip to his chest and traced a slow, idle pattern there. "What about you?"

"Like I discovered a whole new universe," he said, his voice still rough with sleep.

She raised an eyebrow. "That's quite a scientific observation."

"I mean it," he said, and covered her hand with his, holding it still against his heartbeat.

"I suppose we should think about getting ready for work," she said. "Though I'm not entirely convinced that's necessary."

He rested his hand on the curve of her hip beneath the sheet. "I think we have time for another round..."

She didn't argue.

Jack barely noticed the calendar flipping to his one-month anniversary at SPIRE. He had a stack of case files on his desk already, and the satisfaction of his first official debunking. He proved that a reported UFO photographed in the clouds was nothing more than a weather balloon.

Jack watched as colleagues returned from field assignments with windburned faces and stories, their excitement evident in the break room. He was a little disappointed that he hadn't been sent into the field yet.

He and Jess reached a relationship milestone. She broke her lease and moved in with him. This morning he'd opened the shower door to find his once-spartan bathing area transformed.

A small array of products crowded the corners where a single bottle of 3-in-1 had stood sentry before: shampoo, conditioner, exfoliating scrubs, and a pink razor.

He stood there and took it all in. "Hey, how much of these products are really necessary?"

"All of them," she said.

"There are twelve," he said.

"Count again. There are only eleven."

Jack smiled and lifted a bottle. "What is this one even for?" He held up a small bottle with a French label he couldn't pronounce.

"It's an essential oil taken from a plant that only grows in the Atlas mountains of North Africa. For my hair," she said.

Jack sat the bottle back down and shook his head. His bathroom vanity drawers, once home to a lone toothbrush and razor, now housed mysterious tubes and compacts.

But at night, when Jess curled against him in sleep, he found he didn't mind the pink razor or the invasion of French-labeled bottles.

At work, Jack and Jess maintained a careful distance. They would lunch together once in a while, but otherwise restricted themselves to professional nods in the hallway and avoided lingering glances across the conference table. They both knew their charade would have an expiration date, but they worried more about Bob's reaction than whispers around the water cooler. The man who had once posted corporate memos banning workplace relationships might not have softened his stance at SPIRE.

Bob's frustration mounted as their operations hit an unexpected roadblock. His investigators weren't able to reach incident sites fast enough. By the time they arrived at the scene, the trail had already gone cold. Time was working against them, and in this business, fresh data meant everything.

Field assignments beyond driving distance meant surrendering to the whims of commercial airlines: delays, missed connections, and the domino effect of scheduling disasters that followed.

The final straw came when a team of three spent eleven hours in the Atlanta airport chasing a connection that kept getting pushed. By the time they arrived at their destination in rural Virginia, the witnesses grew tired of waiting and went home. Bob had listened to the debrief with his jaw set.

He called in Patty and his operations manager, Dale Hutchins, the following morning.

"I want our own aircraft," he said, before either of them had sat down. "Two of them."

"Two?" asked Dale.

"One mid-size for domestic work. Something nimble that can get a team of eight anywhere in three hours or less. And a long-range jet that won't require a fueling stop to cross the Atlantic."

Dale pulled out a legal pad. "That's a significant capital outlay."

"I'm aware of what it costs, Dale. What I can't afford is another Virginia."

"I know an aircraft broker," said Patty. "Former corporate aviation guy, knows the market. I can have him on the phone this afternoon."

"Do it," said Bob.

The broker was a man named Gerald Fosse, who wore French cuffs and spoke about aircraft the way other men talked about the weather. Bob reviewed the specs on several options presented to him, asking questions that impressed even Fosse. Before long, Bob was the proud owner of two jet aircraft.

The naming took him less time than the purchase. A proud University of Arkansas alumnus who had held season tickets to Razorback games since 1971, Bob christened the larger long-range jet Big Red, after the costumed mascot who whipped crowds into a frenzy at home games in Fayetteville. The nimble mid-size jet became Tusk, named for the living razorback that symbolized the raw, bristling spirit of the athletic program.

When Patty relayed the names to the maintenance crew overseeing the aircraft's customization, there was a brief silence on the other end of the line.

"Did you say Tusk?" the crew chief asked.

"I did," said Patty.

"Like the pig."

"Like the razorback," she said, with the particular patience of someone who had worked for Bob Sinclair long enough to know that this was not the hill to die on.

Both aircraft now stood ready in their hangar at Little Rock National, flight crews hired and on standby. Bob couldn't help but smile at the thought. SPIRE was about to operate on a different level, no longer constrained by commercial air travel.

Jack inched forward on I-630. Red brake lights stretched ahead like an endless chain, surrounding the crumpled metal and flashing emergency vehicles that had brought morning traffic to a standstill.

When cars began creeping onto the shoulder toward the distant off-ramp, he hesitated only briefly before following suit, the tires of his vehicle crunching over gravel. When he reached work, the clock on his dashboard indicated a forty-minute delay to his usual arrival time.

His mind was already at his desk, organizing the day's tasks, when Bob materialized in the corridor, blocking his path to sanctuary. "Got a case that might interest you," he said, leaning in with a conspiratorial smile. "Ever looked into crop circles?"

"Crop circles? They mainly occur in cereal grains, most commonly in England and Western Europe. Some are thought to be man-made hoaxes."

"There's a fresh one that just came in, and I need someone to investigate. How do you feel about getting out of the office for a few days?" he asked. "You'll be the first to break in our new jet."

Jack's eyes lit up. "I'm in! Let me guess—I'm headed to Wiltshire? Or maybe Hampshire?" His voice rose with excitement as he named areas in England that were hotspots for crop circles.

"California," said Bob.

Jack's face fell. "California?"

Bob nodded. "Blythe. Right on the Colorado River. They've got fields of everything there—cantaloupe, lettuce, winter wheat." He tapped his pen against his knuckles. "The LA news vans are already crawling all over it. San Diego too. Thought we might get some positive press if we send our own expert."

Jack's shoulders slumped. So much for his visions of the English countryside. "California, okay then. Will I be flying solo on this one?"

Bob checked his watch. "I'm sending Dr. Winters with you. She's a biologist and knows her plants. Might tell us whether someone trampled that wheat or if it's the real deal." He tapped Jack's shoulder. "Plus a couple of techs will come. Get home and throw some clothes in a bag. Park at the private terminal at Little Rock National Airport. Wheels up at noon."

After tossing shirts and underwear into his overnight bag and grabbing his toothbrush, Jack drove toward Little Rock National with a flutter of anticipation in his stomach. Commercial flights were one thing—cramped seats, recycled air, crying babies—but a private jet? That was virgin territory. He wondered which jet they'd be flying. Bob had christened the aircraft with names from his beloved University of Arkansas. Would he be taking Tusk or Big Red?

Jack preferred the raw power of the NFL to the more random chaos of college games that sent Arkansans into frenzies each fall. Still, he couldn't help but smile at Bob's enthusiasm—maybe there was something to it after all.

Jack had met up with Dr. Lynley Winters and two techs, Bryce and a man who went by the name Whiskers but had no facial hair. A pilot in a crisp white shirt led them across the sun-baked tarmac toward a sleek Cessna Excel—Tusk, the smaller of SPIRE's twin jets. Jack couldn't suppress a grin. He'd flown coach his entire life, wedged between strangers with his knees against the seat ahead. Today, he'd be stretching his legs at 40,000 feet.

As he stepped inside the aircraft, he was taken aback. The cabin stretched before him like a sanctuary, a study in understated opulence where cream and champagne tones melted into one another beneath the soft glow of recessed lighting. Twin rows of oversized seats upholstered in buttery leather faced each other across an aisle carpeted in deep navy.

On the port side, a generous sofa curved against the fuselage, and across from it, individual club chairs swiveled on pedestals.

Jack eased himself into one of the rotating leather chairs. Across from him, Dr. Winters, who asked to be called by her first name, Lynley, took her seat and adjusted it to face him. Bryce and Whiskers sank into a pair of the oversized seats toward the rear of the plane.

Before long, Jack's body pressed deeper into the buttery leather as the jet's engines roared from a whisper to a scream. The world outside blurred into streaks of gray and green through his window, his stomach tightening as the wheels rumbled over the concrete seams. Then came that magical moment. The trembling ceased, the nose lifted, and the ground fell away beneath them like a discarded blanket. They were airborne.

A disembodied voice crackled through hidden speakers. "Folks, we'll be taking her up to 41,000 feet with wheels down in Blythe in three hours unless we run into some stronger headwinds."

He had been fantasizing about dozing off in the plush leather seat, but Lynley leaned forward, her eyes bright with caffeine-fueled intensity.

Jack would have bet good money she was in her late thirties until the night Jess mentioned Lynley was celebrating her forty-ninth birthday next month. He couldn't believe it.

He studied her more closely. Somehow, she possessed a face that seemed to have struck a deal with time. Her skin, warmed by a natural, healthy glow, held a smoothness that defied the decades, etched with only the subtlest lines that fanned outward from her sapphire-blue eyes—eyes that still held the bright, piercing clarity of a woman decades younger.

She wore her blonde hair in a soft, effortless cascade that framed a smile as vibrant as it was genuine. There was a youthful elasticity to her expression. When she laughed, the years seemed to fall away, leaving behind a woman whose spirit remained untouched by the typical wear of life.

Unfortunately for Jack, she'd launched into a detailed explanation of how genuine crop circles showed cellular changes at the nodes of affected plants, complete with emphatic hand gestures. He stifled a yawn behind his fist, watching the sunlight flash across the wing outside his window, knowing sleep would remain a distant luxury for the next three hours.

Stepping onto the tarmac in Blythe felt like a homecoming Jack hadn't asked for, Phoenix all over again. Heat radiated from the concrete in visible waves while the desert air sucked moisture from his skin faster than he could sweat it out. He raised a hand against the harsh glare of the afternoon sun that bounced off every surface. The landscape stretched away in all directions, nothing but sand, scrub, and stone until it dissolved into the shimmer of distant mountains. Their jet sat alone on the runway, miles from the green patchwork of irrigated fields that hugged the Colorado River and a fair distance west of Blythe proper.

Patty had an oversized SUV waiting for them on the tarmac. The baggage handlers, or "rampies" as they called themselves, loaded their bags and gear into the back of the vehicle.

Bryce climbed behind the wheel, with Whiskers riding shotgun. Jack and Lynley relaxed in the back seat. She was still rattling on about the biological effects of UFOs on plants. He thought this might be the third or fourth time he'd heard this part of the lecture.

"Do you guys want to get checked into our motel first?" asked Bryce.

Jack looked at Lynley, and she nodded her approval. "Fine by us," he said. "Did you say motel instead of hotel?"

"Yeah, that's what Patty booked for us. Wasn't my first choice either," said Bryce.

"Lovely. So we flew here in a private jet, and now we're staying in a motor court. The irony..." said Jack.

∽

Jack slid his keycard into the lock, bracing himself for disappointment. To his surprise, the door swung open to reveal gleaming tile floors, crisp white bedding, and the faint scent of lemon cleaner. The Blythe Desert Oasis might lack the private jet's opulence, but its freshly painted walls and modern fixtures suggested Patty hadn't picked a dump after all.

"Okay," he said to nobody in particular, "I can work with this."

Ten minutes later, they were back in the SUV as it rumbled along a rough road south of Blythe toward the winter wheat field where the crop circle had appeared. Jack gazed out the window, regretting that he hadn't thought to look for the formation during their descent.

According to Lynley's briefing, the pattern featured geometric complexities that defied simple human creation, though he remained skeptical. He'd seen what determined pranksters could accomplish with boards and rope under the cover of darkness.

The crop circle announced itself from half a mile away. A circus had descended on this quiet stretch of farmland. Vehicles choked both shoulders of the narrow road, their drivers abandoning any pretense of proper parking. Pedestrians darted between bumpers with the reckless confidence of people who'd forgotten traffic laws existed. In the field itself, a human anthill had formed, with dozens of curiosity-seekers trampling the wheat in their eagerness. At the property entrance, news vans created their own exclusive neighborhood, satellite masts reaching skyward like periscopes. Bryce's knuckles whitened on the steering wheel.

"Christ," he muttered, "this must be the biggest thing to hit Blythe since they installed the second stoplight."

Jack glanced at Lynley. The excitement had drained from her face, replaced by the hollow disappointment of a scientist arriving too late at the laboratory. "Any evidence that might have been here," he said, gesturing toward the trampled wheat, "is long gone now, UFO or otherwise."

Bryce squeezed the SUV into a narrow gap on the side of the road, and they exited the vehicle.

Lynley's shoulders dropped as she surveyed the field. Where the perfect geometric patterns should have been, flattened stalks splayed in chaotic directions, crushed under countless sneakers and boots. Even worse, a ragged pathway now cut through the previously pristine wheat surrounding the formation, the golden stalks bent and broken. She removed her sunglasses, pinched the bridge of her nose, and exhaled through pursed lips.

"It's a total loss, isn't it?" asked Jack.

Lynley's eyes brightened. "Actually, this might work out. Think about it. We now have wheat trampled by humans right next to wheat allegedly flattened by something else. The comparison could be what we need to prove this wasn't some elaborate hoax."

She sprang into action, kneeling in the crop with surgical precision as she snipped stalks and sealed them in labeled evidence bags. Jack traced the formation's edge, noting how the original pattern—a series of interlocking rings with precise geometric offshoots— remained discernible despite the chaos. Several yards away, Whiskers and Bryce hovered, hands in pockets, exchanging glances that asked what their role in this scientific treasure hunt might be.

Later that evening, the crew gathered at El Saguaro, a Mexican restaurant down the street where neon-colored papel picado hung from the ceiling and the scent of sizzling fajitas permeated the air. Over baskets of still-warm tortilla chips and sweating glasses of margaritas, Jack explained that he'd called Bob, describing the trampled wheat and circus-like atmosphere at the site.

On the other end of the line, Bob had fallen into a stunned silence before muttering, "Jesus Christ, what a waste of time."

On a positive note, they had interviewed a few locals who'd arrived after dawn, one of whom had photographed the formation before the human stampede.

Better still, they'd tracked down a Cessna 172 pilot, a Mr. Estrada that had banked low over the field at sunrise, his voice still animated as he described the perfect symmetry of concentric rings radiating from a central hexagon, each line as crisp as if drawn with architectural precision rather than pressed into living wheat.

And they had the plant samples that Lynley had collected, so the trip wasn't a total loss. Their private jet would touch down in Blythe at dawn, whisking them back to Little Rock before the desert heat reached its full, punishing intensity.

A soft rapping at his door pulled Jack from a deep sleep. The bedside clock's red digits glowed 1:17 a.m. He fumbled for his sweatpants in the dark, then squinted through the peephole. Lynley swayed in his view, her smile loose, eyes glassy under the harsh fluorescents in the breezeway. When he opened the door, the unmistakable scent of tequila drifted in with her.

"Hope I didn't wake you," she said in that deliberate way of someone working hard to sound sober. Her hand brushed his arm as she passed, lingering. "I was thinking about those samples we collected..." She perched on the edge of his bed, patting the space beside her. Jack's stomach tightened.

He leaned against the dresser instead, crossing his arms. Lynley twirled a strand of hair around her finger, her shoulders angled toward him as she patted the mattress again. "C'mon, Jack," she said, her voice dropping to a husky whisper. "I have something over here I want to show you." Her lips curved into a smile that had nothing to do with scientific inquiry.

"Lynley, I know what you're doing, and I'm sorry, but I'm involved with Jess. You won't find what you're looking for here."

"Wait!" she said, as she pressed her palm against her forehead, steadying herself. "There's someone else? Jess?" she slurred, waving her hand in the air between them. "No, no. Nobody will ever find out! You don't know what you're missing!"

"I'm sorry, but the answer is no."

Her face crumpled. She stood and swayed on unsteady feet. Jack gripped her shoulders, steering her toward the door.

"Lynley, you're drunk. You need to go back to your room and sleep this off," he said with a firm voice. He followed three paces behind as she zigzagged down the breezeway and waited until her key card found its slot.

Back in his room, Jack twisted the deadbolt and collapsed against the door, sweat cooling on his temples. "Jesus Christ, what the hell was that?"

Tension filled the cabin during the flight back from Blythe. Jack kept glancing over his shoulder, wondering if the alcohol had blurred Lynley's memory of her advances and his refusal. The rigid set of her shoulders told him otherwise. While he remained in his usual seat near the cockpit, she had retreated to the rear of the plane, sandwiched between Whiskers and Bryce, her laptop open but untouched on the tray table.

Back in Little Rock, Lynley had barricaded herself in the lab for days, hunched over her equipment as she analyzed their wheat field samples. Whenever he passed the glass-walled laboratory, she'd either be absorbed in her work or conveniently stepping out for coffee.

The one time he asked about her findings, she glanced up from her clipboard and said, "Monday's meeting, Jack. You'll hear everything then." Then she returned to her calculations.

On a positive note, the one eyewitness had shared his ground-level photographs, and fortune smiled upon their investigation when a commercial satellite imaging service captured high-resolution imagery of the lower Colorado River valley on the very morning the circles first appeared. It was pristine evidence, untouched by the footprints that would soon obliterate it.

The weekend passed in a blur—Friday night with Jess at Sir

Arthur's Prime, where they shared Chateaubriand and a bottle of cabernet, then Saturday surrendering to the tyranny of yard work. Jack's hands blistered on the mower's handle, his back ached from hauling bags of mulch, and his nostrils filled with the scent of severed branches as he pruned away winter's damage. By Sunday evening, dirt lodged beneath his fingernails and sweat-stained T-shirts piled in the hamper, he counted the hours until Monday's return to the office.

The question gnawed at Jack throughout the evening. Should he mention the Lynley situation to Jess? He pictured Jess's eyes narrowing with scrutiny, wondering if he was telling the truth. He sighed. Better to volunteer the awkward truth now rather than have it surface later.

He lowered himself onto the couch beside her, the leather cushion exhaling under his weight. "Jess, I need to tell you something that happened in California." He watched her face shift from relaxed to alert, her eyebrows arching upward as she muted the television.

Jack cleared his throat. "After our group dinner, Lynley showed up at my door at one in the morning. She'd been drinking." He met Jess's eyes. "She was flirting, over the top. Tried to get me to sit on the bed next to her, and I pushed back. I told her no, that I was involved with you." He took Jess's hand and pressed it against his chest, where she could feel his heartbeat. "I've never broken that trust with anyone, and I never would with you."

He winced at the memory. "She wasn't happy about being rejected, but I was firm with her and escorted her back to her own room."

Jess had a look of shock on her face. "Are you fucking kidding me?"

Before she could say anything more, Jack interjected, "I swear to you, nothing happened!"

"I'm not mad at you, Jack. I'm mad at her. Where in the fuck does she get off hitting on my man?"

Jack sighed, "She was intoxicated and not thinking. Now she's avoiding me at work, acting like I somehow wronged her. Making me the villain in this story."

"You were sexually harassed, Jack," Jess insisted. Jack held up a hand dismissively. "No, I mean it. We need to go with this to Bob!"

"Jess, she never touched me, and I wouldn't call it harassment. She was just trying to entice me. I will not ruin somebody's career over a drunken indiscretion," Jack said.

"I won't push you to report it if you're not comfortable, but don't think for a second I'm letting this slide. Lynley and I are having words first thing tomorrow."

Monday morning, Jack and Jess rode the elevator to the fourth floor, where Lynley would unveil her findings to the assembled science team. She had kept him at arm's length throughout her analysis.

When Hendricus noticed Jack's absence from the project, he raised concerns. Lynley had explained, "The specimens were botanical in nature. I have the relevant background."

That fooled everyone but Jack. He recognized the real reason behind his exclusion: retribution for his rejection of her in Blythe.

As they stepped onto the fourth floor, Jess had a look of determination on her face: the physical manifestation of the speech she'd been perfecting since dawn. Last night, he'd persuaded her to save the confrontation for later, somewhere outside work. She had agreed reluctantly. Jack was wondering if she could hold back.

The conference room was packed, with Lynley at the head of the table. Bob stood to her right, Hendricus to her left. The room quieted after a round of forced pleasantries.

Jack slid into a chair along the wall beside Jess. She uncapped her pen with a swift click that sounded deliberate.

Lynley began with a satellite image of the Blythe formation. On the screen was a precise and geometric shape that stood out against the brown patchwork of the Colorado River valley. "On the screen is a formation spanning approximately two hundred and forty feet at its widest point," she began. Lynley carried the confidence of someone who had rehearsed this presentation more than once. "The geometry is precise to a degree that would challenge a team of surveyors working in daylight, let alone in darkness."

She advanced to the ground-level photographs. The eyewitness's shots were good. They were taken early while the formation was still intact, the concentric rings razor-sharp against the flattened wheat.

"These were captured approximately forty minutes after sunrise," Lynley continued. "By mid-morning, the site had been compromised by foot traffic. However, what appeared to be a liability turned out to be an asset."

"When you say asset, are you referring to the comparison samples?" asked Jess.

"Exactly, Dr. Bowden. The human-trampled wheat gave us a control group we couldn't have engineered ourselves."

Lynley advanced to the next slide. "These are microscopic images of the plant nodes from inside the formation," she said. Lynley circled a cluster of cells with her laser pointer. "Note the explosive elongation of the cell walls."

She advanced to the next slide. "What you are seeing here are the samples collected from the area trampled by the public," she said. "Note the clean, compressed breaks.

"The plants inside the circle show signs of exposure to rapid elec-tromagnetic radiation, specifically in the microwave band. The heat generated would cause moisture inside the plant cells to vaporize, producing these expulsion cavities."

"Have you ruled out military microwave systems?" asked Jess.

"Yes, the uniformity of the effect is inconsistent with any known directed energy system."

Hendricus nodded slowly from his position beside Bob. Across the table, two of the physicists exchanged a glance.

Jess considered her next question. "The satellite imagery," she said. "What's the earliest confirmed timestamp before the formation appeared?"

"Eleven forty-two p.m. the previous evening. The field was clear." Lynley clicked to a side-by-side comparison. "By five-seventeen a.m., the formation was complete."

"So a window of roughly five and a half hours," Jess said.

"Correct."

"And your conclusion regarding human fabrication within that window?"

"Categorically impossible. Not for a formation of this complexity, this size, and with this degree of cellular effect. Boards and rope don't rearrange plant biology."

The room went quiet again.

She wrapped up her presentation with a bold statement. "The inescapable conclusion, ladies and gentlemen, is that we are looking at a genuine crop circle. Now, what created it? That is the ultimate question."

The room erupted with questions, which Lynley fielded with ease.

After ten minutes, the meeting dispersed. Scientists drifted toward their workspaces, murmuring among themselves. Jack and Jess had nearly made it back to their offices when she stopped, her shoulders squaring as she pivoted on her heel.

Jack reached for her elbow. "Jess, hold on. Don't do this now."

"I've got this," she hissed through clenched teeth, shaking off his grip. She marched toward the conference room, where Lynley stood alone, gathering her presentation material into a leather portfolio. Lynley's head snapped up at the sound of Jess's determined footsteps crossing the threshold.

~

Jack was sitting in his office, his gut gnawing with anxiety. It had been half an hour since the meeting ended, and he hadn't heard a peep from Jess. He decided to take a walk past the conference room to make sure neither was trying to kill the other. Before he could get up, both of them walked into his office, Jess closing the door behind her.

They both sat down in the leather chairs next to his desk.

Lynley cleared her throat. "Jack, Jess confronted me about Blythe." She smoothed her skirt, eyes fixed on a point past his shoulder. "I'm terribly sorry about what happened. Professional boundaries exist for a reason, and I crossed them." A flush crept up her neck as she met his gaze. "And I had no clue that you two were involved, not that it would have justified my behavior otherwise."

Her fingers twisted around each other in her lap. "That night in Blythe, I was... It had been a long time since I'd been with anyone. The minibar seemed like a good idea." She swallowed hard, her professional veneer cracking. "My judgment was compromised."

Jack started to say something, and Jess motioned for him to wait. Lynley continued, "I was selfish, Jack. I never stopped to consider what it would be like for you, being cornered." She glanced sideways at Jess and continued. "Hell, I'm nearly twice your age, and I'm old enough to be your mother. After you rejected me, I couldn't bear to face you, so I built this wall of professional distance, excluding you from your own work. I told myself it was justified somehow." She looked up, her eyes meeting his. "I was humiliated. And instead of owning that, I punished you for it. That's the truth I've been avoiding."

She buried her face in her hands and said, "If you want me to resign, I'll go straight down to the first floor and do so right now."

Jack had heard enough. "Resign? Listen, Lynley, I think we can put this behind us, and I don't want you to quit. You were drunk, and you hit on me; no harm, no foul. You are a valuable member of this team and a brilliant scientist. SPIRE is a better place because of you."

Tears welled up in Lynley's eyes as Jack continued, "I think you're a good person who exercised poor judgment, and I suppose we've all been guilty of that a time or two in our lives." He glanced at Jess. "Are the two of you able to get over this and work together?"

Jess spoke up before Lynley had a chance. "We've worked things out, haven't we, Lynley? I think we can put this behind us and move forward."

"Indeed," she said.

Maggie's childhood unfolded in River Oaks, where her father's corner office at Texaco had afforded her the upbringing where cotillions and country clubs were part of the calendar. David had been the unexpected variable in her equation, the football captain who'd written her poetry between classes, until their paths diverged when he chose a Navy career while she packed for UT Austin.

After she and Jack divorced, she'd spotted him across the produce section at Kroger, his cart half-filled with single-person portions and a six-pack of Shiner Bock. Their eyes met over a display of Texas citrus. His wedding band was gone. They'd started with coffee that turned into dinner, then breakfast. Soon they were back together again, as if they had never separated.

When David asked her to share his Sugar Land home, Maggie felt like she'd been handed a second chance at happiness. Then reality intruded. Every time he had visited her apartment, he left with watery eyes and a handkerchief pressed to his nose. Annie, her beautiful Persian, triggered sneezing fits that no amount of antihistamines could control.

She stared at the ceiling fan, watching it spin as she weighed her options. David or Annie. A flesh-and-blood man who made her coffee the way she liked it, or the warm, purring weight that had kept her company through the darkest nights after she left Jack. Annie's blue eyes blinked at her from the windowsill, innocent of the dilemma she posed. Then Maggie sat bolt upright, her phone already in hand before the thought fully formed. Of course, Jack had always adored

Annie, even sneaking her treats when he thought Maggie wasn't looking.

She'd lost track of where he'd settled or how to reach him. After three deep breaths, she dialed the National Weather Service in Phoenix. Linda Summers's response left her clutching the edge of her kitchen counter, knuckles white against the granite.

Jack wasn't with the National Weather Service anymore. In fact, he wasn't even in Arizona. How would she find him?

She remembered Pat, the guy he hung around with from that UFO group. "Now, what was his last name? Harper. Pat Harper."

She dug out an old Arizona phone book and started scanning through the directory. There were several people named Pat Harper in the Phoenix area, but only one in Scottsdale—and she was pretty certain that's where he lived.

She crossed her fingers and dialed the number.

"Hello?" said the voice on the other end of the line.

"Hi, is this Pat?" she asked.

"Yeah, who's calling?" he said.

"This is Maggie, Jack's ex-wife. How are you today?"

"Ah, okay, I guess. What can I do for you?" said Pat.

"I'm trying to get in touch with Jack, and I realized that he's not even working for the weather service anymore. Do you know where he is or how to get ahold of him?" she asked.

"Eh, I'm not sure if he would want me to give that to you," he said.

"Please, Pat. We had a cat, and I took her with me to Texas when we divorced. I can't keep her anymore, and I'm trying to see if he would take her back."

Pat sighed. All of this over a cat. "Okay, I'll give you his number. He's working for a UFO research group in Little Rock these days."

Of course Jack would end up with the UFO people. She shook her head. "Any chance you could give me his address?"

Maggie jotted down Jack's address and phone number, then drummed her fingers against the kitchen counter. A phone call would give him the chance to say no. But who could refuse when faced with Annie's blue eyes and plush coat in person? The element of surprise would benefit her and Annie.

The Friday-afternoon sun slanted through her blinds as Maggie's mind clicked into resolve. Seven hours on the road would get her to Little Rock before midnight. She could check into a roadside motel, get some sleep, then show up at Jack's doorstep the next morning with Annie in her carrier. The perfect solution. What could go wrong?

Jack and Jess had been living together for three months, tiptoeing around the office and maintaining separate mailboxes. Lynley knew of their relationship but had so far kept it to herself. There had been a few suspicious glances from other coworkers now and then, but not enough to raise any concerns. As best they could tell, their secret was safe.

After spending a relaxing Saturday morning making love, Jack slipped on a T-shirt and a pair of sweatpants and made his way to the kitchen, while Jess basked in bed. The least he could do was cook breakfast. She might be brilliant with numbers and research, but her culinary experiments typically ended with the smoke alarm blaring.

He had finished frying up bacon and making blueberry pancakes, Jess's favorite, and had set them on the breakfast table. He was about to call her when the doorbell rang. "Who could be here on a Saturday morning?"

Jack opened the door and felt his muscles lock in place. There on his front porch stood Maggie, her familiar perfume hitting him before his brain could process her presence. "What are you doing here?"

Without waiting for an invitation, she brushed past him and strode into the living room. "Jack, we need to talk." The words had barely left her mouth when Jess emerged from the hallway, wearing nothing but a pair of cotton briefs, her bare feet silent against the hardwood. Time suspended as their gazes collided, both women turning to statues in the morning light.

Maggie said, "So, Jack, is this your new plaything? I hope you like hearing about UFOs, honey. That's all he's interested in."

"Maggie!" said Jack.

Jess appeared ready to grab something to cover herself, but instead straightened her spine and let her bare skin catch the morning light.

Without hurrying, she crossed to the kitchen table and lowered herself into a chair, crossing one leg over the other. "Maggie, I presume?" Her voice was level, almost pleasant. "I'm Dr. Jessica Bowden. Astrophysicist." She reached across the table and pulled one of the bacon strips from the plate Jack had just set out, as if this were any other Saturday morning. "And as for UFOs—that's actually my field. So we have that in common." She took a bite and held Maggie's gaze without blinking. "Among other things."

Jack's fingers pressed into Maggie's shoulder as he guided her firmly toward the exit. "If there's something on your mind," he said through clenched teeth, "we can discuss it on the porch."

Jack returned from outside, his jaw still tight from the confrontation. He crossed to where Jess sat, her bare skin glowing in the morning light. "So," he said, running a hand through his disheveled hair, "I need to ask you something important. What's your stance on cats?"

Jess's eyes lit up. "Cats? I adore them. What's this about?"

"When Maggie and I divorced, she took our cat Annie with her to Houston. Turns out, she's got a new man in her life, and he's allergic to cats. She wants to know if I'm willing to take Annie back. If not, she's going to dump her at a shelter, and there is no way I'm going to let that happen. She is a big, fluffy ball of love. If we can't keep Annie, I'll find a home for her. But I'll be damned if she's going to be tossed in an animal shelter. We rescued her from one of those places, and she's not going back!"

A smile crossed Jess's face. "Of course, we'll take Annie. I've had cats most of my life."

Jack relaxed. "Okay, I'll be back in a minute," he said and went outside.

Jack returned several minutes later with many pet supplies from Maggie's car—a litter pan, cat litter, feeding trays, and a bag of cat food. He went back out a second time and returned with a cat carrier containing an unhappy feline. At last, he set the carrier down on the couch and reached in, scooping Annie out.

Annie's ears flattened against her skull as she squirmed in Jack's embrace, her tail twitching nervously. Jack ran his palm along her back, whispering reassurances that seemed to slow her panicked breathing, though her wide eyes still darted around the unfamiliar room. Across from them, Jess rose from her seat and extended her arms, fingers beckoning for a chance to soothe the trembling creature.

Jack watched as Jess transformed before his eyes. Her fingers found the sweet spot behind Annie's ears, and the cat's eyes narrowed to contented slits. "There we go," Jess cooed in a voice Jack had never heard before, high-pitched and musical. "Poor baby, trapped in that awful box." Annie's tail, previously bristling with anxiety, now curved into a relaxed question mark as she settled onto Jess's lap. Fifteen minutes of gentle strokes and nonsensical endearments later, the cat stood on Jess's thighs, her paws kneading the bare skin as if she'd found her rightful place in the world.

Watching Annie settle against Jess's skin, purring as if she'd found home, Jack felt something inside him click into place, as if the universe had finally arranged its stars in the right formation.

Another weekend had come and gone, and it was back to work this morning. Jack finished tucking in his shirt as Jess gathered her things in the kitchen. They'd leave for the office separately again as always. No sense in raising eyebrows at the office yet. The chirp of his phone cut through the quiet of the early hour. Bob's name flashed on the screen, and he answered with a quick flip of his wrist.

Bob's voice came through crisp and businesslike. "Morning, Jack. Still at home?" He glanced at Jess moving about the kitchen. "Grabbing my keys. What's happening?"

Bob cleared his throat. "Change of plans. Skip the office and get packing instead. We've got a situation in the Mediterranean that needs your meteorological expertise. Alec, Jim, and Chris are already there. No timeline yet, so prepare for a week or more. Big Red's on its way into the airport, and the ground crew should have it fueled up and ready to turn around by ten. Don't forget your passport."

"What's the assignment?"

Bob lowered his voice. "Two weeks ago, a private flight out of Alicante, Spain, reported multiple disc-shaped objects suspended over the Mediterranean. Broad daylight, perfect visibility. Chris insists they're lenticular formations, but I need your expert opinion.

The team's investigating other elements—radar signatures, local reports—but your expertise is needed on the meteorological angle."

Jack's pulse quickened. "I'm on it," he said, already cataloging what he'd need to pack. "I'll head straight to the tarmac at ten."

As he hung up the call, he spun around to Jess, who had a look of concern on her face.

She set her cup down with a sharp clink. "Another assignment? Let me guess, somewhere far away, and they don't know when you'll be back."

Jack ran a hand through his hair. "Spain. Mediterranean coast. Could be a week or more from the sound of it."

Jess's shoulders slumped as she traced the rim of her coffee mug with her index finger. Her eyes didn't meet his. "The bed gets cold when you're gone that long."

He stepped closer, his fingers brushing her wrist where her watchband met skin. "I'll set an alarm on my phone—seven your time, every evening." He leaned in, lips grazing her ear. "And I saw that little Spanish restaurant you bookmarked on your computer. Their paella—" He pulled back enough to see her eyes. "I'll bring you the authentic version from Spain."

She lifted an eyebrow, the corner of her mouth curling upward as she pressed a finger into his chest. "Oh, you better bring me something a lot nicer than that." Her voice dipped lower, lingering there as she ran her fingers along his collar.

Jack climbed the metal stairs to the plane, his duffel bag swinging against his thigh. The pilot met him at the top, flight cap tucked under one arm, the skin around his eyes creased from years of squinting into distant horizons. "Morning, sir." He gestured toward a map spread across his clipboard, where a red line arced from Little Rock to a dot labeled St. John's, then stretched east over the vast blue expanse of the Atlantic. His finger tapped Alicante, a tiny point on

Spain's Mediterranean shoreline. "Ten hours with a refueling stop on the Canadian coast. Better get acquainted with that reclining seat back there. And we have a pull-out bed if you want to catch a longer nap."

Jack sank into the leather seat, laptop balanced on his knees. The hours blurred together as he analyzed weather patterns over the Mediterranean from the day in question, barely noticing when they touched down to refuel in St. John's. Somewhere over the Atlantic, he swallowed a sleeping pill with lukewarm coffee, letting the drone of the engines lull him into dreamless sleep until the bump of wheels on the runway announced their arrival in Spain.

He was about to step off the plane when the copilot reminded him of the local time: 3:17 a.m.

Jack followed the flight crew down the metal stairs to where a sleek black sedan idled on the tarmac, its driver standing at attention beside the open rear door. Minutes later, they pulled up to a discreet side entrance of the terminal where a single immigration officer waited with a leather portfolio. No lines, no crowded halls, no fluorescent lighting, only a stamp, a nod, and they were through. The privilege of arriving by private jet never ceased to amaze him.

The digital clock beside the hotel bed flashed 4:11 a.m. when Jack dropped his duffel in the suite overlooking Alicante's marina. He eased open the sliding glass door and stepped onto the balcony, where the Mediterranean's salt-laden breeze washed over him. Below, a cluster of locals spilled from a late-night establishment, their laughter climbing up the building's facade like ivy, unconcerned with the hour or who might be trying to sleep. He knew he should chase a few more hours of rest, but the sleeping pill and fitful dozing on the plane left him wide-eyed in this unfamiliar darkness.

Jack watched dawn break over the marina, surrendering to wakefulness after hours of tossing in sheets. At 8 a.m., he found the team gathered around a cluster of leather armchairs in the lobby. Alec and Jim nodded their hellos while Chris—Dr. Bellini, as the embroidery on his shirt pocket reminded everyone—spread maps and satellite imagery across the coffee table and began walking him through what they'd learned so far.

Chris tapped a flight path traced in red marker on the map. "The pilot departed Alicante at 1300 hours in a Cessna Citation, climbed to 15,000 feet over the Mediterranean, then banked east-northeast toward the island of Ibiza before turning northeast, making his final approach to Mallorca." The entire distance was less than two hundred miles.

Chris slid a transcript across the table. Jack's eyes locked on the highlighted section: "Object One appeared first, metallic, saucer-shaped, reflecting sunlight off its surface. Diameter at least several miles. Stationary at what I estimate to be 25,000 feet. Then I spotted Object Two between Ibiza and Mallorca, to the left of my flight path. Both were hanging there. Silent. No exhaust. No movement. Like someone had painted them onto the sky."

"So you think he saw clouds?"

Chris nodded. "Altocumulus lenticularis."

"I know the look—smooth, saucer-like, and deceptively solid," Jack said. "But for a lenticular cloud to form, you need significant orographic lift—the atmosphere has to be shoved upward by high terrain. The only place we'd see them near here is the Tramuntana range on the north coast of Mallorca, but those peaks are under 5,000 feet. To get a disc-shaped formation sitting at 25,000 feet in a clear blue sky over the open Mediterranean? The physics doesn't work. The location and altitude of this anomaly aren't consistent with weather."

"What about some other type of cloud?" asked Chris.

"I need to investigate further. We could be looking at Kelvin-Helmholtz formations—rare atmospheric phenomena where wind shear creates undulating patterns. But those look like ocean waves frozen in the sky, not hovering discs. And while isolated altostratus clouds might appear disc-shaped from certain angles, but the pilot's description seems inconsistent with that."

Chris folded his arms across his chest. "Jim and I will keep digging into the flight data and radar records. Meanwhile, Jack, I need you and Alec to interview the meteorological stations on both islands. The observers might have caught something our instruments missed." He tapped a finger on the coastline of the map. "And hit the marinas, too: fishermen, charter captains, anyone with eyes on the sky that afternoon who might've seen a phenomenon they couldn't explain."

Chris glanced at his watch, the titanium band catching the light. "The pilots maxed out their flight hours getting you here. I want them to cool their heels until tomorrow morning." He gestured toward the marina visible through the lobby windows. "Take the day. Get your internal clock back in balance. This Mediterranean air might clear your head. Explore the town. Alec, you can show him around."

"Are you hungry?" asked Alec.

"I could eat."

"One thing you need to understand about Spain, Jack. They eat five meals a day. The first breakfast is often just coffee and a pastry, but the main morning meal starts in about half an hour. Are you up for eating like the locals do?"

"Absolutely!"

Stepping through the hotel's revolving door, Jack raised a hand to shield his eyes from the Mediterranean glare. The city that had been a collection of shadows and distant voices when he'd arrived now revealed itself in brilliant splendor, whitewashed buildings rising against a vivid blue sky, the harbor's waters shimmering like scattered diamonds. Alec motioned for him to follow.

They stepped onto the Esplanada de España, which unfurled

before them like a vast mosaic dream. Millions of marble tesserae rolled in endless waves of rust, cream, and slate beneath their feet, as though the Mediterranean itself had crept up from the harbor and frozen into stone. Jack had walked pavements in a dozen cities, but none had ever made him feel quite like this.

Date palms rose on either side in solemn procession, their shaggy crowns filtering the light into something golden and forgiving. Beneath them, the morning had come alive. A boy on a scooter carved arcs across the marble. Couples drifted. Old men watched the yachts. Beyond the rustling palms, the marina glittered. White hulls rocked in their moorings.

Jack paused at a lamppost, one hand resting on its cool iron, and let the promenade carry its noise around him like a current.

Alec gestured at the surrounding panorama. "Once you've spent a few days here, you'll understand why people never want to leave. Spain gets under your skin: the light, the pace of life. Makes life back home feel like another planet."

"Yeah, I'm already getting a sense of that. Maybe we can convince Bob to move our operations over here," Jack said, chuckling.

Alec turned down a side street, and he followed.

The road narrowed, tall residential blocks pressed in on both sides, their facades the color of old bone and tired concrete. During the morning hours, the side streets belonged to no one. A row of motorcycles and scooters lined the right-hand side of the pavement.

Tourists were everywhere here. A tapestry of languages washed over Jack—the rapid-fire consonants of Castilian, the nasal lilt of French, melodic Italian, clipped English, and several other tongues that remained foreign to his American ear.

After another couple of blocks, Alec ducked into a doorway on the left side of the street.

He followed Alec inside. "This is a bar? I thought we were getting breakfast."

"Almost every restaurant around here is a bar. Relax. You're going to get a unique breakfast," Alec said.

The place they'd walked into wasn't large, but a designer had engineered it with the particular genius of Spanish hospitality. Every surface that could hold something did; wine bottles with hand-scrawled labels climbed the shelves in crowded columns, jars of preserves and tins of anchovies jostled for space, and from the ceiling hung jamón, dark and glistening legs of preserved ham.

Alec slid onto one of the wooden stools at the bar and motioned for Jack to join him.

A woman emerged from the rear, her face lined with laugh creases at the corners of her eyes, silver streaking through her dark hair tied back in a practical knot. She wiped her hands on a cloth tucked into her apron as she moved behind the bar. Her eyes, warm and appraising, settled on them. "Sí?"

Alec fumbled with a pocket-sized phrasebook, its cover worn soft at the corners from use.

Jack touched his elbow. "Let me handle this." Alec's eyebrows shot up as Jack leaned forward and addressed the woman in fluid Spanish. The woman's professional politeness melted into something warmer as they spoke, her hands becoming animated. After a brief exchange that left Alec feeling like the foreigner he was, Jack turned back. "Seems she hasn't forgotten your previous visit. Is the last thing you had when you came here still your preference?"

"Yes," said Alec, "dude, I didn't know you could speak Spanish."

He shrugged. "My Spanish is more Mexico City than Madrid. Different rhythm, different words. But the ear adjusts," he said, then pivoted back to the woman behind the bar to continue their exchange.

After a time, María, with whom Jack had become fast friends, returned from the kitchen, balancing two earthenware plates. The main course was a bocadillo, a sandwich made with a rustic, crusty baguette. A thick wedge of Spanish potato omelet filled Alec's sandwich, while Jack had roasted pork loin with melted cheese. She set down several small bowls containing peanuts, pickles, green olives, and spicy peppers, along with something she described as Tinto de Verano—red wine with soda.

The food was delicious, and he thought to himself, This is just breakfast. What further culinary delights await?

They threaded their way back through narrow streets and alleyways and came to a small plaza dominated by a large date palm. A man was seated along a row of benches. He was older, his face pleasant but deeply weathered, the kind of skin that comes from decades of squinting into sun-bleached horizons.

"Jack, this is Hector. He used to fly air cargo over to northern Africa back in the day."

"Hola," said Hector.

Jack extended his hand. "Hola Hector, soy Jack." He switched to English, watching Hector's eyes to gauge his comfort with it. "I'm a meteorologist, and we're trying to determine what these objects were. Alec tells me you've seen them before."

"Sí. More than once." Hector shifted on the bench and folded his hands in his lap. "The first time was in 1984. I was flying a Fokker F27 from Alicante to Oran, loaded with machine parts. Clear day, perfect visibility. And there they were—two of them, suspended above the water. Enormous. Metallic looking. My co-pilot, Fernández, thought I was crazy at first. Then he saw them too."

"What altitude were they at?" Jack asked.

Hector considered this. "We were at 18,000 feet. They were above us. I would say 24,000, maybe 25,000."

Jack leaned forward. "And you reported this?"

Hector let out a short, dry laugh. "We reported it to Alicante approach control. They saw nothing on the radar. Nothing. And afterward, the airline told us to keep quiet. They didn't want passengers reading about their pilots seeing things in the sky." He tapped his temple. "You understand."

"What did you make of them? As a pilot?"

"My first thought was clouds. I know lenticular formations—I've seen them over the Atlas Mountains in Morocco many times. But those are near the ground, near terrain. Out there over open water at that altitude?" He shook his head firmly. "No mountains for hundreds of miles. No mechanism to produce that kind of formation. And clouds don't reflect sunlight the way these did. Like polished aluminum."

Jack glanced at Alec, then back to Hector. "Alec said you had mentioned Fata Morgana when he talked to you the other day."

"Sí." Hector straightened slightly, animated now. "I've thought about this for many years. Fata Morgana is a mirage. It usually occurs near the surface, over water, where you have a temperature inversion. Warm air sitting above cold air. It bends the light and creates false images of objects on the horizon. You've seen this?"

"I've seen the effect, yes," Jack said.

"I am not a scientist, you understand, but I have been wondering about something. Could something similar happen at altitude? The Atlas Mountains in northern Africa rise to over 4,000 meters. On certain days, with the right atmospheric layering, could the light be bent in such a way that an image of those peaks is projected upward into the upper atmosphere? Reflected into a layer where the conditions are right?"

Jack sat back. He thought about that carefully. "That's not how that works. The refraction you're describing would require a very specific inversion layer at extreme altitude. The temperature differential would have to be dramatic and unusually stable."

"But not impossible?"

Jack was quiet for a moment. "Not impossible in principle. I've never encountered documentation of a superior mirage at that altitude over open ocean. But I can't say that it's impossible." He pulled out his notebook. "What was the date of your 1984 sighting? And the approximate time of day?"

Hector provided both without hesitation, as if he'd been keeping them ready for exactly this conversation. Jack wrote them down. "You said you've seen them more than once."

"Three times total. The second was 1989, under similar conditions. The third…" Hector paused. "The third was two years ago. I had retired by then. I was on a ferry from Valencia to Ibiza. It was late afternoon. Same thing. Same altitude, as best I could judge. I had binoculars with me that time."

"And?"

"The surface was not uniform. There were variations in the reflection. There were darker areas and lighter areas. Like a structure. Like panels." He spread his hands. "I am not saying it was a spacecraft, señor. I am saying it did not behave like any weather phenomenon I know. And I know the weather."

Jack tapped his pen against his notebook. "Hector, the pilot whose account brought us here described objects several miles in diameter. Is that similar to what you saw?"

"Sí. The one in 1984. I estimated the size of it and compared it to the horizon. I would say it was three to four kilometers across," he said. "The sky does not produce objects like that."

"No," Jack said quietly, "it does not."

They sat in the shade of the date palm for another forty minutes.

Jack considered every atmospheric scenario he could imagine. Kelvin-Helmholtz instabilities, wave clouds, isolated altostratus, and temperature inversions. Nothing fit the bill.

As they shook hands to leave, Hector said, "You will find that many people here have seen things. They don't speak of it because no one asks seriously. It is good that someone is finally asking."

The day dissolved into a blur of tapas bars and narrow streets. Jack followed Alec's lead as afternoon melted into evening. They stumbled back to their hotel well after midnight.

Daybreak came, and they nursed espressos and throbbing headaches. They arrived at the private airport terminal, bleary-eyed but punctual, via taxi.

The pilot greeted them with a nod, his uniform crisp despite the early hour. "Dr. Bellini mentioned you'd be providing today's flight plan."

"Yes, I want to fly the same route the other plane did, but instead of landing in Mallorca, I want to fly past it and around Menorca, then back again to land in Ibiza. We'll spend an hour or two on the ground, and then we'll fly to Mallorca. I'm not sure what Bob's plans are for the aircraft, but we may be there for a few days."

The Balearic Islands were Spanish territory, composed of three principal islands, Ibiza, Mallorca, and Menorca, aligned in a south-west to northeast fashion. Ibiza was the party island of Europe; Mallorca was a major tourist destination, and Menorca was a lot quieter.

Jack planned to speak to the weather observers at the primary airports in Ibiza and Mallorca to see if they had noted anything unusual that day, in particular any odd-shaped mid-level clouds.

The flight over the islands was smooth, with a pocket or two of light turbulence, and they circled back to land at Aeropuerto Ibiza. After landing, he and Alec made their way across the tarmac toward the airport's meteorological office to interview the weather staff.

Initial wariness melted away when Jack cracked a joke in Spanish that had everyone chuckling behind their hands. Soon they were leaning over desks together, the meteorological team retrieving logbooks and satellite imagery from metal filing cabinets while he translated technical terms for Alec in a low voice.

"Nothing unusual that day," Jack said, flipping through the meticulous logs. "Skies were textbook, not a single formation worth remarking on."

The staff shook their heads at his questions about strange clouds. No, they had never documented such phenomena in their logs. But as they were gathering their things, the youngest technician murmured that mariners from the eastern coves had spoken of strange lights. Circular silhouettes rising from the water after midnight, leaving luminous trails as they disappeared upward.

"If you want these stories," the man said, writing something on a slip of paper, "find Miguel de León at the Santa Eulalia dock. He doesn't speak to just anyone, but tell him Ramón sent you."

With his tip, they informed the pilots of a delay and flagged down a taxi. The cab wound its way along the coastal road for twelve miles before depositing them at the harbor of Santa Eulalia.

Jack had pictured a small wooden dock with maybe a dozen boats. The Santa Eulalia Marina was much larger than that, with nearly 250 boats moored there. Alec found the marina's office, and they went in to inquire about Miguel de León. The reply Jack got was the last thing he wanted to hear.

"Which one?" said the man behind the desk. There were two men there with the same name. Jack explained the situation, and they put him in touch with the right Miguel.

They found him leaning against the railing of his tour boat, a slightly battered vessel with "Aventuras del Mar" painted in fading blue letters on its hull. His tanned face hardened at their approach. At the mention of Ramón, Miguel's eyes narrowed to slits. "¡Ese cabrón!" he spat, launching into a torrent of Spanish that had nearby deckhands turning their heads. Jack caught fragments about Miguel's sister and betrayal, enough to piece together an old romantic wound still festering. Jack raised his palms in surrender, steering the conversation toward the strange lights with careful persistence.

Miguel's tongue loosened after Jack bought him a beer, despite his earlier suspicions. "Lights in the water, sí," he said, "like someone dropped spotlights beneath the waves."

Jack asked about objects breaking the surface or ascending into the sky. "Only below," he said, "maybe three meters across, no more."

Jack and Alec exchanged glances. Whatever Miguel had witnessed was far too small to match their quarry.

This wasn't exactly what they were looking for, but Miguel's tale was intriguing. Jack marked the coordinates on his map before they bid the mariner goodbye. They caught a taxi back to their waiting plane and flew on to Mallorca.

Their visit with the meteorological staff at the Mallorca airport proved fruitless. Whatever the pilot had witnessed, Jack was certain that weather patterns were not the cause of it.

He and Alec decided to remain for a few days, with the goal of approaching local mariners to see if they knew of any phenomena similar to what the pilot had seen. They rented a car and drove around from port to port along the western and southern coastlines. They had struck out time and again, finding no sailors with interesting stories to tell.

As the sun slipped below the horizon, they encountered a harbormaster with salt-crusted eyebrows who gestured northward. "The northern coast," he said, "that's where the old-timers talk about lights coming up from the water. Men who've been sailing these waters since before I was born. Check the smaller villages, but ask around at Puerto de Sóller in particular."

The day's last light stretched their shadows across the harbor as Jack checked his watch. "We'll try the northern coast tomorrow," he said to Alec. They secured a room in Cala Ratjada for the night, then wandered into the evening bustle of the seaside town, following the sound of a distant guitar.

They were up early and had to traverse northward, hugging the eastern shore for over an hour. Finally, the road turned to the east along the northern coast, and they ascended. The landscape unfurled with each bend in the road, stirring something in Jack's memory from those rain-trapped childhood days when he'd escape into glossy National Geographic pages, fingers tracing photographs of places just like this.

On his left, the hillside climbed skyward in a violent disorder of limestone, sharp pinnacles and fractured ridges of pale rock thrust through the sparse vegetation.

As they drove farther, the scenery changed again, wedging them between the Tramuntana mountain range to their left and the coast several miles off to their right.

The terrain smoothed as they continued. Jagged limestone gave way to rolling slopes of pine, olive, and oak, their canopy undulating like a green tide against the road.

Jack eased off the accelerator as the car rounded each bend of the ancient roadway. This was old Mallorca, where sheep paths cut across hillsides, and weathered stone cottages stood unchanged for generations.

The road twisted toward the shoreline, delivering them to a succession of tiny hamlets where inquiries yielded only shrugs and blank stares. By midday, the coastal highway opened onto Puerto de Sóller, its sprawling marina and terraced buildings dwarfing the modest fishing enclaves they'd explored earlier.

The town cascaded up the hillside in tiers of sand-colored buildings and terra-cotta roofs. Below, the Mediterranean's turquoise depths lay still.

Several sailboats floated motionless in the glassy water. A bleached limestone crescent guarded the harbor's mouth. As they rounded the bay, the marina appeared. There were weathered fishing trawlers nestled between gleaming yachts, a forest of masts against the sky.

"We should find the closest tavern to the docks," Alec said. "Fishermen always have their regular spots. A few rounds on us, and their sea stories will flow like the tide."

"Sounds good to me," said Jack.

Tourist bars lined the marina. Jack and Alec circled the waterfront, hope fading at each polished facade. Then they found it...a squat, windowless building wedged between a chandlery and bait shop, its salt-stained walls topped by a weathered wooden sign with the faded letters "B-A-R."

"This looks promising," said Alec.

Amber light pooled across the room, and ancient beams crossed overhead. Tables with blue-and-white checkered cloths stood scattered like anchored vessels on the rust-and-cream tiled floor.

Along the rear wall stood a massive wooden bar, crowned by an iron hood that suggested either a forgotten hearth or deliberate maritime homage. Years of glasses had etched their circular signatures into the bar's surface, now polished to a deep mahogany by time and countless elbows.

Only a handful of men occupied the barstools now. Their faces told stories the sea had written, weather-creased, sun-branded, impassive as stone.

Conversation ceased as they approached the bar. Every head turned. Jack slid pesetas across the counter. "Una ronda para todos," he announced. A round for the house.

After the first round, Jack ordered another and let the silence do its work. The fishermen watched him with the particular wariness of men who have learned that strangers in bars always want something.

He leaned forward and spoke in careful Spanish to the oldest man, a barrel-chested, white-bearded sailor, with hands like dock rope. "I'm Jack, a scientist from the States. I'm here because people have seen things in these waters. I'm not with the press, nor the government. I'm just looking for the truth."

The old man studied him. "What kind of things?"

"Lights. Underwater. Objects in the sky that shouldn't be there."

A long pause. The old man's eyes met those of his companions. Recognition, not skepticism, passed between them.

"You have seen something yourself?" the old man asked.

"I have." Jack set down his beer. "A year and a half ago, in Phoenix, Arizona. I was working as a meteorologist for the government. We got reports of lights crossing the state. My colleague and I went to our roof with cameras." He paused. "A V-shaped craft passed overhead. Completely silent. So massive it blocked out the stars. I measured it at nearly a kilometer wide."

The man with the white beard set down his glass.

"Fighter jets scrambled from the air base and flew toward it," Jack continued. "The moment they got close, it vanished. One second it was there, the next the sky was empty."

The bar was very quiet now.

"The government took our evidence. Broke into my house, took the videotape, the photographs, and the hard drive from my computer. Told us never to speak of it." He spread his hands on the bar. "I lost my job. That's why I'm here now, working for a private research organization. Because I know what I saw, and I want to understand it."

The white-bearded man exchanged a look with his scarred companion, who nodded once.

"I am Antoni," the old man said. "I have fished these waters for fifty years. My father fished them before me." He wrapped both hands around his glass. "What you describe, the silence, the disappearing...I know this."

Jack pulled out his notebook. "Tell me."

Antoni spoke slowly, pausing to search for words in Spanish when the Mallorcan dialect failed him, and Jack translated quietly for Alec as he went. "It was the summer of 1991. We were night fishing, maybe twelve kilometers northwest of this harbor, between here and Dragonera island. Around two in the morning. The sea was flat with no wind or swell. My nephew spotted it first. He thought it was a submarine surfacing."

"What did it look like?"

"A shape beneath the water. Luminous. Not phosphorescence; we know what that looks like. It moves with the current, with the fish. This was different. A defined shape. Circular. Perhaps fifteen meters across, I would estimate. Bright enough to cast light on the underside of our hull." He paused. "It rose slowly, and for a moment I thought it was going to surface completely. Then it accelerated straight up, no angle, just straight up! Then it was gone. No wake. No sound. The water where it had been was completely flat, as if nothing had moved through it."

"How long were you watching it before it went up?"

"Perhaps four minutes. Long enough that all five men on the boat had seen it. Long enough that I am certain of what I saw." He met Jack's eyes. "I have never spoken of this to anyone outside this island. My nephew still won't discuss it."

Jack nodded and wrote. "You said you knew the silence. Was there any sound at all when it left the water?"

"Nothing. That is what frightened me most. Something that size, moving that fast? There should have been a sound. A wave. Something. There was nothing."

The scarred man leaned forward, his accented Spanish deliberate. "I saw the ones in the sky," he said. "Not underwater. Above." He held his palm flat over the bar. "Nineteen eighty-eight. I was sailing from Palma to Menorca with two friends. Midday. Clear sky. We saw two objects. High up. They hovered motionless. No clouds nearby. Round discs. When sunlight struck their surfaces..." He rubbed his fingers together, searching for the word.

"They reflected it?" Jack offered.

"Sí. Like mirrors. Like polished metal." He paused. "After maybe ten minutes, one of them moved. Slow drift, then gone. Vanished. The second one followed minutes later."

Jack put down his pen. "The pilot whose account brought us here described the same thing. Same altitude, same appearance, same disappearance. Over the stretch of water between Ibiza and Mallorca."

The man with the scar stared at him. "It is not the first time, and it will not be the last. These waters have always had them."

Antoni drained his glass and set it on the bar with a quiet click. "What you are looking for is below as well as above. Whatever they are, they move between the sea and the sky. I have thought about this for many years." He tapped the bar with one finger. "The sea is the largest unexplored place on this planet. Larger than all your land combined. If something wanted to stay hidden from human beings, that is where it would be."

Jack stared at his notebook. USO. Unidentified submerged object. The same phenomenon Miguel had described on Ibiza. The same description: defined, luminous, circular, silent, moving in ways that nothing biological or mechanical could explain. Two independent sets of witnesses, two islands apart, separated by years, describing the same thing.

He looked up at Alec, who had been following the translated fragments with growing attention. "Are you getting all of this?"

"Every word." Alec said.

Jack turned back to the fishermen. "One more question. Did these objects affect your instruments? Compasses, electronics?"

Antoni and the scarred man looked at each other again.

"The compass," Antoni said slowly. "After the 1991 sighting. For perhaps twenty minutes afterward, it was useless. Spinning. We had to navigate by the stars until it settled." He frowned. "I had forgotten that detail until now."

Jack wrote it down and underlined it twice. Electromagnetic interference. Consistent with every significant account he'd encountered since Phoenix. The same signature, the same fingerprint, turning up in a fishing bar on the northern coast of Mallorca.

He bought another round. They talked for another hour. Other men at the bar edged closer, offering secondhand accounts...lights off Dragonera, inexplicable radio failures at sea. Nothing matched Antoni's credibility, but the pattern was unmistakable.

Whatever they were dealing with here, it wasn't isolated. It wasn't new. And it wasn't only in the sky.

The night had deepened by the time Jack and Alec felt clear-headed enough to navigate the winding coastal road back toward Palma's airport. They reflected on the stories they had collected.

The waters surrounding the Balearic Islands harbored mysteries worth pursuing, and what they had learned today would add to the mystery.

Jack received the inevitable recall from Bob. Urgent business required his presence in Little Rock. After bidding farewell to Alec in Alicante, he settled into his seat for the long journey home. He watched the last golden thread of the Spanish coastline vanish into the deep blue of the sea, the hollow ache in his ribs reminding him that while he was leaving Spain, the mystery of what lived beneath their waves was coming back to Arkansas with him.

The aircraft banked northward toward its intermediate destination, the Canadian refueling stop before the last leg to Arkansas. Chris and Jim had joined Alec in Alicante, and the time had come to update them on his findings. He flipped open the satellite phone and made the call.

"Chris, can you hear me? The signal is lagging," Jack said, pressing the bulky handset tighter against his ear. The drone of the jet's engines hummed in the background as he looked out at the Atlantic below. "I've gone over the data from the airport observers in Palma and Ibiza again. There was insufficient wind shear for Kelvin-Helmholtz undulating patterns, and the upper-level moisture was nowhere near the threshold for altostratus clouds to form disc shapes like the pilot described. And we can rule out lenticular clouds. Those sightings were in the wrong place and wrong altitude for those. Whatever he saw at 25,000 feet wasn't the weather. We can officially rule out atmospheric anomalies."

"Copy that, Jack," Chris's voice crackled through the static from Alicante. "So we're left with a solid craft and no radar return. Did you get anything from the local mariners before Bob pulled the plug?"

Jack opened his notebook across his knee. "More than I expected. Pull out a map and mark Puerto de Sóller on the north coast of Mallorca." He waited. "I spent last night in a fishing bar there with two men who've been working these waters for decades. The older one described watching a circular luminous object rise from beneath the surface about twelve kilometers northwest of the harbor. 1991. Fifteen meters across, his estimate. Bright enough to light up the underside of his hull. Five witnesses on the boat. It went straight up and disappeared without a wake, without a sound."

"Submerged?" Chris said.

"Submerged, then airborne. The key detail: his compass spun wildly for twenty minutes after the encounter. It was useless. They navigated by stars."

A pause on the line. "Electromagnetic interference."

"Same signature we've been seeing since Phoenix." Jack tapped his pen against the page. "The second man described two disc-shaped objects stationary at high altitude over the Menorca crossing in 1988. Metallic, reflective. One drifted slowly, then vanished instantaneously. The other followed a few minutes later. His description of the disappearance matched the Alicante pilot almost word for word."

"And on Ibiza?" Chris asked.

"Miguel de León at Santa Eulalia described circular silhouettes underwater, about three meters across. Smaller than what the other guy saw, but the same basic profile. Defined shape, luminous, moving in ways nothing biological moves." Jack paused, watching the Atlantic slide past below the wing. "Chris, these aren't isolated incidents. We've got consistent accounts across two islands, spanning a decade, describing objects that transit between the water and the sky. The pilot saw something miles wide at 25,000 feet. The fishermen are describing the same phenomenon at close range from the surface. I think we're looking at two aspects of the same thing."

"You're saying whatever the pilot saw came up from the water."

"I'm saying I can't prove it didn't. And I think Bob needs to authorize a dedicated USO investigation before we close the book on the Mediterranean." Jack closed the notebook. "The compass detail alone is worth following up. If we can cross-reference the sailor's coordinates and date against any anomalous magnetic readings in the Spanish meteorological archive, we might be able to build a pattern."

"I'll flag it for the debrief," Chris said. "Safe flight, Jack."

"Tell the team I'll have a full written summary on Bob's desk by Thursday."

He clicked the phone shut.

ob's key jangled in the ignition as he pulled into his usual spot. He reached for his briefcase but froze. Across the street, two figures in crisp black suits stood unnaturally still, their faces obscured by identical Ray-Bans despite the overcast day. His stomach knotted.

This was the third time this week. He slid lower in his seat, pretending to check his watch while observing their reflection in his side mirror. One of them slightly turned his head, revealing an earpiece. Inside the SPIRE building, Jess was already peering through the blinds, her coffee mug suspended halfway to her lips as she tracked the pair with narrowed eyes.

Not only had they been stalking their headquarters, but on several other occasions team members reported black sedans trailing them through city streets.

Their motives remained a mystery. He'd already circulated an internal memo advising everyone to maintain heightened awareness. Fortunately, these shadowy figures had yet to directly obstruct any of their operations.

Hendricus stared at the men across the street. "Those are the same guys who tossed Jack's place in Phoenix. Broke his lock, stole his evidence." He frowned, leaning closer to Bob. "Why just watch us? Why not kick down our door, too?"

Bob smiled as he pulled out his wallet, flipping it open to reveal a photo of himself shaking hands with the president. Behind them, a framed campaign check hung on the wall, the amount visible even in the small photograph. He murmured, tucking the wallet away, "Some doors cost more to kick down than others."

Hendricus excused himself and walked down the hall to his office. He saw Jess in her office with Dr. Brian Hodges collaborating on an assignment he'd given them.

He had tasked her with collaborating with Dr. Hodges and Dr. Chris Bellini to develop a classification system for the UFO incidents under their investigation. They were also charged with developing preliminary theories about the mechanics behind these crafts' seemingly impossible movements through our atmosphere.

Chris was on assignment in Spain at the moment, so it was only her and Dr. Hodges for the time being.

Jess shook her head at the thought of collaborating with Dr. Hodges again. The man possessed remarkable intellect—his three PhDs and numerous publications proved that much—but his habit of interrupting her while she was speaking during their previous project still rankled.

She recalled how he'd dismissed her hypothesis without even reviewing her data, then presented a strikingly similar theory as his own two weeks later.

In her opinion, he was an arrogant ass. Still, the project demanded her expertise, and she wouldn't let personal grievances compromise scientific discovery, even if it meant tolerating Dr. Hodges's insufferable ego.

Jess and Dr. Hodges initiated a systematic analysis of credible documentation, meticulously sorting through eyewitness accounts, photographic evidence, and video footage that passed their rigorous authentication protocols.

Jess slid a series of photographs across the table to Dr. Hodges. "Historically, we've had saucers and cigar-shaped UFOs, but over the last decade we are seeing descriptions of shapes not previously reported." She took a drink from her coffee mug. "And how about some of the older types we seldom see anymore? Crescent-shaped craft were first seen in 1947 by Kenneth Arnold, but since then, reports have been scarce. And what about diamonds? There was that one famous incident in East Texas in 1980, and very few since. Why?"

"Your logic is flawed, Dr. Bowden. You are confusing the time and frequency of reports with occurrence. I wouldn't have expected someone with your educational background to fall into that trap. Just because they haven't been reported doesn't mean they're not present. They could be over the ocean, the Amazon, or the poles, where they would not be readily observed. Absence of observation does not imply lack of presence," he said.

Prick, she thought to herself. She tapped her pen against the notepad, her brow furrowed in concentration.

Were they looking at an interstellar United Nations of sorts, with each craft design representing a different civilization? Or was this more like Toyota versus Ford versus BMW, diverse engineering approaches from a single species of visitors?

Studying the classification chart, Jess couldn't help but theorize that Earth was being visited by more than one type of non-human species.

Their data revealed clear patterns. While classic disc-shaped craft dominated the historical record, recent years had seen a marked increase in triangular vessels, spheres, and peculiar formations of spheres clustered together like an atomic nucleus.

And were spheres the same as the glowing orbs seen at night? Were those the after-dark version, or were they entirely different?

Dr. Hodges was nowhere to be found whenever the discussion came up regarding propulsion theories. That left Jess to tackle the physics on her own. Of all the unusual craft they documented, the spheres were the ones that caught her interest the most. They defied everything she knew about aerodynamics.

SPIRE was able to gain clearance and access to classified footage through Bob's connections at the Pentagon. Several clips they obtained featured these mysterious spheres, and Jess had been granted unrestricted access to analyze every frame.

She kept returning to the footage of the spheres, fixated on the strange visual rippling that surrounded them. These weren't the expected signs of conventional flight. There were no heat blooms, no atmospheric disturbance, no compression waves. The atmosphere seemed to warp around each object, a thin distortion that clung to its surface like an invisible skin, flowing and reshaping whenever the sphere changed course.

Clutching her findings, Jess entered Dr. Hodges' office where he sat hunched over his desk, writing in the margins of a scientific journal.

Jess loaded the Pentagon footage onto the lab display. "Watch the edges of the sphere," she said. "See that? It's not heat distortion. Not a pressure wave. Not turbulence. But something's there, following the object, changing whenever it changes course. Like it's wearing some kind of...invisible skin."

Hodges finished his annotation, capped his pen, then turned his chair toward the screen. He watched the footage in silence. Then he watched it again.

Hendricus had wandered in during the second viewing. He stood to the side with his arms folded. He leaned closer to the screen and studied the halo surrounding the object. "Look at that visual aberration," he said. "It reminds me of what we see in our deep-space telescopes. When massive stars warp the light passing near them." His posture stiffened as the implication dawned on him. "If that's the same phenomenon..."

"There is a localized gravitational field there," Jess said. "Yes."

Behind his wire-rimmed glasses, Hodges's eyes widened. He

leaned forward and pulled the display closer. "I need to see that footage again," he said.

Hendricus watched Hodges write for a moment, then turned to Jess with a slight raise of his eyebrows. "He's not dismissing it."

"I noticed," she said.

Hodges looked up sharply. "I can hear you both. What I am doing is determining whether this observation is worth the paper it would take to publish it. That requires discipline, not enthusiasm." He returned to his notes. "Leave me the footage."

The next morning, she found him standing before a whiteboard covered edge-to-edge in dense equations. He shook his head and crossed out an entire section with three aggressive strokes. "No, that's not it." By afternoon, his chair was empty and his interest had waned.

Exhausted from Dr. Hodges's continuous dismissals, Jess escaped to the break room. She found Pablo, an aerospace engineer by trade, already occupying a corner of the laminate table.

"From the look on your face, I'd say you're either contemplating the end of all existence or you've been stuck in a room with Dr. Hodges again."

"Just trying to explain how a sphere can pull a ninety-degree turn at Mach 3 without turning the pilot into strawberry jam," she sighed.

Pablo grabbed a napkin and a pen. "Maybe everyone is looking at this all wrong." He sketched a series of concentric circles, adding arrows that bent sharply inward toward the center. "What if they aren't pushing against the air at all? What if they're manipulating the fabric of space itself?"

For two days, Jess wasn't able to shake Pablo's insight from her mind. She barricaded herself at her workstation, working through equations that stretched between several monitors.

When she finally stepped away from her desk, she carried more than a theory. She had scientific ammunition that even Dr. Hodges couldn't dismiss.

The next morning, Jess positioned herself in front of the lab's large display panel. As the simulation materialized, it revealed a luminous sphere hovering in digital space.

The lab door swung open as Dr. Hodges appeared, immediately slipping his wire-rimmed glasses from his face and polishing them with his handkerchief. This was standard procedure for him, buying himself the extra moments he needed to assess a situation.

"We've been looking at this all wrong, Dr. Hodges," Jess said. "All this time, we've been asking the wrong questions. We assumed these craft were breaking the rules, but we need to understand which rules they're playing by."

"Dr. Bowden," said Dr. Hodges, "these objects achieve accelerations that would turn any biological organism, human or otherwise, into organic soup. The G-forces alone would tear apart our most advanced carbon composites. These craft are not bending the laws of physics; they're shattering them entirely."

Jess shook her head. "That's where you're wrong. The physics only breaks if we assume conventional propulsion." She tapped the screen where the sphere glided impossibly through the air. "These objects aren't fighting against reality. They're taking the path of least resistance through the fabric of spacetime itself. A geodesic."

At that moment, Hendricus stepped into the lab, pulling up a chair with interest. "Refresh my memory, Jess. I'm an astronomer, not a theorist. Give me the executive summary on geodesics."

Jess brought up a 3D model of Earth that rotated in the projection space. "A geodesic is nature's version of efficiency," she said. "Imagine tracing the shortest possible line between Tokyo and New York on this globe. From our perspective down on the surface, that flight path appears to arc northward over Alaska. However, it's actually the straightest line possible when you account for Earth's curvature."

Bob materialized in the doorway, arms crossed as he studied the simulation. "So your fancy math keeps our theoretical alien from becoming organic soup. How, exactly?"

Jess turned to face him. "Think about astronauts in space.

They're falling constantly, but they're falling around Earth, not toward it. No rockets pushing them, no engines pulling them. Just pure free fall along nature's highway through the cosmos. That's a geodesic. Zero G-forces because they're not fighting against anything."

She stepped up to the whiteboard. "I'm drawing a sharp right angle here," she said as she tapped on the board. "In a conventional aircraft, this maneuver would liquefy the pilot. But these objects bend the fabric of reality around them, creating their own personal highway through spacetime."

Bob frowned. "Jess, give it to me in chicken-farmer English. Why don't they hit a wall of air and explode?"

She said, "Think of it like this. Instead of pushing through the air, they're creating a downhill path in front of them, folding space itself. The craft isn't moving; it's letting the universe slide beneath it." She continued, "Inside that sphere, the pilot would feel nothing; no acceleration or g-forces. From our perspective as observers, they'd seem to be defying everything we know about physical reality."

With a keystroke from Jess, the classified Pentagon footage bloomed across the display. Her finger traced the strange halo of distortion that outlined the object.

"See this shimmer? Everyone dismisses it as camera artifacts. It's not; that's a gravity signature. It's bending light around itself, the same way massive stars distort the starlight passing near them. What we're observing isn't the vehicle itself but the gravitational lens it's generating to manipulate spacetime," said Jess. "Think about it. Why do we see everything from flying saucers to triangles to these spheres? They're just different housings for the same technology. Like how cars can be sedans or SUVs, but still use internal combustion engines. These craft might come from unique places, different builders, but they've all cracked the same fundamental secret: how to bend gravity to their will."

The lab fell silent.

"Jesus Christ, if you can manipulate spacetime like that, our world changes completely," said Bob.

Hendricus turned to Dr. Hodges. "Does it hold water?

Dr. Hodges slid his glasses back onto his face. He stared at Jess's equations for a long time before clearing his throat.

"It is...an intriguing theory," Dr. Hodges said. "I shall need time to review the calculus myself."

Jess caught Bob's eye. For a man like Dr. Hodges, calling a theory "intriguing" was the equivalent of a standing ovation.

I n Phoenix, Garrett had become somewhat of a pariah at work, affecting his mental well-being both there and outside. Despite his vehement denials and management's official statement exonerating him, the whispers about who leaked the letter to the press followed him through the office like an unwelcome shadow.

Even with assurances that he was not under suspicion, each day he half expected to find his desk cleared and a security escort waiting by the door.

The stress was almost unbearable. He'd been fighting with his wife since Jack's firing, and some days he felt like he was on the verge of losing his mind. At night, Garrett's hand would hover over the liquor cabinet handle, the phantom burn of whiskey already coating his throat. Then he would remember the lost years, the shaking hands, the promises made in a fluorescent-lit church meeting room, and he'd curl his fingers into a fist and walk away.

The silence in his home had become unbearable since his wife had packed an overnight bag that somehow contained two weeks' worth of essentials, promising to "sort things out" from her mother's house across town.

With Jack gone and out of the picture, Garrett decided to follow in his footsteps. He became involved with CAPER, wanting answers as much as Jack did. It was the only thing keeping him grounded these days. Yet when the group began discussing the Phoenix Lights incident, Garrett's face hardened into stone.

"I'll help with anything else," he said, "but I won't touch that, not after what they did to Jack."

CAPER had been hearing reports of mysterious orbs of light being spotted over or near the Palo Verde Nuclear Generating Station in the desert west of Phoenix. They had staked it out multiple times and on one occasion witnessed an orb that appeared over reactor building two, hovered for a while, and then shot off at high speed. They returned the next night, and a security guard chased them off. It was a close call, and after that, the group moved on to other investigations.

But Garrett had become obsessed with the orb of light they'd seen and insisted they find another vantage point. The rest of them thought it was too risky, so Garrett had ventured out on his own. He'd found a good vantage point on a mountain about five miles away. He'd been staking it out for several nights until suddenly he didn't return the next morning.

His absence was noticed from work, and after repeated calls, Marco went over to his house and found nobody there. They raised the alarm and found out from CAPER that Garrett had been staking out the nuclear power plant from a nearby mountain ridge. Pat and Steve from CAPER immediately drove to the area, fearing the worst. When they arrived, a puzzle was waiting for them. Garrett's truck was still there, as was all of his gear, including his keys, but there was no sign of Garrett.

Depression had hit him hard after his wife left. The CAPER group worried about the possibility of suicide. They contacted the Maricopa County Sheriff's Office, which assembled a small search team. Several of Garrett's co-workers and guys from the UFO group joined them. They scoured the area for hours, finding no trace of him.

~

Jack was suffering from jet lag following the trip to Spain. His thoughts were swimming through a haze as Sunday evening settled over Little Rock. He and Jess had barely sunk into the couch cushions when the harsh chirp of her phone cut through their quiet moment.

Hendricus was calling to see if she was up for a trip to her home state of Wisconsin. "There is a mutilation case up there, dairy cattle. Not exactly a hotspot for that type of thing," he said. Jess was ecstatic. She closed her phone and turned to look at Jack. Seconds later, his phone rang, and Hendricus briefed Jack on the same matter.

Grinning at each other, they realized they'd be working their first official case together.

"So where is this farm?" he asked.

"Small town in what I guess you would call central Wisconsin. Looks like we will be taking the jet directly to the Eau Claire and Chippewa Falls area. I think it's almost forty miles away from there. Ever been to that part of the state?"

"No, not that I can recall. Milwaukee, Green Bay, Madison, and the Wisconsin Dells. That's about it for me. How close is this to the Dells?"

"It's at least a hundred miles or so away. We should start packing. Hendricus said we go wheels up at 8 a.m."

After a restful night of sleep, they headed to the airport in the morning and boarded the plane. The flight was smooth, and before they knew it, they were approaching their destination.

Their jet touched down at Chippewa Valley Regional with nothing but clear skies and a light chop to mark the journey. As the engines wound down to a whisper, Jack spotted a vehicle approaching from across the sun-bleached concrete. A black SUV idled on the tarmac, Patty's handiwork, no doubt, saving them the hassle of the rental counter. With hours to kill before the hotel check-in and their one o'clock appointment with the veterinarian, Jess tapped the map in her lap. "Let's head to the farm now," she said. "We can get the farmer's story firsthand, maybe walk the property before the vet shows up."

The SUV cruised eastward toward Thorp, cutting through Wisconsin farmland. Jack glanced at her in the passenger seat, noting how she kept adjusting her seatbelt and staring out the window without seeing the landscape. He'd tried a few casual questions that she'd deflected with vague answers and single-word responses. Finally, after thirty miles of this, she turned to face him.

"Jack, you know my parents live over in the Milwaukee area, about four hours from here."

He didn't like the sound of where this was going. "Okay," he said.

She traced a finger along the edge of her seatbelt. "You remember I told you my folks own a cabin on Lake Holcombe? They're up there this week." She met his eyes. "It's only forty-five minutes from Chippewa Falls. They could drive down and meet us for dinner tonight. What do you think?"

Jack's fingers tightened on the steering wheel. "Meeting the parents already?" He glanced at her, the corner of his mouth lifting. "Alright, I'm game. Remember, I come from Bears territory, and if memory serves, your dad bleeds green and gold. Might need to establish some ground rules before kickoff."

Jess exhaled, her shoulders relaxing as she laughed. "Okay, I'll let them know. Don't worry, Dad saves his real football rage for Vikings fans. Bears supporters only get mild disapproval."

Jack snorted. "A Green Bay Packers fan going easy on a Bears supporter? That's crap, and you know it!" He swept his hand toward the passing farmland. "Maybe they're more forgiving in this part of the state, but Milwaukee folks? Not a chance!"

They exited the highway and pulled into Thorp. They decided to grab some lunch before heading out to the farmer's place.

"This is a charming little town, isn't it?" Jack said.

Jess rolled down her window, letting in the scent of petunias and freshly cut grass. "These little Wisconsin towns compete with each other, you know. See those whiskey barrels?" She pointed to a half-barrel planter where purple and yellow blooms spilled over the edges like a waterfall of color. "A lot of these towns have a garden club that plants them every spring after the last frost. They've got them lined up all the way down the main street. I wouldn't be surprised if the mayor's wife came out every morning to water them herself. Makes you forget you're investigating mutilated cows, doesn't it?"

Jack laughed, "The mayor's wife? Really? Exaggerate much?"

She rolled her eyes, her smile betraying her. "Says the man who convinced half the Phoenix office that Jimmy Buffett came in for a personalized pilot briefing once."

"Well, he was a pilot. It could have happened," he said with a smile.

They were looking for a place to eat, and Jack spotted a restaurant called the Thorpedo. It even had a picture of a torpedo on the sign. He looked at Jess and said, "Okay, now how can I say no to that?"

They went inside and ordered the lunch special. Jack was deep in thought. "So, about tonight, where should we meet your folks? Someplace where I won't embarrass myself by ordering the wrong beer in Packers country?"

"This is Wisconsin, Jack, not Portland. There is no wrong beer," she said. "But let me tell you what I'm hearing from my family. There's this little brewery out of New Glarus that released a brew called the Spotted Cow last year. Order that and you'll impress my dad."

"Spotted Cow? We are literally on our way to look at spotted cows after lunch, dead spotted cows. I don't know about that," he said.

"Trust me on this one!"

~

After a satisfying lunch, they made their way out to the farm, less than a five-mile drive away. A sign greeted them as they pulled in, "Registered Holsteins, Monroe Farm."

Jack double-checked the address and said, "I guess this is the right place."

A man came out of the farmhouse and introduced himself as the owner, Hal Schwebke, as a pair of wary farm dogs trotted out to flank him. They circled at a cautious distance, watching the strangers with alert eyes but offering only an occasional low woof.

"Out of curiosity, how come it says Monroe Farm?" asked Jack.

The farmer dismissed his question with a wave. "Oh, it's been the Monroe Farm going back over a hundred years before my daddy bought the place in 1975."

Jack exchanged a glance with Jess before turning back to the farmer. "So, Mr. Schwebke, what's your current herd size?"

"I got thirty-five milkers plus Rufus, my bull. Well, I had thirty-five. Now I'm down three girls. It's the damndest thing."

Jess cleared her throat. "Mr. Schwebke, would you mind showing us where the animals were found? We'd like to examine what's left of them."

Hal led them across the yard, both dogs in tow, his rubber boots leaving dark prints in a thin layer of mud. "Thing is," he said, squinting against the midday sun, "I locked every last one of them in the barn that night. Double-checked the count, as I always do. Come morning, the barn's still locked tight as a drum, but somehow three of my girls are out in the south pasture, dead as doornails. Makes no sense at all."

"Is there any chance somebody came to your place and let them out?" asked Jess.

Hal shook his head. "Not a chance, miss. See these two?" He gestured toward the dogs who'd settled at his feet, ears perked in their direction. "Don't let the wagging tails fool you. Come nightfall, they turn into different animals. Anyone who sets foot on this property after dark will regret it."

They picked their way across the pasture, sidestepping fresh manure, until they reached the first stiff, motionless Holstein. The dogs kept their distance. "Funny thing is," Hal said, "there was no blood at all. All three were completely drained, and there was none on the ground either."

A horsefly buzzed past them and circled around Hal, landing on his arm. He smacked it and continued on. "The eyes are missing, and the rectum has been cored out in a perfect circle. On one of my girls, the udder has been removed. And again, no blood anywhere. You notice anything else that's off?"

"Shouldn't the corpses be bloated by now?" asked Jack.

"That's right. And not only that, there are no flies, larvae, or any insects on them. Ever seen anything like that?" Hal said.

"Actually," said Jess, "that has been observed with a number of cattle mutilations."

Hal said, "I've heard of these things happening out west in the middle of those ten-thousand-acre tracts, but never anything in a place like this. This pasture here's not that big. These girls were only two hundred yards from my home. I didn't see or hear anything that night. Damndest thing."

Hal continued, his weathered face creasing with worry lines as he waved toward the lifeless Holsteins. "Feed prices are climbing every month, milk checks are shrinking, and equipment is breaking down faster than I can fix it. Now I'm standing here looking at three dead girls. That's nearly ten percent of my revenue sprawled in the dirt." His calloused hand clenched into a fist at his side. "Whoever or whatever did this is killing my livelihood."

Jack and Jess nodded with sympathy. They began circling each carcass, their camera shutters clicking in the silence as they captured close-ups of the precision cuts. Jack was measuring the diameter of the rectal coring when the crunch of tires on gravel drew their attention. A white pickup with "Schultz Veterinary Services" stenciled on the door had pulled into the farmyard.

The dogs bolted toward the newcomer, barking their alert while Hal cupped his hands around his mouth and called out, "Over here, Doc! South pasture!"

The veterinarian shook hands with a firm grip, introduced himself as Dr. Schultz. He then turned his attention to the mutilated carcass as he snapped on a pair of latex gloves. "First things first, no signs of anthrax. Now let's figure out what actually happened here."

He began with an external examination, his gloved fingers probing the stiff hide. He traced the clean-edged wounds, carefully studying the circular space where the rectum had been. "These incisions are impossibly precise," he said. "No tearing, no jagged edges. That is inconsistent with coyotes or any predator I've ever encountered." He pressed against the bloat-free abdomen, his brow furrowing. "And look here, three days dead in summer heat, yet no gas buildup in the cavity. That defies everything I know about decomposition. And where are the flies?"

Then he asked everyone to help turn the cow onto its left side. The carcass rolled with unexpected weight, the stiffened legs jutting out as if they were fence posts. Dr. Schultz unsheathed a gleaming necropsy knife from his case and made a long Y-incision from sternum to pelvis. The hide parted, revealing dry, oddly preserved internal organs instead of the expected rush of bodily fluids.

He examined the abdomen, his gloved fingers probing the desiccated liver and shrunken intestines. Moving to the thoracic cavity, he spread the ribcage wider with an audible crack and leaned in close, his breath fogging his glasses. When he sliced into the heart, a normally blood-saturated muscle, the scalpel met resistance like cutting into cured meat. The organ's chambers gaped open, bone-dry and collapsed like deflated balloons. "In thirty years of veterinary practice," he muttered, "I've never seen anything like this. Every drop of blood appears to be missing from the circulatory system."

Next, he extracted tissue samples with quick, precise snips of his curved scissors, dropping each glistening fragment into labeled vials of clear preservative.

When he sliced open the leathery rumen, a sickly sweet odor of half-digested grass and corn silage wafted upward, yet it was oddly muted compared to normal cattle necropsies. The veterinarian repeated this grim ballet with each desiccated cow, his movements becoming increasingly tense as each animal revealed the same inexplicable anomalies.

The vet peeled off his latex gloves with a snap and tugged his mask down below his chin. He massaged his temples with nicotine-stained fingertips, exhaling a long, defeated sigh that seemed to deflate his entire posture.

Dr. Schultz shook his head, his weathered face creased with confusion. "In all my years, this is a first. Hal, I wish I had answers for you, but these cows..." He pivoted toward Jack and Jess with sudden curiosity. "You folks aren't from the county, are you? Here about those lights people keep seeing?"

Jess's head snapped up, her eyes bright with interest. "You've seen lights around here?" she asked, taking a half-step toward the veterinarian.

The vet nodded, rubbing his chin. "Started about two weeks back. Strange lights hovering over the fields, all across these parts. Lots of folks in town have been talking about it. Funny thing though, I haven't heard a peep about it since these cows turned up dead."

After finishing their examination of the mutilated cattle, Jack and Jess packed their equipment and drove back into Thorp. The list of witnesses Dr. Schultz had scribbled on the back of his business card burned with possibility in Jack's shirt pocket. If these people had seen the same lights, this might provide a compelling link between strange lights and cattle mutilations.

The color had drained from Jess's face, leaving her complexion the same sickly gray as the desiccated cow. "That was rough on you, wasn't it?" Jack asked.

She swallowed hard, her fingers fidgeting with the camera strap.

"Bloodless or not, watching someone slice open a cow like that...sticks with you. Don't worry about me though. I'll be fine," she added, forcing a smile.

Later that afternoon, they met up with several witnesses who told similar stories of strange lights hovering low over the fields, well after dark. Sometimes they would dance around in the sky a bit, and other times they would fade away. They couldn't link any of the lights specifically to the cattle mutilation case, but the relationship between the two left no doubt in Jack's mind.

Jess's parents made dinner plans at Cattleman's Corner, the kind of place where the lighting is kept low and wagon wheels hang overhead as chandeliers. Jack sighed as they approached downtown Eau Claire. "Did you happen to mention to your folks that I spend my free time chasing lights in the sky?"

"They know all about you already. Relax and be yourself! You'll be fine."

He huffed, "Right. Because your dad's going to love the UFO-chasing city boy who's sleeping with his daughter."

He eased the rental SUV into a parking space. His collar suddenly felt too tight against his throat.

"So it's Ken and Susan, right? Or does he go by Kenneth?" Jack asked.

She nudged his arm. "Oh, go with Kenny Boy and throw in a fist bump. He loves that."

"Come on, I'm serious. First impressions are huge," he said as they entered the restaurant.

Jack blinked twice as they stepped inside, the restaurant materializing around him like a photograph developing: first the silhouettes of diners, then the glint of steak knives catching what little light there was. Silverware clinked against plates while the unmistakable sizzle of ribeye on a hot grill drifted from behind the swinging kitchen doors, sending a wave of hunger through him.

A woman with Jess's cheekbones rose from a table and came toward them, her ash-blonde hair falling in loose waves around her face. She pulled Jess into a tight embrace. "Jessica!" The delight in her voice was entirely unperformed. "We've missed you so much!" She turned to Jack, hazel eyes bright with curiosity. "You must be Jack. I'm Susan."

She led them back to the table, where a broad-shouldered man was already on his feet, waiting. Ken Bowden was built like someone who had never slouched in his life. He was wide through the chest, square-jawed, with salt-and-pepper hair combed neatly to one side and a thick mustache. He extended a hand that swallowed Jack's. "Ken Bowden." He gave Jack a good look over, holding the handshake for just a second longer than a casual greeting required.

Jack bit back the urge to say Kenny Boy as the joke flashed through his mind.

They sat down in the booth, trading weather talk and Wisconsin pleasantries, until a waiter in a bolo tie arrived with menus and rattled off the specials.

Drink orders came first, and Jack asked for a Spotted Cow.

Ken's eyebrows lifted. "A man who knows his Wisconsin beer. Maybe there's hope for you yet, even if you are from Chicago."

Jack grinned, leaning forward. "The Bears might be rebuilding for the twentieth straight year, but at least we know real beer when we taste it."

Ken chuckled, relaxing. "Tell you what. You can have our beer. We'll keep the Lombardi trophies."

Frosted glasses clinked against the table as the waiter distributed their drinks, then flipped open his notepad to take their dinner selections before vanishing into the kitchen's swinging doors. Jack raised the glass to his lips, the foam leaving a thin mustache as he swallowed. "Holy cow, pun intended," he said, wiping his mouth with the back of his hand. "Ken, that's good beer! We can't buy that at home."

"Only in Wisconsin, for now. But I'll bet you've got a lot of space on that airplane to take some back with you."

For the next twenty minutes, Ken and Jack traded barbs about the Bears' quarterback woes and the Packers' playoff chokes, each insult drawing genuine laughter from the other until steaming plates arrived at the table.

Dinner went well, and Jack had eased into the witty, charming guy who Jess adored. As the waiter cleared the dishes, the conversation became a bit more pointed.

Ken leaned forward, his forearms forming a V on the table. "Jack, Jessica tells us you two are living together." He paused, his jaw working slightly before he said, "I realize times have changed since I was courting Susan here, but some values stick with you. I guess what I'm asking is..." He glanced at his wife, who gave an almost imperceptible nod. "Where do you see this relationship heading?"

Jack smiled and said, "Ken, your daughter and I have known each other for less than six months." He looked sideways and winked at Jess and took her hand in his. "The first day I met her, I felt something between us. I can't really explain it. It's one of those things. We both felt it. And my feelings for her have only grown stronger."

He looked at Jess again. "We've been talking about, well, what comes next for us." His voice caught, eyes finding Jess's. "I never thought I'd find someone who makes me feel this way. We're figuring it out together. No rush, but no doubt either." He squeezed her hand, thumb brushing over her knuckles. "I wake up every morning and ask myself what I've done to deserve someone as wonderful as she is. That's the honest truth."

Susan's smile tilted at one corner while she blinked, the restaurant's dim light catching on the moisture gathering along her lower lashes. She took Jess's other hand in hers, "Oh, honey, I'm so happy for you. And Jack, you seem like the perfect man for her."

Ken interjected, "But if you hurt my daughter in any way—"

"Daddy!" said Jess.

Jack raised his palms, a smile softening the gesture. "Sir, I promise you, hurting Jess would be like hurting myself. That's not something I would do."

A man in a flannel shirt shattered the gentle hum of conversation as the front doors banged open. He stood silhouetted against the night, his face flushed with excitement. "You've gotta see this," he called out, breathless. "There are some strange lights, a whole cluster of 'em, hanging over the downtown area!"

Jack's eyes locked with Jess's for a fraction of a second before their chairs scraped backward in unison. They bolted toward the entrance, leaving Ken and Susan bewildered at the table. The night air hit his face as they pushed through the door to find the flannel-shirted stranger pointing his finger skyward, his mouth still forming eager words Jack couldn't process over the sudden drumming of his own heartbeat.

There they were, a constellation of amber orbs hovering above the downtown skyline. He tracked their gentle, drifting movement, his initial surge of adrenaline evaporating into the cool night air. He caught Jess's eye, and before either could speak, their shared expertise crystallized into perfect synchronicity. "Chinese lanterns," they announced in unison.

They walked back into the restaurant, where Jess's bewildered parents remained. "False alarm," she said. "Somebody thought they saw a cluster of UFOs. They were Chinese lanterns, probably a wedding."

Susan muttered under her breath, "Eight years of college and you're chasing UFOs. I don't get it."

Jack and Jess had returned to their hotel and turned in for the night. Jack had fallen asleep, and his phone rang. It was Pat, calling from his old UFO-hunting group in Phoenix.

Jack considered ignoring the call. He was tired and needed the rest. With reluctance, he thumbed open his phone and answered it. "Hey Pat, you realize there's a time difference where I'm at now, right?"

"Sorry, buddy. Where are you?"

"Wisconsin, cattle mutilation case."

"Jesus, Jack, you do it all these days, don't you?" he said. "I'd love to talk shop, but the real reason I'm calling is about Garrett."

"Uh-oh. Did something happen?"

"You already knew he had been hanging out with us for a while, but had Steve told you about the orbs over Palo Verde and how we almost got caught?"

"Yeah, that was too close for comfort," Jack said.

"Garrett wanted to go back, and we wouldn't do it. Pissed him off pretty good. So he went off on his own, staking out the power plant by himself."

"Did he get caught by security?" asked Jack.

"No, it's worse than that. He found a vantage point up in a mountain west of there. Went up several times, but the other night he never came home. We found his truck and all his gear out there, but no Garrett. The sheriff's department conducted an extensive search and turned up nothing."

"Oh shit, are you sure the feds didn't nab him?"

"It doesn't look that way," said Pat.

"I heard he and Karen split. You don't suppose he...well, you know."

"I don't think so. His wife says he's been threatening suicide for a while, and I know depression was hanging over him, but I don't think he'd do that. There was no note left, and no trace of him. It's like he vanished into thin air," said Pat. "The cops don't think it was suicide either."

"You don't think a saucer came over and abducted him, do you?"

"I don't know what to think at this point. That makes about as much sense as anything else," said Pat.

"Keep me updated on whatever you guys find. If there's anything I can do to help, let me know, okay?"

"Absolutely, Jack. Sorry if I woke you up! I'll be in touch." Pat ended the call.

Jack realized he was wrong to accuse Garrett of releasing the letter to the press without proof. He wondered if part of Garrett's depression was because of his actions. If he'd gone and done something rash—no, he couldn't even imagine that right now.

The flight back to Little Rock was quiet, Jack's mind still replaying the image of that cow's surgically precise wounds. Beside him, Jess cataloged the tissue and blood samples she'd collected in her lap. "Schultz will send his report next week," she said, "but I want Lynley to look at these too. She might catch something the vet missed."

By 11 a.m., they were back in the office and had called a group meeting to share their preliminary results. The same oddities that were common in so many cases were present in this one as well.

First? Surgically precise wounds that were not from a predator. Next, no blood was present outside or inside the carcass. Finally, no predators or insects were interested in the body.

Dr. Chris Bellini had some wild theories on all of this. As a theoretical physicist, he always seemed a little eccentric, but Jack valued his fresh perspectives. He theorized that an extra-dimensional entity, capable of phasing into our space, was feeding off the cattle's blood.

Perry Boyd, one of the team's engineers, was having none of it. "Come on, Chris, let's be real here. Why the missing eyes? And the cored-out asshole? This makes no sense at all."

"Does any of this make any sense?" asked Jack. "Nobody has

come up with any viable answers to the greater mystery of cattle mutilations over the years, so I think we need to be open-minded and think outside the box."

"What about the strange lights people were seeing in the weeks leading up to this?" asked Lydia Reyes, the team's sociologist. "That points toward UFO involvement, does it not?"

"Correlation does not imply causation," said Hendricus. "We can't tie the two together without better evidence."

Lynley cleared her throat. "I've received the samples Jessica collected: tissue from the carcass, plus vegetation and soil from the surrounding area. I'll begin processing the biological material this afternoon. Priya will handle the soil composition analysis." She tapped her notepad. "You'll all receive my findings as soon as testing is complete."

Dr. Priya Sharma adjusted her glasses. "The soil report will be on your desks by Friday at the latest. I've got three other priority samples ahead of this one."

Hendricus glanced at his watch, rolled back his chair, and stood. "That's all for now, folks. Good work today, especially you, Jessica, getting those samples under less than ideal conditions." He tucked his folio under his arm and was already halfway to the door before anyone else had risen from their seats.

Several days went by before Lynley and Priya were ready to present the findings from the cattle mutilation case. Most of the scientists were in attendance.

Jess slid the veterinarian's report across the conference table while Jack clicked through case photos on the projector, the cow's empty eye socket staring back at them, the bloodless precision cut along its underside gleaming wetly in the camera flash.

"No predator marks," Jack said, pointing to the edge of a wound with his laser pointer. "And Dr. Schultz confirmed there was not a drop of blood left in the entire carcass. And I mean not one single drop. How can that be explained?"

Jess leaned forward. "The vet found something unexpected in his analysis. The tissue samples contained substantial traces of mescaline, the same hallucinogenic compound present in peyote."

Hendricus's eyebrows shot up. "You're telling me there was a psychedelic drug in the cow?"

"That's correct. I can't say where it came from, but peyote does not grow in Wisconsin. In fact, the nearest naturally occurring growth is well over 1200 miles away in Texas," she said. "And now I'll turn it over to Dr. Winters for her lab report."

Lynley tapped her pen against her clipboard. "My analysis confirmed the mescaline, but that's not all I found. The tissue samples contained titanium at concentrations that don't occur naturally. We also detected elevated levels of aluminum and silicon, but the titanium readings were so far beyond normal parameters that I had to recalibrate my equipment twice to be sure. As for what this means..." She looked up, meeting their eyes. "I don't have an explanation."

Lynley adjusted her glasses. "I also detected a fluorescent powder embedded in the hide samples. When I contacted the farmer about it, he was adamant that he'd never used marking substances on his livestock. While I can't rule out ordinary transfer, the animal brushing against something coated with this material, it was present on all three cows. The powder is only visible in the UV spectrum." She glanced toward Priya, yielding the floor with a slight nod.

Priya cleared her throat. "The soil analysis revealed something peculiar. Samples collected beneath the carcasses and within a three-foot radius showed magnetite levels forty times higher than baseline readings. This concentration drops off in samples taken ten feet away." She met their gazes with a troubled expression. "I've run the tests three times to confirm. Whatever caused this magnetic anomaly was localized to the area where the cows were found, but I can't explain why."

Several days later, it was late in the afternoon, and Jack was in his office reading up on a recent UFO investigation from Upstate New York. Bob knocked on his open door and asked, "Got a minute?"

Jack waved him in.

He tossed a manila folder across Jack's desk. "Another dead cow. McAlester, Oklahoma. Both of our jets are tied up, but it's only a four-hour drive. Since you and Jessica did so well in Wisconsin, you two are going to be primary on this one."

Jack hesitated for several seconds, staring at the folder. "I'll do it, Bob, but let me be honest with you. I don't want to become the go-to guy for dead livestock. I'd prefer to investigate something that doesn't involve cattle guts once in a while," he said.

Bob rubbed his temples. "I get it, but you and Jessica are our resident cow corpse specialists now, like it or not." He dropped his hand on the desk. "And speaking of specialists, Priya and Lynley have been hounding me all morning about tagging along. You okay with that?"

"I don't see a problem with that. Makes sense to me."

"Great. Patty has made hotel arrangements. If you guys get on the road within the next hour, you can check in tonight and get a fresh start in the morning," said Bob.

They made their way across Arkansas, stopping once for refreshments and a bathroom break, and continued on into Oklahoma.

Sunset painted the sky in fiery streaks as the team's SUV veered off the interstate, heading south on U.S. Highway 69. Jack bit his tongue as the route number registered, glancing at Lynley in the rearview mirror and then at Priya next to her. Best not to test professional boundaries with juvenile humor today.

McAlester was about another forty miles ahead. As they drove, Jack kept looking at Priya in the mirror, opening his mouth slightly then closing it again. The question hovered in his mind. Would examining a mutilated cow create emotional complications for her? His college roommate had once explained Hindu beliefs about sacred cattle, but he wasn't sure if that applied to all Hindus or if inquiring would make him sound ignorant.

He glanced at Jess, who had fallen asleep in the passenger seat, her head propped between the window and the headrest. He could almost hear her voice in his mind. "Don't even think about asking that question, Jack."

But sometimes he couldn't keep his mouth shut. "Priya," he said, "can I ask you something?"

"Sure, Jack," she said.

"I was thinking about the site visit tomorrow morning and realized this might be a lot heavier for you than it is for the rest of us. My understanding is that the cow has a special significance in your faith. I don't want to overstep, but will you be okay with the fieldwork?" he asked.

Priya collected her thoughts. "I appreciate you asking that. Yes, I'll be fine. I would not have come along otherwise. It is not the death of the cow that troubles me. The cruelty of the death is troubling. To me, it is like a violation of a deep spiritual peace."

He nodded, gripping the steering wheel a little tighter. "Thanks for being straight with me. The Wisconsin cases were..." He shook his head. "I'm hoping this time we find something that makes sense of all this."

They drove the rest of the way in silence.

With a population of around 17,000, McAlester offered limited accommodation options. Jack felt a wave of relief when they pulled into the AmericInn parking lot. Patty had booked lodging at one of the few proper hotels. He dreaded the thought of staying at cheap roadside motels with their flickering neon signs and paper-thin walls.

After dropping their bags in their respective rooms, they reconvened in the lobby's seating area. The night clerk, a woman with reading glasses dangling from a beaded chain, leaned over the counter. "If y'all are looking for dinner, there is a mom-and-pop restaurant up on highway 270. They make some of the best Italian food around these parts."

A collective nod sealed the decision without a word.

The scents of garlic and basil rose from their plates, mixing with the yeasty warmth of fresh bread the waitress kept bringing to the table. Between bites of pasta, they mapped out tomorrow's investigation. Jess suggested arriving at the farm by mid-morning, giving them time to survey the scene before the local veterinarian, courtesy of Patty's arrangements, would join them to examine the remains.

Jack cleared his throat. "One more thing we should consider. Feel that sticky air when we walked in and those gusts that almost ripped the car door from my hand? Classic setup. There's a cold front barreling down from the north that'll collide with all this Gulf moisture tomorrow." He took another bite of pasta. "The Storm Prediction Center has this area under a moderate risk for severe storms, and it looks like the tornado risk is pretty high. We've got a tight window tomorrow. Those storms will be bearing down on us by early afternoon, and I don't want anyone caught in a field when they hit. Let's plan to wrap up by noon at the latest."

"Great, one more thing we need to worry about," said Lynley.

~

Jack woke before his alarm, drawn to the glow of the television where a meteorologist gestured at a map splashed with angry reds and purples. The Storm Prediction Center had upgraded its area to a high risk, the rarest, most dangerous classification. Once he'd have chased these storms with a camera in hand and adrenaline in his veins. Now that he was responsible for a team investigating a dead cow, the same forecast caused his stomach to knot.

The team made its way down to the dining area. Jack eyed the hotel's breakfast spread. Continental breakfasts were never meant to be a culinary adventure. Pale scrambled eggs glistened on his paper plate next to a few extra-crispy strips of bacon and a croissant. There was a lingering sweetness in the air from the waffle maker. They discussed the day's plans while he updated them on the weather.

Fueled by strong coffee, they loaded into the SUV and headed southeast of town. Anderson Road stretched before them, guiding them through Oklahoma farmland toward their grim destination.

The dashboard clock read 9:37 when they arrived at the property, a modest operation of forty acres with freshly painted fences and neatly trimmed hedgerows. Jack steered the SUV up the narrow drive, where a figure in denim overalls stood beside a red pickup truck, arm raised in a beckoning motion.

Gravel crunched beneath the SUV's tires as Jack brought it to a stop. The group climbed out into the humid morning air and made their way toward the waiting man. He flashed a weathered hand in greeting. "Howdy! Name's Cal. Y'all must be the team Bob Sinclair sent."

Jack introduced the group, and the farmer led them to the back pasture. They followed him across the field to the body of a Hereford steer, its brown and white hide dulled by the morning shadow, its massive body turned away from them as if in final refusal.

"Cal, do you know when this happened?" asked Lynley.

"Night before last. I check on my cattle every day, and this one here was just fine. Found 'em like that yesterday morning."

Jack circled the carcass with his camera, the shutter clicking in rapid succession, while Jess documented the scene from various angles. Meanwhile, Lynley knelt in the grass nearby, plucking samples of the surrounding vegetation, as Priya scraped small clumps of soil into labeled containers.

Jack's eyes drifted upward, and his frown deepened. The morning sky had turned ominous. Gray clouds raced southeast to northwest below a thousand feet, while high above them, midlevel clouds streaked perpendicular to the low ones. The conflicting patterns spelled trouble for anyone who knew what to look for.

Jess noticed Jack's gaze fixed on the sky. She moved beside him, following his line of sight. "Something up there bothering you?"

"Wind shear, directional shear to be specific," he said, pointing between the layers of clouds. "When you've got winds moving in layers like that, it's like a crank handle turning. Any storm that forms gets twisted into a rotating one. And that's how you birth a tornado."

Jess stepped closer, her voice barely audible above the wind. "Your storm talk is worrying me, honey."

Jack's jaw tightened. "I don't like what I'm seeing. The atmosphere's locked and loaded. This is the setup that makes storm chasers drive a thousand miles, but we're standing right in the target zone. We need to wrap up this investigation as fast as we can."

The veterinarian was almost an hour late. Jack didn't have time for this today. He checked his watch for the fourth time in ten minutes, his jaw tightening as the veterinarian's truck finally appeared on the horizon.

The vet's methodical dissection followed the same protocol they had witnessed in the Wisconsin field, his gloved hands moving with practiced precision through each step of the grim procedure.

By the time he was completed, the findings mirrored what they'd discovered in Wisconsin with unsettling similarity.

Not a trace of blood remained in the steer's body, nor could they find any spilled across the surrounding soil. Where eyes should have been, only empty sockets stared back at them, and like the Wisconsin cattle, the animal's hindquarters showed the same coring of the rectum. No flies, no insect larvae, no bloating.

A single notable difference between the steer here and the animals in Wisconsin was that flesh had been stripped off one side of the steer's jaw. The vet pointed to where it had been removed on the right-hand side, revealing gleaming bone beneath.

"I've performed thousands of surgeries," he said, shaking his head, "and I couldn't make an excision this clean with the finest medical instruments available."

While Lynley extracted tissue and skin samples, Priya rummaged through her field kit and produced a handheld UV light. "I want to check for fluorescence patterns on the hide," she said, slipped on a pair of protective glasses, and started sweeping the light back and forth across the steer.

The UV light revealed a pattern of tiny glowing specks, particles invisible under normal conditions but unmistakable now, even in the diffuse daylight. Priya looked up at Cal, her brow furrowed. "Have you ever tagged this animal with any kind of marker that might leave residue? Or could it have come into contact with something on your property that would deposit this type of fluorescent trace?"

Cal shook his head. "Not a chance. Never marked my animals with anything that glows, and ain't nothing on this farm that would leave a trace like that either."

Priya looked up from the UV light. "I'd like to examine your other cattle for similar patterns of residue to establish whether this is isolated or widespread."

Cal nodded and gestured toward a cluster of Herefords grazing in the distance. "Got the rest of 'em over yonder. Follow me."

Suddenly, Jack's portable weather radio crackled with an urgent voice, darkening his expression. A severe thunderstorm warning had been issued for an area to their west, with reports of the storm dropping tennis-ball-sized hail near a town named Gerty.

For the past half hour, Jack had tracked the massive thunderhead building on the western horizon, its rapid growth setting off alarm bells in his mind. With nothing else in the atmosphere to steal its energy, this lone storm had the entire sky to itself.

He gestured toward the west, where bulbous white formations pushed upward like boiling cauliflower. "See those sharp edges?" he said to Jess. "That's explosive growth." His finger traced the flattened sheet spreading outward from the storm's crown. "And that anvil there's where the updraft hits the stratosphere and has nowhere else to go but sideways." The storm's center punched upward like a fist through the anvil cloud, a phenomenon Jack recognized as the overshooting top, due to air surging upward with violent momentum, to the extent that it broke through its natural ceiling.

Jess listened to the weather radio. "They're saying it's moving to the northeast, so we should be a little south of that, right?"

He shook his head. "Not exactly. Look at the underside of that anvil." He pointed to where bulbous formations hung like udders beneath the flat cloud. "Mammatus formations. Classic severe weather indicator. And watch the lightning in the anvil. See how it's not just striking down but spreading outward in all directions like a spider web? That's the electrical activity I worry about."

Jess nodded, her eyes fixed on the distant flashes. Jack leaned closer against the rising wind. "That's what we call HF lightning. The electromagnetic signature differs from typical strikes in your average, everyday storm. A team at a university in New York has been tracking these patterns for years, looking for connections between lightning activity and tornado formation."

Jess's eyebrows knitted together as she processed the information. He ran a hand through his wind-tousled hair and sighed. "Bottom line, I've been following this for years, and when I see HF lightning, I start looking for a possible tornado touchdown. The research isn't conclusive yet, but I've seen enough to worry me."

Jess said, "But we're safe right here, aren't we?"

He unfolded a creased paper map, his finger tracing along a line.

"When these monsters spawn tornadoes, they tend to veer rightward of their original path. See this?" He tapped a spot on the map where he'd marked their location. "That deviation would put us on the potential path. We need to find Priya and wrap this up. Now."

"I'll check on her," said Jess. "Looks like Lynley is taking photos while she hits the cows with the UV light."

Jack's weather radio erupted in a harsh electronic tone followed by an automated voice. "The National Weather Service has issued a tornado warning for Pittsburg County, including the city of McAlester." He could now see the storm's massive structure in terrifying detail, clouds twisting upward in spiraling bands like a barber pole around the central updraft, while the entire base of the supercell sagged ominously toward the ground. A line of trees obscured the western horizon, hiding what Jack knew must be there, the telltale wall cloud possibly already spawning a tornado.

The storm had made the right turn, as he had anticipated. He had a sixth sense for these things. The broadcast pinpointed their location, the south side of McAlester and areas southward, directly in the storm's newly projected path.

Jack was getting angry now. Lynley and Priya were still examining the healthy cattle, and Jess was trying to hurry them along. There was no time for this.

He sprinted over toward the team as an outdoor tornado warning siren started to blare somewhere off in the distance. "We need to get the hell out of here right now!"

Cal turned to the group and said, "Y'all better pile into my storm cellar. Don't risk trying to outrun this thing."

Jack mentally traced the storm's trajectory against their position. They could probably outrun it, but gambling with Jess's life—with all their lives—wasn't something he was willing to do, not with a monster thunderstorm bearing down on them. "Grab the samples and gear. Everything comes with us," he said, already moving toward their equipment cases.

The farmer's wife ran out of the house to join them, and they began to pile into a partially buried concrete vault with a sturdy steel door that latched from the inside.

"Jack, it's full of spiderwebs!" Jess said.

He glanced between the cellar and the approaching storm, his jaw set. "Listen, I need to monitor this thing until the last-possible second. You're welcome to stay topside with me, but when I give the word, we're both diving into that hole, spiders and all."

She nodded nervously.

The air transformed into a violent assault, with lightning splitting the sky in rapid succession and thunder merging into one endless, deafening growl. Jack dropped into a crouch and yanked Jess down beside him with an urgent tug of his hand. "Stay low!" he ordered. The rain hammered against them like buckshot. He squinted toward the horizon through the downpour. The tornado remained hidden from view, but its presence was unmistakable, betrayed by the rapid inflow of low scud clouds spiraling into the rotating wall cloud that hung from the storm's underbelly.

The storm's continued approach revealed its true horror, a churning wedge of destruction half a mile wide, its dark mass scraping the earth clean. Blue-white flashes erupted in staccato bursts as the vortex devoured power lines less than a mile distant, each flash briefly illuminating the monster's rotating wall. Chunks of ice slammed into the surrounding ground, pea-sized at first but rapidly swelling to golf balls, each impact sending up tiny explosions of mud and grass. Jack knew the hail would only get larger, becoming soft-ball-sized missiles that could crack skulls.

The hailstones were merely harbingers of what approached. Jack calculated the tornado's path, its massive circulation edging toward them. A slight wobble in its trajectory might spare them or doom them.

"Bunker! Let's go!" he shouted to Jess, his voice fighting against the storm's deafening symphony of wind and thunder that had fused into one continuous roar.

She scrambled into the cellar. Jack followed, batting away spider-webs that clung to his face. The heavy door fought him as he hauled it closed, each gust threatening to tear it from his grip before the latch finally clicked into place.

The hailstones hammered against the steel door in rapid-fire percussion, like artillery on a battlefield. Outside, the storm's rage swallowed every other noise in the world.

Then it came, that sound storm chasers always described but no recording could capture. Not merely a freight train passing nearby but as if they were crouched between the rails while the locomotive thundered directly overhead, vibrating through bone and tooth. Their ears popped violently as the pressure plummeted. Above them, the steel door convulsed against its hinges, shrieking as the vortex hurled ice and debris against it like machine-gun fire.

After some cussing and hand-wringing, the tornado's roar faded to silence. Jack waited several minutes before reaching for the latch, glancing at Cal for confirmation. The farmer gave a terse nod. He pushed against the steel, only to meet unyielding resistance. He threw his shoulder into it, grunting with effort.

"Something's blocking us," he said, voice tight. Cal and Jess crowded behind him, adding their weight to his. It refused to give even an inch. They were sealed in.

Lynley started to panic. Jack placed a steady hand on her shoulder. "Take a breath," he said, his voice low and even. "That vent up there means we've got air. And out here?" He gestured vaguely upward. "First people checking damaged properties won't be paramedics or firefighters. It'll be folks from down the road with chainsaws and pickup trucks. Rural code. They're probably already on their way."

Within ten minutes, they heard a man yelling for Cal. "In here," he said at the top of his lungs. "We're blocked in!"

A short time later, the growl of a diesel engine approached, followed by the metallic jingle of heavy chains dragging across debris. Something massive scraped against the cellar door with an ear-splitting shriek of metal on metal. "Y'all are clear," called a gruff voice.

Jack heaved the door upward, metal grinding against metal. He emerged into a landscape that could have been plucked from old newsreels of bombed-out European villages—splintered wood where homes had stood, trees snapped like matchsticks, and household items scattered across muddy ground that no longer resembled the farm they'd walked on just a few hours before.

Cal emerged from the shelter and froze. His wife stumbled out behind him, her knees buckling as she took in the wasteland where their livelihood had stood minutes earlier.

A massive oak had pinned their door shut, its trunk dragged clear by a neighbor's John Deere. Jack scanned the devastated landscape for their vehicle, but the SUV they'd driven from Arkansas had vanished completely, likely scattered across the county in a thousand twisted pieces.

McAlester was their only hope now. They needed a working phone to reach Bob. "I can get y'all into town," Cal's neighbor offered, gesturing to his mud-caked truck. "Roads are a mess. We might have to take a few detours, but I'll get you there."

He squeezed them into his mud-splattered pickup for the silent drive back to McAlester. The city stood eerily untouched, as if existing in another world from the devastation they'd witnessed. With cell service knocked out across the county, Jack hunched over the hotel room's yellowed landline phone, relief flooding through him when Bob's voice finally crackled through the receiver.

His voice was mixed with static, but his message came through clear enough. Their smaller jet, Tusk, had returned to Little Rock, and he could have it ready within the hour to extract them from this nightmare.

Jack said, "No, Bob, the tornado tore through south of town and clipped the airport. There's nothing left but twisted metal and debris. We need ground transport. Send someone with a vehicle who can get us out of here. After what we witnessed...we're done and need to get home."

Two vehicles screeched into the hotel parking lot barely three and a half hours after their phone call. Perry was behind the wheel of a Ford Explorer, and Whiskers piloted a Chevrolet Suburban. Jack figured it should have taken them at least four hours to get there. He checked his watch and said nothing about their arrival time. After what they'd survived, a few traffic laws seemed trivial by comparison.

Jess and Jack joined Perry, and Lynley and Priya rode with Whiskers.

As they sped eastward, he recounted their brush with death, his voice flat while Perry's eyes widened with each new detail of the tornado's fury. The most interesting conversation was taking place in the other vehicle.

In the Suburban, Whiskers listened intently as Priya and Lynley detailed their discovery: a single additional cow in the herd bore the telltale fluorescent markings, while every other animal showed no trace of the substance.

"I'd bet anything that the other cow would have ended up the same way within weeks," said Lynley. "Someone, or more likely some *thing* had marked them."

"We will never know now," said Priya. "The entire herd was wiped out by the tornado. Such a senseless loss."

A day after their harrowing ordeal in Oklahoma, Jack and Jess collapsed onto their couch after another long day at the office. The question of dinner hung between them. He rubbed his eyes. "I'm too beat to cook tonight. Is there a restaurant that sounds good to you?"

Jess sighed and let her head fall back against the couch. "God, I'm too tired to even think about what I want to eat."

Jack's phone buzzed in his pocket. The caller ID displayed an unfamiliar number with a Little Rock area code. It could be work-related, he thought. He answered it with reluctance.

Dave Pruett was calling, an old colleague from his days at the weather service in Texas. He knew Dave was at the Little Rock office now but hadn't reached out to him since moving.

"Jack, good to hear your voice! I heard you're working with some UFO group now, right?"

"As a matter of fact, I am. Best decision I ever made. No more of those damn rotating shifts!"

"I recently found out you're living in Little Rock, and Rudy and I —you remember Rudy, right?" Dave asked.

"Rudy? Of course!"

"We wanted to see if you were free to go out and grab a few beers one of these nights."

"I'd love to. How about tonight? My girlfriend and I were just sitting here, trying to decide whether we wanted to eat tonight. You guys up for dinner and drinks?"

"Yeah! That's great. Wait, what girlfriend? I thought you were married?" said Dave.

"Not anymore. That didn't work out the way I thought it would. Long story. So what do you guys like?"

They quickly made arrangements to meet up.

A half hour later, Jack and Jess walked into a sports bar in North Little Rock that Dave had suggested. Squinting through the bar's murky interior, he caught sight of Dave's enthusiastic arm-waving from a booth near the back. "Over there." He nodded toward his old friend.

They exchanged pleasantries, and he introduced Jess to Dave and Rudy. They had a couple of rounds of beer, engaged in small talk, and ordered food.

While they were waiting, Dave said, "The reason I was so eager to meet you is that we had a strange incident up in Perry County a week ago. I think there may have been a UFO crash."

"Wait, here in Arkansas?" asked Jack.

"Yeah, outside Perryville. The radar picked up a massive plume of something from the surface. We assumed it was smoke. And the weather satellite detected a white-hot fire in the same location. This was no ordinary fire; it was hotter than hot. We contacted the Arkansas Department of Emergency Management because we thought something major had exploded up there. They sent a state trooper up there to check it out, and he said there was no visible smoke anywhere."

Jack was a little confused. "Okay, but what does that have to do with a UFO?"

"This has been puzzling all of us for a week. How could we detect a huge fire yet find nothing there? One of our guys was off work yesterday and drove up to poke around. He didn't see any obvious signs of a fire, so he started asking questions. One guy told him that a flaming object crashed from the sky and landed in a wooded area. Then he said the Air Force came in, closed everything off for a day or two, and hauled something out of there on a flatbed in the middle of the night. That's pretty much all we know right now."

Jack was quiet for several seconds. "Okay, are you guys screwing with me? Is this payback for that tarantula thing I did back in San Antonio? Because if it is, you've got me. But if you're serious—"

"Jack, I swear on my grandmother's grave this isn't a joke. However, in case you're wondering, yes, I am still pissed about the tarantula thing. And the fake rattlesnake." He glanced at Jess. "Ask him about that one sometime."

Jack chuckled, "Okay, let me give you my new email address, and I want you to send me everything you've got on this."

"Okay, but I thought you might want these printouts instead."

Jack's eyes widened. "You brought actual printouts? Here?" His hand shot across the table, fingers already grasping at air. "Let me see."

Rudy reached beneath the table, pulled out a manila folder from his backpack, and slapped it down between their beer glasses. He flipped it open, revealing a dozen glossy color printouts of radar screens and satellite images. Jack and Jess hunched over the table, their faces bathed in the glow of neon beer signs as they studied the evidence.

Jack squinted, looking at data from the satellite. "Wow, that is a hot fire. Off the charts. And no smoke plume on visible imagery?" Both of them shook their heads. "And this radar cross section, holy moly, something was lofting up high in the atmosphere. It wasn't smoke?"

Rudy shrugged. "Whatever it was, our equipment picked it up clear as day, but nobody on the ground could see a damn thing with their own eyes."

Jess leaned in closer to the images, her finger tracing the anomaly's arc. "What about a meteor?" she asked, glancing up at the men. "Couldn't this be something burning up as it hit our atmosphere?"

Dave shook his head, pushing the folder closer to Jack. "Look, I track thunderstorms, not whatever the hell this is. That's why I called. If anyone can make sense of this, it's you guys."

"Okay, we'll make sure this gets looked into."

Consciousness returned to Garrett in fragments. First, the bite of rock against his spine. Then, the wind, not just blowing but tearing across whatever exposed place he'd ended up in. Darkness enveloped him, broken only by pinpricks of starlight and scattered clouds hanging in the middle distance. Each breath brought a knife edge of pain through his ribs. His fingers scrabbled against the ground, finding nothing but stone in every direction.

"Where the hell am I?" His voice disappeared into the empty night.

His tongue felt like sandpaper against the roof of his mouth. Water. He needed water. The world faded to black, then flickered back. How many times, he couldn't say. Minutes or hours passed in this half-alive state, the stars wheeling overhead in the moments his eyes focused.

A thin blade of dawn light cut across his vision, though his sight remained a smeared watercolor painting. Somewhere beyond the ringing in his ears came human sounds, voices carried on the wind. Garrett's throat constricted, his parched vocal cords straining as primal instinct took over and he rasped out a desperate plea into the vastness.

The voices grew closer, one of them calling out, asking where he was. His lungs burned as he forced another sound from his throat, a raw animal noise that tore through his chest. The effort sent black spots swimming across his vision, and the world tilted to the side before dissolving.

Consciousness found Garrett again beneath harsh lights, a needle piercing the crook of his arm. The ambulance wailed, lurching through mountain switchbacks that sent tremors through the gurney straps across his chest. Through the haze, a face materialized above, masked, concerned, clinical.

Garrett's lips cracked as they parted. "What happened to me?" The question barely escaped his throat.

The paramedic's eyes crinkled above her mask. "That's what we're trying to figure out," she said, adjusting something on the IV line. "But you're with us now. Nothing else matters at the moment. We're taking you to the hospital in Montrose."

"Montrose?" Garrett asked weakly. "Colorado?"

"What other Montrose is there?"

The evidence from McAlester's cattle mutilation had yielded results too startling to share over email. Lynley's fingers had trembled as she'd typed the meeting invitation, while Priya had paced the lab, repeatedly checking the analysis outputs. Now, with the conference room filling with scientists, they exchanged a glance that acknowledged the weight of what they were about to present.

With everyone in place, Lynley began, "We have the results back from the cattle mutilation in McAlester, Oklahoma. These findings are similar to our previous results from cattle that were mutilated in Wisconsin. Long story short, everything is almost exactly the same. Drugged with mescaline. Eyes were removed, rectum was cored out, no blood was present."

Everyone in the room had a look of astonishment.

"Seven hundred miles away and it's almost identical. High levels of titanium, high levels of magnetite in the soil. The hide was marked with fluorescent powder. One difference is that the skin and tissue were flayed from the right jaw region of the animal. The vet said the cuts were so precise that he couldn't perform them with the finest medical instruments."

She turned it over to Priya, who stepped forward. "Our team

inspected every head of cattle on the property, thirty-seven animals in total. All appeared normal except for a single heifer that displayed identical fluorescent markings to our mutilated specimen. We believe this animal was tagged for future extraction, but nature intervened. The F4 tornado that devastated the property last week left nothing but carcasses scattered across the area. Whatever intelligence was studying these animals has lost its laboratory."

Multiple questions arose from overlapping voices, each struggling to reconcile these findings with their understanding of the natural world.

The clamor of scientific voices eventually subsided. Jack rose from his chair, ready to present his newest case.

He relayed the data his weather service colleagues had shared with him the previous night. He'd scanned the hard copies into digital format and was displaying them on the screen. "This happened in our backyard, and we're just hearing about it now. I'm not convinced this was a UFO, but I think we would be fools not to check it out, especially since it happened right here."

Bob leaned forward, elbows on the conference table. "Makes sense to me, Jack. Take Naden and a couple of the techs up there this morning and see what you can find."

The team volleyed questions about the Arkansas case for several minutes before gravitating back to the cattle incident in Oklahoma.

After a time, the chatter wound down. Jack's phone rang in his pocket, and he excused himself from the meeting and stepped into the hallway. It was Pat calling from Phoenix again.

"Jack, they found Garrett! He's alive and okay," he said.

"Where was he?"

"Colorado. He was found perched on a ledge a thousand feet up in the Black Canyon of the Gunnison. I didn't even know what that was until I looked it up this morning."

"Holy shit, how did he get there?" asked Jack.

"I think he was abducted by a UFO. How else would he end up in such a strange place?" Pat said.

"Where is he now?" asked Jack.

"Hospital in Montrose. Steve and I are going to hit the road soon to go up there."

Jack's pulse quickened. "Pat, wait. Don't leave yet. I think I can arrange transportation that'll get us there a lot faster," he said, already turning back toward the conference room door.

Jack ducked back into the conference room, caught Bob's eye, and gestured toward the door with a quick tilt of his head. In the hallway, he laid out what Pat said. "Is there any chance we could use the jet? If this is a genuine abduction, we need to get Dr. Benton up there. His hypnosis techniques have pulled details from dozens of cases while the memories were still accessible."

Bob reached for his phone. "Get moving. I'll make sure the jet's fueled and ready by the time you reach the airfield."

Jack told Pat and Steve to get to Scottsdale Airport fast. They would pick them up for the final hop to Montrose.

With Jack needing to jet off to Colorado on short notice, Hendricus led the expedition to Perry County. As far as he was concerned, this whole incident reeked of wishful thinking. He'd pored over the radar and satellite data this morning until his eyes burned. The data was compelling but inconclusive. His scientific instincts told him this would be something mundane as usual. Had this report originated from Kazakhstan or Indonesia, he would have dismissed it with a quick email and returned to more pressing matters, but seeing as it was in their own backyard, a closer look seemed prudent.

The four-man team consisted of Hendricus, Bill Naden, and a pair of technicians; they departed just after 9 a.m. in a large SUV. They were bound for Perry County, a rural stretch northwest of Little Rock where, according to Jack's report, an unidentified object had crashed onto farmland outside the minuscule settlement of

Aplin. Hendricus doubted the place even had a population of one hundred.

A multi-vehicle pileup on Interstate 40 forced them onto a winding state highway instead. The detour carried them westward out of Little Rock's concrete sprawl and into the undulating forest of the Ouachita foothills. They reached the Aplin area around ten o'clock.

They drove around the area for an hour and had spotted nothing burned by fire. The area Jack had highlighted was in the middle of a large farm, private land, and the owner had posted "No Trespassing" signs. There was a large area of dense tree cover, perhaps twenty acres or more, surrounded by miles of open farmland. There was no way to get a closer look at the wooded area.

Barry, a technician with an extensive military background, gestured for them to stop. At the junction where the blacktop road met a narrow dirt lane cutting through the farmland, he climbed out of the vehicle and motioned for the others to follow. He pointed out subtle disturbances in the ground.

"These markings suggest recent barricades," he said, crouching to examine the soil. "Military-style blockade, if I had to guess."

He knelt down, brushing his fingertips over the compressed soil. "See these depressions? Military vehicles have a distinctive footprint. These were made by something heavy, likely a deuce and a half, parked at each intersection around the perimeter."

"A deuce and a half?" Bill asked.

Barry raised an eyebrow. "Military transport truck. Big green beast weighing about five thousand pounds. The kind that rumbles down highways during wartime with canvas-covered soldiers in the back."

"Got it," replied Bill.

Barry swept his hand toward the edge of the road. "Look over there. What else do you see?"

"Piles of cigarette butts," Hendricus observed.

Barry nodded. "Exactly. My guess? Military personnel on

perimeter duty were stationed here." He stood, brushing dirt from his knees. "If you connect the dots where these checkpoints were positioned," he said, tracing an invisible perimeter in the air with his finger, "the area Jack highlighted would be dead center of the restricted zone."

Tall dead grass lined the roadside, reaching knee high in patches. Hendricus dropped to all fours and began combing through the dead stalks with his fingers. The team fell silent, watching until he straightened, pinching something small and white between his thumb and forefinger.

"What's that?" asked Bill.

"A clue, a big one. It's a dosimeter badge, the kind they issue to personnel working near radiation sources. This isn't standard equipment for farmhands or forest rangers." Hendricus pulled out his phone and punched in the office number. When the line connected, his instructions left no room for discussion. "Send half a dozen techs to my location. I want them knocking on every door within a five-mile radius before sundown."

Something happened out here, and he was determined to get to the bottom of it.

The flight to Arizona was uneventful, and the jet's engines were still winding down as the two men jogged across the tarmac.

Pat froze at the top of the stairs, taking in the leather seats and polished wood. "Holy shit, Jack," he said, his voice dropping to a reverent whisper, "when did you start rolling with the Learjet crowd?"

"It's Bob's aircraft. This is just one of two we have at our disposal."

Once onboard, the jet taxied back to the runway and took off, headed for Southwestern Colorado.

"Allow me to introduce you to Dr. Henry Benton, our resident shrink," Jack said.

Henry grimaced. "The term is psychologist, as I have mentioned several times." He extended his hand to Pat and Steve. "My specialty is recovering suppressed memories through hypnosis. I've had considerable success with individuals who've experienced unexplained gaps in their timeline, particularly those who believe they've been abducted."

The jet landed with a jolt at Montrose Regional Airport. Pat's face was ashen. They had a turbulent flight through thunderstorms over Northern Arizona. As the cabin door swung open, the group exhaled, grateful for the solid tarmac beneath them. A black SUV with tinted windows approached the aircraft, its tires crunching on the asphalt.

Jack gestured toward the approaching vehicle with a slight grin. "Bob doesn't spare any expense. First class for us all around," he said to Pat and Steve.

They made their way to the hospital to check on Garrett. The nurse explained that only two were allowed in at a time, so he and Henry held back.

After twenty minutes, Steve came out to talk to the others. "He remembers nothing. The last thing he knew, he was scoping out the Palo Verde nuclear plant at night, looking for orbs. Felt a sharp pain in his neck, and then he woke four days later, 450 miles away, on a rocky ledge suspended a thousand feet above the bottom of the canyon."

Jack shook his head. "How do you explain something like that?"

"He's got a lot of cuts and contusions, two broken ribs, and a mild concussion. Maybe a hairline fracture in his forearm. Can you imagine what would have happened if he'd rolled off that ledge?" asked Steve.

After a while, Jack and Henry took their turn. The antiseptic smell hit him first as they pushed through the door, followed by the rhythmic beeping of monitors. Garrett was propped against stark white pillows, his skin nearly matching the sheets except where purple-yellow bruises bloomed across his temple. Clear tubing snaked from the wall to his nostrils, and an IV bag dripped into his arm, which rested motionless atop the thin blanket. He cracked open his eyes and saw Jack.

His eyes narrowed as they found Jack's face, his cracked lips barely moving. "Well, look who it is. The last thing I remember before all this, you were telling me to fuck off. Guess it takes me nearly dying for you to give a damn."

Jack's shoulders slumped as he stepped closer to the bed. "Garrett," he murmured, eyes glassy, "you have every right to be mad at me. I wrongly accused you of something, and that's on me. Sorry, my old friend. I was wrong. Will you accept my apology?"

Garrett blinked. "Yeah, but still—fuck you for not believing me."

Jack leaned forward. "Is there anything you recall between Palo Verde and waking up on that ledge? Lights in the sky? Strange craft? Even the smallest detail could help us understand what happened to you."

Garrett's hand drifted to the side of his neck, fingers probing gently. "I remember feeling this stabbing sensation over here. Doctors didn't find anything there. They tested my blood, but whatever they used is gone now." He paused, eyes drifting toward the window. "Could've been them, you know. Aliens."

Jack rubbed his chin, eyes narrowing. "I don't know, Garrett. We need to figure out exactly what happened. This is Dr. Benton, a colleague of mine. He specializes in hypnosis. He could help you recover lost memories."

"Sure, go ahead," answered Garrett.

Henry shook his head. "Not while you're hospitalized. The doctor says you'll be discharged tomorrow. We'll wait."

The sun was low on the horizon, and Jack pushed open the door to his motel room in Montrose, revealing two double beds with faded burgundy bedspreads and a laminate desk beneath a buzzing fluorescent light. Pat, Steve, and Henry all had adjacent rooms.

Jack clinked beer bottles into the ice bucket, the motel's neon sign still burning pink against the darkening sky outside. Pat dragged a chair across the carpet, its wooden legs leaving temporary impressions in the fibers. Steve and Henry followed suit, arranging themselves in a loose circle.

They engaged in conversation about Garrett's situation, pausing whenever they heard any footsteps shuffling past Jack's door. They would wait in silence until the breezeway fell quiet again.

Jack stared into his beer, searching for alternative explanations. "What if Garrett got here under his own power somehow? Maybe he had a breakdown, some kind of fugue state where he traveled all this way without remembering, then wandered up to that ledge, confused?"

Pat shook his head, peeling the label from his bottle with his thumbnail. "No way he got here on his own. His wife checked; no credit card charges for flights or rental cars. Unless he was carrying a wad of cash or stuck out his thumb for 450 miles, I don't see it happening."

Henry spoke up for the first time. "By the way, where is his wife?"

Pat's eyes flicked to Jack. "His wife left him over the UFO stuff. Hits a little close to home, doesn't it?"

Jack's smile tightened at the corners. "I've made peace with my past, Pat. Let's focus on Garrett."

Steve chimed in, "As crazy as it sounds, I think a UFO abduction is the most logical conclusion, and they dumped him in a bad spot."

Jack pinched the bridge of his nose then looked up. "Advanced beings capable of interstellar travel wouldn't make such a careless mistake, would they? Leaving him exposed on that ledge? It's like they wanted him to be found in that condition, or someone did."

Steve's finger traced a spot behind his own ear as he stared at the carpet. "You know what bothers me most? That neck pain he was talking about. Right here." He pressed his index finger into the soft hollow beneath his skull. "Perfect spot to inject something." He met Jack's eyes. "That's not alien technology. It's a syringe wielded by a human who knows anatomy."

Pat leaned forward, elbows on his knees. "What about the wife? They weren't on good terms. Never met her myself. Jack, you know her. What's she like?"

Jack rubbed his jaw. "I've met her a few times. I never had a good opinion of her. She micromanages everything in Garrett's life, very controlling. And she's a nurse who gives injections every day."

The four men sat motionless, the only sound the hum of the fluorescent light and the occasional creak of ice shifting in the bucket. Each seemed lost in his own mental calculation of probability and betrayal.

They debated in circles until their theories grew as tepid as their drinks. Midnight found them staring at beers bobbing in what had once been ice, now just a bucket of water. The wastebasket in the corner stood as a monument to their consumption—brown glass necks poking out at odd angles. One by one, they pushed back their chairs, mumbled goodbyes, and shuffled off to their separate rooms.

The morning was growing late. The nurse's promise of Garrett's imminent discharge had stretched into an hour-long wait. Jack grimaced through the last bitter sip of his third vending-machine coffee as a staff member finally appeared with Garrett's paperwork.

Despite his protests that his legs worked fine, hospital regulations required him to exit in a wheelchair, pushed by a nurse whose expression suggested she'd heard these objections a thousand times before. The procession moved through the hospital's sliding doors and out to their waiting car.

Within the hour, they were guiding Garrett up the metal stairs of the private jet, his steps uncertain despite his earlier protests. Jack gave the flight crew their destination with a weary nod: back to Scottsdale.

The aircraft touched down just after lunch. Steve and Pat had shared a ride to the airport and whisked Garrett back to his home in Steve's Honda. Jack and Henry picked up the keys to a rental car and joined them shortly thereafter.

Back at Garrett's house in Chandler, Henry dimmed the lights and drew the blinds halfway, casting the living room in a muted amber glow. He explained the hypnosis procedure to Garrett in a low, measured voice while arranging two chairs to face each other.

Garrett nodded, his fingers tapping nervously against his thigh as he settled into the worn leather recliner. A small digital recorder blinked red on the coffee table between them. In the adjacent kitchen, Pat paced on a creaky floor while Steve leaned against the refrigerator, arms folded. Jack sat motionless at the breakfast bar, watching the second hand tick around his watch face.

Henry's voice dropped to a hypnotic cadence, each word measured and rhythmic. Garrett's eyelids fluttered then grew heavy, his breathing deepening until his chest rose and fell in a slow, steady pattern. But despite his apparent trance state, his responses remained vague. His brow would furrow at certain questions, lips parting only to mumble disconnected fragments—"light," "cold," "can't see"— before lapsing into prolonged silence. After twenty minutes of circular questioning that yielded nothing but these cryptic whispers, Henry's shoulders sagged. He glanced at Jack with a slight shake of his head before leaning forward to guide Garrett back to consciousness with a series of gentle commands.

Garrett excused himself to the restroom, his socked feet dragging across the carpet. Henry waited until the bathroom door clicked shut before sidling up to Jack.

"I'm not getting anywhere with him," Henry whispered, his silver-rimmed glasses catching the amber light as he glanced toward the hallway. "That doesn't mean he wasn't abducted by aliens. He still has a mental block in place and is suffering from trauma. We might want to give this a while and try again."

Pat and Steve were listening in.

"So let's play a theory I have and say it wasn't aliens. Who then?" Pat asked, shaking his head. "And more importantly, why?"

Steve had an idea. "The wife, or soon-to-be ex-wife."

Jack rubbed his chin. "Well, Steve, I suppose that's something to follow up on. Maybe we can hire a detective to keep tabs on her and see what she's been up to. At this point in time, I don't know what else to do."

Garrett shuffled back into the living room, his face pale and drawn. Henry walked him through a sanitized version of what might have happened—aliens, memory-wiping drugs, possible interrogation —carefully avoiding any speculation about Garrett's estranged wife. As the afternoon shadows lengthened across the apartment floor, Jack checked his watch and nodded to Henry. They gathered their things, promised to follow up soon, and left Garrett in Pat and Steve's capable hands before heading back to return their rental car at Scottsdale Airport. A few hours later, they were back in Little Rock.

The town of Aplin was in the Fourche La Fave River valley, a slender corridor that snaked from the Arkansas River into the heart of the Ouachita Mountains. Even at its broadest stretch, barely five miles across, the search area remained deceptively compact. Bill traced his fingers across the map, his options dwindling with each X he marked. They'd combed almost every inch of accessible terrain and still had nothing.

A volunteer fire station appeared on their right as they cruised through town, a small brick building with its bay doors open to the afternoon sun. A man in coveralls bent over the exposed engine of a red pickup truck parked in the driveway. Bill caught Hendricus's eye, nodded once, and swung their car around in a tight U-turn without a word between them.

The man straightened up from the engine as they approached, wiping his hands on a rag. "Howdy there," Bill called out, his voice sliding into that easy Arkansas drawl he reserved for locals.

The firefighter straightened, rag still in hand. "Help you fellas with somethin'?" he asked, wary.

Bill introduced himself and Hendricus. He leaned against the truck's fender. "We're tracking reports of unusual military activity in the valley last week. Bright lights, helicopters, that sort of thing." He studied the man's face. "You boys get called out for anything strange recently? Maybe there was a big fire you had to put out?"

His head swiveled from side to side so vigorously that his neck tendons stood out like cables. "Ain't been no fires worth mentionin' since a couple of months ago," he said. His gaze fixed on a point somewhere over Bill's left shoulder. "And I sure as hell ain't seen no military. No sir. Not a single helicopter or Humvee or nothin' else with government plates." His Adam's apple bobbed as he swallowed hard.

Bill continued to ask more specific questions. With each new one, the firefighter's eyes darted more frantically between them and the road.

The man's twitchy demeanor and evasive eyes screamed that he was holding something back. Whatever knowledge he possessed remained locked behind clenched teeth and that white-knuckled grip on his wrench. Something, or someone, had gotten to him first.

Bill gripped Hendricus's elbow and steered him a few paces away. "This is getting us nowhere," he muttered, glancing back at the firefighter. "Guy's scared stiff. Military types have a way of making sure people keep quiet, threats, intimidation, whatever it takes. Let's try the gas station down the road. In small towns like this, there's always someone with loose lips."

Hendricus sighed and slid back into the passenger seat, leaving Bill to smooth things over. "Appreciate your help," Bill called to the firefighter with a smile. "Sorry to interrupt your work."

The man grunted, already turning back to his truck's engine.

So far, they were getting the same story from the town's residents. Nothing unusual had taken place. And yet Hendricus didn't believe it.

At the intersection of highways 10 and 60 in Perryville was a gas station with an attached mini-mart. The team filed in, hoping for information. The clerk behind the counter shook his head when they described what they were looking for but mentioned that Janise, who worked the graveyard shift, had been telling similar stories all week.

Janise wasn't working today, but the clerk sketched out directions to find her place on the outskirts of town. Following his map, they headed east down Highway 60 until they spotted the mailbox he'd described. The tires crunched over loose gravel as they made their way up the long drive toward what appeared to be an aging single-wide trailer, its metal siding patched in places with mismatched panels.

"Jesus Christ, somebody lives here?" asked Hendricus.

Bill shrugged. "Gas station clerk on the graveyard shift? This is probably the palace that minimum wage built."

A rusty chain-link fence enclosed the patch of dirt in front of the trailer. Two pit bulls erupted from beneath the structure, their muscular bodies tensed as they hurled themselves against the metal barrier, jaws snapping and eyes fixed on the visitors.

"The hell with this shit, man!" said Barry. "Those guys will take a limb off you!"

The trailer door swung open, revealing a man in a stained tank top. "What the hell you people want?" he called out, his voice like gravel under tires.

Hendricus shouted over the snarling dogs, "We need to speak with Janise. She home?"

The man's eyes narrowed to slits as he looked them over. "Y'all cops?"

He shook his head. "We're journalists. I heard Janise witnessed something unusual during her shift and we want to ask her a few questions."

The man disappeared inside. Moments later, the door creaked open again as a woman emerged—rail-thin with a silver ring through her nostril and a tank top that hung loosely from her shoulders. She shoved at the dogs with her knee, commanding them back with a practiced gesture before unlatching the gate and slipping through.

She squinted at them through the afternoon sun, arms crossed over her chest. "What's this about?"

Hendricus stepped forward, keeping one eye on the dogs. "Name's Hendricus. We're looking into some strange stuff going on with the military around here." He gestured back toward the direction of the gas station. "Guy at the counter said you might've spotted something during your shift the other night."

Janise's eyes narrowed as she pulled a pack of cigarettes from her pocket, tapping one out. "Two in the morning. Dead quiet, like always. I was out back by the dumpsters having my smoke when it happened." She rolled the unlit cigarette between her thumb and forefinger, gaze fixed on some middle distance.

Hendricus said, "Go ahead."

She lit her cigarette, inhaled deeply, and blew smoke toward the sky. "Middle of the night, dead quiet, then this rumble hit my ears. Like thunder, but it don't stop. Coming down 60 from Aplin way." She gestured with her cigarette. "Military convoy. Humvees leading —desert camo, like Iraq shit. Then this massive flatbed. Whatever they had under that tarp was huge. Wide enough they needed escort vehicles with flashers." She took another drag. "More humvees bringing up the rear. Whole damn parade rolled through the intersection, hung a left on 10. Heading north to the interstate, I guess. It was weird. Seen nothing like it around these parts before."

They wrapped up their conversation with her and left.

Hendricus was beside himself. "I knew it! The military hauled something out in the middle of the night. Anyone want to take bets on what it was?"

There were no takers.

The next morning, Bob gathered everyone in the fourth-floor conference room.

Hendricus launched into a recap of what they'd found. Bob held up a hand to stop him.

"Hold up, Hendricus. I've got some information that might save us all some time." The room fell silent as every head swiveled toward him, eyebrows raised.

Bob leaned back in his chair, fingers laced across his stomach. "I have connections in influential circles. Well, 'connections' may be too strong a word. Perhaps it's more accurate to say there are individuals in Washington who are financially indebted to me. I had a brief conversation this morning with a distinguished senator from Arkansas concerning the situation in Perry County."

Hendricus's face darkened as he leaned back in his chair, while his colleagues around him sat forward, eyes widening and lips parting.

Bob drummed his fingers on the table. "You were sniffing around the right tree. The military definitely recovered something outside Aplin," he said, letting his gaze drift across their expectant faces. "But it wasn't little gray aliens. The senator confirmed that a Chinese surveillance satellite went haywire. It came down right in our backyard. Top brass swooped in and locked it down tight. That's all they'd give me, even off the record." He slapped his palm on the table. "So I'd say we can close the book on this one."

Hendricus snorted, his eyes narrowing to slits. "A Chinese satellite? Really, Bob?"

Bob leaned forward, his voice dropping to a confidential rumble. "Yes, Hendricus. The senator has been cashing my campaign contribution checks for fifteen years now. When I call, he picks up. Trust me on this one."

"If you say so." He bit his tongue, but the math didn't add up. He'd estimated at least thirty military vehicles and what looked like a mobile command center, all for some downed spy satellite? He didn't buy it.

But without Bob's support, this investigation would proceed no further.

Jack and Henry had been back in Little Rock since last week, and things had returned to normal. It was now Friday, and Bob had called for a morning meeting of the scientists in the conference room.

Bob and Hendricus unveiled their vision, a complex operation they'd been orchestrating for months. The scale of what they proposed left little doubt that this would be their most ambitious project yet, with the added complication of operating south of the border.

Bob addressed the room, "We've investigated internationally before, but this is going to be on a much larger scale. We are going to attack this in two phases. First, an initial team will deploy to assess the project's viability. If it looks good, we will deploy a much larger second wave of investigators. We're working to get the initial team deployed as soon as possible, hopefully in a few days." He turned to Jack. "You speak fluent Spanish, do you not?"

"About ninety percent fluency," he said. "I can carry on a conversation with the average person on the street, but I do struggle with the less frequently used verb tenses, and when it comes to technical language, outside of meteorology, I'm—"

Bob held up a hand to cut him off. "Okay, that's good enough for me, Jack. We're sending a team to Mexico to investigate. We don't need you to give a presentation to the institute of technology down there." That drew a round of muffled laughter from the room.

Bob continued, "Many of you may already know of this event, but in 1974, a UFO allegedly collided with a small plane outside a small town in Chihuahua, Mexico." He adjusted his glasses and peered more closely at a printed sheet in his hand. "On a ranch outside the town of Coyame, the crash site was less than fifty miles from the U.S. border. As the story goes, our Air Force or some other military unit swept in there and scooped it all up before the Mexican authorities could get to it. The ranch down there is under new owner-ship, and they've been finding small metallic debris at the surface, probably dug up by burrowing rodents. Could this be something from the UFO that our government missed?"

Dr. Chris Bellini raised a hand and asked, "Presumably we have permission from the new owners to come in and dig around?"

"Well, yes, and no. They don't mind us coming in with shovels and metal detectors, but bulldozers and backhoes are out of the question."

Hendricus took over. "The initial team will be composed of scientists who speak Spanish fluently," and he turned to Jack with a slight smile, "or at least ninety percent." Jack's face reddened. "So that group would be Lydia, Perry, Pablo, Tomás, and Jack."

"As you all know, our larger jet, Big Red, is deployed down in Australia, and we found out this morning that Tusk needs an engine overhaul. It will be out of service for at least a few days. I don't want us to sit on deployment too long, so the initial team will fly commer-cial to El Paso, rent a car, and drive into Mexico."

Sighs and murmured complaints rippled through the conference room at the mention of commercial flights.

Jack shifted in his seat, hesitating before raising his hand. "Hen-dricus, don't most rental companies prohibit taking their vehicles into

Mexico? I've heard there are insurance and liability issues at the border."

"Good question, Jack. You're right. Most of the big companies won't allow that. Patty located a few specialized agencies in El Paso that permit a vehicle to be taken across the border, but it will cost us extra. Plus, we will have to purchase Mexican auto insurance in case anything goes wrong on the other side."

Alec leaned back in his chair with a smirk. "Make sure that insurance covers acts of God and federales with creative interpretations of traffic laws," he said, triggering scattered laughter around the table.

Bob pushed back and rose to his feet. "That's all for now, folks. We will start drafting the expedition schedule and travel arrangements. We'll circulate the details once we have something, hopefully sooner rather than later."

The travel arrangements materialized with unexpected haste. By late afternoon, Bob had summoned the initial deployment team to his office. Jack's stomach tightened as Bob slid five manila folders across the gleaming surface—each containing boarding passes for a 1:15 PM flight to El Paso. The group exchanged grimaces; after months of stretching out in the luxury accommodations of Bob's private jets, the prospect of cramped economy seats and security lines felt like a demotion to the minor leagues.

Jack jolted awake as the plane bucked through a pocket of rough air. He'd dozed off not long after takeoff, lulled by the drone of engines at thirty thousand feet. Blinking away sleep, he pressed his forehead against the cool window, orienting himself in the vastness below. Nothing but sun-bleached earth extended to the edges of his vision, an endless canvas of tans and browns, occasionally interrupted by the ruler-straight lines of distant roads. *We must be over the central or western part of Texas*, he thought.

Tomás occupied the middle seat beside him with Lydia in the aisle. Their Spanish flowed between them in hushed tones. Jack caught most of what Lydia said. Her Mexican accent was familiar territory despite his rustiness. Tomás was another matter entirely. The Chilean's distinctive cadence and clipped consonants transformed the language Jack thought he knew into something beyond his complete comprehension. He'd need weeks of exposure before those sounds would make sense to him, or he and Tomás would have to resort to English.

The plane's engines changed pitch, their roar softening to a muted growl as the aircraft tilted earthward. A chime echoed through the cabin, followed by the illumination of the seatbelt icons overhead.

He glanced at his watch. They would be on the ground in El Paso in twenty or thirty minutes.

Lydia caught Jack's eye and switched to English. "Sleeping Beauty awakens," she said with a hint of amusement. "Good nap?"

Jack rubbed his eyes. "I usually can't sleep on these things. I guess I didn't exactly get my full eight hours last night." The corner of Lydia's mouth twitched upward as she glanced at Tomás, who raised an eyebrow in return.

"So, amigo, it seems like you and Dr. Bowden have gotten pretty close lately."

Heat crept up Jack's neck and bloomed across his cheeks. "Uh, well, we've become friends. We worked together on those cattle mutilation cases." He shifted in his seat, suddenly aware of how transparent his expression might be. Did they know?

Tomás continued to press on. "I noticed that you arrived right after each other this morning. A coincidence?"

"I hadn't really noticed."

Lydia pressed her lips together, failing to suppress a smile. Tomás leaned in slightly. "Jack, amigo," he said, his voice dropping conspiratorially, "People have been whispering about you two for a while. Last night, I was at the Rev Room in Little Rock, and I saw you two there—together—and it was obvious you were more than just friends."

Jack's face fell. "Oh, shit..."

Lydia and Tomás exchanged glances, both struggling to contain their amusement. "Relax," Tomás said, leaning closer, "your secret is safe with me." He offered Jack a conspiratorial smile and a gentle nudge with his elbow. "Though I must say, she is a fine catch. You should be proud. How long have you been involved? Since Wisconsin, is that where it happened?"

Jack's face was completely flushed. He gripped the armrests, wishing the seat would swallow him whole, then sighed and met their eyes. "Jess and I hit it off on day one. She moved in with me a month after that. We really didn't want to make a public announcement about our relationship. We don't know where Bob stands on all of that."

Tomás's eyebrows shot up. "Day one? And she moved in a month later? Wow! That would bring you respect even back in Santiago, my friend!"

Lydia waved a dismissive hand. "Your personal life is your own, although I must say, you two make a cute couple. In any event, we're colleagues first, and we have more important matters to focus on." She leaned forward, her expression shifting to one of professional interest. "Tomás and I were discussing some theories about the crash site. I'd value your perspective."

Jack relaxed somewhat as they began discussing the case file.

Their plane touched down smoothly in El Paso, and after collecting their baggage from the carousel, they discovered they needed to catch a shuttle to the rental car facility. Their agency didn't operate directly out of the terminal.

Perry and Pablo had flown together in another section of the plane and appointed themselves in charge of procuring the vehicle. Perry pulled Jack aside while they waited for the shuttle. "Heads up —Patty called me before we boarded. The specialty agency she found that allows vehicles across the border couldn't get us anything suitable. Apparently their only available unit was a cargo van with a cracked windshield and 140,000 miles on it."

"Of course it was," said Jack.

"So the new plan is: we rent something decent here at the airport, drive it to Presidio, and walk across. She's already lined up a rental on the Mexican side."

Tomás nodded. "Smart. Mexican roads south of Ojinaga are not kind to vehicles. Better to abuse something that belongs to them."

Enterprise had them sorted in under thirty minutes—a silver sedan with enough room for the team and their gear, no arguments required. The only catch, as expected, was that the insurance wouldn't cover a single inch south of the Rio Grande.

"Which brings us to the parking problem," Perry said, spreading a map across the hood of the sedan while Pablo loaded the last of the bags. "There's no rental return center in Presidio. Patty already checked."

Jack studied the map. "So we leave it there for however long this takes and hope nobody strips it."

"Patty thought of that too," said Perry. "She called ahead to our motel in Presidio. She says we can work out the details with the owner, but she thinks he'll let us leave it in their lot, maybe for twenty bucks a day." He folded the map. "She also said to tell you that the owner's name is Ruben, and he speaks English, so don't embarrass her."

"Patty thinks of everything," said Lydia.

"Patty thinks of everything and then apologizes for what she missed," said Jack. "Which means she's already worried she forgot something."

They loaded up and pulled out of the rental lot into the El Paso afternoon, the Franklin Mountains rising to the north and the broad flat sprawl of the border city stretching in every other direction. Presidio was still nearly two hours southeast down Highway 67, and somewhere on the other side of the Rio Grande, a ranch outside Coyame was waiting for them.

They made it to the border without incident. Patty had secured them rooms at the Cactus Inn, a no-frills establishment that, after hours of travel, looked like the Ritz-Carlton to their exhausted eyes.

Jack negotiated with the motel manager, who agreed to let them leave the car in the back lot. "It'll be waiting for you when you return," he assured them, "twenty dollars a day."

Jack hauled his suitcase into the room, where a cockroach lay belly up on the thin carpet, its legs curled inward like a tiny monument to the motel's housekeeping standards. When he plopped onto the mattress, it yielded with a wheezing protest of ancient springs that sank down several inches.

He had barely closed his eyes when three sharp raps at the door yanked him from the edge of sleep. He stumbled to answer it, only to find Pablo standing there.

"Hey, we're all going to get something to eat and grab a few drinks. You interested?"

"Oh, hell yeah, I'm starving. I could go for some of the local Mexican flavor here."

Pablo shrugged. "Lydia's got her heart set on this pizza joint she spotted on the way in. When she gets that look in her eye, it's best not to argue."

Jack raised an eyebrow. "We're on the border, and we're getting pizza?" He shook his head with a tired smile. "Fine by me, but they better have cold beer."

Twenty minutes later, the five of them piled into their rental and headed for a neon cactus sign marking Sancho's Pizza Palace. Inside, they found themselves in what could only be described as a glorified diner—mismatched tables and chairs with chipped veneer, walls adorned with flickering neon beer logos, and linoleum floors that crunched underfoot with each step. The group agreed on a large pepperoni with an extra-thick crust. While the beer was indeed cold, the pizza's absence from their table stretched from minutes into what felt like an eternity.

Several rounds of beer had come and gone from the table until finally the pizza arrived. The deep-dish pepperoni pie glistened under the fluorescent lights, pools of orange grease collecting in the dimples of the cheese. Nobody commented on its appearance. After hours on the road, hunger had a way of silencing criticism.

The group deferred to Lydia, who slid the first slice onto her plate. Pablo was last, and when he selected a piece, his hand suddenly went rigid, the metal utensil and pizza slice suspended in midair.

Pablo's fork clattered against his plate. "Jesus Christ, nobody eat this!" His head whipped around, scanning for the server. "Hey! Camarero! Over here, now! Rápido!"

The waiter rushed over, his face a mask of concern. "Is there a problem, señor?" Everyone at the table leaned forward, craning to see what had caught Pablo's attention. When the server finally glimpsed it, his expression collapsed into horror. "Oh! I'm so sorry. Please, we can make you another one."

Pablo rotated the pizza server around so everyone could see the dead cockroach baked into the crust.

Perry froze while chewing, his eyes widening as he stared at the half-eaten slice in his hand. Lydia pressed a napkin to her mouth, turning green. Jack's gaze locked onto the waiter, his voice dropping to a dangerous growl. "Do you honestly think we'd let you make us another pizza after you served us this?"

A stocky man in a grease-stained apron burst through the kitchen doors, his face flushed with indignation. "What seems to be the problem here?" he barked, planting himself beside their table. Pablo thrust the pizza server toward him, launching into rapid-fire Spanish that grew louder with each syllable. As their voices escalated, Jack gave a nod to the rest of the team, and they headed toward the door. The four of them slipped out, leaving Pablo arguing with the manager, and hurried across the gravel to their waiting vehicle.

Pablo stormed out minutes later, slamming the car door behind him. "Can you believe that pendejo? Tried to make us pay for the beer after serving us roach pizza!" He shuddered, wiping his hands on his jeans as if still trying to remove the memory. "I told him where he could stick it!"

The car hummed with tense silence until Perry's stomach growled. He patted it sheepishly. "I hate to be that guy, but we never actually got dinner." Lydia turned to face Perry. "You just saw a cockroach baked into a pizza and are still hungry?"

"Well, it's not like we actually ate it!" he said.

Jack sighed, "Come on, folks. We're a stone's throw from Mexico. There's gotta be authentic food somewhere in this town."

He caught Lydia's eye in the rearview mirror. "And if your stomach's still turning, I'll cover your drinks all night. Hell, the first round's on me for everyone after what we went through."

The promise of free drinks was all it took. Five minutes later, they pulled into the gravel lot of an establishment with a hand-painted sign reading "Lucy's Cantina y Cocina Auténtica" illuminated by a string of multicolored bulbs.

They pushed through the screen door and stepped into another world. Gone was the antiseptic glare of the "roach pizza" joint; here, mismatched wooden chairs crowded around tables draped in bright oilcloth, and hand-painted saints watched from their niches between faded family photos. The scent of cilantro and sizzling meat filled the air. Spanish flowed around them in musical currents, punctuated by ranchero music from the lone overhead speaker.

A waitress stepped up to their table. Her silver-streaked hair framed a face that had seen decades of seasons. When Jack addressed her in Spanish, the woman's initial assessment melted into warmth.

She distributed menus, her hospitality transforming the simple restaurant into something like hallowed ground after their long day.

Platters arrived in waves, cast iron skillets hissing with peppers and onions beneath strips of caramelized beef. Corn husks unfurled to reveal golden masa treasures, and the tortillas were so fresh they steamed when torn. The chips came stacked in woven baskets, flanked by molcajetes of salsa that promised both pleasure and pain.

As the night deepened, so did the group's thirst, amber tequila disappearing in swift backward tilts of heads, beer pitchers emptying and refilling like tides, salt-rimmed glasses leaving rings on the wooden tabletop. Only Jack maintained his vigil over a single, sweating bottle, watching his colleagues shed their sobriety with each toast.

By the time they stumbled out of Lucy's, the night had grown old. The tequila shots and pitchers of beer had done their work on everyone but Jack.

As they stumbled into the vehicle, his focus shifted to a vehicle parked across the street. A black sedan idled under a flickering street-light, its windows tinted enough to obscure but not hide the silhou-ettes of two men in suits. As they turned their heads in unison to track the group's movements, Jack's throat tightened. The tableau triggered an immediate flashback to the pair who'd appeared without warning at the Phoenix weather office, asking pointed questions about what he and Garrett had observed. Were these similar govern-ment agents?

Jack locked eyes with the sedan's occupants until the engine hummed to life and the vehicle pulled away into the night. The hair on his neck stood on end—men in suits lurking outside a border town cantina at midnight weren't tourists or locals. They were watching, waiting. But for what?

As the last passenger tumbled into the back seat, the car filled with slurred nonsense, pulling Jack's attention away from the mysterious sedan and back to his intoxicated companions. Lydia seemed to be in the worst shape of all. Her head lolled against the window as they drove, her consciousness fading in and out with each streetlight they passed.

They made it back to the motel after a short drive. Once parked, Tomás and Pablo flanked her like reluctant pallbearers, half-dragging her limp body up the concrete steps and through the doorway of her room.

By morning, they straggled one by one into the motel's breakfast nook, faces ashen, eyes bloodshot. Jack moved around the buffet comfortably, having nursed only a single beer the night before. He couldn't help but feel a twinge of humor as he watched his colleagues wince at every clink of silverware against ceramic.

Their ambitious plans for an early border crossing dissolved as quickly as the morning sun. By the time they'd showered away the regret of the night before, packed their scattered belongings, and assembled in the parking lot, it was eleven o'clock. The border station had seemed walkable when they checked in, but they hadn't realized it was over two miles away. With throbbing temples and queasy stomachs, they agreed that the best course of action was to hire a taxi to drive them across to the other side.

Once they crossed the border, things looked better. The automobile rental process went smoothly, thanks to Patty's arrangements. The team reached the town in the early afternoon. Coyame was barely a dot on the map, with a population of 1,500 on a good day. Sun-bleached storefronts and crumbling stucco spoke of prosperity long past.

Their vehicle kicked up dust as they left the highway behind, Pablo navigating the narrow streets of Coyame while everyone scanned for any sign of their lodging.

From the passenger seat, Lydia squinted at a printed sheet of paper. "Take this all the way down Del Pilar," she told Pablo, who drummed his fingers impatiently on the steering wheel. "There should be a plaza with large palm trees coming up. The hotel is on the other side."

The town square opened before them, and Pablo guided the vehicle along its perimeter. As they made their way around it, a low-rise structure was on the left, the color of dried clay, crowned with curved roof tiles and adorned with intricate metal scrollwork. Lydia's finger jabbed toward the building. "Look, that has to be it."

Pablo eased off the gas, squinting at the building. "I don't see a name or a hotel sign anywhere on that place." He continued forward until the plaza's edge forced him to turn.

Lydia grabbed the dashboard. "Stop the vehicle! We just passed it, that building with the tile roof!"

Pablo threw his hands up in exasperation. "How are we supposed to find lodging in this damn town? Not a single sign!" He yanked the vehicle to the curb while Jack leapt out, taking the ornately tiled steps two at a time. The others waited, squinting through the windows at the typical-looking building. Moments later, Jack reappeared at the entrance, beckoning with a wide sweep of his arm. Pablo muttered under his breath, backing the car into an empty space in front of the hotel.

After the confusion outside, the group found themselves surprised once they'd checked in and located their rooms. Hand-woven rugs covered terracotta floors, wrought-iron fixtures cast intricate shadows across whitewashed walls, and ceiling fans turned lazily overhead. The crisp sheets and absence of mysterious stains made everyone grateful they'd left the roach-infested Cactus Inn back across the border.

Their contact, José, had agreed to meet them at a local cantina at two o'clock before guiding them to the crash site. Perry kept checking his watch, pacing back and forth. Lydia reached out and caught his arm. "Have a drink first," she said, nodding toward the bar in the corner. "Time is a philosophical concept in Mexico. Our guy could show up anytime between now and sunset."

Jack said, "Or later."

José arrived a little after three, sliding into their booth with an easy smile that suggested no awareness of his tardiness. After exchanging pleasantries over mezcal shots that burned all the way down, they piled into their vehicles and headed back toward the highway. The ranch, he explained over the crackling two-way radio, was about ten miles outside town, requiring them to retrace part of their route from Ojinaga.

José's pickup veered off the pavement onto what barely qualified as a road, twin ruts carved through scrubland. After unlocking a rusted gate and crossing a cattle guard that rattled their teeth, they bounced along for another half mile, the vehicle pitching and yawing over rocks and washouts. Finally, they stopped beside a circular patch of ground enclosed by a barbed wire fence strung between crooked posts; the whole arrangement no wider than a backyard swimming pool.

The group climbed out of their vehicles into the afternoon sun. José gestured toward a round depression surrounded by the makeshift fence, its soil darker than the surrounding earth as if burned by an ancient fire.

"Why is the ground scorched?" asked Jack.

"The older folks claim the crash happened in this area and that small pieces of airplane debris can be found scattered in every direction," he said, making a sweeping gesture with his left arm. "This fenced area, everyone has been warned to stay away. Nobody seems to know why anymore." José then walked around to the back of his pickup and dropped the tailgate. "Señor Bob arranged for these metal detectors, shovels, and pickaxes to be brought to you, and I trust you will put them to good use."

Pablo said, "Bob also said something about a ground-penetrating radar unit?"

"Yes, he arranged for a portable GPR, but it will not arrive until tomorrow." The group had gathered everything from the back of José's truck. "If there is nothing else, I will leave it to you."

With that, José rumbled away down the dirt track and departed.

Jack said, "It looks like we only have two or three hours of daylight remaining. How do we want to proceed here? Do we split up into groups, or should we stick together?"

Tomás suggested, "Let's call our starting point right here ground zero. Pablo, you and Perry are engineers. The two of you should spiral outward from here, mark any aircraft debris you identify with these little white survey flags, and anything metallic or suspicious with the orange flags. You have a Geiger counter with you. If you encounter any hot spots, mark them with these neon-green flags. I want to examine ground zero to see if I can determine what happened. Lydia, if you're okay with it, I think you should start sweeping the area with a metal detector. Jack, I want to run a theory by you."

Everyone agreed. Tomás approached Jack with a topographic map. "This crash, or whatever it was, happened almost twenty-five years ago," he said, gesturing to the map. "Do you see these dry washes all across the map? You're the expert. How often do you think it rains hard enough to create a flash flood around here?"

"Probably twice per year, but a huge one? Maybe once every ten or twenty years." Jack nodded, seeing what Tomás was hinting at.

"These floods, especially the big ones, could wash metallic debris downstream, far from the original crash site. I think you should focus on checking the dry washes for any crash remnants," said Tomás.

"I'm on it," said Jack.

Over an hour had passed, and the sun was getting lower. Pablo and Perry had been spiraling outward from ground zero, marking a few areas with white flags and placing only one orange flag. Tomás was busy in the fenced-off area, and Lydia was sweeping the surrounding ground with a metal detector.

Jack had made his way almost half a mile downstream on the dry wash that ran next to ground zero. So far, he'd detected nothing unusual. Finally, the dry streambed he was following opened into a wider one. According to the topographic map, this wash drained a much larger area extending back toward the mountains, and it looked like a dozen smaller ones, like the one he was in, fed into it upstream. He looked at the lowering sun and wondered if he should quit or keep moving forward. He decided to soldier on.

Jack swept the metal detector with his right arm while he took readings with the Geiger counter in his left. He'd gone less than fifty feet downstream and got a small hit on the metal detector. After zeroing in on the area, he removed his trowel and started digging.

He found nothing at first, so he grabbed the pinpoint metal detector from his belt loop. After a short while, he found the culprit: a small coin. He brushed it off and used some water from his canteen to wash away the dirt. It was a Mexican fifty-centavo piece from 1967, heavily worn. This didn't seem significant, but for the sake of completeness he bagged it, documented the location, and placed it into his fanny pack.

A hundred feet forward, the detector pinged again on the opposite side of the wash. This one was deep, buried under a rock the size of a bowling ball. Jack froze when the pinpoint metal detector led him to the object, a misshapen metallic nodule no bigger than his thumbnail with the appearance of having been subjected to extreme heat until it liquefied and then cooled again into this strange form. Now, what was this?

He passed the Geiger counter over the sample. The device's soft clicking suddenly transformed into an insistent staccato. Jack recoiled, his hand jerking away instinctively. The metal nodule was emitting radiation, not enough to cause immediate harm but well above normal background levels.

He knew there were natural uranium deposits in the area, but this had to be something else. He marked the spot with a neon-green flag and placed the sample into a special, lead-lined bag Tomás had provided. Another look at the sun near the horizon, and Jack started the long trek back toward ground zero.

As the last rays of sunlight stretched across the desert, the team reconvened at the fenced-in circle, their tools stowed away in the SUV's cargo area. Faces dusty and tired, they formed a loose huddle to compare discoveries. Lydia's metal detector had yielded only a handful of rusted steel fragments scattered around ground zero—nothing surprising considering that this was ranch land.

Pablo and Perry found one suspicious item and bagged it, but didn't think it looked too promising. Their search turned up aviation debris, though. As they reached the outer edge of their spiral pattern, they'd uncovered small fragments they thought belonged to an aircraft's tail assembly, along with several hydraulic line connectors. The evidence pointed to an aircraft incident, though nothing yet suggested anything extraterrestrial had fallen from the sky. They were searching in the right area, for certain.

Jack revealed his findings. The coin drew little interest, but the radioactive metal fragment was another story. Tomás took out his Geiger counter and examined it. "Hmm, interesting," he said as he turned the object over in his hands. "The radioactivity is very unusual, but it's not dangerous, at least not for short-term exposure. I wouldn't recommend walking around with it in your pocket all day, though. I'd guess this is magnesium, or an alloy by the looks of it. For what it's worth, naturally occurring magnesium is not radioactive."

Lydia asked, "What do you think it's from?"

Tomás said, "Possibly whatever crashed out here, although I couldn't rule out something else, like a meteorite impact. We'll have to take it back to the lab for a full analysis."

"Now, let me tell you about ground zero. This place is a puzzle. There is a narrow shaft here extending into the earth. It's unstable, and I can't judge its depth. Maybe it was an old mine shaft. The entire area around the fence is depressed a foot lower than the surrounding terrain. Perhaps there was an underground collapse. The small passage is full of debris, dirt, rocks, lids from fifty-five-gallon drums, and some other metal fragments that appear to be steel. This area was burned in the past, a hot, prolonged fire. There are several reasons this could be here, and most aren't noteworthy."

Tomás continued, "But there's something radioactive down there. In case you didn't know it, there are significant uranium ore deposits here in the Chihuahuan Desert. However, this area right here isn't known for it. Those mountains could contain some minor deposits, but I wouldn't expect to find any here on the valley floor, unless it was washed down in the streambed. But whatever I'm picking up on the Geiger down that shaft, I don't think it's natural uranium ore."

Everyone stared at each other for a second. Finally, Jack asked, "So what could it be then?"

"That," Tomás said with emphasis, "is the big question. To get to the radioactive source, we'll need to move a lot of earth, and I have serious concerns about our safety given the ground's instability. My guess is that an underground chamber, possibly associated with a mine shaft, collapsed. To be honest, a mine on the valley floor makes little sense. There is no mineral, gem, or precious metal that should be present here."

They packed up and headed back to Coyame, returning to the hotel to clean up. A half-hour later, they trickled into the lobby. Perry feigned starvation and wanted to know where they were eating.

Jack gestured toward the hotel's front windows. "We have a choice of three restaurants in town. After a week, we'll be sick and tired of them all."

Lydia said, "There's a place on Del Pilar when you first come off the highway with a big pine tree in front of it. You know which one I mean? I'd like to try that out tonight."

Pablo raised his hand with a grin. "Count me in, but let's skip the pizza this time."

Chuckles rippled through the group, and they set off on foot toward the restaurant four blocks away.

The enchiladas and tamales disappeared quickly, and the group settled into a comfortable rhythm of cold cervezas and tall tales until Tomás leaned forward, his expression shifting from relaxed to resolute. "I called Bob and spoke to him for a bit when we got back to the hotel. He agrees that we need to excavate the area around ground zero and recognizes that it's too much of a risk for our group to handle, at least with shovels. He's going to talk to the new owners again and see if we can get permission to bring in a backhoe to dig up that one small area. Otherwise, we need to continue searching for surface debris. For tomorrow's plan, Jack won't be alone out there in those dry streambeds. Lydia and I will join him. Finding one radioactive fragment like that? No way it's sitting out there all by itself. That's a big clue that the streambeds are transporting larger, heavier materials during floods."

Jack said, "And we need to search upstream in that big wash as well. I don't think that element came down the streambed I was following. If one or two of us follow it upstream, we might be lucky enough to trace the source back to a smaller area."

The next morning, the team was on the job bright and early. Tomás had taken a six a.m. call from Bob. After an intense discussion with the scientists in Arkansas, they had agreed to send a group of technicians to assist with the project. Given the rental car nightmare they'd already endured, Bob wasn't taking any chances this time. He'd arranged for a small chartered plane to deliver the reinforcements to Presidio.

It fell to Lydia to take the SUV and make the trek back to Ojinaga to collect the incoming technicians and transport them to the Coyame site. Bob was still working with the ranch owners to secure permission to conduct a limited backhoe dig.

There had been a change of plans from the night before. José had delivered the ground-penetrating radar, and Tomás had Lydia assist him with it to see if they could detect anything underground near ground zero. Perry and Pablo would continue searching for aircraft debris, and Jack would work his way farther down the dry streambed, looking for any additional anomalies.

By late afternoon, Perry and Pablo had identified a long debris field from the downed plane, although not much remained; spread out over a mile were small aircraft pieces in a northeast-to-southwest direction. They could estimate the approximate area where the collision occurred, providing a starting point for searching for any remaining UFO debris.

Jack had worked his way downstream three-quarters of a mile and had made it to the Federal Highway 16 bridge. He hadn't come up with anything significant: just small bits of rusted metal, which were nothing more than trash. By the time the dry streambed reached the bridge, it had become narrow, and he thought that during floods, the water would rage through this area. Beyond that point, he figured the narrow channel would widen and fan out, where the rushing water would slow and drop debris caught in the turbulent flow.

Lydia had returned with the techs who had flown to Presidio and went back to assisting Tomás. "Find anything unusual while I was gone?" she asked.

"I'm not sure what to make of it all," said Tomás. "The ground-penetrating radar is showing a number of small voids underground. Could be a natural cave system, or it could be evidence that the area was excavated and filled in hastily."

"Are caves natural in this area?"

"I wouldn't think so," he said, studying the readout. "Hmm, that's strange. I'm also getting a horizontal return about ten feet down, right in the middle of ground zero. Very dense. It could be a rock, but it seems out of place. We'll have to excavate to know for sure."

A few hours of daylight remained, and Tomás had assigned two techs to metal-detect downstream from where Jack had left off. He had Lydia sweeping for radiation with a Geiger counter. Jack would return to where his original wash emptied into the larger one and start looking for radioactivity upstream. Two additional techs would man the metal detectors, walking behind Jack. Tomás joined Perry and Pablo in the hunt for any UFO debris.

The ranch owners told Bob that burrowing rodents had been digging up odd metal fragments in their burrows, but so far nothing of the sort had been found.

About a thousand feet up the larger wash, Jack froze. The Geiger counter in his hand had stuttered, its rhythm of clicks speeding up like a nervous heartbeat as he moved forward. He raised his hand, signaling the techs to stop in their tracks, then crept forward with deliberate steps, sweeping the counter in a methodical arc to pinpoint the radiation's origin.

The clicks merged into an urgent staccato, the counter's needle jumping to a borderline dangerous level. Jack crouched down, holding the Geiger counter above the ground, moving it in tight circles until the frantic clicking reached its peak. There it was, a tiny black orb nestled in the dirt, perfect in its roundness, no larger than a pea. The Geiger counter's frantic response left no doubt this thing was pulsing with radiation. His fingers fumbled for the two-way radio, unclipping it from his belt with urgency.

"Attention," he called into the receiver, "I need everyone at my location now." He took several steps back to minimize his exposure.

The team converged on Jack's position within minutes. Tomás arrived last, his boots kicking up dust as he skidded to a halt, sweat darkening his shirt collar. Between labored breaths, he asked, "What have you found?"

Jack pointed toward a gap between two stones. "See that tiny black sphere the size of a pea? The counter's going crazy, Tomás. That thing's putting out radiation levels I've never seen before." He switched on the Geiger counter and started walking toward it.

The group tensed as the Geiger counter's frantic clicking filled the air. Tomás stepped forward, his hand outstretched toward Jack. "Let me see that," he said, taking the device and studying its reading with narrowed eyes. "Sweet Mary, mother of Jesus!" he exclaimed.

Pablo spoke up from behind. "Could it be plutonium?"

Tomás shook his head. "I do not know, amigo. Whatever it is, we have to be very careful with it. I need a lead bag and a set of tweezers. We're going to get this contained, and we'll need to send it back to Little Rock right away." As he picked up the object, he remarked, "This is heavy. It's extremely dense." He placed it in the safety of the protective pouch and turned to face the group.

Tomás raised his palm toward the technicians. "Stay put. We need to check what's ahead before any of you guys move forward." He pivoted to Jack and the others, the lead bag dangling from his fingers. "Everyone takes a counter. We spread out, move slowly, eyes on the readings. No more surprises like this little nightmare," he said, giving the bag a gentle shake that belied its potential danger. He grimaced. "If there's a bigger piece out there, we'd be walking into a radiation field that could fry us."

The group spread out in a line, moving slowly upstream. They had gone just twenty steps before Perry called out from the far right-hand side of the group. "I'm getting some elevated readings. Looks like it's coming from over here," he said, gesturing to an area out of the dry stream bed.

Everyone stopped in their tracks and watched as he climbed up onto the bank and started walking forward. About five feet in, Perry squatted down and swept the meter back and forth. "There's something over here, and I think it's buried."

Pablo and Jack made their way over to him, and as he dug, Jack used his Geiger counter to sweep the small dirt pile. Finally, the culprit was revealed. A small, dull, silvery piece of metal with a slight curve to it, about an inch long and as thin as an eggshell.

The Geiger counter stuttered over the metal, its rhythm slower than the frantic drumbeat of the black sphere, but still fast enough to make Jack's pulse quicken.

Farther up the dry streambed, Lydia hollered, "Over here! I've found another one of those black spheres, radiation levels matching the first!"

The next fifteen minutes yielded two more spheres and four radioactive metal fragments, each marked with a fluttering green flag. Tomás squinted at the darkening horizon then checked his watch. "That's it for today," he announced, wiping sweat from his brow. "Daylight's almost gone, and Little Rock needs to know about this."

Bob was on the phone when a sharp rap at the door preceded Patty's anxious face in the doorway. "I have Tomás on line two," she said, her voice tight. "Says it's urgent, a significant development down in Coyame."

He held up one finger to Patty, wrapped up his call with a clipped goodbye then jabbed the blinking button for the other line. "Talk to me, Tomás."

"Bob, you won't believe what we found," he said, his voice crackling with tension over the line. "We've uncovered something that defies explanation: four small black spheres, each barely the size of a pea, emitting radiation levels that sent our Geiger counters into a frenzy. These objects are emitting levels that put us at significant risk with prolonged exposure. I've zipped them in a lead-lined bag for now. We also discovered metallic debris around the site, unusual alloy fragments giving off lower radiation signatures than the spheres, but still concerning. We don't know what they are. I've never seen anything like it before."

"Are we looking at something from the UFO?" asked Bob.

"I've no idea what else it could be from. They're not natural, and I can't imagine a man-made item resembling anything like it," he said.

Bob gripped the phone tighter. "We've got Tusk back from maintenance. I can have it waiting for you in Presidio by eight a.m. tomorrow."

"Thank God," Tomás exhaled. "These samples need to be in a proper containment facility. But will we have any issues getting these across the border?"

Bob gave that some thought. "Shit, we might. Pack everything and have it ready for transport. We're bringing it all back to Little Rock. Maybe we need to fly the jet to Chihuahua and have you meet us there. Oh, and one last thing. You should have a backhoe on the site sometime tomorrow morning with an operator and an assistant. We've got permission to dig, but only right around the area you're calling ground zero."

"That's good news. You know, with all of that going on, we could use a couple more scientists on site. We haven't had any luck identifying these rodent burrows we've heard about, so maybe Dr. Winters could come in handy with that. And maybe Dr. Bowden could be useful in finding UFO material?"

"Okay, I'll take that into consideration. Call me at six a.m., and I'll let you know where the jet is headed."

Jess paced from the kitchen to the living room, checking her phone every few minutes. Jack had been calling nightly right around this time. When the phone rang, she snatched it up without looking at the screen, only to hear Bob's voice instead of Jack's on the other end.

"Jessica, it's Bob. How are you tonight?" he asked.

"Fine, I was just watching a little television," she lied.

"Listen, we've had some major developments down in Mexico and could use another scientist or two on site. How would you like to fly down there early tomorrow morning? We have Tusk back. Maintenance has been completed, so it will be a direct flight. I realize this is short notice, but Tomás requested you and Dr. Winters."

Jess gripped the phone, her pulse quickening at the thought of not needing to be separated from Jack for a month. She took a deep breath to steady her voice. "Yes, I'd be very interested in joining the team in Mexico."

"Excellent. You might lose a few hours of sleep tonight, but be at the office at five-thirty, and we will get you and Dr. Winters over to the jet waiting at Little Rock National. We'll go wheels up at six a.m. I'm going along for the ride, but I won't be staying."

After hanging up with Bob, Jess clutched the phone to her chest, a smile spreading across her face. Jack's temporary exile to Mexico wouldn't be so bad after all. She was thinking of calling him herself when the device suddenly rang. It was Jack.

"Hey, honey! Guess what? I'm coming to Mexico tomorrow with Lynley. We're going to join you guys in Coyame," she gushed.

"Wait, you're coming down here? Tomorrow? How?"

Jess couldn't suppress a smile. "Tusk is back in service. We leave at six tomorrow morning."

"Where are you flying into? Presidio?" he asked. "Because there isn't an airfield anywhere near here, especially one that can handle a small jet."

"Honestly, I don't know. Bob called and told me to be ready to fly out at six in the morning."

Jack's voice softened. "I thought we were going to be apart for a month or more. This is fantastic!"

"See you tomorrow!"

Bob had directed the aircraft to Chihuahua. He didn't want to risk bringing radioactive materials across a U.S. border crossing.

Jack had volunteered to bring the samples to the airport and to receive Dr. Bowden and Dr. Winters.

The jet's wheels touched the tarmac, and now the aircraft was taxiing toward the private terminal where they'd stretch their legs during refueling. Bob checked his watch. Jack ought to have arrived with the samples already.

As soon as the cabin door opened and the stairs were deployed, the group deplaned. Sure enough, Jack was inside waiting for them. He extended a hand and said, "Good work, Jack. I heard you discovered the first sphere."

"Thanks. These are puzzling," he said, motioning to the lead-lined bags as he handed them to Bob. "We don't know what they're made of. According to Tomás, the decay rate suggests these spheres were originally much larger and emitted higher radiation levels, assuming they are from the UFO crash. Of course, we have some other items in there which are equally puzzling. Some make no sense at all," he said, handing them to Bob.

"I'll get Drs. Hao and Mokena on it right away. If they can't crack the code, nobody can."

At that moment, Jack caught sight of Jess walking toward him, beside Lynley. He nodded to them. "Welcome to Mexico, Jessica, Lynley."

The corner of Jess's mouth twitched upward. "Thank you, Jack," she said, her voice carrying a hint of eagerness that hadn't been there before. "Mexico is exactly where I need to be right now."

Everyone retreated to the private terminal, where they continued discussing the ongoing case while the plane was refueling. Bob's phone rang, and he stepped aside to take the call.

He completed his call when the pilot approached with a thumbs-up gesture. "Aircraft is topped off and ready for departure, sir.

"Okay, everyone, it looks like it's time for me to head back. I'll get these samples to the lab, and hopefully we can find some answers."

Back at the ranch outside Coyame, José led the way as a dust-covered pickup hauling digging equipment rumbled toward ground zero. Tomás had sent everyone else out searching the dry streambeds with metal detectors and Geiger counters, while he remained behind to supervise the excavation.

The truck carrying the backhoe tilted precariously at one point on the deeply rutted road. José had jumped out of his vehicle and was waving his arms, trying to get the driver's attention, shouting, "Aguas! Cuidado!" José's heart was in his throat as one set of wheels lifted off the ground. After the white-knuckle navigation through the worst sections, they finally reached the site and eased the heavy machinery down the flatbed's ramp.

Addressing Tomás, José called out, "Okay, amigo! I'll leave it to you. When these guys depart, make sure they close the gate up front." Tomás waved as he left and began discussing the plan with the excavation crew.

The assistant spray-painted many markings on the ground, which apparently made sense to the backhoe operator, because Tomás couldn't decipher them.

Slowly, methodically, they started peeling back layers of dirt as Tomás kept a close watch.

Jack pulled up in the SUV. His hopes of sitting beside Jess were quickly dashed as Lynley swooped in and settled in the front passenger seat. "I get carsick on bumpy roads and have to ride in the front," she said quickly. "I know you'd rather sit with her, but I don't want to get sick."

"It's all paved highway to Coyame from here, Lynley," said Jack. "You rode in the back seat in Blythe, and those were dirt roads there, and you didn't get sick."

"This isn't my first time in the Mexican backcountry. We start hitting bumps, and I'm puking my guts out," she said.

"Well, I don't want to see that."

As they made their way out of town, he caught Jess's eye in the rearview mirror, exchanging a private smile that made his pulse quicken. The crash site beckoned with its mysteries, but his thoughts kept drifting to later tonight when they'd finally have time alone. Two days apart had felt like an eternity, leaving an ache in his chest that only her presence could soothe.

Jack stopped at the hotel so Jess and Lynley could unpack and freshen up then drove them to ground zero. As he made his way down the rutted road, he could see a rectangular pit where the backhoe clawed through the earth. They must have found something, because Tomás was now joined by Lydia, Perry, and Pablo.

As they exited the vehicle, they exchanged brief pleasantries, and Jack asked, "Find anything yet?"

Tomás had a grim expression. "Bones, lots of bones. I think several men were thrown in here. I'm not sure if they were dead or alive when that happened, but they were burned extensively."

"Holy shit," Jack muttered.

Several of the bones had been pulled aside, and Lynley knelt beside to examine one. She was a biologist, so the sight of death didn't bother her much. "What's the deal with these pockmarks all over the bones? Did you guys notice that?"

"Yeah, we did," said Tomás. "We were hoping you might tell us more about that. Did these guys have a disease, or could that be from the fire?"

"I've never seen anything like this before, and it's not from the fire. I'll need to get a closer look using some of the equipment I brought." She continued to scan over the pile of bones when she pointed toward one of them and exclaimed, "What is that?"

"What's what?" asked Tomás.

"That bone there doesn't look like a human bone, and at first glance it doesn't look like any animal that should be in this part of the world either. The proportions and sizing are all wrong, and I can tell right away the density is very different. If this were human, the bone material would primarily be composed of calcium and phosphate. There may be calcium and phosphate in here, but the proportions are all off," she said.

"Do you mean to tell me you've been here less than five minutes and have discovered an alien bone?" Tomás asked incredulously.

"I'm not sure yet, but this isn't right. And notice that it doesn't have the pockmarks like all the rest do."

Tomás looked around the group, astonished faces staring back at him. "Okay, well, do what you need to do to test it. We'll continue with the excavation."

Jack interjected, "Hey, I thought there was something radioactive down there."

"There is, and we are getting close to it. We need to be careful."

With the technicians' help, Lynley erected a portable field laboratory beneath a canvas shelter. She arranged her makeshift workspace, two collapsible tables flanked by folding chairs, while an array of scientific instruments awaited her investigation. Tomás watched as she performed a series of unfamiliar procedures, her hands moving with practiced precision over equipment he couldn't name. Though the tests were beyond his expertise, her confident actions reassured him that if answers existed, she would find them.

After the team identified the non-human bone, Tomás signaled for the backhoe operator to stop all operations. Its mechanical arm had nearly extended to its maximum reach anyway, so they couldn't go much deeper even if they wanted to.

The possibility of additional non-human remains lurking beneath the surface sent a chill through him, and he couldn't risk damaging them with the excavator. From this point forward, careful hands and shovels would replace the backhoe. Many hours of daylight remained, and Tomás intended to mobilize every available technician for the painstaking task. The radiation source lurking beneath their feet was a concern. They'd need to keep close tabs on their progress. There was something significant and dangerous down below.

Next, Jack teamed up with Pablo and Perry. The three of them spread out to search for scattered remains of what might once have been an otherworldly craft. In the area where the first radioactive sphere was found, they successfully mapped a crossing of the dry streambed at nearly a forty-five-degree angle, about forty feet wide, that contained a treasure trove of artifacts. They were retracing their steps eastward to see how far the debris field extended.

Next, they planned to follow the craft's likely westward trajectory from the streambed, hoping to pinpoint the final impact site where the UFO had crashed to Earth. Jack could picture military personnel working at a frantic pace, hauling away anything substantial enough to load onto trucks but missing the scattered pieces that blended with the desert floor. What the government had overlooked would now fill in crucial gaps in their investigation.

Their collection grew by the hour. Fragments of unknown metal and composite materials littered their sorting tables, while the Geiger counter's persistent clicking marked the location of each new radioactive sphere they unearthed from the desert floor. Jack remembered his earlier modest hope of finding even a single piece of evidence. Now, surrounded by tables laden with otherworldly debris, he realized how dramatically their expectations had been surpassed.

The day was growing short in Coyame, and Tomás had asked everyone to gather at ground zero for an end-of-shift briefing. The first report was from Pablo about the artifacts and the extent of the debris field that had been mapped. Next, Tomás gave his report to the group.

"We have recovered many additional bones, several intact skulls, and numerous fragments of bone. No more non-human remains that I'm aware of, but we still have quite a way to go. The source of radiation remains a major concern of mine, but it appears to be buried deeper than we've gone. As much as I hate to do this, I think we need to get Dr. Hodges down here. I know he has a rather... Well, he's the kind of man who corrects your grammar and tells you your methodology is flawed before you've even finished explaining it."

Before Tomás could complete his spiel, Perry blurted out, "He's an asshole!" Everyone laughed.

Tomás continued, "Yes, that may be true, but he is a nuclear expert, and whatever is down there has me concerned. For all I know, it's some mysterious alien power source that could fry us all in an instant. I think we need his expertise."

Next up was Lynley. "I have two areas of focus right now. The non-human bone, which I believe may be the equivalent of a femur, and the pockmarks on the human bones. The non-human bone's composition is unlike anything I've ever seen. We won't know exactly what that is until we get it back to Little Rock, but the ratios of calcium and phosphates are way off, and there are elements in there that aren't present in humans or any animal I'm familiar with."

Pablo said quickly, "So are you saying it's not from a terrestrial species?"

"I think it would be premature to make that conclusion at this time, but that's possible. If we assume it's from a bipedal life form, and it's the equivalent of a human femur, this bone would be capable of supporting upright mobility in an environment that has five to six times the gravity of Earth. Its density is remarkable, like petrified wood compared to balsa, and the internal lattice structure visible in the cross-section resembles a honeycomb reinforced with something I can't even identify."

The assembled group exchanged wide-eyed glances, their whispered exclamations creating a ripple of excitement through the gathering.

"And that's only the first thing I'm focusing on. Every single human bone we've pulled out of this pit is covered with strange pockmarks. My primary thought was that an ionizing beam, perhaps a weapon, had been used. But the more I look at it, I don't know," she said. "If I had a complete body to analyze, I might find some answers. As it stands, I don't have enough to go on. I hate to bring this up, but there is another possibility. A remote possibility, but I would be irresponsible if I didn't mention it. There is a chance this was caused by a biological pathogen, though I can't think of any known terrestrial virus or bacteria that could do anything like this."

Lynley continued, "I just remembered something. Years ago, prehistoric remains turned up in Siberia with markings almost identical to these. The leading theory was a now-extinct virus. Perhaps from a comet or meteorite."

"So, since we may be dealing with an alien species here...it's something to keep in mind," she said.

B ob had brought a cache of recovered objects back from the project site in Coyame. Of principal interest were three categories of artifacts.

First, obsidian-like orbs no larger than garden peas; second, metallic shards with the delicate thinness of cracked eggshells; and third, several nuggets of metal that appeared to have liquefied and reformed. The Geiger counter ticked across all specimens, but when passed over the black spheres, it erupted into a frantic chatter that sent everyone reaching for their lead-lined gloves.

Dr. Thabo Mokena was a South African materials scientist who was working with Dr. Chris Bellini and Dr. Brian Hodges in the nuclear lab, trying to determine the composition of the substances. Dr. Chen Hao was examining their properties in the chemistry lab.

Chen had already performed density and magnetic tests on the items before retreating to his lab.

Thabo thought the melted nuggets were likely magnesium or a magnesium alloy. He was preparing the sample for analysis with the X-ray fluorescence spectrometer, or XRF, which would bombard it with X-rays to identify the elements present. It was a fast, nondestructive process, and he was looking forward to seeing if his guess was correct.

While he was awaiting results, he stepped over to the chemistry lab to see how Chen was doing, where he was performing a comprehensive chemical analysis on small pieces of the samples.

A few minutes later, the XRF was complete, and Thabo's eyebrows raised at the findings. It was an alloy of magnesium, scandium, and lithium with trace elements of gadolinium and yttrium. They were shocked. The composition defied both natural formation and current metallurgical capabilities, a material that had no business existing on Earth. An alloy with this makeup had no terrestrial explanation for its presence in the barren expanse of the Chihuahuan Desert.

He called Chris over to his station.

"How is this alloy possible?" asked Chris. "Are you sure this is correct?"

"Yes, I am. This is an alloy that does not exist on Earth," Thabo said.

"We need to run this through gamma spectroscopy so we can get the specific isotopes," said Chris, shaking with excitement.

In the adjacent chemistry lab, Chen tested the peculiar alloy Thabo had identified. After hearing about the impossible combination of magnesium, scandium, and lithium, Chen's experiments had revealed equally baffling properties. When he applied an acetylene torch to the sample, the metal refused to ignite, defying the characteristic flammability of magnesium. Even more remarkably, when subjected to temperatures exceeding 300 degrees Celsius, the alloy maintained structural integrity that would have reduced conventional metals to malleable putty.

Unlike typical magnesium, which shatters under pressure, Chen discovered this alloy could be bent, twisted, and manipulated without breaking, a property that should have been impossible under standard laboratory conditions.

The aerospace industry would pay billions for this material if they could reverse-engineer its manufacturing process. A lightweight, heat-resistant, non-flammable, and malleable magnesium alloy would revolutionize everything from commercial aircraft to space exploration overnight.

Dr. Brian Hodges hunched over his workstation, scowling at the readout from the mass spectrometer. The black spheres had defied categorization across seven different analytical protocols. Their density measurements placed them well beyond any element on the periodic table, suggesting something that would make headlines in every scientific journal on Earth, if he could only determine what the hell they were made of.

The data suggested a solution beyond the boundaries of known physics, an element occupying theoretical space that most colleagues dismissed as speculative fantasy. Nuclear theory predicted an "island of stability" where superheavy elements might exist with atomic weights exceeding 164, far beyond anything ever synthesized in a laboratory.

Yet the readings from these obsidian spheres aligned with those predictions. Dr. Hodges felt his pulse quicken. He could be staring at the first tangible evidence of that theoretical island.

He scribbled on his notepad, double-checking the decay curve calculations. If his math was correct, and it always was, the mysterious element would have a half-life of approximately 1.7 years.

He removed his glasses and pinched the bridge of his nose. The academic paper documenting this discovery would not be forthcoming soon.

Dr. Hodges sketched a hasty regression curve on his notepad. Based on the half-life and current size, he calculated backward to 1974, the year of the alleged Coyame incident. The implications were staggering. At the time of impact, the sphere would have been roughly the diameter of a bowling ball.

Could he be looking at the fuel element used by these cosmic visitors?

Across the laboratory, Thabo and Chris were now hunched over the eggshell-thin metallic fragments, their instruments probing for secrets locked within the impossibly light, strong, yet ductile material.

The XRF was giving them some very puzzling results. Only two elements were being returned: hydrogen and lithium. The only known compound containing those elements was lithium hydride, LiH. Yet this was not lithium hydride, a highly reactive crystalline solid.

"What do you think we are dealing with here, Chris?" asked Thabo.

Chris's sudden laugh earned him a blank stare from Thabo. "Remember that theoretical physics conference in Kyoto? There were those two researchers presenting on metallic hydrogen, pure speculation at the time." He leaned closer to the sample, his reflection distorted on its surface. "But what if this is it? A lithium-metallic hydrogen alloy? The technology to create an alloy like this shouldn't exist, not on this planet anyway."

Thabo said, "How would we even go about confirming something like that?"

Chris thrust his hands deep into his lab coat pockets and exhaled a long, defeated sigh. "I don't know, Thabo. I don't know."

José had been monitoring the group's progress from afar and would get a complete report tonight. The gringos didn't know it, but both of the men on the excavating crew worked for his boss too. Apparently, Bob had never discussed the identity of the nameless and faceless landowner. He probably didn't want them to know about the deal he made with *la Alianza del Pacífico Rojo*, the Alliance of the Red Pacific cartel, or just the "Reds."

If anything of value was taken from the land, half the money went straight to his boss, the infamous Rodrigo Salazar Vega, better known as "El Toro."

José's burner phone buzzed twice; the signal that El Toro was calling, not requesting.

He stepped away and pressed the phone to his ear. "Jefe."

"How much longer?" the voice on the other end asked.

"They are making progress. The backhoe operator says they are close to something significant underground. The radiation concerns them, but they are pushing forward."

A pause. "Radiation?"

"Sí. The gringos have Geiger counters. They found small

spheres, black colored, dense, the size of a pinto. Very hot. They sealed them in lead bags and shipped them north."

"And the bone?" El Toro said it quietly, as if savoring the word.

José glanced back at the barn where the two excavation workers sat around the table, their voices low. "One of their biologists, the woman, examined it for hours. She says it is not human, and it's not from any animal in this part of the world. The density is strange, something she has never seen before." He hesitated. "She believes it may be from something that did not originate on this planet."

The silence on the line stretched long enough that José pulled the phone away to check the connection.

"How much," El Toro finally said, "would something like that be worth?"

"I made some inquiries. Private collectors, the kind who do not ask questions about provenance. There are men in Hong Kong, in Dubai, in São Paulo who would pay." José paused. "Millions, jefe. Perhaps more, depending on what the scientists ultimately determine it to be."

"Then I want it." The tone remained level. "And whatever else they pull out of that ground."

"There is a complication. The team is larger than expected. Eleven, possibly twelve people on site at any given time. Scientists, technicians. Some of them are not soft."

"That is not a complication," El Toro said. "That is a detail. One more day, José. Let them finish digging. Let them do the hard work of identifying what is valuable and what is not." Another pause. "Then clean it up. All of it. I want no loose ends walking back across that border."

José stared at the ground. "And the radioactive material? The spheres they sent north are gone, but if there is more underground..."

"Leave the radiation. I have no use for something that will kill my men." A dry sound that might have been a laugh. "The bone, the artifacts, whatever currency this American billionaire's team has decided is worth shipping home, that is what I want. The rest can stay buried."

"Understood."

"José." The voice sharpened just slightly. "The scientists? They are guests on my land until tomorrow night. After that, they are a liability. Make sure your men understand the difference."

The line went dead.

José stood in the warm desert dark for a moment, listening to the insects and the sound of the excavation crew's conversation. He thought about the American meteorologist, the one who spoke decent Spanish and made the others laugh. And the woman scientist who had held the alien bone up to the light.

He put the phone back in his pocket and walked back inside.

The next morning, the group was back at it again with fresh orders from Bob. He wanted them to excavate toward the radiation source. If they could figure out what it was and clear it out of the way, he would be much more comfortable with them sifting through the dirt looking for additional alien bones.

Tomás had the crew working toward that goal this morning with shovels and wheelbarrows. Scientists and techs alike toiled under the blistering sun, except for the three ladies. Truth be told, Tomás came from a culture that didn't favor women in those roles, though he recognized American values were different. Instead, he insisted that the women continue working on examining the human remains and the alien bone. Some scientists back in Little Rock insisted on using clinical terminology like "unidentified osseous fragment," but Tomás wasn't having any of it. It was an alien bone, plain and simple.

Hours had passed, and the sun was almost directly overhead when Perry made contact with the object. A dull metal surface emerged from the soil, not some exotic alien alloy but what looked like ordinary steel, pitted and oxidized from decades in the ground.

For the next hour, several of them brushed away soil until the object's full contours emerged.

He froze, his brush in hand. "Holy fuck!" he exclaimed. The unmistakable cylindrical shape with its distinctive nose cone told a story none of them wanted to hear. They were looking at a nuclear warhead.

They had been taking readings with the Geiger counter throughout the excavation, and the numbers were higher than they were comfortable with but not yet in the danger zone.

Everyone stood frozen, staring at the object as if their brains couldn't quite process what their eyes were seeing. Alien bones? Sure. Strange artifacts? Absolutely. But a nuclear warhead buried in Mexican soil? That was beyond their wildest expectations.

The bomb looked to be about seven feet long with faded stenciling on the exterior. Despite the oxidized metal, Cyrillic lettering was still visible. Perry stooped to brush off a caked area, revealing smaller lettering. He used some water from his canteen to make it clearer.

"This is an old Soviet nuclear device. Back in college, I had a roommate who was a Russian language major. I had to help him study. I think I recognize some of these letters here. If I'm right, the yield looks like…" There was a dramatic pause while Perry continued to buff away at the faded lettering with his fingers. He let out a low whistle. "100 kilotons, if my Russian is correct. That's at least five times greater than the shit we dropped on Japan."

Pablo turned to the others. "So the American military was never here. It must have been the Mexicans who made the recovery. That makes sense. If the Americans were here, there wouldn't be so many small artifacts left behind. They picked Roswell clean back in '47. But where did they get a Russian nuke? And why is it still here, undetonated?"

The group concluded that the Mexicans must have found extraterrestrial remains but lacked the proper containment to transport them safely. Their solution? Bury the evidence, burn what they could, then when that wasn't thorough enough, leave behind a nuclear device programmed to vaporize every cell and trace. A desperate attempt at sterilization through atomic fire.

But why leave it here? They must have aborted the mission, a last-minute stand-down order from Mexico City, but that didn't explain why they'd abandon a weapon of mass destruction in the desert.

The human remains presented another mystery. Had these people been abducted, subjected to extraterrestrial examination, and died aboard the craft before it crashed? The specifics remained frustratingly unclear. Dr. Winters frowned, tapping her pen against her clipboard. She wasn't buying the abduction theory, but the alternatives swimming in her mind seemed equally far-fetched.

They retreated to the shade of the equipment tent, passing around lukewarm water bottles as the reality of their discovery settled over them. Jack wiped sweat from his forehead with his bandana then gestured toward the excavation. "So we've got an abandoned nuclear warhead sitting on Mexican soil. Anyone want to explain how we're supposed to secure that thing before some random guy stumbles across our dig site?"

Pablo wiped dust from his hands onto his jeans. "If that weapon hasn't gone off in a quarter century, I doubt tonight's the night it goes," he said with an uneasy shrug. "I say we leave it alone."

Jack opened his mouth, but Tomás cut him off with a raised palm. "I hear what you're saying, but look at that thing, corroded, unstable. It stays buried. You want to bounce a decades-old nuke around in the back of our truck over these washboard roads? We can cover it up with a foot or two of loose soil for the night, but we need to leave it in place."

The Aplin case gnawed at Hendricus like an ulcer. Every instinct in his bones told him the "Chinese spy satellite" explanation was bureaucratic horseshit, and the abrupt termination of his investigation only deepened his suspicions. Furthermore, he wasn't happy about Bob being involved with a U.S. senator.

Bob had dismissed the store clerk's account without a second thought. "Just some local yokel making up stories," he'd said with a wave of his hand. But Hendricus couldn't shake what the woman had told him, how she'd been halfway through her cigarette at 2 a.m. when the rumble of engines drew her attention to the road, where military Humvees flanked an oversized semi hauling something massive under a tarp as it lumbered north onto Highway 10 toward the interstate.

That night he called Bill Naden. They'd worked the initial investigation together, and Hendricus knew exactly which buttons to push. Ten minutes later, Bill was in.

The plan was to have Bill drop him nearby, and he would sneak in to investigate the site. There was a risk that he might get arrested by the sheriff for trespassing, but he had to know what crashed in those woods.

An hour later, Bill's SUV crawled along the dark country road, headlights off for the final stretch. "Give me two hours," Hendricus whispered as he slipped out, night vision goggles fitted over his head, and a flashlight clutched in his palm. "Then get the hell out if I'm not back."

He slowly moved forward across a pasture, his sights set on a line of trees nearly six hundred yards in the distance. Little did he know that a U.S. KH-11 CRYSTAL spy satellite was watching the property from two hundred miles above his head right now.

Hendricus reached the tree line and slipped between two wide oaks. Through the green haze of his night-vision goggles, the forest materialized as ghostly silhouettes against the darkness. He cursed under his breath as his boot sank into unseen undergrowth with a soft squelch.

Something snagged his pant leg, a blackberry vine. He yanked free and pushed forward, wincing as thorns raked across his calf. Three steps later, a greenbrier snagged him again, this time tearing through denim. Warm wetness trickled down his shin as he pressed deeper into the tangle.

Fifty yards in, Hendricus's boot caught on nothing. The thorny undergrowth had vanished. Through his goggles, he saw charred stumps where bushes should be, their remains crumbling to ash at his touch.

Blackened pillars that used to be trees towered along the edge. His boots crunched across glass-like earth as he approached a depression in the ground that stretched wider than a basketball court. It sloped down until the bottom disappeared in shadow beneath the green glow of his vision.

Whatever had scorched this ground hadn't occurred because of a fallen satellite.

~

Bill checked his watch for the fourth time. Forty minutes. Hendricus had said two hours, but something about the stillness coming from those trees was wrong in a way he couldn't articulate. He remained parked at the end of the dirt track with the engine off, window down, listening to the Arkansas night: crickets, frogs, a distant dog, and the occasional rush of a vehicle on the highway half a mile east. Normal sounds, the kind that could lull you into a false sense of security.

Then they stopped.

Not gradually, the way sounds fade when a storm front moves through. All at once, as if someone had thrown a switch. The crickets went silent first, followed by the frogs a few seconds later. Bill sat up straighter in his seat.

He raised the night vision scope Hendricus had left him and swept it across the field toward the tree line. Nothing moved. The perimeter of the forest sat six hundred yards away, a dark wall against a slightly less dark sky.

He was about to lower the scope when he caught a glimpse of something. A halo of displaced air to the north, low and fast, moving without sound. He adjusted the focus. Two shapes resolved out of the darkness, matte black against black, rotors turning but producing almost nothing in the way of noise. Not silent exactly, but wrong: a faint mechanical whisper where there should have been the heavy beat of helicopter blades.

Bill held his breath.

They came in low over the far tree line and settled into the field between the road and the woods with rapid precision that spoke of many rehearsals. No running lights. No identifying markings that he could see through the scope. The downdraft flattened the dead grass in a wide circle as the skids touched down, and before the dust had even begun to settle, figures were already moving: dark-clad, helmeted, weapons at the low ready, spreading out in a practiced fan toward the tree line.

He counted eight. Then four more from the second aircraft. Twelve total.

His hand went to his phone before he remembered. No devices. Hendricus had been explicit. If anything electronic was transmitting from their location, whoever was watching the property would know within minutes. Bill set the phone back on the seat and gripped the scope with both hands, his knuckles pale.

The figures disappeared into the trees.

He counted seconds in his head, gave up around ninety, and started counting again. The night vision scope showed him nothing but the two helicopters sitting in the field, rotors still turning at idle, and two figures who had remained outside as perimeter. They stood completely still, facing outward, rifles across their chests. Not military police, Bill thought. Not the National Guard, not the regular Army.

Six minutes by his watch. Then movement at the tree line.

The figures emerged in a cluster, and in the center of the cluster was Hendricus. Bill could tell it was him by the height, by the slight forward lean that was just his natural posture, though now that lean was being assisted by two sets of hands gripping his arms, his wrists pinned behind him. His head was down. He was on his feet but not quite under his own power, his legs moving but not setting the pace.

They crossed the field quickly and efficiently. One of the perimeter men fell in behind the group. The other swept a final arc with his weapon before following.

Hendricus was lifted through the side door of the nearest helicopter. The door slid shut as the rotors increased their pitch, that strange, near-silent whine building to something just below what it should have been. Both aircraft lifted simultaneously, banked north, and were gone. No lights or radio chatter that Bill could hear. Within twenty seconds, there was nothing in the field but flattened grass and the sound of crickets beginning to chirp again.

Bill sat motionless for a full minute, scope still raised, as if the helicopters might come back into frame.

They didn't.

He lowered the scope slowly and looked at his hands. They were steady, which surprised him. His mind, however, was running through everything at once. *Should I call someone? Who? And what would he even say?*

He started the engine, kept the headlights off, and eased the SUV backward down the track until he reached the county road. Only then did he turn on the lights. He allowed himself to think. Whoever these people were, they hadn't been surprised to find Hendricus in those woods. They already knew he was there.

Bill arrived at the office early, his stomach in knots. This news might cost him his job. Still, there was no way to deliver the grim update about Hendricus except face-to-face.

He stepped off the elevator onto the first floor, where Patty sat guarding the entrance to Bob's inner sanctum. He managed a tepid smile in her direction. "Is the boss available?"

"He's a little busy this morning, Bill. Do you have an appointment?"

He leaned across her desk. "It's about Hendricus," he said. "There's been an incident."

Patty's eyes widened. She rose from her chair and ushered him toward the heavy wooden door, her hand light but insistent against his back. Two sharp knocks later, he stood before Bob.

Bill stammered through the events of the previous night, his voice dropping to a whisper as he described the stealth helicopters that had descended and spirited Hendricus away. Bob's expression hardened, then slackened, then hardened again as he listened, the tension obvious in his facial expressions.

Bill swallowed hard, the lie sticking in his throat like a fishbone. "Sir, I only realized at the last minute, right before leaving Hendricus in that field, that this operation wasn't sanctioned. Had I known earlier, I never would have taken part."

Bob's face darkened to a dangerous crimson. "That's the flimsiest excuse I've heard in twenty years of management," he said. "Get out. Don't come back until I contact you and don't expect a paycheck while you wait."

Pat leveraged a connection at the Palo Verde Nuclear Generating Station, a security technician who owed a friend a favor. Over a round of cold ones at the Desert Mirage Bar, he convinced him to review archived surveillance footage from the night of Garrett's disappearance.

Pat's friend called three days later. "You need to see this." The recording revealed a luminous object hovering over Garrett's last-known location in the time frame when he disappeared.

Armed with this evidence, Pat persuaded Dr. Henry Benton to give hypnotic regression another chance.

After collecting Dr. Benton from his flight at Sky Harbor, Pat and Steve drove him to the Scottsdale resort where a suite had been reserved for them. They'd asked for a suite specifically, ensuring it met all of Dr. Benton's exacting conditions: blackout curtains, minimal outside noise, and lights that can be dimmed. Garrett paced inside, having arrived an hour earlier to prepare himself for what was to come.

After brief pleasantries and settling in, Dr. Benton started the hypnotic regression.

The recorder clicked as he set it on the side table, its small red light blinking to life. He eased into the leather chair opposite Garrett, who was on the couch. He had a thin blanket over his lap. A single lamp glowed from the corner.

Pat and Steve had retreated to the adjoining space, leaving them alone. Dr. Benton removed the cap from his pen and balanced his notepad on one knee.

"Breathe in slowly through your nose, Garrett. That's it. Now hold...and release through your mouth." He watched Garrett's chest rise and fall. "Once more. Perfect. Let everything else fall away. No problems to solve, no questions to answer. Your breath and the sound of my voice are filling this space between us."

The grip Garrett had on the blanket relaxed. The rigid set of his jaw softened, the tension melting away like ice under a gentle flame. He fought the process initially, as he had during their previous session.

Benton's voice flowed like water over smooth stones. "As I count backward from ten," he said, "each number will carry you deeper into that space between waking and dreaming. You won't sleep. Your mind stays alert, responsive, but your body will surrender its tensions. Ten..." Garrett's eyelids grew heavy. "Nine...eight..." The cushions seemed to soften beneath him. "Seven...six..." His arms melted into the couch. "Five...four..."

The outside world ceased to exist. "Three...two..." Benton's voice became the only link to consciousness. "One."

The suite was dead quiet now. The only sound was Garrett's breathing as his body surrendered to the trance, eyelids motionless, mouth slack with relaxation.

Benton leaned forward. "That's it," he murmured. "Now picture yourself at the top of a staircase, solid beneath your feet, warmly lit. Down below waits your sanctuary. A place of absolute security." His cadence slowed. "We'll descend together. Each step carries you deeper. Shall we begin?" He guided Garrett downward with gentle verbal nudges. "Another step...and another," until they'd reached the bottom. Then he fell silent, allowing half a minute to pass unmarked while he floated in the depths of his trance.

Benton's voice lowered to a gentle command. "Return to that night on the Arizona mountainside, Garrett. You're watching the power plant from above. Open your memory and describe what surrounds you."

Garrett's brow creased slightly.

His voice emerged, distant and monotone. "Not much light. Enough moonlight to make out the hillside. Down below, I can see the power plant, all those lights. Steam rising from the squat cooling towers. Boulder under me. Trail nearby. Binoculars in hand. Been watching for hours already."

"Why were you there, Garrett?"

"Days earlier...we were there observing the plant. A glowing orb appeared, hanging motionless above the cooling towers. Orange-white glow. Not aircraft. No helicopter moves like that: instant acceleration, no sound." His throat worked visibly. "Security patrol almost nabbed us. Everyone scattered, but I couldn't let it go, so I returned alone for several nights after that. Just me, binoculars, flashlight. Waited for hours in the dark. Watching."

Benton leaned closer. "Tell me what you witnessed that night, Garrett, before everything changed. Did you see something?"

"Yeah, I did," he said. "A pinprick at first, out where the mountains meet the sky. So faint I blinked three times, thinking my eyes were playing tricks on me." His breathing quickened. "Then it... swelled. No wing lights. No blinking. No sound. This silent thing bearing down. My legs went watery. I fumbled with the binoculars, almost dropping them. And through the lens... God, I'd spent months praying to see something up close again, and suddenly all I wanted was to be anywhere else."

"What did it look like through the binoculars?"

"A perfect circle, but the outline...wouldn't stay still in my vision, like trying to focus on something underwater. And there was this glow that came from inside." He paused for several seconds. "Then it...hung there maybe four hundred yards away. Suspended. Watching me the way I was watching it."

"And then?"

"My flashlight died at the same moment. Then came the light.

Not directed at me, more like it saturated everything. The air itself turned luminous. I tried to run. But my legs wouldn't move."

"And then?"

Garrett's expression flattened in a way that Benton associated with the moment a subject crossed a threshold, when they stopped narrating and started reliving.

"The light...it's not a beam or a spotlight. It's just...there. Everywhere. Surrounding me. And all of a sudden I'm rising. The boulder I was sitting on shrank beneath me. The whole mountainside fell away. I can see the power plant getting smaller, all those lights dwindling." He paused again. "The strangest part is I feel nothing. No terror. No panic. It's like someone reached inside me and flipped a switch, disconnecting whatever part of me should be screaming right now."

"You're doing well. Keep breathing. What happens next?"

"The air bites at my skin. I'm in some kind of chamber. Everything's bathed in this dim...not even light, more like an absence of total darkness. Shouldn't be able to see anything, but somehow I can." Garrett shifted his head back and forth, as if he was searching for something. "Figures. Two of them. Standing by the wall. Maybe there were three. Their gaze isn't human, not curious or emotional. It's clinical, like scientists examining a specimen."

"Can you describe them?"

His fingers dug into the blanket. "Like saplings. No, like something that only eats when it has to. Their limbs were long, and their heads..." His voice faltered. "Misshapen. Not human proportions at all. And those eyes, not the solid black ones from TV. These had... layers, like peering into a well where you can't see the bottom but know something's down there. Somehow their intentions reached me anyway. I can't explain it."

"What do they want?"

"They want me to lie down."

Benton kept his voice level. "And do you?"

"I didn't want to, but somehow I did. I'm lying flat on something that should be cold but feels like...nothing at all. One of them hovers above me, staring. Not blinking. Not speaking. There's this question burning in my throat that I can't quite remember. Then it starts, this vibration. Not something I hear exactly. More like my ribcage has become a tuning fork, humming from the inside out."

"Does anything happen while you're on the table?"

A longer pause this time, and Benton watched Garrett's face cycle through something difficult and unresolved.

"They take me somewhere else. Show me something. Not through a window; the wall just dissolves. And suddenly there's Earth, the entire planet."

"It's all there, suspended, this blue-green marble so tiny I could cup it in my hand. And I realize everyone who's ever mattered to me is on that sphere. Mom. That mutt I had in fifth grade. And it looked so fragile, like a child's toy."

The room was still.

Benton set his pen aside altogether.

After a while, he said, "Garrett, it's time to return now. I'll guide you back. Picture that staircase we discussed earlier. We'll ascend together. Each step will reconnect you to the present. The experience will remain intact but contained, no lingering presences pursuing you up those stairs, only recollections kept at a comfortable remove. Are you prepared? Take one step up. Now another..."

Benton guided him back through the numbers, his voice growing firmer with each descending digit. "When you feel anchored again, Garrett, let your eyes find the present."

Garrett remained motionless, as though returning to his body required careful navigation. When his eyelids fluttered open, he rotated his head with the deliberate caution of someone emerging from a darkened theater. Tears had gathered at the edges of his eyes, yet he seemed oblivious to their presence.

"The Earth," he said. His voice was his again, rough and quiet. "I saw the whole Earth."

Benton nodded and reached over to stop the recorder. "I know. I heard."

After a few minutes of recovery, they stepped out into the other room where Pat and Steve were waiting.

Pat gave a knowing look to Benton. "Well?"

Benton cleared his throat and met Garrett's gaze. "What you shared in there...it's significant, but I'd like your permission before discussing it with the others."

"Yeah, go ahead," said Garrett.

Benton cleared his throat. "Your experience matches patterns we've documented before. The physical descriptions, the sensation of paralysis, the examination table—these align with hundreds of accounts I've studied. What you encountered appears consistent with what researchers in our field have categorized as encounters with the elongated entities called the 'Tall Greys.'"

The room fell silent as jaws slackened and eyes widened.

Benton adjusted his glasses, his voice measured. "We've only scratched the surface of your lost time. Four days is substantial, but what we have uncovered today gives us solid ground to work from."

José stepped away from his men before dialing. El Toro answered on the second ring.

"Talk to me, José."

"The source of the radiation is not from the crash. It's not what we thought," he said. "It is an old Soviet nuclear warhead, buried deep at the site. The Americans estimate a hundred kilotons."

José was met with silence. For El Toro, silence was never empty; it was a room filling with something.

"Say that again?" asked El Toro.

"A Soviet nuclear device. An old one, it's corroded but intact. The Americans believe our military buried it here decades ago, intending to destroy the crash site and the remains. They never detonated it. They don't know why."

Another silence. When El Toro spoke again, something in his voice had shifted—not excitement exactly, but the particular focus of a man recalculating the value of everything he thought he already owned. "A functioning weapon."

"Possibly. The Americans are treating it as if it is. They are being very careful."

"José," he said. "Do you understand what I am telling you when I say that certain parties in the Middle East have been asking questions about our operation? Parties with resources and patience and no particular attachment to international law?"

"Sí, jefe."

"If we recover a Soviet warhead with clean provenance, that is recovered quietly, with no paper trail? That conversation changes completely. The alien specimens were worth millions. This..." He stopped. "This is a different category of transaction entirely."

José looked back toward the pit, where the backhoe had gone quiet. "The bone fragments and artifacts. The SPIRE team has catalogued everything. Photographs, measurements, written records."

"Then we take the records with everything else. The warhead first. But nothing leaves that site without my inventory. Every bone, every fragment, every piece of paper those scientists have touched. I want it all."

"And the Americans?"

A pause just long enough to feel deliberate. "They came a long way to do our excavating for us. I think we owe them a debt of gratitude." Another pause. "Settle it in the morning."

José understood perfectly. "It will be done."

"José." The voice sharpened in that particular way that meant the next words were the ones that actually mattered. "Do not let your men near that warhead without a specialist present. I do not want a giant hole in the Chihuahuan Desert."

The line went dead.

José stood in the dark for a moment, phone in hand. He looked up at the stars. The same stars the Americans were probably looking at from their hotel rooms in Coyame right now, with no idea that their work had just made them the most dangerous loose ends in northern Mexico.

He put the phone away and went to find Navarro.

~

With their headlights extinguished, seven vehicles materialized from the darkness, their suspension systems groaning as they navigated the half-mile stretch of rocky road.

José counted the men as they emerged from the vehicles. Five more than he'd requested. El Toro didn't send extra muscle unless the stakes warranted it.

The men slipped from their vehicles and fanned out across the site like shadows. They moved with the confidence of those who had crossed into many places uninvited.

José directed them to the edge of the pit, and the backhoe operator climbed into the cab.

José checked his watch then locked eyes with Navarro. The crew chief stood motionless, broad shoulders squared beneath his work shirt. "Three a.m. is our window for the device," José said. "Until then, I want every scoop of dirt examined. Nothing gets missed. Any bone fragment, anything, you find it."

Metal teeth tore into the desert floor as the men arranged themselves in formation, their latex-covered fingers sifting methodically through each scoop of excavated earth, their handheld lights cutting geometric patterns through the darkness as they worked.

He had briefed the men on the nature of their search: skeletal remains that defied normal classification. José could read the skepticism in their eyes, but that wouldn't compromise their efforts.

The men knew that their pay depended on his approval. Whatever Navarro had shared about him ensured their compliance. José strolled the perimeter, listening to the backhoe work. Three hours and seventeen minutes until they moved to the warhead.

The minutes crawled by. Finally, the backhoe brought up something that wasn't all earth. The team had already bagged several bone-like fragments, but this was different.

As they brushed away the soil, a complete skeleton emerged from its ancient bed. José stared at the compact frame, the oblong cranium with cavernous orbital hollows that once housed eyes nothing like his own. His pulse quickened. El Toro would reward them well; the bonus would be enough to set them up for years.

The team continued to dig for another fifty minutes when José retreated to his pickup. The cellular phone mounted inside rang with an incoming call. He reached for the handset when the night split open with a scream from the excavation pit. What in the name of God was happening over there?

Another solitary cry tore through the night, then another and another, until the air vibrated with terror. José watched as the first worker collapsed, his legs giving out. Then a second man dropped. A third. In the space of a breath, bodies were collapsing across the excavation site like dominoes.

José froze in place. Human voices transformed into something primal and bestial. Workers tore at their own flesh, leaving bloody furrows across their forearms as if trying to extract an invisible poison.

Their spines contorted at unnatural angles, testing the limits of what human anatomy could endure before breaking.

A thousand needles of agony ignited beneath José's skin, each pulse of his heart pushing the torment deeper into his marrow. He clawed at his forearms, a silent prayer dying on his lips as the terrible truth dawned that the same invisible horror devouring his men had found him too.

Arms and legs spasmed without coordination. Black fluid trickled from nostrils and ear canals while frothy crimson-tinged spittle formed at their lips, their jaws clicking involuntarily between urgent attempts to breathe.

Men convulsed in the dirt, their fingers carving desperate trenches in the soil. José's bloodied hands clawed at nothing as his spine bent backward at an impossible angle, his joints rotating in directions nature never intended.

Their genetic code was being overwritten, cell by cell, as calcium leached from their bones like sugar dissolving in hot coffee.

Dormant for nearly a quarter century in the alien remains, the pathogen had awakened when disturbed, silently colonizing their bodies for almost an hour before announcing its presence.

From the first contortion to the final collapse, the alien contagion required less than five minutes to transform two dozen armed men into a grotesque tableau of broken figures scattered across the desert floor.

Tomás scraped the last of his huevos rancheros onto his fork as he glanced at Lydia. She raised an eyebrow at Jack and Jess's empty chairs. The knowing smirks they'd exchanged earlier had faded as the minutes rolled by. Most of the excavation team had already loaded their vehicles and headed toward the site, leaving only Perry, Pablo, and Lynley lingering by the breakfast bar. Tomás sighed, pushed back his chair, and stood.

"I'll go get them," he said, already dreading the conversation.

Tomás rapped on Jack's door. From inside came a muffled thud, followed by hushed voices and the rustle of fabric. After what felt like minutes, the door cracked open to reveal Jack's disheveled face.

Jack squinted against the light streaming in from the hallway. "What time is it?" "Late enough. Everyone has been waiting on you two," Tomás said, not bothering to hide his irritation. "The rest already left for the site. We'll be waiting in the vehicle. Don't take long."

Tomás trudged back to the waiting vehicle where Lydia, Perry, Pablo, and Lynley sat in uncomfortable silence. Two minutes passed, then five. Nobody mentioned the obvious, but their shared glances and suppressed smiles said everything. Jack and Jess weren't fooling anyone anymore.

Pablo fidgeted in his seat. "So, is this a new thing or…"

Tomás snorted. "Day one. The guy barely had dust on his boots."

Perry let out a low whistle. "Jack didn't waste any time, did he?"

After several minutes, Jack and Jess emerged from the hotel, hastily tucking in shirts and adjusting their collars. They slid into the back seat without making eye contact with anyone. The flush on their cheeks matched the desert sunrise. The vehicle dipped with their weight as the rest of the team clicked their seatbelts, lips pressed together to suppress smiles.

Jack cleared his throat. "Look, some of you already know about us, but as for the rest, keep it between us for now, alright? No need for Little Rock to hear about this yet."

Gravel popped beneath their wheels as they pulled away from the hotel, already an hour behind the others who would be hard at work at the dig site by now.

Tomás eased the vehicle off the highway onto a dirt access road that ended at a metal gate. Perry jumped out, fumbled with the padlock for a moment, then heaved the gate open with a metallic scrape. Tomás drove through, the vehicle's undercarriage rattling as they crossed the cattle guard, coming to a stop as Perry secured the gate then hopped back in.

The vehicle jostled along the rutted road toward the excavation area. Lynley leaned forward between the front seats, squinting through the windshield. A cluster of unfamiliar trucks and SUVs surrounded their dig site, along with their own vehicles. No movement. No people. Her stomach tightened.

"Tomás, stop!" she cried out, one hand flying out to brace herself.

Tomás slammed on the brakes, sending them lurching forward against their seatbelts as the vehicle skidded to a halt. Dust billowed around them like smoke. "What is it?"

"Something's wrong. What are all those vehicles doing out here?

And where is the rest of our team? I don't see anyone moving around."

Pablo twisted in his seat, fumbling through the equipment bag for binoculars. Jack leaned forward, tense. "Tomás, see that dry streambed alongside the road? Pull the vehicle down there. They won't spot us from the dig site."

Tomás nodded, his throat suddenly dry. "Good call," he said, already easing the vehicle toward the concealment of the lower terrain.

Pablo belly-crawled to the edge of the streambed, raising the binoculars to his eyes and adjusting the focus on the dig site. His body went rigid. He lowered the binoculars and beckoned to Tomás with a sharp jerk of his hand. "We've got trouble," he whispered over the desert wind.

Tomás pressed the binoculars against his face, blinking hard as the image came into focus. His breath caught. Motionless bodies were scattered across the excavation site. The distance obscured their features, but dark stains spread across the pale earth around them. Not a single figure stirred in the warm morning air.

The binoculars trembled in his hands. Behind him, gravel crunched softly as the others slithered up the embankment. Tomás turned to face them. "Our team," he said, his voice cracking. "They're not moving."

Jack asked, "Are they dead?"

Tomás shook his head. "I don't know, but it doesn't look good. We need to get a closer look."

Lynley said, "I wouldn't go any closer." She knelt beside them, a high-powered spotting scope pressed to her eye. She'd retrieved it from the vehicle with no one noticing. "Remember that alien pathogen theory I talked about?" Her finger remained steady on the focus dial. "It might not be a theory anymore."

"I thought you said it was only a remote possibility?" Tomás's voice rose sharply.

She adjusted the scope. "I was working with all the information I had. But looking at the situation now…" Her voice tightened. "No bullet wounds. No external injuries. There's blood seeping from their eyes, ears, noses, bodies twisted." She pulled back from the scope, her face pale. "Whatever killed them worked fast, too quick for radiation poisoning."

Jack made an observation. "If this is airborne, we need to think about what happens when, not if, the winds shift. Right now, it's at our backs. That's been the case almost every day out here, which is a typical morning downslope flow in a mountainous environment. As the sun heats the landscape, the flow will reverse. The wind will blow upslope right at us."

Tomás said, "We can't leave. What if someone's still breathing out there?"

Lynley shook her head. "If anyone were still alive out there, we'd see movement. There's nothing but stillness."

A retching sound hit their ears. They turned to see Jess doubled over beside the vehicle, one hand braced against the rear tire, the other held out to stop Jack's approach. Panic set in as they thought she might be affected by whatever killed the rest of their team.

"Don't," she managed between gasps, "I'll be okay."

Tomás ran a hand through his sweat-damp hair, his voice low and strained. "There is a nuclear bomb out there. If we leave now, what happens next?"

Jack said, "I say we leave." He wiped sweat from his forehead with a trembling hand. "The town's not safe if the wind shifts. Our best bet is the highway straight to Presidio then across the border. Whatever's out there, including that bomb, is not our problem anymore. It can't be, not if we want to survive."

Perry agreed. "Call Bob and brief him on everything that's happened. They'll have no choice but to get the authorities involved, Mexican or American."

Lydia said, "If we call in the Americans, they'll connect the dots about our operation here. You think they'll thank us and walk away?

They'll have our offices emptied before we even cross back over the border."

Tomás was rubbing his eyes, trying to think. "Lynley, correct me if I'm wrong, but don't you have a couple of biohazard suits?"

Lynley nodded. "There are two in my storage trunks in the back, but they're rated for known pathogens, not whatever turned our colleagues into corpses."

Tomás said, "We have to risk it. We could use the suits to retrieve the nuke."

"You want to walk into that death trap?" asked Jack.

"That town has families, children, over a thousand people who'll die screaming if this reaches them. And after that? Cities? States? We have a chance to end it here with that bomb," said Tomás.

Jack's fingers went numb as he gripped the binoculars. "Brilliant plan, except for the part where we don't have a way to detonate it without being vaporized ourselves. Assuming we could even get to it without being exposed to the alien virus or whatever it is. I don't have a death wish."

"First, get the bomb. Then we'll figure out how to survive," said Tomás.

The group fractured into a storm of angry debate. Lynley shook her head vehemently while Pablo made slashing motions with his hands. Jack turned his back, shoulders rigid with refusal. Only Tomás remained steadfast, his eyes fixed on the distant site where their colleagues lay motionless.

Finally, Tomás said, "Humor me. Let's get a biohazard suit out to see if it fits me. If it fits, I will volunteer to go in there myself. The bomb is buried under loose soil. It will take no more than five minutes to dig out."

"And it weighs several hundred pounds. You can't leave it where the virus is, and you can't get it back here without some manpower," said Jack.

Tomás waved him off as he struggled with the biohazard suit, forcing his limbs through the resistant material while sweat beaded on his forehead.

Lynley grabbed the sleeve of the biohazard suit. "Even if you make it back alive, we're still screwed. That bomb's been rotting for twenty-five years. We have no manual, no codes, nothing. And the radiation leak means every second you spend near it is burning through your cells, suit or no suit."

Perry said, "I might have a solution." He leaned forward, eyes locked on Tomás. "Give me the other suit. I had a good look at it yesterday, and I think the safety measures may have been bypassed. I think I can figure out how to detonate it. Engineering backgrounds come in handy."

Jack said, "You guys are nuts. Let's say we detonate it. Do we have any idea what the yield is? The minimum safe distance? What's going to happen to Coyame?"

"I saw the specs on that casing, 100 kilotons in its prime but far less now. It's degraded. About a one-mile vaporization radius, tops. The town will get hit with the shockwave and the fallout, yes. Some cases of cancer down the line, but they'll have twenty years to live before that happens," said Perry. He locked eyes with Jack. "This virus? They won't have twenty minutes."

Perry suited up and took his place beside Tomás, whose faces disappeared behind the fogged visors as they sealed the final closures.

Tomás raised a gloved hand toward the others. "Take our truck. Cross the border. Alert Bob. If we make it, we'll use one of the vehicles at the site. Now move before the wind changes!"

Choked farewells hung in the air as Jack slid behind the wheel. Jess climbed in beside him, her face streaked with tears, while Pablo, Lynley, and Lydia squeezed into the back seat. The engine roared to life, and the vehicle lurched forward, kicking up a plume of dust as they fled the nightmare behind them.

"Perry, you stay behind," said Tomás. "I'll bring the bomb back here, assuming I survive. There is no sense exposing both of us to the virus."

He checked the seals on his suit one final time, tugging at the wrist closures until they bit into the material, then adjusted the visor.

"Half a mile," Tomás said, his voice muffled inside the helmet. "Give me forty-five minutes. If I'm not back by then..."

"You'll be back," Perry said.

Tomás looked at him for a moment, then turned and started walking.

Perry watched him go. The biohazard suit was bright yellow. It made Tomás look absurd out here in the brown desert. Perry lost him twice in the waves of heat rising off the ground before the terrain dipped and swallowed him entirely.

He checked his watch: 8:47 a.m.

The wait was its own particular kind of punishment. Perry had nothing to do but stand in the thin shade of the truck and think about everything that could be happening a half mile away. He thought about the bodies lying on the ground. Whatever had hit them had hit all of them at once. He thought about the black fluid at the nostrils, the contorted spines. He thought about the fact that Tomás was walking into the middle of that right now with nothing but a suit rated for terrestrial pathogens.

At 9:04 a.m., he heard the backhoe start up.

The backhoe's engine carried across the desert...first a groan, then a stutter, finally a sustained roar. Perry exhaled for what felt like the first time in seventeen minutes. The machine was running, which meant Tomás was alive. He gripped that fact and held onto it.

The engine's sound changed pitch. Perry could picture it without seeing it: the mechanical arm extending, the bucket biting into soil, the chain pulling taut against something that didn't want to move. He found himself leaning forward slightly as if those few inches of posture might help.

Then the engine eased. Metal groaned as the backhoe crawled toward him across the uneven ground.

It took twenty minutes for the backhoe to cross the distance from the pit. Perry tracked its progress by sound long before he could see it, the diesel note rising and falling as Tomás negotiated the terrain, the occasional metallic scrape of the chain dragging its cargo over rock. When the machine came closer, Perry had to force himself not to run.

Tomás was upright in the cab. Alive and moving with purpose.

Behind the backhoe, trailing on the chain like something dredged from a river, was the warhead. It was uglier than Perry remembered. The soil brushed away now revealed the full extent of the corrosion, the pitted oxidized steel streaked with rust and mineral deposits, the Cyrillic stenciling faded to near-illegibility. A relic, forgotten by design.

Tomás brought the machine to a halt and cut the engine. The sudden silence was jarring. He climbed down from the cab with the careful movements of a man who has been managing his adrenaline for the past thirty minutes.

Perry grabbed his toolkit from the truck and walked to the warhead, crouching beside it. Up close, the casing was in worse condition than he'd imagined, yet better than he'd feared. The nose cone was intact. The arming panel was corroded but present, the cover plate seized in place by decades of oxidation. He pulled a flathead from the kit and began working the edge of the panel, applying steady pressure until he felt the first give of metal that had been locked in place since the Ford administration.

"Talk to me," Tomás said, standing behind him. "Tell me what you see."

"I'm seeing a very old weapon that someone decided not to use." Perry worked the panel loose and set it aside. The components inside were dusty but intact, with no obvious corrosion on the internal contacts. The wiring insulation was cracked in places but not severed.

He pulled a penlight from his pocket and leaned in close. "I have no way of knowing if the primary inside is still viable. If the fissile material has degraded too far, we get a fizzle yield—dirty but not catastrophic. If it hasn't..."

"How do we know which?"

Perry sat back on his heels and looked up at Tomás. "We don't. Not without equipment I don't have." He was quiet for a moment. "But the spheres were still radioactive after twenty-five years in the ground. So there's hope."

Tomás stared at the warhead. Somewhere behind them, half a mile away, the bodies of their colleagues lay in the morning sun, and somewhere beyond that, in a town of fifteen hundred people, children were probably eating breakfast right now.

"Can you arm it?" Tomás asked.

Perry looked at the panel for a long moment. "I think so. The timer mechanism is the question. If the clock circuit is seized..."

"How long would you need?"

"Twenty minutes. Maybe thirty." He picked up his tools again. "Give me room to work."

Tomás stepped back and turned to face the horizon, watching for dust clouds on the road, listening for engines. The desert gave him nothing but heat and silence and the small precise sounds of Perry working behind him.

He checked his watch. The wind, which had been at their backs all morning, had not yet shifted.

They still had time. Not much, but some.

The team had made it back to Ojinaga, and Jack was in the queue to cross the border back into the U.S. He knew painfully that they had a ton of artifacts packed into their gear in the back, many of them radioactive. He was telling everyone else to "act natural."

Lydia said, "And how the hell are we supposed to do that, Jack? Most of our team is dead. Perry and Tomás have almost zero chance of survival, and we have a vehicle loaded with radioactive material attempting to cross the U.S. border."

The vehicles were inching forward ahead of them. "Follow my lead and trust me," he said. Finally, a border agent waved them into the fourth lane, and another approached the window.

A border agent in mirrored sunglasses leaned into their window. "Citizenship?" he asked, his breath smelling of coffee.

Jack nodded toward each person as he spoke with an exaggerated drawl. "American. American. American. Mr. Castillo and Ms. Reyes here have their green cards." Lydia and Pablo produced their papers. The agent flipped through all the documents, holding each one up to catch the light.

"Anything to declare today?" he asked, eyes scanning the cramped interior of their vehicle.

Jack flashed his most professional smile. "Some geological survey work for Rio Tinto," he said, gesturing toward their equipment. "Looking for potential copper deposits. Nothing interesting, unless you're into rocks, which unfortunately for my social life, I am."

He held his breath as the agents rummaged through their bags, their bare hands inches from the lead-lined cases. One agent lifted a sample container, flipping it over casually before setting it back down. After a few tense moments, the senior officer nodded and waved them forward. "You're clear to proceed," he said, already turning his attention to the next vehicle in line.

The tension drained as they crossed into Presidio. Jack's tight grip on the steering wheel relaxed. When the neon cactus sign of Sancho's Pizza Palace appeared on their left, Jack caught Lydia's eye in the rearview mirror. A snort escaped him, triggering an eruption of laughter between himself, Lydia, and Pablo that bordered on hysteria. Jess and Lynley exchanged confused glances, completely lost on the private joke.

As their laughter subsided, Jess cleared her throat. "So what's the plan now?" she asked.

Jack rubbed the back of his neck. "We should swing by the Cactus Inn. Got a rental sitting in their lot. Let's head toward Midland afterwards and have Bob bring the plane there. Enterprise has a drop-off at the airport."

Lynley's jaw dropped. "A rental car? That's what you're thinking about right now? Jesus Christ, Jack. We lost nearly our entire team!"

Lydia leaned forward from the back seat. "Forget the car. Bob can write off the entire thing as a rounding error. And speaking of our benefactor, shouldn't we be updating him on this catastrophe?"

Jack's eyes remained fixed on the road ahead. "Jesus, where do I even start?" He exhaled slowly. "But you're right. Time to make the call to Little Rock."

He continued north out of town and found a good spot to pull over on the highway. The vehicle idled on the shoulder with the hazards blinking while eighteen-wheelers blew past and rocked the vehicle on its springs. He'd wanted to be stopped for this one. The news he had to deliver required his full attention, and the highway demanded the same.

Bob answered quickly, his tone crisp and businesslike. "Jack. Update me on the excavation."

Jack had stared through the windshield at the flat Texas scrubland and said, "Bob, I need you to sit down."

A pause. "I'm already sitting."

"I mean somewhere private."

The sound of a door closing. "Go ahead."

He'd laid it out as plainly as he could, in the order it had happened, without editorializing. The vehicles at the site. The bodies. Lynley's assessment through the spotting scope. The pathogen theory. The warhead. Tomás and Perry suiting up. The drive to Ojinaga. The border crossing. He kept his voice level and his sentences short, the way you do when you're afraid that if you pause too long, you'll lose the ability to continue.

Bob had not interrupted once.

When Jack finished, the line went quiet. He'd watched the second hand on his watch tick through eleven seconds before he pulled the phone away from his ear to check the signal. Four bars. The call was live.

"Bob?"

"I'm here." The voice was different now. Flatter. The brisk energy was gone. "How many got out?"

"We left with five. Tomás and Perry stayed behind." Jack glanced in the rearview mirror at Jess, who was watching him. "The rest of the team that was already at the site when we arrived—all of them—we saw them through binoculars. Lynley doesn't think anyone was still alive."

Another silence. Shorter this time.

"The pathogen." Bob's voice was careful now. "Lynley thinks it came from the remains?"

"From disturbing them, yes. She said it could have been dormant in the bone material for decades. Maybe longer."

"And Tomás and Perry went back into that?"

"In the biohazard suits. Tomás didn't want anyone else exposed. He was going to use the backhoe to retrieve the warhead, and Perry was going to attempt to arm it." Jack pressed his thumb and forefinger against the bridge of his nose. "Bob, if they pull it off, there won't be much left of that site. The pathogen, the remaining artifacts, the warhead itself. All of it."

"And them."

"They're going to try to get clear. But I don't know if there's any hope of that."

The highway stretched out ahead, empty and indifferent under the West Texas sun. Someone in the back seat—he thought it was Lydia—had started crying quietly. He hadn't turned around.

"The artifacts you have with you," Bob said. "The lead cases."

"In the back. We got through the border. They didn't scan the vehicle."

"When you get to Midland, don't check the cases into any storage facility. Don't let them out of your sight. I'll have Tusk on the ground within two hours of your arrival." A pause. "Are all of you okay? Physically?"

"We're okay. None of us were at the site when it happened." He hesitated. "Jess was sick at the scene, but she thinks it was a stress reaction. She's been fine since."

"I want a doctor to assess everyone when you land. No exceptions." Bob's voice had recovered some of its authority, the executive instinct reasserting itself over the grief. Jack could hear it happening in real time: the man reaching for the tools he knew how to use. "I'll have the containment lab prepped by the time you're wheels down. Chen and Thabo will be standing by."

"Understood."

A long exhale on the other end of the line. Then, quietly: "Christ, Jack. Do I call in the military?"

Jack had sat with that question for a moment before answering. "I don't know, Bob. If Perry got that warhead armed and it went off, there may not be anything left to call them about. Otherwise..." He stopped. "If not, we've got a live Soviet warhead sitting in a Mexican desert next to an active alien pathogen. Either way, I don't think we get to keep this to ourselves much longer."

Bob said nothing to that. Just a quiet acknowledgment, a sound that wasn't quite a word, and then they'd ended the call.

Now, as they pulled back on the road to Midland, Bob's last question still hung in the air between them. Jack kept both hands on the wheel and his eyes on the vanishing point where the road met the horizon, trying not to think about a yellow biohazard suit moving alone across a half mile of Mexican desert.

Perry's Russian was limited to a handful of words and Cyrillic characters, but he knew enough to make sense of the labels inside the aging Soviet nuclear bomb. Kneeling before the open panel, he rocked back on his heels to get a better look at the tangle of wiring.

This was no factory-standard device. The interior was a mess of severed wires reconnected in haphazard configurations, with after-market circuit boards wedged into spaces not designed for them. Whoever had done this work had circumvented the fail-safe systems built into the original Soviet design.

His gloved finger traced the Cyrillic lettering, following each stroke until the meaning crystallized in his mind. Perry froze, his breath catching in his throat. The modified device would arm upon connection to an eighteen-volt power source.

He thought about the requirement for eighteen volts. They had nothing like that on hand. He twitched his fingers against his thigh, eyes scanning the horizon beyond the dig site, then stopped. His lips curled into a thin smile.

"Tomás, I need you to take the backhoe up to those vehicles up there," he said, gesturing toward ground zero, "and extract two car batteries for me. I'm going to require them to power this up."

Tomás nodded and jumped into action.

Perry knew a way to make an eighteen-volt circuit out of two car batteries, but it would be dangerous. He traced the chaotic nest of wires, following each connection to its terminus. A new question surfaced in his mind. Would connecting the power source trigger immediate detonation? His eyes narrowed as he found a small junction box with disconnected leads. He exhaled. The bomb would arm but not detonate...yet.

His relief vanished as he traced a second modified circuit, one that would trigger detonation once armed, and it would detonate the bomb the second it received power.

Perry wiped sweat from his brow. The eighteen-volt connection would need to be made manually, with no timer mechanism in sight. His gaze drifted to the horizon, calculating distances and blast radius. Someone would have to stay behind to complete the circuit, unless he could come up with an alternative.

The backhoe's diesel engine growled closer, and Perry glanced up to see Tomás in his biohazard suit maneuvering toward him, the front loader cradling two salvaged car batteries like precious cargo. Tomás eased the machine forward until the bucket rested on the ground a few feet from where Perry knelt.

Now came the hard part. Perry needed to breach the plastic shell of one battery to access what was beneath. He knew the architecture by heart: six chambers of chemical reaction, each generating over two volts of electrical potential. If he could tap into the midpoint after the third cell, he'd harvest six volts to combine with the intact battery's twelve, giving him what the bomb required.

Perry motioned Tomás away with a sharp wave of his hand. "Get way back." He picked up a utility knife from his kit. "I need to breach this battery casing, and when I do, there'll be hydrogen gas. Sulfuric acid. All it takes is one tiny spark for us to become part of the crater." His finger traced an explosive arc in the air.

Perry didn't hesitate once Tomás was clear. He pressed the utility knife down, cutting into the top of the casing. The plastic yielded with a soft pop, releasing a serpentine hiss. He was thankful that he had the biohazard suit on. His hand trembled as he continued the incision, knowing that one spark from the blade against the lead plates would turn this crater into his final resting place.

Once the lead bridge gleamed through the jagged hole, Perry's breath caught. He needed a connection. His fingers fumbled through his kit, his gloved hands making it difficult to grasp smaller objects. He scattered small tools across the tarp until his hand closed around a self-tapping screw. Sweat beaded on his forehead, trickling down into his eyebrows as he positioned the metal point against the soft lead.

The screwdriver slipped once then twice in his gloved hand before catching. One spark and this would be over. Each careful turn sent his pulse hammering in his ears.

Metal bit into soft lead with a final turn, creating a solid connection point. Perry exhaled through his nose, allowing himself only this momentary reprieve. The most dangerous part still was ahead.

Now came the moment of truth. Perry trembled as he extracted a coil of red and black wiring from his kit, the plastic insulation worn thin in places from years in his field bag. He stripped the ends with the utility knife and pressed the exposed copper to the negative post of the intact battery. Then he tightened the connection with a small wrench.

He ran the wire like a lifeline to the positive terminal of the modified battery. Then he attached the ground of the entire system to the negative terminal and laid it aside. This would attach to the bomb.

Finally, the screw he'd driven into the lead plate waited for the last connection, eighteen volts of raw electrical potential hovering inches from completion. He made the attachment and set that wire aside. This would attach to the bomb as well.

He eased back on his haunches, lungs burning as he allowed himself to exhale. Half a mile was all that separated them from the epicenter. Even degraded, the yield would be enough to turn everything within the blast radius into superheated vapor. His fingers twitched against his thigh. One mistake now and there wouldn't be dental records to identify.

Working in the biohazard suit was proving to be much more difficult than he'd imagined. It wasn't built for dexterity, and the gloves were thick and cumbersome. He took a deep breath. Now for the hard part.

With the makeshift power source ready, Perry turned his attention to the arming circuit. He held the wire poised above the connection point, his gloved hand steady despite the hammering in his rib cage. Science told him the bomb wouldn't detonate yet, but science hadn't accounted for Soviet engineers and whoever had modified their work. His fingers traced a small cross over his chest before he pressed the wire against the terminal.

Inside the device, a constellation of tiny red LEDs blinked awake in sequence, accompanied by a soft electronic chirp that seemed loud in the silence. Perry's lungs burned as he exhaled. He hadn't even realized he'd been holding his breath since the moment the connection was made.

Perry waved Tomás closer. "I need cigarettes," he called through his respirator, voice muffled but clear. "And a lighter. Check the vehicles at ground zero. While you're there, secure us transportation, something rugged with a full tank. When this goes, we'll have maybe three to five minutes to clear the radius."

Perry wired up a second set of copper wires to the battery terminal, struggling with the thick gloves. These would power the detonator. Next, he stripped the hot wire attachment on the bomb casing.

He returned to his kit. He dug around and found some nylon fishing wire. It was a twenty-pound test, clear monofilament, the type you'd use for bass.

Now he needed a spring with enough tension to snap the contact wire forward when released. His eyes moved around his kit bag and fished out a cheap ballpoint pen. He unscrewed the barrel and shook out the ink cartridge, letting it fall to the ground.

The spring fell into his gloved palm, small and silvery. He tried to test it between his fingers, but it kept falling out. He didn't have enough dexterity. His options were limited; he had to use it, however weak it was. A pen spring was designed to push a ballpoint tip forward with enough force to write, nothing more.

He moved with as much precision as the gloved suit would allow, which wasn't a lot, as he assembled the crude timer that would give them enough time to escape. The physics were sound, but doubt crept in. The entire fate of the world might rest upon this bomb detonating.

With difficulty, he mounted the spring to the bomb's hot wire receptacle. He attached a copper filament to the free end of the spring, trying to bend its tip into a small hook. His fingers were too cumbersome. He grasped the screwdriver and was able to make the bend. Using the same methodology, he shaped the power source's hot wire into a matching hook, and when ready he would position it far enough away so that the two metal ends hung suspended in the air, like adversaries waiting for the signal to clash.

With a steady hand, he completed the circuit, connecting the negative terminal wire to the detonator's ground port, the final electrical handshake between power source and destruction.

He did his best to tension the spring until it quivered with resistance, far more strain than such a delicate coil should endure, and fastened the fishing line to the copper hook at its end. It took almost four tries to get it attached. Finally, the monofilament stretched taut as he secured its opposite end to the immovable mass of the backhoe, creating a deadly equation of potential energy waiting to be solved.

Perry held his breath as he positioned the last component. The hooked wire from the battery needed to hover in space, close enough to its spring-loaded counterpart to ensure contact when released, yet sufficiently far that the slightest vibration wouldn't trigger premature connection. He measured the gap three times with the tip of his screwdriver. When the heat severed the fishing line, the tensioned spring would slam forward, copper would meet copper, and the circuit would complete. In that instant, kilotons of destructive potential would awaken beneath his hands.

The crunch of tires on the rocky ground announced the return of Tomás. A mud-splattered pickup idled behind him as he approached. He tossed a crumpled pack of cigarettes and a plastic lighter that arced through the air before landing in Perry's gloved palm.

"I hope you know what you're doing, amigo," said Tomás.

"Me too!" he said.

Near the backhoe, Perry constructed a small cairn of stones, balancing the cigarette so its lit end extended over the edge. He positioned it beneath the taut fishing line. The burning ember would sever the monofilament, releasing the spring-loaded contact wire. If his calculations were correct, the circuit would complete, and the detonation sequence would begin.

Perry studied the cigarette, calculating. Unlike the reliable smokes of his youth that would burn to the filter, these modern ones had safety features—chemical rings in the paper that choked the ember if left unattended.

Five minutes, maybe less, before it would put itself out. He needed precision, which was going to be hard to come by; enough time to clear the blast radius, not enough to extinguish it. He positioned the cigarette, hoping the burning ember would sever the line within the narrow window between escape and annihilation.

Lighting the tobacco presented a fresh problem. He was inside a sealed suit. How could he draw air through it to light it? His gloved hands returned to the kit, emerging with a rubber desoldering bulb. Perfect, he could place the suction end of the bulb on the filter of the cigarette and create suction while he lit it. Everything was in place and ready to go. The last step was to apply power to the other end of the trigger hook. One wrong move and the bomb would detonate instantly. He tried to keep his hands from shaking when he made the last connection. "Steady, Perry. You've done stuff like this a thousand times," he said to himself. Finally, he hooked it up, and the bomb was ready to explode as soon as the monofilament line was severed.

"Get ready," he said to Tomás, who had returned to the driver's seat of the pickup truck.

Perry made one final visual sweep, confirming sufficient distance between himself and the battery. He tried to flick the lighter through his gloved hand, but it was too cumbersome. It wouldn't strike properly. He tried again and again.

Finally, success; it sparked to life. He touched the flame to the cigarette's tip while pressing the suction end of the desoldering bulb against the filter, coaxing the tobacco to catch. Two quick draws, and the ember glowed angry red. The timer was set!

Perry bolted across the uneven ground, boots kicking up dust as he rounded the truck's hood. He flung himself into the passenger seat. The door barely latched before Tomás stomped on the accelerator. The pickup lurched forward with a scream of protesting metal, tires spinning before finding purchase on the rocky ground.

Their biohazard suits squeaked against the vinyl seats as the truck bounced over the terrain, helmets knocking against the roof with each jolt. The digital watch on Perry's wrist ticked down their remaining window of survival.

As they continued the gradual climb away from Presidio, Lydia interrupted the silence.

"Damn, Jack. I just realized something. If you two hadn't kept us waiting this morning with your...whatever that was, we'd be dead out there with the others."

Jess whipped around, her cheeks flushing. "It wasn't whatever you think it was. The alarm didn't go off. And for the record..."

Jess didn't have a chance to finish her sentence. Without warning, the world turned white. Total, sourceless, all-consuming white that erased shadows and depth and the distinction between the road and the sky. It lasted less than a second, but in that second Jack's hands locked on the wheel and his foot came off the accelerator. The vehicle coasted as his brain tried to process what his eyes had just seen.

Then the white was gone, and the world was back, the shadows swinging wildly as his vision readjusted, and Jack realized he'd drifted toward the shoulder.

"Holy shit!" he said. "That was a nuclear detonation! They did it. They actually did it."

Nobody answered. Jess had turned back to face forward, one

hand pressed flat against the dashboard. In the rearview mirror, Pablo's mouth was open. Lydia and Lynley sat completely still.

"Don't look directly south," Jack said, though there was nothing left to see in that direction, just the ordinary, blinding West Texas sun. "Give it a minute."

He checked the clock on the dashboard. They were approximately fifty miles north-northeast of the site. He did the math without wanting to.

"The shockwave," he said. "Brace yourselves. It's going to be..."

The sound arrived before he finished the sentence. It came from everywhere at once, a concussive pressure that crashed against the vehicle. Not a bang but a sustained crack that rolled through the air and then kept rolling, the way thunder does when it's directly overhead. The sound built and then subsided and then built again as the pressure wave bounced off the terrain. The windows flexed in their frames, and something in the cargo area shifted and knocked against the side panel. Jess made a sharp involuntary sound and grabbed the door handle.

The ground didn't shake, not exactly. It was more that the air pressure changed so completely and so suddenly that the road itself seemed to drop half an inch and come back, a sensation Jack felt in his chest and his back teeth simultaneously.

Then it passed. The silence that followed differed from the silence before.

"Everyone okay?" asked Jack.

A series of murmured affirmations from the back seat. Jess nodded without speaking.

The road curved upward through the foothills north of Presidio, and as they crested the rise, the view opened southward. Jack slowed without thinking about it, the vehicle dropping to thirty, then twenty, then barely rolling as five sets of eyes found the horizon.

Fifty miles distant, a column of smoke and debris was climbing into the sky. The cap was already forming, that unmistakable broadening at the top, the shape that the human eye instantly recognizes.

Against the pale blue of the West Texas morning it looked almost peaceful, the way a photograph of something catastrophic can look peaceful when the sound has been removed.

"Forty kilotons, Perry predicted," Pablo said. "Maybe fifty."

"Degraded yield," Jack said. "It could have been less."

"Tomás," Lydia said. Just the name. Nothing else.

Jack pulled back onto the road. There was no point in lingering here.

"You think they got clear?" Lydia asked. It was the same question she'd asked in Ojinaga, worded slightly differently.

Nobody offered one this time.

The mushroom cloud was still visible in the rearview mirror twenty minutes later, the column dispersing at altitude now, spreading into the high atmosphere. Jack watched it in three-second glances. By the time it had faded to an indistinct smear against the sky, they were well north of Presidio and the road had straightened out into the long, flat nothingness between there and Midland.

The rest of the drive passed with only the sound of tires on asphalt and the occasional clearing of a throat.

Every television channel blazed with the same story, news anchors leaning forward in their seats, pundits gesturing with their hands, all speaking in that tone reserved for civilization-altering events.

In northern Chihuahua, the nuclear detonation transformed miles of desert into a hellish wound on the Earth's surface.

A Mexican rancher captured it with his camcorder, filming the apocalyptic plume that towered over the sierra, an atomic fist punching through the sky. The footage spread like wildfire, reaching millions before government officials could even plan a response.

Space agencies worldwide scrambled their orbital assets, redirecting every available satellite to document the smoldering pit.

The world's desperate need for answers circled the smoking crater. Which nation or group unleashed such devastation? What made this empty stretch of borderland their target? Had someone miscalculated? Was this deliberate? Had the first shot of an unthinkable conflict been fired?

Every network carved the screen into frantic quadrants. On CNN, gray-haired military men and intelligence veterans took turns painting doomsday scenarios.

ABC News hypnotized viewers with an endless loop of heat-mapped satellite imagery, the wound in the earth pulsing angry orange against desert blue.

Over at CBS, disheveled physicists argued over the long-term health effects of the blast.

On call-in radio shows across the country, listeners offered explanations that ranged from the biblical to the extraterrestrial.

In the Pentagon's subterranean war rooms, intelligence analysts leaned forward under the blue glow of monitors displaying the mile-wide crater from orbit. F-16s launched from bases in Arizona and New Mexico cut tight ovals through borderland skies, their instrument packages sampling air for radiation signatures.

Deep beneath the White House, the commander-in-chief sat stone-faced as uniformed officers with star-clustered shoulders delivered assessment after assessment, each one more dire than the last, yet none answering the fundamental question of what had actually happened.

The United States government crafted a carefully worded press release, pushing the theory that a drug cartel deployed a Soviet-era tactical nuke against a rival faction.

Everyone knew the cartels had graduated from rifles to RPGs to armored vehicles. That one of them had gotten their hands on a portable nuclear device was terrifying, but not unthinkable. The story gave the news networks what they needed, a villain they could put a face on.

When Jack and his team reached Midland, they found an empty tarmac where their extraction aircraft should have been. The mushroom cloud that had bloomed over northern Mexico had knocked out communications across the border region. Though they'd placed 250 miles between themselves and ground zero, their phones only occasionally flickered to life with a single, wavering bar of service.

Jack punched Bob's number into his phone again. The connection finally went through.

"Tell me," Bob asked, "was that us?"

"It was our payload. They got the job done," he said. "We don't know if they got clear in time."

"They're going to hunt us down like dogs when they figure out what we did. Life in a black site somewhere, if we're lucky," said Bob.

Jack closed his eyes. "How's the world taking it?"

Bob let out a humorless laugh. "The news is running with a drug cartel playing with old Soviet nukes. CNN already has a special graphic for it."

Jack said, "We should keep our heads down, Bob. The cartel narrative helps us. After what happened out there, nobody will find a shred of evidence pinning us to what went down."

"Maybe," said Bob. "The FAA has grounded all air traffic over a dozen states out of an abundance of caution. I can't get the jet to you for a while. It might be faster for you to drive back here. Is it about ten hours?"

"That's about right. The only problem is we have a vehicle with Mexican plates. I'm not feeling too good about driving it all the way back to Arkansas right now," said Jack.

"Christ. Okay, find a place to hunker down in Midland. I'll have the jet out there as soon as the FAA allows flights to resume," he said. "And figure something out with the truck. We don't need this coming back on us."

After securing rooms at a roadside motel in Midland with peeling paint and buzzing neon, Pablo pulled Jack aside.

Pablo's eyes narrowed. "We take that truck to the bad part of Odessa, park it with the windows down, keys dangling from the ignition. Twenty minutes tops before it vanishes into someone's chop shop."

Jess's brow furrowed. "The rental paperwork has all our information on it."

Pablo rubbed his jaw, considering. "File a police report in

Presidio. Tell them we crossed the border and came back to find the truck gone. Simple story, minimal details. The less we elaborate, the more believable it sounds."

Jack said, "Okay, we don't have time for a debate right now. Pablo and I will ditch the vehicle and get a taxi ride back. You ladies strategize on how we can make a report of it being stolen. Sound good?"

There were no objections.

West Odessa became their target, a lawless stretch beyond city jurisdiction where stolen vehicles disappeared without a trace. They navigated through streets lined with chain-link fences and homes with boarded windows, selecting a corner where stripped cars already littered an empty lot.

Working quickly, they rolled down all the windows, erased their presence with shirt sleeves across every surface they'd touched, and left the keys dangling from the ignition.

As they made their way toward the highway, Jack felt the weight of hostile stares following their every step. Men lounged on porches and leaned against fence posts, eyes narrowing beneath the brims of worn caps. Jack fumbled with his phone, squinting at the taxi company number he'd scrawled on his palm.

"Damn it," he muttered, tapping the screen. "No signal again."

Several locals started following them at a distance.

"Of course the signal drops now. Keep moving and don't look back," said Pablo. "If any of these bad hombres give us trouble, I'll handle it."

After trudging several more blocks, they spotted a Mexican restaurant with the paint peeling off the side, along with a dim neon "Open" sign in the front window. Jack caught Pablo's eye, and they veered toward the entrance, shoulders hunched as they slipped inside.

"I'm not hungry, but we should try to blend in until we can get a taxi," said Pablo.

The vinyl booth squeaked as they slid in, Jack ordering carne asada and Pablo a plate of enchiladas, both men nursing cold Dos Equis bottles that sweated rings onto the laminate tabletop.

When the waitress returned with their food, Jack pulled out his phone again. The signal bars were steady.

Three minutes later, he pocketed the device, nodding to Pablo. "Taxi's coming. Twenty minutes tops."

Pablo stabbed his fork into the enchilada, releasing a plume of steam. "Clock's ticking. Don't let it get cold."

They had nearly finished when the taxi pulled up outside. Not wanting to miss their ride, Jack stood up and threw a couple of twenties on the table, and they both hurried to the waiting vehicle.

Fifteen minutes later, they reunited with the ladies.

The FAA had removed flight restrictions, and Bob was en route on Tusk to retrieve the crew in Midland.

Jack had talked to Bob before he left Little Rock. He was worried about himself and SPIRE being drawn into this, but he seemed pleased with how his team had handled a difficult situation. "The world may never know it," he said, "but we probably saved it by detonating that weapon."

Jack had called a taxi, and they were waiting for it to arrive to take them to the airport. His phone rang, a Mexican number he didn't recognize. He flipped it open anyway.

The call was full of static and garbled, but he heard the unmistakable sound of Perry's voice.

"Perry, you guys are alive?" he said.

His voice crackled through the static. "Made it about nine miles from ground zero before we ditched the truck in this arroyo. A huge rock face gave us a lot of cover from the thermal blast and shockwave. We're alive, but Christ, Jack, the radiation exposure... We won't be buying any ten-year savings bonds."

Jack gripped the phone tighter. "What's your location?"

Perry's voice faded in and out through the static. "We've been sticking to dirt roads. Made it all the way to the border near Candelaria. We found an abandoned ranch with a landline. Our cell phones are fried. Do you know where Candelaria is?" The line crackled.

"I do. Did a hydrologic survey on the river there in my Texas days. There is a place about two or three miles north of town where you can cross the river on foot. You'll know you're in the right spot when you see a rocky bluff right there on the other side. It runs up against the river. Hold up there. We're in Midland now, and Bob is on his way with the jet. We can fly to Presidio from here and drive up and rescue you guys. While you're waiting, scrub off in the river. Get as much of that nuclear shit off of you as you can."

They met Bob at the aircraft when it landed and explained the situation to him.

Bob had briefed them on what he knew about the blast effects. The bomb had indeed been degraded, which was fortunate. According to CNN, the initial death toll was under ten people. Coyame was hit badly by the shockwave, which knocked down a number of buildings. On the other side of the blast, the town of Cuchillo Parado was also hit but spared from the thermal blast. Several smaller villages were also within the radius of the shockwave, but their status was unknown. Windows were blown out of homes and automobiles as far as forty to fifty miles away.

CNN reported victims had died not from radiation or the blast itself but from crumbling adobe walls and vehicles thrown off the desert highways.

The cabin fell silent. People were dead. Jack stared at his hands, wondering if they were now instruments of murder or salvation. Pablo's jaw clenched, his eyes fixed on some distant point. Lydia's fingers trembled as she twisted a loose thread on her sleeve.

The cold calculus said ten casualties against a global pandemic was a bargain. But each of those killed had names, families, and dreams that would never be realized. Jack wondered if he'd ever sleep again, knowing what they'd done, even to save millions.

There was no comfort to be had.

Bob said grimly, "We need to focus on what's next." He was eager to fly to Presidio, but wasn't sure how they would get to Candelaria, which was forty miles upriver.

"I have a rental car still sitting in the back lot at the Cactus Inn. We can grab that and drive up there," said Jack.

Lydia started laughing. "You and that damn rental car. Looks like it was a genius move to leave it there after all!"

The flight to Presidio was quick. Bob stayed with the women on the jet while Jack and Pablo caught a taxi to the Cactus Inn. The manager's eyebrows shot up when he saw Jack again. He paid him an extra fifty for the vehicle storage, which eliminated any questions about why they needed it now.

They made good time to Candelaria on smooth asphalt, but the car's low clearance would be tested beyond the town limits. The route to the crossing point was nothing but rutted dirt tracks carved into the harsh landscape, territory that demanded heavy-duty suspension and four-wheel drive.

Pablo shrugged, eyeing the battered path ahead. "What's the worst that happens? We wreck a rental car, and Bob writes a check. These guys need us."

They bounced and scraped over the rough terrain for two miles, wincing at every rock that struck the undercarriage. Then the dirt track disappeared into a flowing creek bed, twenty feet wide and two and a half feet deep, cutting across their path. Pablo killed the engine and stared through the windshield. The rental sedan might as well have been facing the Grand Canyon.

"Stay here with the vehicle, Pablo. The crossing is about a half mile up. I'll sprint up ahead and bring them back."

Jack waded across the creek bed and sprinted forward until he reached the rocky outcropping that met the water's edge. He was out of breath and gasping for air as he called out for Perry or Tomás.

The river flowed past, but no sign of human life appeared on either bank. His hand was already reaching for his phone when movement caught his eye: two figures wading through the shallows, their clothes plastered to their bodies as they emerged from the current.

Jack's throat closed up as he sprinted toward them, his boots kicking up dust. Perry's face was sunburned and raw, his garments stiff with river water and sweat. They collided hard, arms wrapping around each other, fists bunching the fabric of Perry's shirt. Jack's chest heaved against his friend's shoulder, the salt of unexpected tears stinging the corners of his eyes. Then he and Tomás embraced.

He pulled back enough to look at their faces, his voice breaking. "You crazy bastards. I thought you were gone."

Perry's skin had a waxy pallor beneath the sunburn, and dark crescents hung beneath bloodshot eyes. When he tried to stand straighter, a violent tremor passed through him. "Jack, Tomás got lucky. Me? Been emptying from both ends since the blast. Can't keep water down." He wiped his cracked lips with a sleeve that bore rusty-brown stains. "I took a higher dose of radiation than he did."

"Can you make it the half mile back to the car?"

He nodded then doubled over, one hand braced against his knee, the other pressed against his mouth. When the spasm passed, he straightened with effort, revealing a fresh crimson streak on his palm. "Half a mile," he whispered, eyes glassy with fever. "Get me somewhere with an IV and a doctor who won't ask questions."

Jack half carried Perry through the scrubland, his friend's arm draped across his shoulders, each labored breath hot against Jack's neck. Twice they stopped when Perry's knees buckled, his body convulsing as he coughed crimson onto the parched earth. Tomás trudged ahead, scanning the horizon.

When Pablo's silhouette appeared beside the dust-covered sedan, he waved his arms overhead, the rental car's dented hood gleaming like a beacon in the merciless sun. They forded the creek and made it to the car safely. Pablo crawled back over the rutted path, the vehicle's undercarriage screaming against rocks, Perry's head lolling against the window with each violent jolt. Once they hit the pavement, they made it to the aircraft in short order.

Back at the aircraft, emotions overflowed as Perry and Tomás stepped aboard. Lynley, Jess, and Lydia rushed toward them with choked sobs, wrapping the men in desperate embraces. Bob stood back, jaw clenched tight before finally stepping forward to grip each man's shoulder, his weathered face betraying the moisture gathering at the corners of his eyes.

Perry slumped against the cabin wall, his breathing shallow and rapid. Crimson flecks dotted the handkerchief clutched in his trembling hand. Bob leaned toward the cockpit. "Radio Little Rock. A private ambulance on the tarmac when we land. No sirens, no questions." Bob addressed the occupants of the aircraft. "I think we've spent enough time in this godforsaken corner of nowhere. Time to go home."

Jack said, "And what becomes of our battle-scarred rental down there, Bob?"

"Leave it! I'll buy them a new one."

They had saved the world, but at what cost? At least they were headed back home now.

Once the plane leveled off, Bob motioned Jack to the galley. "You won't believe this," he said, glancing over his shoulder. "Hendricus went back to Perry County a few nights ago. Midnight operation, totally unauthorized. He'd started poking around when these unmarked choppers appeared out of nowhere. Military types. They took him. No word since."

Jack's mouth fell open.

Bob's eyes narrowed as he leaned in closer. "So I called in some favors with my contacts in D.C., the ones who usually pick up on the first ring. Straight to voicemail, every one of them. But that nuclear detonation south of the border will have their undivided attention for the next several weeks, so I don't expect to hear from them soon."

Jack ran his hand over his jaw, a chill crawling up his spine. "Let me get this straight. We're not dealing with Chinese space debris in Arkansas, are we?"

Bob shook his head. "Chinese space debris was apparently a cover story. As for who's holding Hendricus now..." He lowered his voice to a whisper. "Pentagon black ops? Some CIA ghost unit? Your guess is as good as mine."

Jack said, "He's a Dutch citizen. Maybe they'll deport him back to the Netherlands."

"If only we could be so lucky."

The plane's engines hummed. Jack gritted his teeth. "You know, everyone in the UFO circles always insisted Coyame '74 was an American operation. But that Soviet warhead changes everything. If the Americans had been first on the scene, that nuke would've been whisked to Sandia or Los Alamos decades ago. So the Mexicans must have gotten there before anyone else." He frowned, rubbing his thumb across his lower lip. "But how the hell did Mexico end up with Russian nuclear tech fifty miles from the U.S. border?"

Bob eyed him. "You know, before that nuke went off, my Washington contacts weren't dodging my calls. I made some discreet inquiries, and I think I've pieced together how a Soviet warhead ended up buried in Mexican desert soil. Interested in the backstory?"

"Absolutely!"

"Do you remember from your history classes what was going on in 1973? Ever heard of Watergate?"

"That was the thing Nixon got impeached over, right?" said Jack.

Bob shook his head. "Nixon wasn't impeached. He resigned before they could finish the process. But yes. While America was distracted by its internal chaos, Moscow was making moves south of the border. According to my contacts, Brezhnev flew to Havana under the cover of night for closed-door talks with Castro and Mexican President Álvarez."

"I hadn't heard of that."

"This isn't something you'd find in textbooks. We're talking classified material buried in CIA archives. Remember the Cuban Missile Crisis? When Kennedy nearly went to war after discovering Soviet nukes ninety miles from Florida?" He glanced around. "Well, intelligence suggests Brezhnev made a similar play in '73, trying to convince President Álvarez to let them stash nuclear weapons in Mexico."

"That would have been another Cuban Missile Crisis all over again. Maybe worse," said Jack.

Bob nodded. "Álvarez refused the official proposal, but according to intercepted CIA cables, a handful of smaller yield warheads still made their way to certain Mexican military commanders. Not ICBMs, we're talking bombs like the one you found. That warhead they found could be one of those. Though it begs the question, who abandons a functioning nuclear device in the middle of nowhere for a quarter century?"

Jack nodded. "What if knowledge of the warhead was compartmentalized? A handful of officers sent to secure it then wiped out by whatever extraterrestrial contagion they encountered at the crash site."

Bob rubbed his temple. "There's another possibility. What if Soviet operatives took part in the recovery alongside Mexican forces? They could have been on-site when the pathogen was released. Maybe they planted the warhead as a failsafe, but when it malfunctioned, they abandoned the operation, cutting their losses rather than risking further exposure or detection so close to American soil."

"Seems like we may never know for sure," said Jack.

"No, I suppose it's a little too late for answers now."

Hendricus's eyelids peeled apart, sticky with sleep or something worse. Blackness. He blinked twice. Shapes refused to materialize. Only a faint red dot glowed in the distance, a camera? An exit sign? His head throbbed where it pressed against something unyielding.

Cold seeped through his shirt, numbing his shoulder blades while his spine braced against something flat and unyielding. When he tried to shift position, pain shot through his ribs, his wrists, and the back of his skull. His fingers twitched, grazing a rough surface that scraped his fingertips like sandpaper. Concrete.

He tilted his head, ear flattened against the chill concrete. A murmur filtered through the walls—two voices, maybe three. Between their pauses came the steady drip, drip, drip of water striking metal somewhere to his left, each drop marking seconds in this timeless dark.

Shadows swam before him, sharpening from murky soup into hard edges as his pupils fought to dilate. Six feet in front of him, a rectangular outline emerged, darker than the surrounding darkness, with a tiny red dot floating at chest height. The walls pressed in, their rough texture visible now as his fingertips confirmed it was poured concrete, still damp in places, the corners meeting at perfect right angles like the inside of a shoebox.

The air clung to his nostrils like wet newspaper, carrying hints of mildew and something metallic—blood, perhaps his own. Each shallow breath felt thick in his lungs, neither warming his body nor refreshing it, as if the room existed in that uncomfortable space between refrigeration and room temperature.

Pine needles crunched beneath his boots as the memory flickered back of moonlight illuminating the raw earth of the crater, his hand touching something smooth and warm under the soil.

The forest had gone silent before the beam of flashlights cut through the trees. A voice barked, "Hands where I can see them!" Another spoke into a radio. Rough gloves gripped his arms, pushing him forward at gunpoint as he struggled to keep up. The helicopter's rotors had whipped his hair against his face, the vibration rattling his teeth until the sharp pinch at his neck spread cold numbness through his veins. Then darkness befell him.

The geography of his imprisonment remained a mystery, as did the identity of his captors in their unmarked fatigues. Minutes or days might have passed in this lightless vault. His body offered no reliable clock.

His questions multiplied in the darkness, breeding like bacteria in a petri dish, while answers stayed as absent as the sun.

As soon as Perry and Tomás made it back to Little Rock, they were rushed straight from the tarmac to the University of Arkansas Medical Center by private ambulance.

Tomás had received a lower dose of radiation and recovered within days. Perry wasn't so lucky. His condition deteriorated rapidly. The medical team found his bone marrow struggling to produce blood cells, his digestive tract inflamed and bleeding, and his hands trembling with nerve damage.

"About half of the patients with this level of exposure don't make it," the physician told Jack. "And those who do are never quite the same."

Behind the glass partition, monitors beeped a fragile rhythm as Perry slept, his skin waxy under the fluorescent lights.

By the third day following the blast, the border had become a circus. Thousands of Mexican civilians living within the fallout radius had been evacuated to hastily erected tent cities in Chihuahua City and Ojinaga. Their faces were blurred on American television as they described the flash, the roar, the way the ground itself seemed to liquefy beneath their feet. El Paso hospitals reported a surge of patients presenting with radiation anxiety, though actual exposure levels on the U.S. side remained negligible. The governor of Texas declared a state of emergency and deployed the National Guard to the border, ostensibly for "public safety" but unmistakably a political move. Arizona and New Mexico followed within hours.

In the weeks that followed, Bob slid manila envelopes across kitchen tables throughout the state. Inside were large cashier's checks, documents for college funds already established for the children, and statements to paid-off mortgages. The widows nodded, tucking away both the money and any questions about what their husbands had really been doing in Mexico.

Patty walked into Bob's office and set a stack of folders on the corner of his desk and didn't leave. Bob recognized the stance: she had something to say and was deciding how to say it.

"Still nothing on Hendricus?" she asked.

"Nothing." He turned the empty scotch glass in his hand then set it down. "The investigators checked in this morning. They're following a lead in Florida, but..." He shook his head. "I don't know, Patty."

"Chris asked about him again this morning. So did Priya."

"What did you tell them?"

"Amsterdam. His mother." She paused. "Bob, I've told them Amsterdam several times now. Lydia asked me yesterday if his mother had a name."

He looked at her. "What did you say?"

"I said I didn't know her first name. Which is true. But I don't know how much longer that holds. People aren't stupid."

"I know." He pushed back from the desk and moved to the window. Below, the parking lot was filling up with vehicles he didn't recognize. The cars of the industry people, the titans Patty had spent three weeks coordinating.

"The satellite story is worse. I can feel it fraying every time I say it. Hendricus didn't believe it for a second and he's not here to keep quiet about it anymore," said Bob. "How many people in this building do you think have already connected the dots?"

"Most of the scientists on four. Maybe all of them," she said. "They're loyal, Bob. But loyalty has a shelf life when the story keeps changing."

He nodded slowly. On his desk, the stack of newspapers with their border-incident headlines sat beside the marked-up map of Chihuahua, beside the empty glass, beside the encrypted laptop he checked every morning for messages that never came. The debris field of everything that had happened in the last several weeks, arranged neatly by Patty's hands.

"And Jack and Jessica," he said.

Patty's expression shifted almost imperceptibly. She'd been waiting for this particular topic. "You figured that out," she said.

"I figured that out about three weeks after everyone else, apparently." He almost smiled. "How long?"

"Day one, from what I understand."

He was quiet for a moment, watching two of the industry visitors cross the parking lot below, their suits out of place in the Arkansas heat. "I was going to cite the handbook," he said. "Fraternization policy, all of that."

"I figured," she said.

"I'm not going to."

"I figured that, too." She picked up the stack of folders. "They've earned some grace, Bob. They both have."

He looked at her. Patty had worked for him since before Elaine died. She knew him well enough to say things plainly.

"Alright," he said. "Let's go upstairs. Are they all signed?"

"NDAs, every one. I watched them do it."

"Any pushback?"

"Morrison from Lockheed tried to negotiate the scope of the confidentiality clause." She moved toward the door. "I told him the scope wasn't negotiable."

"What did he say?"

"He signed it."

Bob picked up his jacket from the back of his chair and followed her out.

A handful of scientists and industry titans were gathered in the conference room. They were going to go over everything they had discovered that was important, with the focus on the artifacts recovered from Coyame.

Chris, Chen, and Thabo kicked things off with the melted metal fragments recovered in Coyame.

Chris held up a silvery fragment that caught the light oddly, almost as if it were absorbing rather than reflecting it. "This here defies conventional metallurgy," he said, turning the sample between his fingers. "The composition reads as primarily magnesium, lithium, and scandium bonds, plus trace elements I had to look up, gadolinium and yttrium. We've bent it, heated it past the melting point of titanium, and hit it with forces that would shatter magnesium. Nothing. It remembers its shape."

Chen turned the sample in his hands. "Our manufacturing capabilities can't even approach this. Any of you who could replicate it would dominate aerospace for decades. The market value?" He gave a small, incredulous laugh. "Incalculable, if you ask me."

Thabo said, "This sample is radioactive, likely from the crash. We believe it is from the UFO, but at this time I couldn't speculate what its specific use was."

There were many questions from the group. Even Bob, who prided himself on professional detachment, leaned forward in his chair.

Chen and Chris returned to their seats, leaving Thabo alone at the head of the table. "If you thought that was incredible, wait until you see this."

He held up the thin, silvery material that was slightly curved and as thin as an eggshell. "I believe this might have been from the skin of the alien craft."

He had everyone's attention.

Thabo balanced the material on his fingertips. "Hold out your hand," he instructed the CEO of Boeing in the front row. When he did, he placed it on his palm. His eyebrows shot up.

"Feels like nothing, right? Yet it withstood temperatures that would vaporize tungsten." He reclaimed the sample, eyes sweeping across their transfixed faces. "And its composition? Just two elements, lithium and hydrogen."

That elicited some puzzled looks from the group.

"Now, only one compound of lithium and hydrogen is known to science, and that would be lithium hydride. For those of you who don't know, lithium hydride is a crystalline solid, and this is clearly not that. I believe what we are looking at here is an alloy of metallic hydrogen and lithium."

From the back of the room, the CEO of Raytheon called out, "You're claiming that's metallic hydrogen? That's only theoretical!"

Thabo turned the sample so the light caught its surface. "Metallic hydrogen exists in textbooks as a hypothetical substance, something that might form in the crushing pressure at Jupiter's core. It shouldn't exist in a laboratory, much less here at one standard atmosphere." He paused for effect. "Yet the evidence defies everything we thought we knew."

"The technological gap between this material and our most advanced manufacturing capabilities is like comparing stone tools to supercomputers. Within our current scientific framework, we can't even imagine what applications this might have."

Thabo was peppered with questions, CEOs rising from their seats, professional composure forgotten. He raised his hands, waiting for the commotion to subside. When the voices finally quieted, he gestured toward the back of the room with a slight smile. "Dr. Hodges has findings that make even this look conventional."

Dr. Hodges took the floor. He approached the podium with a

sample case clutched to his chest like a religious relic. "What I'm about to show you," he said, "represents an energy density that makes uranium look like a double-A battery."

A photograph appeared on screen, solid-black orbs against a white background, each no larger than a garden pea. "This here is likely the most concentrated energy source ever discovered on Earth. These spheres emit radiation signatures unlike anything in our periodic table, with a decay rate suggesting a half-life of approximately 1.7 years. All evidence points to these being the power cells that once fueled the craft we recovered from the desert floor."

Dr. Hodges cupped his hands to demonstrate. "When the craft crashed in '74, each power cell was roughly the size of a bowling ball. What you see now is what remains after twenty-five years of radioactive decay." He opened his palm to reveal the obsidian pea.

"This is highly radioactive, so if you will permit me, I will put it back in its lead-lined case," he said. "But here's what defies everything we know about nuclear physics. This is an element that shouldn't exist. On our periodic table, anything from element 104 and beyond breaks down almost instantly. This?" He tapped the case. "It has a half-life of 1.7 years."

Dr. Hodges raised the case slightly. "What you're looking at is an element so far beyond our periodic table that it shouldn't exist: element 171. For decades, nuclear physicists have only dreamed of reaching the island of stability beyond element 164. Today, that island is no longer theoretical. We're standing on its shores."

Some of their guests stood from their seats, questions overlapping in a crescendo of disbelief.

"Alright, people!" Bob shouted. "We have two more things we need to get through, and then we can open the floor to questions." He gestured to Lynley to return to the front.

"Ladies and gentlemen, we are not alone in this universe. I'm sure we've already determined that from the artifacts that were recovered, but this here," she said, as the screen shifted to display a small white fragment, "is part of a bone that belongs to an alien species." A murmur moved through the assembled group.

Lynley's hands trembled as she held up the bone fragment. "Under the electron microscope, I saw what looked like spider silk woven into the calcium matrix, thin strands glinting like metal." She tapped a key, bringing up a magnified image where silvery threads crisscrossed through honeycombed structures. "These fibers are pure titanium integrated into bone tissue. Either someone engineered this creature molecule by molecule, or it evolved somewhere that would crush a human like tissue paper."

A stunned hush overcame the room, punctuated only by scattered whispers and the occasional half-formed question that seemed to die in the air.

Lynley's eyes gleamed. "Imagine a soldier with bones that wouldn't shatter under any impact, or an astronaut who could withstand forces that would crush an ordinary human skeleton. If you could replicate this technology..."

Bob stepped to the front. "Now we have one more discovery to present, and it's a theoretical take on how these UFOs are able to move through space, our atmosphere, and even underwater. Dr. Bowden...the floor is yours."

Jess stepped forward and sketched a curved line across the whiteboard, then another intersecting it. "Imagine space-time as this rubber sheet," she said, gesturing to the curves. "The craft doesn't push through it. It pinches two points together, like this." She folded her notes, creating a crease between distant corners, and launched into her theory of geodesics.

Several CEOs exchanged skeptical glances. The Boeing executive scribbled something. "Fascinating theory," he said finally, "but what's the practical application timeline?"

Jess hesitated. "This is all still theoretical."

Bob checked his watch, tapping its face twice before raising his hand. The barrage of questions—about metallic hydrogen, element 171, alien biology—gradually died down as he stepped to the podium. He pulled a Mont Blanc pen from his breast pocket and clicked it open, his eyes scanning the room of aerospace executives and defense contractors whose expressions had transformed from skepticism to barely contained avarice. He thanked his team of scientists and dismissed them.

"I believe we've established the authenticity of our findings," he said, sliding forward a stack of folders with more detailed information inside.

"Gentlemen, ladies, digest what you've witnessed today, and we'll meet again to discuss potential collaborations." He noted the calculating gleam in their eyes. "And before you mistake my intentions, my bank accounts already overflow. This isn't about profit. It's about pushing humanity forward with what we've found buried in that desert."

In Arizona, Garrett had started seeing a therapist to process the findings uncovered by Dr. Benton. While his fellow CAPER members had doubted his abduction story early on, it now appeared to have been genuine.

Pat and Steve were more determined than ever to return to Colorado to investigate the Black Canyon of the Gunnison. Was there a reason why Garrett was dumped in that particular place after the abduction?

They had more questions than answers.

At SPIRE, Tomás was back to work at his desk, diving into work. The medical team had upgraded Perry's status to stable, assuring everyone he'd pull through, though his hospital bracelet wouldn't be coming off anytime soon.

The injuries had permanently altered Perry's life trajectory. After weighing his options, he chose to step away from the team and relocate near his family, who could provide the ongoing support his condition required. Bob, ever the responsible leader, had ensured a generous financial package that acknowledged Perry's sacrifice and service.

Bob looked up from the stack of reports on his desk when Patty appeared in his doorway. "There's someone on line two," she said, her voice pitched higher than usual. "I think you should take it."

Bob picked up the receiver and punched in line two. A voice crackled on the other end of the line in heavily accented English.

"Ah, so this must be the infamous Señor Bob!"

"Who is this?" asked Bob.

"Me? I am nobody. I am everybody. I am El Cajón. The Americans and the Federales have killed my patrón, and now I am in charge of the cartel."

Bob glanced at the phone, cringing. "What do you want with me?"

El Cajón let out a long belly laugh. "Do you think I don't know who killed our men in Coyame? You set off a nuclear weapon on our land, and we get blamed for it. Now we are being hunted down like dogs. And then you plot to sell the things you collected from our land, for billions of dollars no less. And you ask what I want? We are coming for you and every one of you gringos who took what was rightfully ours!"

Bob stammered and started to reply before the connection went dead.

"Oh, shit..." he whispered. It was time to hire more security—a lot more security.

Jack took Jess to a minor-league baseball game featuring the Arkansas Travelers. They both loved baseball, but it was hot and sticky, and Jess wanted to leave, especially since their team was down by six runs.

"Jack, can we go? The mosquitoes are eating me alive, and it's so damn hot and humid out here," said Jess.

"We have to wait until the middle of the fifth inning," he said.

"What's so special about the fifth inning?"

"There's going to be a special giveaway, and I want to be here when it happens," he said. She shook her head.

Jack nursed his third beer while Jess picked at the congealing cheese on their eight-dollar nachos. The final out of the top of the fifth brought a halfhearted cheer from the remaining crowd, players trudging toward their dugout in the sweltering evening heat. The stadium lights flickered once, and the Jumbotron transitioned from the dismal score to a message that made the few thousand fans suddenly fall silent.

Jess, will you marry me?
Your true love,
Jack

Jess froze, a nacho chip suspended halfway to her mouth. She turned to find Jack kneeling in the sticky concrete aisle, balancing a small wooden box in his palm. Inside nestled a diamond that caught the stadium lights in prismatic bursts. Her mouth opened, closed, opened again. The nachos tumbled to the ground as she lunged forward, nodding frantically before finding her voice. The crowd's cheers washed over them as she pulled him up.

"Yes!" The emotion in her voice was lost in the roar but unmistakable in her eyes.

Good news travels fast, and bad news even faster—or so they say.

Jack and Jess hadn't anticipated how quickly word of their engagement would circulate, though in retrospect, perhaps a baseball stadium proposal splashed across a sixty-foot jumbotron wasn't exactly keeping things under wraps.

The next morning, they stepped into the office where everyone was waiting for their arrival.

A wave of enthusiastic well-wishes met them at every turn.

Women from accounting to HR clustered around Jess's left hand, their collective gasps and sighs audible through the hallways as the diamond caught the fluorescent light.

"Is that a cushion cut?" said Donna from accounting, seizing Jess's wrist with both hands and angling the ring toward the nearest light fixture with the focused intensity of a gemologist.

"Actually, it's an emerald cut," said Jess.

Donna dropped Jess's hand as if it had suddenly become too hot to touch and pressed both palms to her cheeks. "Oh my God," she breathed, her voice rising an octave. She spun toward the woman hovering behind her. "Sandra, you have to see this ring."

And so went the rest of the morning for Jess. Jack was about to excuse himself to the fourth floor when Patty materialized from the direction of the reception desk. Before he'd processed what was happening, she had both arms around him and was squeezing him. "I am so happy for you both. So happy." She pulled back and held him by both shoulders, examining his face. "You look terrified."

"I'm not terrified."

"You look a little terrified," she said.

"It's the fluorescent lighting."

She laughed and released him, then turned immediately to join the cluster around Jess.

Before Jack could make a tactical retreat, Bob approached him from behind.

"My office," Bob said. "When you get a chance."

"Lead the way," he said.

Jack stepped into the familiar warmth of Bob's office.

Bob took Jack's hand in both of his own, grip firm and steady, eyes meeting Jack's with unmistakable sincerity.

"Congratulations!" He squeezed Jack's hand once before releasing it, gesturing toward the chairs. "Jess is exceptional. You both deserve this." They settled into their seats, and Bob's expression shifted to something more reflective. "When you first walked through that door, I wasn't completely sure what I had."

"What I know now," Bob said, "is that you're the best field investigator I've got, and you're a good man. And Jess..." He paused, choosing words with the care of someone who felt strongly and didn't want to overdo it. "Jess is the kind of scientist who makes everyone around her sharper. The two of you together..." He shook his head. "I don't know what you'll figure out, but I want front-row seats."

"Thank you, Bob."

Bob leaned forward, the chair creaking slightly beneath him. "Just so we're clear on one thing," he said. "Marriage doesn't change the nature of what we do here. The late nights, the field work in places where I can't always guarantee your safety. That's still the job." He tapped his index finger once on the desk. "But I want you to know I see the sacrifice that represents. For both of you. I don't take that lightly."

Jack nodded. There wasn't much to say to that, and Bob seemed to know it, because he let the silence sit for a moment and then leaned back and returned to the register of a man wrapping up a meeting.

"Now. Is there anything you need from me on the personal side? Time, arrangements..."

"I can't think of anything right now. Jess's parents are flying in from Wisconsin," Jack said. "Not sure exactly when, but soon. I've only met them once before, when we were up there on the cattle mutilation case. Let's just say her dad is a little intimidating."

Bob smiled. "When they get here, take the time you need. Strange phenomena have a way of waiting for us." He rose from his chair, the leather creaking softly beneath him. "And Jack? Ask Jess to stop by when she can break free from her admirers. I'd like to offer my congratulations in person."

Jack stood and shook his hand again at the door. In the hallway, the cluster around Jess had grown by two people and migrated several feet down the corridor, and someone had apparently produced a phone showing the jumbotron footage, because three women were gathered around a small screen making the kind of sounds that Jack suspected would follow him for the rest of his career at SPIRE.

He caught Jess's eye again across the hallway.

For a moment, her professional veneer slipped away. The careful mask she'd maintained all morning vanished, replaced by something genuine that transformed her entire face—eyes bright, laugh lines deepening, shoulders relaxing just enough that only he would notice. It was a private signal meant solely for him, lasting just long enough to matter before she turned back to Donna, who was gesturing at the diamond with renewed enthusiasm.

Jack thought to himself, *I'm the luckiest man in the world.*

The next morning, Tomás stood at the threshold of Bob's office, his gaze lingering on the two men flanking the doorway. Their dark suits couldn't quite conceal the bulges beneath their jackets, and their eyes tracked his movements.

Tomás's hand tightened around his coffee mug as he stepped inside. "New decor?" he asked, nodding toward the men.

Bob's smile didn't reach his eyes. "Security detail. That Mexican cartel everyone's pinning the nuclear blast on has made it clear we're on their radar."

"How would they know who we are?"

Bob waved. "Certain people talk when they shouldn't. We can discuss the details later." He gestured to the chair across from his desk. "What can I do for you this morning?"

"Some of my family members back in Chile are telling me there is something big going on down in Puerto Montt."

"Tomás, I'm a little weak on South American geography. Where is that exactly?"

"It's about five hundred miles south of Santiago in the green part of Chile. It lies at the northern extent of the fjords."

"Okay, I'm still not sure where that's at, but what's happening?"

He said, "My cousin is with the port authority down there. Look what he sent." His fingers pushed a manila folder across the table's surface. Inside were several blurry photographs showing three slate-gray American naval ships dominating Puerto Montt's usually tranquil waters.

Tomás's eyes darted toward the door before continuing. "Four days ago, these warships arrived carrying equipment for deep-sea salvage operations. My sister-in-law works maintenance in Puerto Montt's government complex and was emptying trash bins when she heard officials having a heated discussion. They kept mentioning 'the discs' resting on the seabed and expressing doubts about whether the Americans would keep their promises after recovery."

Tomás grinned. "That's not all. She heard them discussing some massive American-funded installation high in the Atacama. They called it 'the Nave.' Billions of dollars are pouring into something in the northern desert. Whatever they're fishing for in those waters connects directly to what's happening up there in the mountains."

Bob settled back in his chair. "Now that's something worth looking into. Let's come up with a plan here. Maybe we can put together two teams. One for Puerto Montt, and another to investigate this business in the Atacama."

To be continued...

Daniel Koch spent thirty-two years as a government meteorologist, tracking storm fronts, writing scientific papers, and issuing forecasts that people actually relied on. Though his former colleagues call it retirement, he prefers to think of it as a career change—one where storm fronts and pressure systems have given way to plot points and character arcs.

The written word has called to him since childhood, though the relentless demands of operational forecasting left little room for fiction until now.

These days, Daniel dedicates most of his time to crafting fiction, drawn primarily to the pulse-quickening worlds of techno-thrillers, though the vast frontiers of science fiction and the shadowy corners of horror also beckon.

He lives in Arkansas with his wife, a dog, and a cat that thinks she owns the place.

For more information, see the author's website at: danieljkochbooks.com or scan the code on this page with your phone or smart device.

Thrillers:

Classified Skies Book 2: Silent Descent

Classified Skies Book 3: Convergence

The Accidental Spy

Horror:

Revenge of the Mothman

Historical Fiction:

Washington's Life Guards

Non-Fiction:

Tales from the Weather Service

If you enjoyed *Deadly Artifact*, I'd be grateful if you'd take a few minutes to leave a review on Amazon. Even a sentence or two makes an enormous difference for an independent author.

Reviews help other readers discover the book, and for a debut novelist without a major publisher behind him, they're truly everything.

If you'd like to stay connected and be the first to hear about Book 2 in the *Classified Skies* series, visit danieljkochbooks.com and join the reader list.

Thank you for taking a chance on a new author. It means more than you know.

— Dan